DAVID GIBBINS has worked in underwater archaeology all his professional life. After taking a PhD from Cambridge University he taught archaeology in Britain and abroad, and is a world authority on ancient shipwrecks and sunken cities. He has led numerous expeditions to investigate underwater sites in the Mediterranean and around the world. He currently divides his time between fieldwork, England and Canada.

By David Gibbins

Atlantis
Crusader Gold
The Last Gospel

ATLANTIS

DAVID GIBBINS

headline

First published in Great Britain in 2005
by HEADLINE PUBLISHING GROUP

First published in paperback in 2005
by HEADLINE PUBLISHING GROUP

This edition published in 2008
by HEADLINE PUBLISHING GROUP

1

Cataloguing in Publication Data is available from the British Library

ISBN 978 0 7553 4791 9

Typeset in Aldine 401BT by Avon DataSet Ltd,
Bidford-on-Avon, Warwickshire

Printed in the UK by CPI Mackays, Chatham, ME5 8TD

Headline's policy is to use papers that are natural, renewable and recyclable
products and made from wood grown in sustainable forests. The logging
and manufacturing processes are expected to conform to the environmental
regulations of the country of origin.

HEADLINE PUBLISHING GROUP
An Hachette Livre UK Company
338 Euston Road
London NW1 3BH

www.headline.co.uk
www.hachettelivre.co.uk

Acknowledgements

With heartfelt thanks to my agent, Luigi Bonomi, to my editors Harriet Evans and Bill Massey, and to Jane Heller. Also to Amanda Preston, Amelia Cummins, Vanessa Forbes, Gaia Banks, Jenny Bateman and Catherine Cobain. To the many friends, colleagues and institutions who have helped make my fieldwork such an adventure over the years, and have made real archaeology as exciting as fiction. To Ann Verrinder Gibbins, who took me to the Caucasus and Central Asia, and then provided the perfect haven for writing. To Dad, Alan and Hugh, and to Zebedee and Suzie. To Angie, and to our lovely daughter Molly, who arrived when this book was just an idea and has seen me through it.

Present-day map of the Mediterranean

'A mighty empire once ruled the larger part of the world. Its rulers lived in a vast citadel, up against the sea, a great maze of corridors like nothing seen since. They were ingenious workers in gold and ivory and fearless bullfighters. But then, for defying Poseidon the Sea God, in one mighty deluge the citadel was swallowed beneath the waves, its people never to be seen again.'

Prologue

The old man shuffled to a halt and raised his head, as awestruck as he had been the first time he stood before the temple. Nothing like this had yet been built in his native Athens. High above him the monumental doorway seemed to carry all the weight of the heavens, its colossal pillars casting a moonlit shadow far beyond the temple precinct into the shimmering expanse of the desert. Ahead loomed rows of huge columns, soaring into the cavernous antechamber, their polished surfaces covered with hieroglyphic inscriptions and towering human forms scarcely visible in the spluttering torchlight. The only hint of what lay beyond was a whispering, chilling breeze which brought with it the musty odour of incense, as if someone had just opened the doors of a long-sealed burial chamber. The old man shuddered in spite of himself, his philosophical demeanour momentarily giving way to an irrational fear of the unknown, a fear of the power of gods whom he could not placate and who had no interest in the well-being of his people.

'Come, Greek.' The words hissed out of the darkness as the attendant lit his torch from one of the doorway fires, its leaping flame revealing a lithe, wiry physique clad only in a loincloth. As he padded ahead, the bobbing flame was the only mark of his progress. As usual he stopped at the entrance to the inner sanctum and waited impatiently for the old man, whose stooped form followed behind through the antechamber. The attendant had nothing but contempt for this *hellenos*, this Greek, with his bald head and unkempt beard, with his endless questions, who kept him waiting in the temple every night far beyond the appointed hour. By writing on his scrolls, the Greek was performing an act properly reserved for the priests.

Now the attendant's contempt had turned to loathing. That very morning his brother Seth had returned from Naucratis, the busy port nearby where the brown flood-water of the Nile debouched into the Great Middle Sea. Seth had been downcast and forlorn. They had entrusted a batch of cloth from their father's workshop in the Fayum to a Greek merchant who now claimed it was lost in a shipwreck. They were already full of suspicion that the wily Greeks would exploit their ignorance of commerce. Now their foreboding had hardened to hatred. It had been their last hope of escaping a life of drudgery in the temple, condemned to an existence little better than the baboons and cats that lurked in the dark recesses behind the columns.

The attendant peered venomously at the old man as he approached. Lawmaker, they called him. 'I will show you,' the attendant whispered to himself, 'what my gods think of your laws, you Greek.'

The scene within the inner sanctum could not have been in greater contrast to the forbidding grandeur of the antechamber. A thousand pinpricks of light, like fireflies in the night, sprang from pottery oil lamps around a chamber hewn from the living rock. From the ceiling hung elaborate bronze incense burners, the wispy trails of smoke forming a layer of haze across the room. The walls were set with recesses like the burial niches of a necropolis; only here they were filled not with shrouded corpses and cinerary urns but with tall, open-topped jars brimming over with papyrus scrolls. As the two men descended a flight of steps, the reek of incense grew stronger and the silence was broken by a murmur that became steadily more distinct. Ahead lay two eagle-headed pillars which served as jambs for great bronze doors that opened towards them.

Facing them through the entrance were orderly rows of men, some sitting cross-legged on reed mats and wearing only loincloths, all hunched over low desks. Some were copying from scrolls laid out beside them; others were transcribing dictations from black-robed priests, their low recitations forming the softly undulating chant they had heard as they approached. This was the scriptorium, the chamber of wisdom, a vast repository of written and memorized knowledge passed down from priest to priest since the dawn of history, since even before the pyramid builders.

The attendant withdrew into the shadows of the stairwell. He was forbidden from entering the chamber, and now began the long wait until the time came to escort the Greek away. But this evening, instead of whiling away the hours in sullen resentment, he took a grim satisfaction in the events planned for the night.

The old man pushed past in his eagerness to get on. This was his final night in the temple, his last chance to fathom the mystery that had obsessed him since his previous visit. Tomorrow was the beginning of the month-long Festival of Thoth, when all newcomers were barred from the temple. He knew that an outsider would never again be granted an audience with the high priest.

In his haste the Greek stumbled into the room, dropping his scroll and pens with a clatter which momentarily distracted the scribes from their work. He muttered in annoyance and glanced around apologetically before collecting together his bundle and shuffling between the men towards an annexe at the far end of the chamber. He ducked under a low doorway and sat down on a reed mat, his previous visits giving him the only intimation that there might be another seated in the darkness before him.

'Solon the Lawmaker, I am Amenhotep the high priest.'

The voice was barely audible, little more than a whisper, and sounded as old as the gods. Again it spoke.

'You come to my temple at Saïs, and I receive you. You seek knowledge, and I give what the gods will impart.'

The formal salutations over, the Greek quickly arranged his white robe over his knees and readied his scroll. From the darkness Amenhotep leaned forward, just enough for his face to be caught in a flickering shaft of light. Solon had seen it many times before, but it still sent a shudder through his soul. It seemed disembodied, a luminous orb suspended in the darkness, like some spectre leering from the edge of the underworld. It was the face of a young man suspended in time, as if mummified; the skin was taut and translucent, almost parchment-like, and the eyes were glazed over with the milky sheen of blindness.

Amenhotep had been old before Solon was born. It was said

that he had been visited by Homer, in the time of Solon's great-grandfather, and that it was he who told of the siege of Troy, of Agamemnon and Hector and Helen, and of the wanderings of Odysseus. Solon would have dearly loved to ask him about this and other matters, but in so doing he would be violating his agreement not to question the old priest.

Solon leaned forward attentively, determined not to miss anything in this final visit. At length Amenhotep spoke again, his voice no more than a ghostly exhalation.

'Lawmaker, tell me whereof I spoke yesterday.'

Solon quickly unravelled his scroll, scanning the densely written lines. After a moment he began to read, translating the Greek of his script into the Egyptian language they were now speaking.

'A mighty empire once ruled the larger part of the world.' He peered down in the gloom. 'Its rulers lived in a vast citadel, up against the sea, a great maze of corridors like nothing seen since. They were ingenious workers in gold and ivory and fearless bullfighters. But then, for defying Poseidon the Sea God, in one mighty deluge the citadel was swallowed beneath the waves, its people never to be seen again.' Solon stopped reading and looked up expectantly. 'That is where you finished.'

After what seemed an interminable silence, the old priest spoke again, his lips scarcely moving and his voice little more than a murmur.

'Tonight, Lawmaker, I will tell you many things. But first let me speak of this lost world, this city of hubris smitten by the gods, this city they called Atlantis.'

Many hours later the Greek put down his pen, his hand aching from continuous writing, and wound up his scroll.

Amenhotep had finished. Now was the night of the full moon, the beginning of the Festival of Thoth, and the priests must prepare the temple before the supplicants arrived at dawn.

'What I have told you, Lawmaker, was here, and nowhere else,' Amenhotep had whispered, his crooked finger slowly tapping his head. 'By ancient decree we who cannot leave this temple, we high priests, must keep this wisdom as our treasure. It is only by command of the *astrologos*, the temple seer, that you are able to be here, by some will of divine Osiris.' The old priest leaned forward, a hint of a smile on his lips. 'And Lawmaker, remember: I do not speak in riddles, like your Greek oracles, but there may be riddles in what I recite. I speak a truth passed down, not a truth of my own devising. You have come for the last time. Go now.' As the deathly face receded into the darkness Solon slowly rose, hesitating momentarily and looking back one last time before stooping out into the now empty scriptorium and making his way towards the torchlit entranceway.

Rosy-fingered dawn was colouring the eastern sky, the faint glow tinting the moonlight which still danced across the waters of the Nile. The old Greek was alone, the attendant having left him as usual outside the precinct. He had sighed with satisfaction as he passed the temple columns, their palm-leaf capitals so unlike the simple Greek forms, and glanced for the last time at the Sacred Lake with its eerie phalanx of obelisks and human-headed sphinxes and colossal statues of the pharaohs. He had been pleased to leave all that behind and was walking contentedly along the dusty road towards the mud-brick village where he was staying. In his hands he clutched the precious scroll, and over his shoulder hung a satchel weighed down by a heavy purse. Tomorrow, before leaving, he would make his offering of gold to the goddess Neith, as he had promised Amenhotep when they first spoke.

He was still lost in wonderment at what he had heard. A Golden Age, an age of splendour even the pharaohs could not have imagined. A race who mastered every art, in fire and stone and metal. Yet these were men, not giants, not like the Cyclops who built the ancient walls on the Acropolis. They had found the divine fruit and picked it. Their citadel shone like Mount Olympus. They had dared defy the gods, and the gods had struck them down.

Yet they had lived on.

In his reverie he failed to notice two dark forms who stole out from behind a wall as he was entering the village. The blow caught him completely unawares. As he slumped to the ground and darkness descended, he was briefly aware of hands pulling off his shoulder bag. One of the figures snatched the scroll from his grasp and tore it to shreds, throwing the fragments out of sight down a rubbish-strewn alley. The two figures disappeared as silently as they had come, leaving the Greek bloodied and unconscious in the dirt.

When he came to he would have no memory of that final night in the temple. In his remaining years he would rarely speak of his time in Saïs and never again put pen to paper. The wisdom of Amenhotep would never again leave the sanctity of the temple, and would seem lost for ever as the last priests died and the silt of the Nile enveloped the temple and its key to the deepest mysteries of the past.

1

'I've never seen anything like it before!'

The words came from a drysuited diver who had just surfaced behind the stern of the research vessel, his voice breathless with excitement. After swimming over to the ladder, he removed his fins and mask and passed them up to the waiting barge chief. He hauled himself laboriously out of the water, his heavy cylinders causing him momentarily to lose balance, but a heave from above landed him safe and sound on the deck. His dripping shape was quickly surrounded by other members of the team who had been waiting on the dive platform.

Jack Howard made his way down from the bridge walkway and smiled at his friend. He still found it amazing that such a bulky figure could be so agile underwater. As he negotiated the clutter of dive equipment on the aft deck he called out, his mocking tone a familiar part of their banter over the years.

'We thought you'd swum back to Athens for a gin and tonic beside your father's pool. What've you found, the lost treasure of the Queen of Sheba?'

Costas Kazantzakis shook his head impatiently as he struggled along the railing towards Jack. He was too agitated even to bother taking off his equipment. 'No,' he panted. 'I'm serious. Take a look at this.'

Jack silently prayed that the news was good. It had been a solo dive to investigate a silted-up shelf on top of the submerged volcano, and the two divers who had followed Costas would soon be surfacing from the decompression stop. There would be no more dives that season.

Costas unclipped a carabiner and passed over an underwater camcorder housing, pressing the replay button as he did so. The other members of the team converged behind the tall Englishman as he flipped open the miniature LCD screen and activated the video. Within moments Jack's sceptical grin had given way to a look of blank amazement.

The underwater scene was illuminated by powerful flood-lights which gave colour to the gloom almost one hundred metres below. Two divers were kneeling on the seabed using an airlift, a large vacuum tube fed by a low-pressure air hose which sucked up the silt covering the site. One diver wrestled to keep the airlift in position while the other gently wafted sediment up towards the mouth the tube, the action revealing artefacts just as an archaeologist on land would use a trowel.

As the camera zoomed in, the object of the divers' attention came dramatically into view. The dark shape visible upslope was not rock but a concreted mass of metal slabs laid in interlocking rows like shingles.

'Oxhide ingots,' Jack said excitedly. 'Hundreds of them. And there's a cushioning layer of brushwood dunnage, just as Homer described in the ship of Odysseus.'

Each slab was about a metre long with protruding corners, their shape resembling the flayed and stretched hide of an ox. They were the characteristic copper ingots of the Bronze Age, dating back more than three and a half thousand years.

'It looks like the early type,' one of the students on the team ventured. 'Sixteenth century BC?'

'Unquestionably,' Jack said. 'And still in rows just as they were laden, suggesting the hull may be preserved underneath. We could have the oldest ship ever discovered.'

Jack's excitement mounted as the camera traversed down the slope. Between the ingots and the divers loomed three giant pottery jars, each as tall as a man and over a metre in girth. They were identical to jars that Jack had seen in the storerooms at Knossos on Crete. Inside, they could see stacks of stemmed cups painted with beautifully naturalistic octopuses and marine motifs, their swirling forms at one with the undulations of the seabed.

There was no mistaking the pottery of the Minoans, the remarkable island civilization that flourished at the time of the Egyptian Middle and New Kingdoms but then disappeared suddenly, around 1400 BC. Knossos, the fabled labyrinth of the Minotaur, had been one of the most sensational discoveries of the last century. Following close on the heels of Heinrich Schliemann, excavator of Troy, the English archaeologist Arthur Evans had set out to prove that the legend of the Athenian prince Theseus and his lover Ariadne was as grounded in real events as the Trojan War. The sprawling palace just south of Heraklion was the key to a lost civilization he dubbed Minoan after their legendary king. The maze of passageways and chambers gave extraordinary credence to the story of Theseus' battle with the Minotaur, and showed that the myths of the Greeks centuries later were closer to real history than anyone had dared think.

'Yes!' Jack punched the air with his free hand, his normal reserve giving way to the emotion of a truly momentous discovery. It was the culmination of years of single-minded passion, the fulfilment of a dream that had driven him since boyhood. It was a find that would rival Tutankhamun's tomb, a discovery that would secure his team front place in the annals of archaeology.

For Jack these images were enough. Yet there was more, much more, and he stood transfixed by the screen. The camera panned down to the divers on a low shelf below the clump of ingots.

'Probably the stern compartment.' Costas was pointing at the screen. 'Just beyond this ledge is a row of stone anchors and a wooden steering oar.'

Immediately in front was an area of shimmering yellow which looked like the reflection of the floodlights off the sediment in the water. As the camera zoomed in, there was a collective gasp of astonishment.

'That's not sand,' the student whispered. 'That's gold!'

Now they knew what they were looking at, the image was one of surpassing splendour. In the centre was a magnificent golden chalice fit for King Minos himself. It was decorated in relief with an elaborate bullfighting scene. Alongside lay a life-sized golden statue of a woman, her arms raised in supplication and her headdress wreathed in snakes. Her bare breasts had been sculpted from ivory, and a flickering arc of colour showed where her neck was embellished with jewels. Nestled in front was a bundle of golden-handled bronze swords, their blades decorated with fighting scenes made from inlaid silver and blue enamel.

The most brilliant reflection came from the area just in front of the divers. Each waft of the hand seemed to reveal another gleaming object. Jack could make out gold bars, royal seals, jewellery and delicate diadem crowns of intertwined leaves, all jumbled together as if they had once been inside a treasure chest.

The view suddenly veered up towards the ascent line and the screen abruptly went blank. In the stunned silence that followed, Jack lowered the camera and looked at Costas.

'I think we're in business,' he said quietly.

Jack had staked his reputation on a far-flung proposal. In the decade since completing his doctorate he had become fixated on discovering a Minoan wreck, a find that would clinch his theory about the maritime supremacy of the Minoans in the Bronze Age. He had become convinced that the most likely spot was a group of reefs and islets some seventy nautical miles north-east of Knossos.

Yet for weeks they had searched in vain. A few days earlier their hopes had been raised and then dashed by the discovery of a Roman wreck, a dive Jack expected to be his last of the season. Today was to have been a chance to evaluate new equipment for their next project. Once again Jack's luck had held out.

'Mind giving me a hand?'

Costas had slumped exhausted beside the stern railing on *Seaquest*, his equipment still unbuckled and the water on his face now joined by rivulets of sweat. The late afternoon sun of the Aegean drenched his form in light. He looked up at the lean physique that towered over him. Jack was an unlikely scion of one of England's most ancient families, his easy grace the only hint of a privileged lineage. His father had been an adventurer who had eschewed his background and used his wealth to take his family away with him to remote locations around the world. His unconventional upbringing had left Jack an outsider, a man most at ease in his own company and beholden to nobody. He was a born leader who commanded respect on the bridge and the foredeck.

'What would you do without me?' Jack asked with a grin as he lifted the tanks off Costas' back.

The son of a Greek shipping tycoon, Costas had spurned the playboy lifestyle which was his for the asking and opted for ten years at Stanford and MIT, emerging as an expert in submersible technology. Surrounded by a vast jumble of tools and parts that only he could navigate, Costas would routinely conjure up wondrous inventions like some latter-day Caractacus Pott. His passion for a challenge was matched by his gregarious nature, a vital asset in a profession where teamwork was essential.

The two men had first met at the NATO base at Izmir in Turkey when Jack had been seconded to the Naval Intelligence School and Costas was a civilian adviser to UNANTSUB, the United Nations anti-submarine warfare research establishment. A few years later Jack invited Costas to join him at the International Maritime University, the research institution which had been their home for more than ten years now. In that time Jack had seen his remit as director of field operations at IMU grow to four ships and more than two hundred personnel, and despite an equally burgeoning role in the engineering department, Costas always seemed to find a way to join Jack when things got exciting.

'Thanks, Jack.' Costas slowly stood up, too tired to say more. He only came as high as Jack's shoulders and had a barrel chest and forearms inherited from generations of

Greek sponge fishermen and sailors, with a personality to match. This project had been close to his heart as well, and he was suddenly drained by the excitement of discovery. It was he who had set the expedition in train, using his father's connections with the Greek government. Although they were now in international waters, the support of the Hellenic Navy had been invaluable, not least in keeping them supplied with the cylinders of purified gas which were vital for trimix diving.

'Oh, I almost forgot.' Costas' round, tanned face broke into a grin as he reached into his stabilizer jacket. 'Just in case you thought I'd faked the whole thing.'

He extracted a package swaddled in protective neoprene and handed it over, a triumphant gleam in his eye. Jack was unprepared for the weight and his hand momentarily dropped. He undid the wrapping and gasped in astonishment.

It was a solid metal disc about the diameter of his hand, its surface as lustrous as if it were brand new. There was no mistaking the deep hue of unalloyed gold, a gold refined to the purity of bullion.

Unlike many of his academic colleagues Jack never pretended to be unmoved by treasure, and for a moment he let the thrill of holding several kilogrammes of gold wash through him. As he held it up and angled it towards the sun, the disc gave off a dazzling flash of light, as if it were releasing a great burst of energy pent up over the millennia.

He was even more elated when he saw the sun glint off markings on the surface. He lowered the disc into Costas' shadow and traced his fingers over the indentations, all of them exquisitely executed on one convex side.

In the centre was a curious rectilinear device, like a large letter H, with a short line dropping from the crossbar and four lines extending like combs from either side. Around the edge of the disc were three concentric bands, each one divided into twenty compartments. Each compartment contained a different symbol stamped into the metal. To Jack the outer circle looked like pictograms, symbols that conveyed the meaning of a word or phrase. At a glance he could make out a man's head, a walking man, a paddle, a boat and a sheaf of corn. The inner compartments were aligned with those along the edge, but instead contained linear signs. Each of these was different but they seemed more akin to letters of the alphabet than to pictograms.

Costas stood and watched Jack examine the disc, totally absorbed. His eyes were alight in a way Costas had seen before. Jack was touching the Age of Heroes, a time shrouded in myth and legend, yet a period which had been spectacularly revealed in great palaces and citadels, in sublime works of art and brilliantly honed weapons of war. He was communing with the ancients in a way that was only possible with a shipwreck, holding a priceless artefact that had not been tossed away but had been cherished to the moment of catastrophe. Yet it was an artefact shrouded in mystery, one he knew would draw him on without respite until all its secrets were out.

Jack turned the disc over several times and looked at the inscriptions again, his mind racing back to undergraduate courses on the history of writing. He had seen something like this before. He made a mental note to email the image to Professor James Dillen, his old mentor at Cambridge University and the world's leading authority on the ancient scripts of Greece.

Jack passed the disc back to Costas. For a moment the two men looked at each other, their eyes ablaze with excitement. Jack hurried over to join the team kitting up beside the stern ladder. The sight of all that gold had redoubled his fervour.

The greatest threat to archaeology lay in international waters, a free-for-all where no country held jurisdiction. Every attempt to impose a global sea law had ended in failure. The problems of policing such a huge area seemed insurmountable. Yet advances in technology meant that remote-operated submersibles, of the type used to discover the *Titanic*, were now little more expensive than a car. Deep-water exploration that was once the preserve of a few institutes was now open to all, and had led to the wholesale destruction of historic sites. Organized pillagers with state-of-the-art technology were stripping the seabed with no record being made for posterity and artefacts disappearing for ever into the hands of private collectors. And the IMU teams were not only up against legitimate operators. Looted antiquities had become major currency in the criminal underworld.

Jack glanced up at the timekeeper's platform and felt a familiar surge of adrenalin as he signalled his intention to dive. He began carefully to assemble his equipment, setting his dive computer and checking the pressure of his cylinders, his demeanour methodical and professional as if there were nothing special about this day.

In truth he could barely contain his excitement.

2

Maurice Hiebermeyer stood up and wiped his forehead, momentarily checking the sheen of sweat that was dripping off his face. He looked at his watch. It was nearly noon, close to the end of their working day, and the desert heat was becoming unbearable. He arched his back and winced, suddenly realizing how much he ached from more than five hours hunched over a dusty trench. He slowly made his way to the central part of the site for his customary end-of-day inspection. With his wide-brimmed hat, little round glasses and knee-length shorts he cut a faintly comic figure, like some empire builder of old, an image that belied his stature as one of the world's leading Egyptologists.

He silently watched the excavation, his thoughts

accompanied by the familiar clinking of mattocks and the occasional creak of a wheelbarrow. This may not have the glamour of the Valley of the Kings, he reflected, but it had far more artefacts. It had taken years of fruitless search before Tutankhamun's tomb had been discovered; here they were literally up to their knees in mummies, with hundreds already revealed and more being uncovered every day as new passageways were cleared of sand.

Hiebermeyer walked over to the deep pit where it had all begun. He peered over the edge into an underground labyrinth, a maze of rock-cut tunnels lined with niches where the dead had remained undisturbed over the centuries, escaping the attention of the tomb robbers who had destroyed so many of the royal graves. It was a wayward camel that had exposed the catacombs; the unfortunate beast had strayed off the track and disappeared into the sand before its owner's eyes. The drover had run over to the spot and recoiled in horror when he saw row upon row of bodies far below, their faces staring up at him as if in reproach for disturbing their hallowed place of rest.

'These people are in all likelihood your ancestors,' Hiebermeyer had told the camel drover after he had been summoned from the Institute of Archaeology in Alexandria to the desert oasis two hundred kilometres to the south. The excavations had proved him right. The faces which had so terrified the drover were in reality exquisite paintings. Some were of a quality unsurpassed until the Italian Renaissance. Yet they were the work of artisans, not some ancient great master, and the mummies were not nobles but ordinary folk. Most of them had lived not in the age of the pharaohs but in the centuries when Egypt was under Greek and Roman rule. It was a time of increased prosperity, when the introduction of coinage spread wealth and allowed the new middle class to afford gilded mummy casings and elaborate burial rituals. They lived in the Fayum, the fertile oasis which extended sixty kilometres east from the necropolis towards the Nile.

The burials represented a much wider cross-section of life than a royal necropolis, Hiebermeyer reflected, and they told stories just as fascinating as a mummified Ramses or Tutankhamun. Only this morning he had been excavating a family of cloth-makers, a man named Seth and his father and brother. Colourful scenes of temple life adorned the *cartonnage*, the plaster and linen board that formed the breastplate over their coffins. The inscription showed that the two brothers had been lowly attendants in the temple of Neith at Saïs but had experienced good fortune and gone into business with their father, a trader in cloth with the Greeks. They had clearly profited handsomely to judge from the valuable offerings in the mummy wrappings and the gold-leaf masks that covered their faces.

'Dr Hiebermeyer, I think you should come and see this.'

The voice came from one of his most experienced trench supervisors, an Egyptian graduate student who he hoped one day would follow him as director of the institute. Aysha Farouk peered up from the side of the pit, her handsome, dark-skinned face an image from the past, as if one of the mummy portraits had suddenly sprung to life.

'You will have to climb down.'

Hiebermeyer replaced his hat with a yellow safety helmet and gingerly descended the ladder, his progress aided by one of the local *fellahin* employed as labourers on the site. Aysha was perched over a mummy in a sandstone niche only a few steps down from the surface. It was one of the graves that had been damaged by the camel's fall, and Hiebermeyer could see where the terracotta coffin had been cracked and the mummy inside partly torn open.

They were in the oldest part of the site, a shallow cluster of passageways which formed the heart of the necropolis. Hiebermeyer fervently hoped his student had found something that would prove his theory that the mortuary complex had been founded as early as the sixth century BC, more than two centuries before Alexander the Great conquered Egypt.

'Right. What do we have?' His German accent gave his voice a clipped authority.

He stepped off the ladder and squeezed in beside his assistant, careful not to damage the mummy any further. They had both donned lightweight medical masks, protection against the viruses and bacteria that might lie dormant within the wrapping and be revived in the heat and moisture of their lungs. He closed his eyes and briefly bowed his head, an act of private piety he carried out each time he opened a burial chamber. After the dead had told their tale he would see that they were reinterred to continue their voyage through the afterlife.

When he was ready, Aysha adjusted the lamp and reached into the coffin, cautiously prising apart the jagged tear which ran like a great wound through the belly of the mummy.

'Just let me clean up.'

She worked with a surgeon's precision, her fingers deftly manipulating the brushes and dental picks which had been neatly arranged in a tray beside her. After a few minutes clearing away the debris from her earlier work she replaced the tools and edged her way towards the head of the coffin, making room for Hiebermeyer to have a closer look.

He cast an expert eye over the objects she had removed from the resin-soaked gauze of the mummy, its aroma still pungent after all the centuries. He quickly identified a golden *ba*, the winged symbol of the soul, alongside protective amulets shaped like cobras. In the centre of the tray was an amulet of Qebeh-sennuef, guardian of the intestines. Alongside was an exquisite faience brooch of an eagle god, its wings outstretched and the silicate material fired to a lustrous greenish hue.

He shifted his bulky frame along the shelf until he was poised directly over the incision in the casing. The body was facing east to greet the rising sun in symbolic rebirth, a tradition which went far back into prehistory. Below the torn wrapping he could see the rust-coloured torso of the mummy itself, the skin taut and parchment-like over the ribcage. The mummies in the necropolis had not been prepared in the manner of the pharaohs, whose bodies were eviscerated and filled with embalming salts; here the desiccating conditions of the desert had done most of the job, and the embalmers had removed only the organs of the gut. By the Roman period even that procedure was abandoned. The preservational characteristics of the desert were a godsend to archaeologists, as remarkable as waterlogged sites, and Hiebermeyer was constantly astonished by the delicate organic materials that had survived for thousands of years in near perfect condition.

'Do you see?' Aysha could no longer contain her excitement. 'There, below your right hand.'

'Ah yes.' Hiebermeyer's eye had been caught by a torn flap in the mummy wrapping, its ragged edge resting on the lower pelvis.

The material was covered with finely spaced writing. This in itself was nothing new; the ancient Egyptians were indefatigable record-keepers, writing copious lists on the paper they made by matting together fibres of papyrus reed. Discarded papyrus also made excellent mummy wrapping and was collected and recycled by the funerary technicians.

These scraps were among the most precious finds of the necropolis, and were one reason why Hiebermeyer had proposed such a large-scale excavation.

At the moment he was less interested in what the writing said than the possibility of dating the mummy from the style and language of the script. He could understand Aysha's excitement. The torn-open mummy offered a rare opportunity for on-the-spot dating. Normally they would have to wait for weeks while the conservators in Alexandria painstakingly peeled away the wrappings.

'The script is Greek,' Aysha said, her enthusiasm getting the better of her deference. She was now crouched beside him, her hair brushing against his shoulder as she motioned towards the papyrus.

Hiebermeyer nodded. She was right. There was no mistaking the fluid script of ancient Greek, quite distinct from the hieratic of the Pharaonic period and the Coptic of the Fayum region in Greek and Roman times.

He was puzzled. How could a fragment of Greek text have been incorporated in a Fayum mummy of the sixth or fifth century BC? The Greeks had been allowed to establish a trading colony at Naucratis on the Canopic branch of the Nile in the seventh century BC, but their movement inland had been strictly controlled. They did not become major players in Egypt until Alexander the Great's conquest in 332 BC, and it was inconceivable that Egyptian records would have been kept in Greek before that date.

Hiebermeyer suddenly felt deflated. A Greek document in the Fayum would most likely date from the time of the Ptolemies, the Macedonian dynasty that began with Alexander's general, Ptolemy I Lagus, and ended with the suicide of Cleopatra and the Roman takeover in 30 BC. Had he been so wrong in his early date for this part of the necropolis? He turned towards Aysha, his expressionless face masking a rising disappointment.

'I'm not sure I like this. I'm going to take a closer look.'

He pulled the angle-lamp closer to the mummy. Using a brush from Aysha's tray, he delicately swept away the dust from one corner of the papyrus, revealing a script as crisp as if it had been penned that day. He took out his magnifying glass and held his breath as he inspected the writing. The letters were small and continuous, uninterrupted by punctuation. He knew it would take time and patience before a full translation could be made.

What mattered now was its style. Hiebermeyer was fortunate to have studied under Professor James Dillen, a renowned linguist whose teaching left such an indelible impression that Hiebermeyer was still able to remember every detail more than two decades after he had last studied ancient Greek calligraphy.

After a few moments his face broke into a grin and he turned towards Aysha.

'We can rest easy. It's early, I'm sure of it. Fifth, probably sixth century BC.'

He closed his eyes with relief and she gave him a swift embrace, the reserve between student and professor momentarily forgotten. She had guessed the date already; her master's thesis had been on the archaic Greek inscriptions of Athens and she was more of an expert than Hiebermeyer, but she had wanted him to have the triumph of discovery, the satisfaction of vindicating his hypothesis about the early foundation of the necropolis.

Hiebermeyer peered again at the papyrus, his mind racing. With its tightly spaced, continuous script it was clear this was no administrative ledger, no mere list of names and numbers. This was not the type of document which would have been produced by the merchants of Naucratis. Were there other Greeks in Egypt at this period? Hiebermeyer knew only of occasional visits by scholars who had been granted rare access to the temple archives. Herodotus of Halicarnassos, the Father of History, had visited the priests in the fifth century BC, and they had told him many wondrous things, of the world before the conflict between the Greeks and the Persians which was the main theme of his book. Earlier Greeks had visited too, Athenian statesmen and men of letters, but their visits were only half remembered and none of their accounts had survived first-hand.

Hiebermeyer dared not voice his thoughts to Aysha, aware of the embarrassment that could be caused by a premature announcement which would spread like wildfire among the waiting journalists. But he could barely restrain himself. Had they found some long-lost lynchpin of ancient history?

Almost all the literature that survived from antiquity was known only from medieval copies, from manuscripts painstakingly transcribed by monks in the monasteries after the fall of the Roman Empire in the west. Most of the ancient manuscripts had been ruined by decay or destroyed by invaders and religious zealots. For years scholars had hoped against hope that the desert of Egypt would reveal lost texts, writings which might overturn ancient history. Above all they dreamed of something that might preserve the wisdom of Egypt's scholar priests. The temple scriptoria visited by Herodotus and his predecessors preserved an unbroken tradition of knowledge that extended back thousands of years to the dawn of recorded history.

Hiebermeyer ran excitedly through the possibilities. Was this a first-hand account of the wanderings of the Jews, a document to set alongside the Old Testament? Or a record of the end of the Bronze Age, of the reality behind the Trojan

War? It might tell an even earlier history, one showing that the Egyptians did more than simply trade with Bronze Age Crete but actually built the great palaces. An Egyptian King Minos? Hiebermeyer found the idea hugely appealing.

He was brought back to earth by Aysha, who had continued to clean the papyrus and now motioned him towards the mummy.

'Look at this.'

Aysha had been working along the edge of the papyrus where it stuck out from the undamaged wrapping. She gingerly raised a flap of linen and pointed with her brush.

'It's some kind of symbol,' she said.

The text had been broken by a strange rectilinear device, part of it still concealed under the wrapping. It looked like the end of a garden rake with four protruding arms.

'What do you make of it?'

'I don't know.' Hiebermeyer paused, anxious not to seem at a loss in front of his student. 'It may be some form of numerical device, perhaps derived from cuneiform.' He was recalling the wedge-shaped symbols impressed into clay tablets by the early scribes of the Near East.

'Here. This might give a clue.' He leaned forward until his face was only inches away from the mummy, gently blowing the dust from the text that resumed below the symbol. Between the symbol and the text was a single word, its Greek letters larger than the continuous script on the rest of the papyrus.

'I think I can read it,' he murmured. 'Take the notebook out of my back pocket and write down the letters as I dictate them.'

She did as instructed and squatted by the coffin with her pencil poised, flattered that Hiebermeyer had confidence in her ability to make the transcription.

'OK. Here goes.' He paused and raised his magnifying glass. 'The first letter is Alpha.' He shifted to catch a better light. 'Then Tau. Then Alpha again. No, scratch that. Lamna. Now another Alpha.'

Despite the shade of the niche the sweat was welling up on his forehead. He shifted back slightly, anxious to avoid dripping on the papyrus.

'Nu. Then Tau again. Iota, I think. Yes, definitely. And now the final letter.' Without letting his eyes leave the papyrus he felt for a small pair of tweezers on the tray and used them to raise part of the wrapping that was lying over the end of the word. He blew gently on the text again.

'Sigma. Yes, Sigma. And that's it.' Hiebermeyer straightened. 'Right. What do we have?'

In truth he had known from the moment he saw the word, but his mind refused to register what had been staring him in the face. It was beyond his wildest dreams, a possibility so embedded in fantasy that most scholars would simply disown it.

They both stared dumbfounded at the notebook, the single word transfixing them as if by magic, everything else suddenly blotted out and meaningless.

'*Atlantis.*' Hiebermeyer's voice was barely a whisper.

He turned away, blinked hard, and turned back again. The word was still there. His mind was suddenly in a frenzy of speculation, pulling out everything he knew and trying to make it hold.

Years of scholarship told him to start with what was least contentious, to try to work his finds into the established framework first.

Atlantis. He stared into space. To the ancients the story could have occupied the tail end of their creation myth, when the Age of Giants gave over to the First Age of Men. Perhaps the papyrus was an account of this legendary golden age, an Atlantis rooted not in history but in myth.

Hiebermeyer looked into the coffin and wordlessly shook his head. That could not be right. The place, the date. It was too much of a coincidence. His instinct had never failed him, and now he felt it more strongly than he ever had before.

The familiar, predictable world of mummies and pharaohs, priests and temples seemed to fall away before his eyes. All he could think about was the enormous expenditure of effort and imagination that had gone into reconstructing the ancient past, an edifice that suddenly seemed so fragile and precarious.

It was funny, he mused, but that camel may have been responsible for the greatest archaeological discovery ever made.

'Aysha, I want you to prepare this coffin for immediate removal. Fill that cavity with foam and seal it over.' He was site director again, the immense responsibility of their discovery overcoming his boyish excitement of the last few minutes. 'I want this on the truck to Alexandria today, and I want you to go with it. Arrange for the usual armed escort, but nothing special as I do not want to attract undue attention.'

They were ever mindful of the threat posed by modern-day tomb robbers, scavengers and highwaymen who lurked in the dunes around the site and had become increasingly audacious in their attempts to steal even the smallest trifle.

'And Aysha,' he said, his face now deadly serious. 'I know I can trust you not to breathe a word of this to anyone, not even to our colleagues and friends in the team.'

Hiebermeyer left Aysha to her task and grappled his way up the ladder, the extraordinary drama of the discovery suddenly compounding his fatigue. He made his way across the site, staggering slightly under the withering sun, oblivious to the excavators who were still waiting dutifully for his inspection. He entered the site director's hut and slumped heavily in front of the satellite phone. After wiping his face and closing his eyes for a moment he composed himself and switched on the set. He dialled a number and soon a voice came over the headphone, crackly at first but clearer as he adjusted the antenna.

'Good afternoon, you have reached the International Maritime University. How may I help you?'

Hiebermeyer quickly responded, his voice hoarse with excitement. 'Hello, this is Maurice Hiebermeyer calling from Egypt. This is top priority. Patch me through immediately to Jack Howard.'

3

The waters of the old harbour lapped gently at the quayside, each wave drawing in lines of floating seaweed that stretched out as far as the eye could see. Across the basin, rows of fishing boats bobbed and shimmered in the midday sun. Jack Howard stood up and walked towards the balustrade, his dark hair ruffled by the breeze and his bronzed features reflecting the months spent at sea in search of a Bronze Age shipwreck. He leaned against the parapet and gazed out at the sparkling waters. This had once been the ancient harbour of Alexandria, its splendour rivalled only by Carthage and Rome itself. From here the grain fleets had set sail, wide-hulled argosies that carried the bounty of Egypt to a million people in Rome. From here, too, wealthy merchants had despatched chests of gold and silver across the desert to the Red Sea and beyond; in return had come the riches of the east, frankincense and myrrh, lapis lazuli and sapphires and tortoiseshell, silk and opium, brought by hardy mariners who dared to sail the monsoon route from Arabia and far-off India.

Jack looked down at the massive stone revetment ten metres below. Two thousand years ago this had been one of the wonders of the world, the fabled Pharos of Alexandria. It was inaugurated by Ptolemy II Philadelphus in 285 BC, a mere fifty years after Alexander the Great had founded the city. At one hundred metres it towered higher than the Great Pyramid at Giza. Even today, more than six centuries after the lighthouse had been toppled by an earthquake, the foundations remained one of the marvels of antiquity. The walls had been converted into a medieval fortress and served as headquarters of the Institute of Archaeology at Alexandria, now the foremost centre for the study of Egypt during the Graeco-Roman period.

The remains of the lighthouse still littered the harbour floor. Just below the surface lay a great jumble of blocks and columns, their massive forms interpersed with shattered statues of kings and queens, gods and sphinxes. Jack himself had discovered one of the most impressive, a colossal form broken on the seabed like Ozymandias, King of Kings, the toppled image of Ramses II so famously evoked by Shelley. Jack had argued that the statues should be recorded and left undisturbed like their poetic counterpart in the desert.

He was pleased to see a queue forming at the submarine port, testimony to the success of the underwater park. Across the harbour the skyline was dominated by the futuristic Bibliotheca Alexandrina, the reconstituted library of the ancients that was a further link to the glories of the past.

'Jack!' The door of the conference chamber swung open

and a stout figure stepped onto the balcony. Jack turned to greet the newcomer.

'Herr Professor Dr Hiebermeyer!' Jack grinned and held out his hand. 'I can't believe you brought me all the way here to look at a piece of mummy wrapping.'

'I knew I'd get you hooked on ancient Egypt in the end.'

The two men had been exact contemporaries at Cambridge, and their rivalry had fuelled their shared passion for antiquity. Jack knew Hiebermeyer's occasional formality masked a highly receptive mind, and Hiebermeyer in turn knew how to break through Jack's reserve. After so many projects in other parts of the world, Jack looked forward eagerly to sparring again with his old tutorial partner. Hiebermeyer had changed little since their student days, and their disagreements about the influence of Egypt on Greek civilization were an integral part of their friendship.

Behind Hiebermeyer stood an older man dressed immaculately in a crisp light suit and bow tie, his eyes startlingly sharp beneath a shock of white hair. Jack strode over and warmly shook the hand of their mentor, Professor James Dillen.

Dillen stood aside and ushered two more figures through the doorway.

'Jack, I don't think you've met Dr Svetlanova.'

Her penetrating green eyes were almost level with his own and she smiled as she shook his hand. 'Please call me Katya.' Her English was accented but flawless, a result of ten years' study in America and England after she had been allowed to travel from the Soviet Union. Jack knew of Katya by reputation, but he had not expected to feel such an immediate attraction. Normally Jack was able to focus completely on the excitement of a new discovery, but this was something else. He could not keep his eyes off her.

'Jack Howard,' he replied, annoyed that he had let his guard down as her cool and amused stare seemed to bore into him.

Her long black hair swung as she turned to introduce her colleague. 'And this is my assistant Olga Ivanovna Bortsev from the Moscow Institute of Palaeography.'

In contrast to Katya Svetlanova's well-dressed elegance, Olga was distinctly in the Russian peasant mould. She looked like one of the propaganda heroines of the Great Patriotic War, thought Jack, plain and fearless, with the strength of any man. She was struggling beneath a pile of books but looked him full in the eyes as he offered his hand.

With the formalities over, Dillen ushered them through the door into the conference room. He was to chair the proceedings, Hiebermeyer having relinquished his usual role as director of the institute in deference to the older man's status.

They seated themselves round the table. Olga arranged her load of books neatly beside Katya and then retired to one of the chairs ranged along the back wall of the room.

Hiebermeyer began to speak, pacing to and fro at the far end of the room and illustrating his account with slides. He quickly ran through the circumstances of the discovery and described how the coffin had been moved to Alexandria only two days previously. Since then the conservators had worked round the clock to unravel the mummy and free the papyrus. He confirmed that there were no other fragments of writing, that the papyrus was only a few centimetres larger than had been visible during the excavation.

The result was laid out in front of them under a glass panel on the table, a ragged sheet about thirty centimetres long and half as wide, its surface densely covered by writing except for a gap in the middle.

'Extraordinary coincidence that the camel should have put its foot right in it,' Katya said.

'Extraordinary how often that happens in archaeology.' Jack winked at her after he had spoken and they both smiled.

'Most of the great finds are made by chance,' Hiebermeyer continued, oblivious to the other two. 'And remember, we have hundreds more mummies to open. This was precisely the type of discovery I was hoping for and there could be many more.'

'A fabulous prospect,' agreed Katya.

Dillen leaned across to take the projector remote control. He straightened a pile of papers which he had removed from his briefcase while Hiebermeyer was speaking.

'Friends and colleagues,' he said, slowly scanning the expectant faces. 'We all know why we are here.'

Their attention shifted to the screen at the far end of the room. The image of the desert necropolis was replaced by a close-up of the papyrus. The word which had so transfixed Hiebermeyer in the desert now filled the screen.

'Atlantis,' Jack breathed.

'I must ask you to be patient.' Dillen scanned the faces, aware how desperate they were to hear his and Katya's translation of the text. 'Before I speak I propose that Dr Svetlanova give us an account of the Atlantis story as we know it. Katya, if you will.'

'With pleasure, Professor.'

Katya and Dillen had become friends when she was a sabbatical fellow under his guidance at Cambridge. Recently they had been together in Athens when the city had been devastated by a massive earthquake, cracking open the Acropolis to reveal a cluster of rock-cut chambers which contained the long-lost archive of the ancient city. Katya and Dillen had assumed responsibility for publishing the texts relating to Greek exploration beyond the Mediterranean. Only a few weeks earlier their faces had been splashed over front pages all round the world following a press conference in which they revealed how an expedition of Greek and

Egyptian adventurers had sailed across the Indian Ocean as far as the South China Sea.

Katya was also one of the world's leading experts on the legend of Atlantis, and had brought with her copies of the relevant ancient texts. She picked up two small books and opened them at the marked pages.

'Gentlemen, may I first say what a pleasure it is for me to be invited to this symposium. It is a great honour for the Moscow Institute of Palaeography. Long may the spirit of international co-operation continue.'

There was an appreciative murmur from around the table.

'I will be brief. First, you can forget virtually everything you have ever heard about Atlantis.'

She had assumed a serious scholarly demeanour, the twinkle in her eye gone, and Jack found himself concentrating entirely on what she had to say.

'You may think Atlantis was a global legend, some distant episode in history half remembered by many different cultures, preserved in myth and legend around the world.'

'Like the stories of the Great Flood,' Jack interjected.

'Exactly.' She fixed his eyes with wry amusement. 'But you would be wrong. There is one source only.' She picked up the two books as she spoke. 'The ancient Greek philosopher Plato.'

The others settled back to listen.

'Plato lived in Athens from 427 to 347 BC, a generation after Herodotus,' she said. 'As a young man Plato would have known of the orator Pericles, would have attended the plays of Euripides and Aeschylus and Aristophanes, would have seen the great temples being erected on the Acropolis. These were the glory days of classical Greece, the greatest period of civilization ever known.'

Katya put down the books and pressed them open. 'These two books are known as the *Timaeus* and the *Critias*. They are imaginary dialogues between men of those names and Socrates, Plato's mentor whose wisdom survives only through the writings of his pupil.

'Here, in a fictional conversation, Critias tells Socrates about a mighty civilization, one which came forth out of the Atlantic Ocean nine thousand years before. The Atlanteans were descendants of Poseidon, god of the sea. Critias is lecturing Socrates.

'There was an island situated in front of the Straits which are by you called the Pillars of Hercules; the island was larger than Libya and Asia put together. In this island of Atlantis there was a great and wonderful empire which had rule over the whole island and several others, and over parts of the continent, and, furthermore, the men of Atlantis had subjugated the parts of Libya within the Columns of Hercules as far as Egypt, and of Europe as far as Tyrrhenia. This vast power, gathered into one, endeavoured to subdue at a blow our country and yours and the whole of the region within the Straits.'

Katya took the second volume, looking up briefly. 'Libya was the ancient name for Africa, Tyrrhenia was central Italy and the Pillars of Hercules the Strait of Gibraltar. But Plato was neither geographer nor historian. His theme was a monumental war between the Athenians and the Atlanteans, one which the Athenians naturally won but only after enduring the most extreme danger.'

She looked again at the text.

'And now the climax, the nub of the legend. These final few sentences have tantalized scholars for more than two thousand years, and have led to more dead ends than I can count.

'But afterwards there occurred violent earthquakes and floods; and

*in a single day and night of misfortune all your warlike men in a
body sank into the earth, and the island of Atlantis in like manner
disappeared in the depths of the sea.'*

Katya closed the book and gazed quizzically at Jack. 'What
would you expect to find in Atlantis?'

Jack hesitated uncharacteristically, aware that she would be
judging his scholarship for the first time. 'Atlantis has always
meant much more than simply a lost civilization,' he replied.
'To the ancients it was a fascination with the fallen, with
greatness doomed by arrogance and hubris. Every age has had
its Atlantis fantasy, always harking back to a world of
unimagined splendour overshadowing all history. To the
Nazis it was the birthplace of *Überman,* the original Aryan
homeland, spurring a demented search around the world for
racially pure descendants. To others it was the Garden of
Eden, a Paradise Lost.'

Katya nodded and spoke quietly. 'If there is any truth to this
story, if the papyrus gives us any more clues, then we may be
able to solve one of the greatest mysteries of ancient history.'

There was a pause as the assembled gathering looked from
one to the other, anticipation and barely repressed eagerness
on their faces.

'Thank you, Katya.' Dillen stood up, obviously more
comfortable speaking on his feet. He was an accomplished
lecturer, used to commanding the full attention of his audience.

'I suggest the Atlantis story is not history but allegory.
Plato's intention was to draw out a series of moral lessons. In
the *Timaeus*, order triumphs over chaos in the formation of
the Cosmos. In the *Critias*, men of self-discipline, moderation
and respect for the law triumph over men of pride and
presumption. The conflict with Atlantis was contrived to
show that Athenians had always been people of resolve who

would ultimately be victorious in any war. Even Plato's pupil Aristotle thought Atlantis never existed.' Dillen put his hands on the table and leaned forward.

'I suggest Atlantis is a political fable. Plato's account of how he came by the story is a whimsical fiction like Swift's introduction to *Gulliver's Travels*, where he gives a source which is plausible but could never be verified.'

Dillen was playing devil's advocate, Jack knew. He always relished his old professor's rhetorical skills, a reflection of years spent in the world's great universities.

'It would be useful if you could run over Plato's source,' Hiebermeyer said.

'Certainly.' Dillen looked at his notes. 'Critias was Plato's great-grandfather. Critias claims that his own great-grandfather heard the Atlantis story from Solon, the famed Athenian lawmaker. Solon in turn heard it from an aged Egyptian priest at Saïs in the Nile Delta.'

Jack did a quick mental calculation. 'Solon lived from about 640 to 560 BC. He would only have been admitted to the temple as a venerated scholar. If we therefore assume he visited Egypt as an older man, but not too old to travel, that would place the encounter some time in the early sixth century BC, say 590 or 580 BC.'

'If, that is, we are dealing with fact and not fiction. I would like to pose a question. How is it that such a remarkable story was not known more widely? Herodotus visited Egypt in the middle of the fifth century BC, about half a century before Plato's time. He was an indefatigable researcher, a magpie who scooped up every bit of trivia, and his work survives in its entirety. Yet there is no mention of Atlantis. Why?'

Dillen's gaze ranged around the room taking in each of them in turn. He sat down. After a pause Hiebermeyer stood up and paced behind his chair.

'I think I might be able to answer your question.' He paused briefly. 'In our world we tend to think of historical knowledge as universal property. There are exceptions of course, and we all know history can be manipulated, but in general little of significance can be kept hidden for long. Well, ancient Egypt was not like that.'

The others listened attentively.

'Unlike Greece and the Near East, whose cultures had been swept away by invasions, Egypt had an unbroken tradition stretching back to the early Bronze Age, to the early dynastic period around 3100 BC. Some believe it stretched back even as far as the arrival of the first agriculturalists almost four thousand years earlier.'

There was a murmur of interest from the others.

'Yet by the time of Solon this ancient knowledge had become increasingly hard to access. It was as if it had been divided into interlocking fragments, like a jigsaw puzzle, then packaged up and parcelled away.' He paused, pleased with the metaphor. 'It came to reside in many different temples, dedicated to many different gods. The priests came to guard their own parcel of knowledge covetously, as their own treasure. It could only be revealed to outsiders through divine intervention, through some sign from the gods. Oddly,' he added with a twinkle in his eye, 'these signs came most often when the applicant offered a benefaction, usually gold.'

'So you could buy knowledge?' Jack asked.

'Yes, but only when the circumstances were right, on the right day of the month, outside the many religious festivals, according to a host of other signs and auguries. Unless everything was right, an applicant would be turned away, even if he arrived with a shipload of gold.'

'So the Atlantis story could have been known in only one temple, and told to only one Greek.'

'Precisely.' Hiebermeyer nodded solemnly at Jack. 'Only a handful of Greeks ever made it into the temple scriptoria. The priests were suspicious of men like Herodotus who were too inquisitive and indiscriminate, travelling from temple to temple. Herodotus was sometimes fed misinformation, stories that were exaggerated and falsified. He was, as you English say, led up the garden path.

'The most precious knowledge was too sacred to be committed to paper. It was passed down by word of mouth, from high priest to high priest. Most of it died with the last priests when the Greeks shut down the temples. What little made it to paper was lost under the Romans, when the Royal Library of Alexandria was burnt during the civil war in 48 BC and the Daughter Library went the same way when the Emperor Theodosius ordered the destruction of all remaining pagan temples in AD 391. We already know some of what was lost from references in surviving ancient texts. The *Geography* of Pytheas the Navigator. The *History of the World* by the Emperor Claudius. The missing volumes of Galen and Celsus. Great works of history and science, compendia of pharmaceutical knowledge that would have advanced medicine immeasurably. We can barely begin to imagine the secret knowledge of the Egyptians that went the same way.'

Hiebermeyer sat down and Katya spoke again.

'I'd like to propose an alternative hypothesis. I suggest Plato was telling the truth about his source. Yet for some reason Solon did not write down an account of his visit. Was he forbidden from doing so by the priests?'

She picked up the books and continued. 'I believe Plato took the bare facts he knew and embellished them to suit his purposes. Here I agree in part with Professor Dillen. Plato exaggerated to make Atlantis a more remote and awesome place, fitting for a distant age. So he put the story far back in the past, made Atlantis equal to the largest landmass he could envisage, and placed it in the western ocean beyond the boundaries of the ancient world.' She looked at Jack. 'There is a theory about Atlantis, one widely held by archaeologists. We are fortunate in having one of its leading proponents among us today. Dr Howard?'

Jack was already flicking the remote control to a map of the Aegean with the island of Crete prominently in the centre.

'It only becomes plausible if we scale it down,' he said. 'If we set it nine hundred rather than nine thousand years before Solon we arrive at about 1600 BC. That was the period of the great Bronze Age civilizations, the New Kingdom of Egypt, the Canaanites of Syro-Palestine, the Hittites of Anatolia, the Mycenaeans of Greece, the Minoans of Crete. This is the only possible context for the Atlantis story.'

He aimed a pencil-sized light pointer at the map. 'And I believe the only possible location is Crete.' He looked at Hiebermeyer. 'For most Egyptians at the time of the Pharaohs, Crete was the northerly limit of their experience. From the south it's an imposing land, a long shoreline backed by mountains, yet the Egyptians would have known it was an island from the expeditions they undertook to the palace of Knossos on the north coast.'

'What about the Atlantic Ocean?' Hiebermeyer asked.

'You can forget that,' Jack said. 'In Plato's day the sea to the west of Gibraltar was unknown, a vast ocean leading to the fiery edge of the world. So that was where Plato relocated Atlantis. His readers would hardly have been awestruck by an island in the Mediterranean.'

'And the word *Atlantis*?'

'The sea god Poseidon had a son Atlas, the muscle-bound colossus who carried the sky on his shoulders. The Atlantic Ocean was the Ocean of *Atlas*, not of Atlantis. The term

Atlantic first appears in Herodotus, so it was probably in widespread currency by the time Plato was writing.' Jack paused and looked at the others.

'Before seeing the papyrus I would have argued that Plato made up the word Atlantis, a plausible name for a lost continent in the Ocean of Atlas. We know from inscriptions that the Egyptians referred to the Minoans and Mycenaeans as the people of Keftiu, people from the north who came in ships bearing tribute. I would have suggested that Keftiu, not Atlantis, was the name for the lost continent in the original account. Now I'm not so sure. If this papyrus really does date from before Plato's time then clearly he didn't invent the word.'

Katya swept her long hair back and gazed at Jack. 'Was the war between the Athenians and the Atlanteans in reality a war between the Mycenaeans and the Minoans?'

'I believe so,' Jack looked keenly back at her as he replied. 'The Athenian Acropolis may have been the most impressive of all the Mycenaean strongholds before it was demolished to make way for the buildings of the classical period. Soon after 1500 BC Mycenaean warriors took over Knossos on Crete, ruling it until the palace was destroyed by fire and rampage a hundred years later. The conventional view is that the Mycenaeans were warlike, the Minoans peaceable. The takeover occurred after the Minoans had been devastated by a natural catastrophe.'

'There may be a hint of this in the legend of Theseus and the Minotaur,' Katya said. 'Theseus the Athenian prince wooed Ariadne, daughter of King Minos of Knossos, but before taking her hand he had to confront the Minotaur in the Labyrinth. The Minotaur was half bull, half man, surely a representation of Minoan strength in arms.'

Hiebermeyer joined in. 'The Greek Bronze Age was rediscovered by men who believed the legends contained a kernel of truth. Sir Arthur Evans at Knossos, Heinrich

Schliemann at Troy and Mycenae. Both believed the Trojan wars of Homer's *Iliad* and *Odyssey*, written down in the eighth century BC, preserved a memory of the tumultuous events which led to the collapse of Bronze Age civilization.'

'That brings me to my final point,' Jack said. 'Plato would have known nothing of Bronze Age Crete, which had been forgotten in the Dark Age that preceded the classical period. Yet there is much in the story reminiscent of the Minoans, details Plato could never have known. Katya, may I?' Jack reached across and took the two books she pushed forward, catching her eye as he did so. He flicked through one and laid it open towards the end.

'Here. Atlantis *was the way to other islands, and from those you might pass to the whole of the opposite continent.* That's exactly how Crete looks from Egypt, the other islands being the Dodecanese and Cycladic archipelagos in the Aegean and the continent Greece and Asia Minor. And there's more.' He opened the other book and read out another passage.

'*Atlantis was very lofty and precipitous on the side of the sea, and encompassed a large mountain-girt plain.*' Jack strode over to the screen which now displayed a large-scale map of Crete. 'That's exactly the appearance of the southern coast of Crete and the great plain of the Mesara.'

He moved back to where he had left the books on the table.

'And finally the Atlanteans themselves. *They were divided into ten relatively independent administrative districts under the primacy of the royal metropolis.*' He swivelled round and pointed at the map. 'Archaeologists believe Minoan Crete was divided into a dozen or so semi-autonomous palace fiefdoms, with Knossos the most important.'

He flicked the remote control to reveal a spectacular image of the excavated palace at Knossos with its restored throne room. 'This surely is the *splendid capital city halfway along the coast.*' He advanced the slides to a close-up of the drainage system in the palace. 'And just as the Minoans were excellent hydraulic engineers, so the *Atlanteans made cisterns, some open to the heavens, others roofed over, to use in winters as warm baths; there were the baths for the kings and for private persons and for horses and cattle.* And then the bull.' Jack pressed the selector and another view of Knossos appeared, this time showing a magnificent bull's horn sculpture beside the courtyard. He read again. '*There were bulls who had the range of the temple of Poseidon, and the kings, being left alone in the temple, after they had offered prayers to the god that they might capture the victim which was acceptable to him, hunted the bulls, without weapons but with staves and nooses.*'

Jack turned towards the screen and flicked through the remaining images. 'A wall painting from Knossos of a bull with a leaping acrobat. A stone libation vase in the shape of a bull's head. A golden cup impressed with a bull-hunting scene. An excavated pit containing hundreds of bulls' horns, recently discovered below the main courtyard of the palace.' Jack sat down and looked at the others. 'And there is one final ingredient in this story.'

The image transformed to an aerial shot of the island of Thera, one Jack had taken from *Seaquest*'s helicopter only a few days before. The jagged outline of the caldera could clearly be seen, its vast basin surrounded by spectacular cliffs surmounted by the whitewashed houses of the modern villages.

'The only active volcano in the Aegean and one of the biggest in the world. Some time in the middle of the second millennium BC that thing blew its top. Eighteen cubic kilometres of rock and ash were thrown eighty kilometres high and hundreds of kilometres south over Crete and the east Mediterranean, darkening the sky for days. The concussion shook buildings in Egypt.'

Hiebermeyer recited from memory from the Old

Testament: ' "And the Lord said unto Moses, stretch out thine hand toward heaven, that there may be darkness over the land of Egypt, even darkness which may be felt. And Moses stretched forth his hand toward heaven; and there was a thick darkness in all the land of Egypt three days." '

'The ash would have carpeted Crete and wiped out agriculture for a generation,' Jack continued. 'Vast tidal waves, tsunamis, battered the northern shore, devastating the palaces. There were massive earthquakes. The remaining population was no match for the Mycenaeans when they arrived seeking rich pickings.'

Katya raised her hands to her chin and spoke.

'So. The Egyptians hear a huge noise. The sky darkens. A few survivors make it to Egypt with terrifying stories of a deluge. The men of Keftiu no longer arrive with their tribute. Atlantis doesn't exactly sink beneath the waves, but it does disappear for ever from the Egyptian world.' She raised her head and looked at Jack, who smiled at her.

'I rest my case,' he said.

Throughout this discussion Dillen had sat silently. He knew the others were acutely aware of his presence, conscious that the translation of the papyrus fragment may have unlocked secrets that would overturn everything they believed. They looked at him expectantly as Jack reset the digital projector to the first image. The screen was again filled with the close-set script of ancient Greek.

'Are you ready?' Dillen asked the group.

There was a fervent murmur of assent. The atmosphere in the room tightened perceptibly. Dillen reached down and unlocked his briefcase, drawing out a large scroll and unrolling it in front of them. Jack dimmed the main lights and switched on a fluorescent lamp over the torn fragment of ancient papyrus in the centre of the table.

4

The object of their attention was revealed in every detail, the ancient sheet of writing almost luminous beneath the protective glass plate. The others drew their chairs forward, their faces looming out of the shadows at the edge of the light.

'First, the material.'

Dillen handed round a small plastic specimen box containing a fragment removed for analysis when the mummy was unwrapped.

'Unmistakably papyrus, *Cyperus papyrus*. You can see the criss-cross pattern where the fibres of the reed were flattened and pasted together.'

'Papyrus had largely disappeared in Egypt by the second century AD,' Hiebermeyer said. 'It became extinct because of the Egyptian mania for record-keeping. They were brilliant at irrigation and agriculture but somehow failed to sustain the reed beds along the Nile.' He spoke with a flush of excitement. 'And I can now reveal that the earliest known papyrus dates from 4000 BC, almost a thousand years before any previous find. It was discovered during my excavations earlier this year in the temple of Neith at Saïs in the Nile Delta.'

There was a murmur of excitement around the table. Katya leaned forward.

'So. To the manuscript. We have a medium which is ancient but could date any time up to the second century AD. Can we be more precise?'

Hiebermeyer shook his head. 'Not from the material alone. We could try a radiocarbon date, but the isotope ratios would probably have been contaminated by other organic material in the mummy wrapping. And to get a big enough sample would mean destroying the papyrus.'

'Obviously unacceptable.' Dillen took over the discussion. 'But we have the evidence of the script itself. If Maurice had not recognized it we would not be here today.'

'The first clues were spotted by my student Aysha Farouk.' Hiebermeyer looked round the table. 'I believe the burial and the papyrus were contemporaneous. The papyrus was not some ancient scrap but a recently written document. The clarity of the letters attests to that.'

Dillen pinned the four corners of his scroll to the table, allowing the others to see that it was covered with symbols copied from the papyrus. He had grouped together identical letters, pairs of letters and words. It was a way of analysing stylistical regularity familiar to those who had studied under him.

He pointed to eight lines of continuous script at the

bottom. 'Maurice was correct to identify this as an early form of Greek script, dating no later than the high classical period of the fifth century BC.' He looked up and paused. 'He was right, but I can be more precise than that.'

His hand moved up to a cluster of letters at the top. 'The Greeks adopted the alphabet from the Phoenicians early in the first millennium BC. Some of the Phoenician letters survived unaltered, others changed shape over time. The Greek alphabet didn't reach its final form until the late sixth century BC.' He picked up the light pointer and aimed at the upper right corner of the scroll. 'Now look at this.'

An identical letter had been underlined in a number of words copied from the papyrus. It looked like the letter A toppled over to the left, the crossbar extending through either side like the arms of a stick figure.

Jack spoke excitedly. 'The Phoenician letter A.'

'Correct.' Dillen drew his chair close to the table. 'The Phoenician shape disappears about the middle of the sixth century BC. For that reason, and because of the vocabulary and style, I suggest a date at the beginning of the century. Perhaps 600, certainly no later than 580 BC.'

There was a collective gasp.

'How confident are you?' asked Jack.

'As confident as I have ever been.'

'And I can now reveal our most important dating evidence for the mummy,' Hiebermeyer announced triumphantly. 'A gold amulet of a heart, *ib*, underneath a sun disc, *re*, together forming a symbolic representation of the pharaoh Apries' birth name *Wah-Ib-Re*. The amulet may have been a personal gift to the occupant of the tomb, a treasured possession taken to the afterlife. Apries was a pharaoh of the Twenty-sixth Dynasty who ruled from 595 to 568 BC.'

'It's fantastic,' Katya exclaimed. 'Apart from a few fragments we have no original Greek manuscripts from before the fifth century BC. This dates only a century after Homer, only a few generations after the Greeks began to use the new alphabet. This is the most important epigraphical find in decades.' She paused to marshal her thoughts. 'My question is this. What is a papyrus with Greek script doing in Egypt in the sixth century BC, more than two hundred years before the arrival of Alexander the Great?'

Dillen looked round the table. 'I won't beat about the bush any longer. I believe we have a fragment of the lost work of Solon the Lawmaker, his account of his visit to the high priest at Saïs. We have found the source of Plato's story of Atlantis.'

Half an hour later they stood in a group on the balcony overlooking the Great Harbour. Dillen was smoking his pipe and fondly watching Jack talk to Katya apart from the others. It was not the first time he had seen this, but perhaps Jack had found someone serious at last. Years before, Dillen had seen the potential in an unruly student who lacked the credentials of a conventional education; it was he who had pushed Jack towards a spell in military intelligence on condition that he return to make archaeology his career. Another former student, Efram Jacobovich, had provided an endowment from his software fortune that funded all of IMU's research, and Dillen quietly delighted in the chance this gave him to be involved in Jack's adventures.

Jack excused himself to make a satellite call to *Seaquest*, putting his hand briefly on Katya's arm and striding off towards the doorway. His excitement at the papyrus discovery competed with his need to keep up with the wreck excavation. It had been only two days since Costas had uncovered the golden disc, yet already the site was producing riches that threatened to overshadow even that find.

During a lull in the conversation while he was away the others had been diverted by a TV monitor set up in a niche in the wall. It was a CNN report of yet another terrorist attack in the former Soviet Union, this one a devastating car bomb in the capital of the Republic of Georgia. Like most other recent outrages it was not the work of fanatics but a calculated act of personal vengeance, another grim episode in a world where extremist ideology was being replaced by greed and vendetta as the main cause of global instability. It was a situation of special concern to those standing on the balcony, with stolen antiquities being used to lubricate deals and black market operators increasingly audacious in their attempts to acquire the most prized treasures.

On his return, Jack resumed the conversation he had been having with Katya. She had revealed little about her background but had confided her craving to become more involved in the battle against antiquities crime than her present position allowed. Jack discovered she had been offered prestigious university posts in the west but had chosen to remain in Russia at the forefront of the problem, despite the corrupt bureaucracy and ever present threat of blackmail and reprisal.

Hiebermeyer and Dillen joined them and the discussion reverted to the papyrus.

'I've always been perplexed by the fact that Solon left no account of his visit to Egypt,' Katya said. 'He was such a prominent man of letters, the most learned Athenian of his day.'

'Could such a record have been made within the temple precinct itself?' Jack looked enquiringly at Hiebermeyer, who was cleaning his glasses and visibly perspiring.

'Possibly, though such occasions must have been few and far between.' Hiebermeyer replaced his glasses and wiped his forehead. 'To the Egyptians the art of writing was the divine gift of Thoth, scribe to the gods. By making it sacred, the priests could keep knowledge under their control. And any writing by a foreigner in a temple would have been considered sacrilegious.'

'So he would not have been popular,' Jack commented.

Hiebermeyer shook his head. 'He would have been met with suspicion by those who disapproved of the high priest's decision to reveal their knowledge. The temple attendants would have resented his presence as a foreigner who appeared to defy the gods.' Hiebermeyer struggled out of his jacket and rolled up his sleeves. 'And the Greeks weren't exactly flavour of the month. The Pharaohs had recently allowed them to establish a trading post at Naucratis on the Delta. They were wily traders, experienced from their dealings with the Phoenicians, whereas Egypt had been closed off for years from the outside world. The Egyptians who entrusted their goods to Greek merchants were ignorant of the harsh realities of commerce. Those who didn't profit immediately felt they had been tricked and betrayed. There was a lot of resentment.'

'So what you're suggesting,' Jack interrupted, 'is that Solon did make this record but it was somehow taken from him and trashed?'

Hiebermeyer nodded. 'It's possible. You can picture the kind of scholar he was. Single-minded to the point of obsession, making little allowance for those around him. And naïve about the real world. He must have been carrying a weighty purse of gold, and the temple staff would have known it. He would have been easy prey during those night-time treks across the desert from the temple precinct to the town where he would have been staying.'

'So what we're saying is that Solon is ambushed and robbed in the desert. His scroll is ripped up and thrown away. Soon afterwards a few scraps are collected together and reused as mummy wrapping. The attack takes place after Solon's final visit to the temple, so his entire record is lost.'

'And what about this,' Hiebermeyer rejoined. 'He's so badly knocked about that he can only remember bits of the story, perhaps nothing at all of that final visit. He's already an old man and his memory is dimmed. Back in Greece he never again puts pen to paper, and is too ashamed to admit how much he may have lost through his own stupidity. He only ever tells a garbled version of what he can remember to a few close friends.'

Dillen listened with visible satisfaction as his two former students carried the argument forward. A gathering like this was more than the sum of its parts; the meeting of minds sparked off new ideas and lines of reasoning.

'I had come to much the same conclusion myself from reading the texts,' he said, 'from comparing Plato's story with the papyrus. You will see what I mean shortly. Let us reconvene.'

They filed back into the conference chamber, the cool dampness of the ancient walls refreshing after the searing heat outside. The others looked on expectantly as Dillen composed himself in front of the papyrus fragment.

'I believe this is the transcript of a dictation. The text has been hastily written and the composition is not especially polished. It is only a shred of the original scroll which could have been thousands of lines long. What has survived is the equivalent of two short paragraphs divided by a gap about six lines wide. In the centre is this symbol followed by the word Atlantis.'

'I've seen that somewhere before.' Jack was leaning over the table and peering at the strange symbol in the centre of the papyrus.

'Yes, you have.' Dillen looked up briefly from his notes.

'But I'll leave that for a little later, if I may. There is no doubt in my mind that this was written by Solon in the temple scriptorium at Saïs as he sat in front of the high priest.'

'His name was Amenhotep.' Hiebermeyer was flushed with excitement again. 'During our excavation last month at the Temple of Neith we found a fragmentary priest list for the Twenty-sixth Dynasty. According to the chronology, Amenhotep was over a hundred years old at the time Solon would have visited. There's even a statue of him. It's in the British Museum.

Hiebermeyer reached over and tapped the multimedia projector, revealing a figure in classic Egyptian pose holding a model *naos* shrine. The face seemed at once youthful and ageless, concealing more than it revealed, with the mournful expression of an old man who has passed on all he has to give before death enfolds him.

'Could it be,' Katya interjected, 'that the break in the text represents a break in the dictation, that the writing above represents the end of one account, perhaps one day's audience with the priest, and the writing below the beginning of another?'

'Exactly.' Dillen beamed. 'The word Atlantis is a heading, the start of a new chapter.' His fingers tapped the laptop he had connected to the multimedia projector. They could now follow a digitally enhanced image of the Greek text alongside his English words. He began to read the translation he and Katya had been working on since they had arrived the previous day.

'And in their citadels were bulls, so many that they filled the courtyards and the narrow corridors, and men danced with them. And then, in the time of Pharaoh Thutmosis, the gods smote the earth with a mighty crash and darkness came over the land, and

Poseidon threw up a mighty rushing wave that swept away all before it. Such was the end of the island kingdom of the Keftiu. And next we will hear of another mighty kingdom, of the sunken citadel they called Atlantis.

'And now for the second section,' Dillen went on. He tapped a key and the image scrolled down below the gap. 'Remember, this is pretty unpolished stuff. Solon was translating Egyptian into Greek as he wrote. So for us it's relatively straightforward, with few complex phrases or obscure words. But there is a problem.'

Their eyes followed his to the screen. The text had scrolled to the end, the words petering off where the papyrus had torn away. Whereas the first paragraph had been well preserved, the second was progressively truncated as the ripped edges converged in a V shape. The final lines contained only fragments of words.

Katya now began to read.

'*Atlantis.*' Her accent gave the syllables added emphasis, somehow helping to bring home the reality of what they had before them.

'The first sentence is uncontentious.' She focused on the screen and spoke under her breath.

'Dia tōn nēson mechri hou hē thalatta stenoutai.' The vowels almost sounded Chinese as she recreated the lilt of the ancient language.

'*Through the islands until the sea narrows. Past the Cataract of Bos.*'

Hiebermeyer frowned in puzzlement. 'My Greek is good enough to know that *katarraktēs* means a down-rushing or waterfall,' he said. 'It was used to describe the rapids of the upper Nile. How could it refer to the sea?'

Dillen walked to the screen. 'At this juncture we begin to lose whole words from the text.'

Katya again read. '*And then twenty dromoi along the southern shore.*'

'A *dromos* was about sixty *stades*,' Dillen commented. 'About fifty nautical miles.'

'It was in fact highly variable,' Jack said. '*Dromos* means "run", the distance a ship could sail in one day while the sun was up.'

'Presumably it varied from place to place,' Hiebermeyer mused. 'According to winds and currents and the time of year, taking into account seasonal changes in climate and daylight hours.'

'Precisely. A run was an indication of how long it would take you to get from A to B in favourable conditions.'

'*Under the high bucranion, the sign of the bull,*' Katya went on.

'Or bull's horns,' Dillen suggested.

'Fascinating.' Hiebermeyer spoke almost to himself. 'One of the most redolent symbols in prehistory. We've already seen them in Jack's pictures of Knossos. They also appear in Neolithic shrines and all over the Bronze Age palaces of the Near East. Even as late as the Roman period the *bucranium* is everywhere in monumental art.'

Katya nodded. 'The text now becomes fragmentary, but the professor and I agree on the likely meaning. It will be easier for you to understand if you see where the breaks occur.'

She switched the projector to overhead mode, at the same time placing a transparent sheet on the glass plate. The screen showed her neatly written words below the V shape of the lower part of the papyrus.

'*Then you reach the citadel. And there below lies a vast golden plain, the deep basins, the salt lakes, as far as the eye can see. And two hundred lifetimes ago Poseidon wreaked vengeance on the Atlanteans for daring to live like gods. The cataract fell, the great golden door of the*

citadel shut for ever, and Atlantis was swallowed beneath the waves.'
She paused. 'We believe these last sentences were a way of linking the story with the end of the land of Keftiu. Perhaps the high priest's theme was the wrath of the sea god, the vengeance taken by Poseidon on men for their hubris.'

She aimed the pointer at the screen. 'The next section was probably the beginning of a detailed description of Atlantis. Unfortunately there are just a few disconnected words. Here, we think, is *golden house* or *golden-walled*. And here you can clearly read the Greek letters for *pyramid*. The full phrase translates as *immense stone pyramids.*' She glanced questioningly at Hiebermeyer, who was too stunned to comment and could only gawp at the screen.

'And then these final words.' She pointed at the ragged tail of the document. '*House of the gods*, perhaps *hall of the gods*, which is again *kata boukerōs*, meaning *under the sign of the bull.* And there the text ends.'

Hiebermeyer was the first to speak, his voice quivering with excitement. 'Surely that clinches it. The voyage through the islands, to a place where the sea narrows. That can only mean west from Egypt, past Sicily to the Strait of Gibraltar.' He slapped his hand down in affirmation. 'Atlantis was in the Atlantic Ocean after all!'

'What about the cataract?' Jack asked. 'The Strait of Gibraltar is hardly a raging torrent.'

'And the vast golden plain, and the salt lakes,' Katya added. 'In the Atlantic all you would have is the sea on one side, high mountains or desert on the other.'

'Southern shore is also perplexing,' Jack said. 'Since there is no obvious southern shore to the Atlantic, that would imply that Atlantis was in the Mediterranean, and I can hardly imagine a citadel on the barren shore of the western Sahara.'

Dillen unhooked the overhead and flicked the projector to

slide mode, reloading the digital images. A range of snow-capped mountains filled the screen, with a complex of ruins nestled among verdant terraces in the foreground.

'Jack was correct to associate Plato's Atlantis with Bronze Age Crete. The first part of the text clearly refers to the Minoans and the eruption of Thera. The problem is that Crete was not Atlantis.'

Katya nodded slowly. 'Plato's account is a conflation.'

'Exactly.' Dillen stepped back behind his chair, gesticulating as he spoke. 'We have fragments of two different histories. One describes the end of Bronze Age Crete, the land of Keftiu. The other is about a much more ancient civilization, that of Atlantis.'

'The dating difference is unambiguous.' Hiebermeyer mopped his face as he spoke. 'The first paragraph on the papyrus dates the destruction of Keftiu to the reign of Thutmosis. He was a pharaoh of the Eighteenth Dynasty, in the late sixteenth century BC, exactly the time Thera erupted. And for Atlantis "two hundred lifespans" in the second paragraph is in fact a fairly precise calculation, a lifetime meaning about twenty-five years to the Egyptian chroniclers.' He made a swift mental calculation. 'Five thousand years before Solon, so about 5600 BC.'

'Incredible.' Jack shook his head in disbelief. 'A whole epoch before the first city states. The sixth millennium BC was still the Neolithic, a time when agriculture was a novelty in Europe.'

'I'm puzzled by one detail,' Katya said. 'If these stories are so distinct, how can the bull symbol figure so prominently in both accounts?'

'Not a problem,' Jack said. 'The bull was not just a Minoan symbol. From the beginning of the Neolithic it represented strength, virility, mastery over the land. Plough-oxen were vital to early farmers. Bull symbols are everywhere in the early agricultural communities of the region.'

Dillen looked pensively at the papyrus. 'I believe we have discovered the basis for two and a half thousand years of misguided speculation. At the end of his account of Keftiu, the high priest, Amenhotep, signalled his intention for the next session, giving a taste of what was to come. He wanted to keep Solon in a high state of anticipation, to ensure he returned day after day until the final date allowed by the temple calendar. Perhaps he had an eye on that purse of gold, on ever more generous donations. I think we have a foretaste here of the story of Atlantis in the final sentence of the account of Keftiu.'

Jack immediately caught his mentor's drift. 'You mean that in Solon's confusion the word Atlantis may have replaced Keftiu whenever he recalled the story of the end of the Minoans.'

'You have it.' Dillen nodded. 'There's nothing in Plato's account to suggest Solon remembered anything of the second section of text. No cataract, no vast plain. And no pyramids, which would be difficult to forget. Someone must have hit him pretty hard on the head that final night.'

The sun was now setting, its rays casting a rosy hue on the waters of the Great Harbour below. They had returned to the conference room for a final session following a late afternoon break. None of them showed any sign of exhaustion despite the hours they had spent huddled round the table with the precious document. They were all bound up in the elation of discovery, of uncovering a key to the past which might change the entire picture of the rise of civilization.

Dillen settled back and spoke. 'And finally, Jack, to that symbol you said you had seen before.'

At that moment there was a loud knocking on the door and a young man looked in.

'Excuse me, Professor, but this is very urgent. Dr Howard.'

Jack strode over and took the cellphone that was offered to him, positioning himself on the seafront balustrade out of earshot of the others.

'Howard here.'

'Jack, this is Costas. We are on Red Alert. You must return to *Seaquest* at once.'

5

Jack eased back on the control and the Lynx helicopter stood still in the air, the normal whirr of its rotor reduced to a shuddering clatter. He adjusted the audio on his headset as he gently feathered the left pedal, at the same time giving the tail propeller a quick burst to bring the machine broadside on to the spectacular sight below. He turned to Costas and they both peered out of the open port-side door.

A thousand metres below lay the smouldering heart of Thera. They were hovering over the flooded remnant of a gigantic caldera, a vast scooped-out shell with only its jagged edges protruding above the sea. All round them cliffs reared up precipitously. Directly below was Nea Kameni, 'New Burnt', its surface scorched and lifeless. In the centre were telltale wisps of smoke where the volcano was once again thrusting through the earth's crust. It was a warning beacon, Jack thought, a harbinger of doom, like a bull snorting and pawing before the onslaught.

A disembodied voice came over the intercom, one that Jack was finding increasingly irresistible.

'It's awesome,' Katya said. 'The African and Eurasian plates grind together to produce more earthquakes and volcanoes than virtually anywhere else on earth. No wonder the Greek gods were such a violent lot. Founding a civilization here is like building a city on the San Andreas fault.'

'Sure,' Costas replied. 'But without plate tectonics limestone would never have turned into marble. No temples, no sculpture.' He gestured at the cliff walls. 'And what about volcanic ash? Incredible stuff. The Romans discovered if you add it to lime mortar you get concrete that sets underwater.'

'That's true,' Katya conceded. 'Volcanic fallout also makes incredibly fertile soil. The plains around Etna and Vesuvius were breadbaskets of the ancient world.'

Jack smiled to himself. Costas was a ladies man, and he and Katya had discovered a shared passion for geology which had dominated the conversation all the way from Alexandria.

The Lynx had been on a return flight to the Maritime Museum in Carthage when Costas had received an emergency signal from Tom York, *Seaquest*'s captain. Costas had immediately put in the call to Jack and diverted south to Egypt. That afternoon beside the harbour he had watched as Jack said quick farewells to Dillen and Hiebermeyer, any disappointment they may have felt masked by the anxiety clearly etched on their faces.

Jack had learned that Katya was an experienced diver

and when she approached him on the balcony to ask if she could join him, he had seen no reason to refuse.

'It's my chance to join the forefront of the fray,' she had said, 'to experience first-hand what modern archaeologists are up against.'

Meanwhile, her assistant Olga would return on urgent business to Moscow.

'There she is.'

The forward tilt of the helicopter directed their gaze towards the eastern horizon. They were now out of sight of Thera and could just make out *Seaquest* in the distant haze. As they flew closer the deep blue of the Mediterranean darkened as if under a passing cloud. Costas explained that it was a submerged volcano, its peak rising from the abyss like a gigantic atoll.

Jack flicked on the intercom. 'This is not where I expected to find a site,' he said. 'The top of the volcano is thirty metres underwater, too deep to have been a reef. Something else wrecked our Minoan ship.'

They were now directly over *Seaquest* and began to descend towards the helipad on the stern. The landing markings became clearer as the altimeter dropped below five hundred feet.

'But we're incredibly lucky the ship sank where it did, at a depth where our divers can work. This is the only place for miles around where the seabed is less than five hundred metres deep.'

Katya's voice came over the intercom. 'You say the ship went down in the sixteenth century BC. This may be a long shot, but could it have been the eruption of Thera?'

'Absolutely,' Jack enthused. 'And oddly enough, that would also account for the excellent state of preservation. The ship was swamped in a sudden deluge and sank upright about seventy metres below the summit.'

Costas spoke again. 'It was probably an earthquake a few days before the volcano blew. We know the Therans had advance warning and were able to leave with most of their possessions.'

Jack nodded. 'The explosive discharge would have destroyed everything for miles around,' Costas continued. 'But that was only the beginning. The rush of water into the caldera would have rebounded horrifically, causing hundred-metre tsunamis. We're pretty close to Thera and the waves would have lost little of their power. They would have smashed any ship in their path to smithereens, leaving only mangled fragments. Our wreck survived on the sea floor only because it got wedged in a cleft below the depth of the wave oscillations.'

The helicopter hovered a hundred feet above *Seaquest* while Jack awaited permission to land. He took the opportunity to cast a critical eye over his pride and joy. Beyond the helipad and the Zodiac inflatables was the three-storey accommodation block, able to house twenty scientists and the crew of thirty. At 75 metres *Seaquest* was almost twice the length of Cousteau's *Calypso*. She had been custom-built in the shipyards in Finland that produced the famous *Akademic*-class vessels for the Russian Institute of Oceanology. Like them she had bow and lateral thrusters for dynamic positioning ability, allowing her to hold over a precise fix on the seabed, and an automated trimming system to maintain stability by regulating the flow of water in her ballast tanks. She was now more than ten years old and due for a refit but still vital to IMU's research and exploration around the world.

As he nudged the stick forward, their attention was caught

by a dark silhouette on the horizon ahead. It was another vessel, low-set and sinister, lying motionless several kilometres off *Seaquest*'s bows.

They all knew what they were looking at. It was the reason why Jack had been recalled so urgently from Alexandria. Katya and Costas went silent, their minds reverting from the excitement of archaeology to the sobering problems of the present. Jack set his jaw in grim determination as he made a perfect landing inside the orange circle on the helipad. His calm assurance belied the rage that welled up inside him. He had known their excavation would be discovered, but he had not expected it quite so soon. Their opponents had access to ex-Soviet satellite surveillance that could make out a man's face from an orbital height of four hundred kilometres. *Seaquest* was totally exposed in the cloudless summer skies of the Mediterranean, and the fact that she had stayed put for several days had obviously excited interest.

'Check this out. It came up yesterday before I flew out.'

Costas was leading Jack and Katya through the maze of tables in *Seaquest*'s conservation lab. The tungsten bulbs in the overhead gantry cast a brilliant optical light over the scene. A group of white-coated technicians were busy cleaning and recording the dozens of precious artefacts that had come up from the Minoan wreck over the last two days, preparing them for conservation before being readied for display. At the far end Costas stopped beside a low bench and gingerly lifted the covering from an object about a metre high.

Katya drew in her breath with astonishment. It was a life-sized bull's head, its flesh black steatite from Egypt, its eyes lapis lazuli from Afghanistan, its horns solid gold capped with sparkling rubies from India. A hole in the mouth showed it was a rhyton, a hollowed-out libation vessel for offerings to the gods. A rhyton as sumptuous as this could only have been used by the high priests in the most sacred ceremonies of the Minoan world.

'It's beautiful,' she murmured. 'Picasso would have loved it.'

'A brilliant centrepiece for the exhibit,' Costas said.

'In the maritime museum?' Katya asked.

'Jack earmarked one of the trireme sheds for his long-cherished Minoan wreck. It's almost full and the excavation's hardly begun.'

IMU's Mediterranean base was the ancient site of Carthage in Tunisia, where the circular war harbour of the Phoenicians had been magnificently reconstructed. The sheds once used for oared galleys now housed the finds from the many ancient shipwrecks they had excavated.

Jack suddenly seethed with anger. That such a priceless artefact should fall into the hands of the criminal underworld was unconscionable. Even the safe haven of the museum was no longer an option. When that silhouette had appeared on the horizon, it had been decided to abandon the regular helicopter shuttle. The Lynx had a supercharge capacity, enabling it to outrun virtually any other rotary-winged aircraft over short distances, but it was as vulnerable as any subsonic aircraft to laser-guided ship-to-air missiles. Their enemy would pinpoint the crash site with GPS and then retrieve the wreckage using submersible remote-operated vehicles. Any surviving crew would be summarily executed and the artefacts would disappear forever as attacker's booty.

It was a new and lethal form of piracy on the high seas.

Jack and his companions made their way to the captain's day cabin. Tom York, the vessel's master, was a compact, white-

haired Englishman who had finished a distinguished career in
the Royal Navy as captain of a jump-jet carrier. Opposite him
sat a ruggedly handsome man whose physique had been
honed as a rugby international for his native New Zealand.
Peter Howe had spent twenty years in the Royal Marines and
Australian Special Air Service and was now IMU's chief
security officer. He had flown in from IMU's Cornwall
headquarters in England the night before. Howe had been a
friend of Jack's since schooldays and all three had served
together in naval intelligence.

'I couldn't fit in our climbing gear.' Howe gave Jack a rueful
look.

'No problem.' Jack's face creased into a smile. 'I'll have it
airfreighted out. We'll find a mountain to climb when this is
done.'

On the table lay a two-way UHF radio and an Admiralty
Chart of the Aegean. Costas and Katya squeezed in beside
York and Howe. Jack remained standing, his tall frame filling
the doorway and his voice suddenly terse and to the point.

'Right. What do we have?'

'It's a new one on us,' Howe said. 'His name is Aslan.'

Katya visibly shuddered, her eyes widening in disbelief.
'*Aslan.*' Her voice was barely audible.

'You know this man?' Jack asked.

'I know this man.' She spoke haltingly. 'Aslan – it means
Lion. He is . . .' She hesitated, her face pale. 'He is a warlord,
a gangster. The worst.'

'From Kazakhstan, to be precise.' Tom York pulled out a
photograph and slapped it down on the chart. 'I received this
by email from the IMU press agency in London a few
minutes ago.'

It showed a group of men in combat fatigues and traditional
Islamic gear. The backdrop was a barren landscape of

sun-scorched ravines and scree slopes. They held Kalashnikovs and the ground in front was piled high with Soviet era weaponry, from heavy-calibre machine guns to RPG launchers.

It was not so much the bristling arsenal that caught their attention, such images being commonplace since the early days of the mujahedin in Afghanistan; it was the figure sitting in the centre. He was a man of awesome bulk, his hands grasping his knees and his elbows jutting out defiantly. In contrast to the khaki that surrounded him, he wore a billowing white robe and a close-fitting cap. The hint of a moustache showed on either side of his mouth. The face had once been fine-featured, even handsome, with the arched nose and high cheekbones of the nomads of central Asia. The eyes that stared out of sunken sockets were jet-black and piercing.

'Aslan,' York said. 'Real name Piotr Alexandrovich Nazarbetov. Father a Mongolian, mother from Kyrgyzstan. Based in Kazakhstan but has a stronghold on the Black Sea in Abkhazia, the breakaway province of the Georgian Republic. A former Soviet Academician and Professor of Art History at Bishkek University, would you believe.'

Howe nodded. This was his area of expertise. 'All manner of people have been seduced by the huge profits of crime in this part of the world. And it takes an art historian to know the value of antiquities and where to find them.' He glanced at the newcomers. 'I'm sure you're all familiar with the situation in Kazakhstan.' He gestured at the map on the wall behind him. 'It's the usual story. Kazakhstan gains independence following the collapse of the Soviet Union. But the government's run by the former Communist Party boss. Corruption is rife and democracy a farce. Despite oil reserves and foreign investment, there's a progressive breakdown in internal security. A popular uprising gives the Russians an excuse to send in the army, which is withdrawn after a bloody war. The nationalist forces are severely weakened and the place is left in anarchy.'

'And then the warlords move in,' Costas interjected.

'Right. The insurgents who once fought together against the Russians now compete with each other to fill the vacuum. The idealists of the early days are replaced by thugs and religious extremists. The most ruthless murder and pillage their way across the country. They carve out territories for themselves like medieval barons, running their own armies and growing fat on drug and gun money.'

'I read somewhere that Kazakhstan is becoming the world's main opium and heroin producer,' Costas said.

'That's right,' said Howe. 'And this man controls most of it. By all accounts he's a charming host to journalists invited to meet him, a scholar who collects art and antiquities on a prodigious scale.' Howe paused and looked round the table. 'He's also a murderous psychopath.'

'How long has he been eyeballing us?' Jack asked.

'They hove into visual range twenty-four hours ago, immediately before Costas called you in Alexandria,' York responded. 'SATSURV had already warned us of a potentially hostile intrusion, a vessel of warship configuration which answered no international call signs.'

'That's when you shifted position.' *Seaquest* now lay off the far side of the atoll two nautical miles from the wreck.

'Not before we bubble-mined the site,' York replied.

Katya looked questioningly at Jack.

'An IMU innovation,' he explained. 'Miniature contact mines the size of ping-pong balls joined together by monofilaments like a screen of bubbles. They're triggered by photoelectric sensors which can distinguish the movement of divers and submersibles.'

Costas shifted his gaze to York. 'What are our options?'

'Whatever we do now may be pointless.' York's voice was bleak and emotionless. 'We've been issued an ultimatum.' He handed Jack a sheet of paper which had just come through by email. Jack quickly scanned the text, his face betraying nothing of the turmoil he felt inside.

'*Seaquest*, this is *Vultura*. Depart by eighteen hundred hours or be annihilated.'

Costas peered over at the paper. 'Doesn't mess around, does he?'

As if on cue, there was an immense rushing sound like a low-flying jet followed by a thunderous crash off the starboard bow. Tom York spun round to the nearest porthole just as a towering column of white water lashed the windowpane with spray. The shell had only narrowly missed them.

'*You bastards.*' York spoke through clenched teeth with the rage of a professional naval officer who was powerless to respond in kind.

At that moment the two-way radio began to crackle, and York angrily punched the intercom so they all could hear.

'This is *Seaquest*.' York's voice was barely controlled, almost a snarl. 'Make your intentions clear. Over.'

After a few moments a voice came over the intercom, its drawling, guttural tones unmistakably Russian.

'Good afternoon, Captain York. Major Howe. And Dr Howard, I presume? Our felicitations. This is *Vultura*.' There was a pause. 'You have been warned.'

York switched off the receiver in disgust and flipped open a lid beside him. Before he pulled down the lever inside, he looked up at Jack, his voice now coldly composed.

'We're going to battle stations.'

★

Within minutes of the klaxon sounding, *Seaquest* had transformed from a research vessel into a ship of war. The diving equipment which usually cluttered the deck had been stowed as soon as *Vultura* appeared on the scene. Now, in the hold forward of the deckhouse, a group of technicians in white anti-flash overalls were arming *Seaquest*'s weapons pod, a Breda twin 40mm L70 modified to IMU specifications. The successor of the renowned Bofors anti-aircraft gun of the Second World War, the 'Fast Forty' had a dual-feed mechanism which fired high-explosive and armour-piercing shells at a rate of 900 rounds per minute. The pod was concealed in a retracted shaft which was elevated moments before use.

In the hold all non-essential personnel were assembling beside *Seaquest*'s escape submersible *Neptune II*. The submersible would quickly reach Greek territorial waters and rendezvous with a Hellenic Navy frigate which would set sail from Crete within the hour. It would also take away the bull's head rhyton and other artefacts which had come up too late for the final helicopter shuttle to Carthage.

York quickly led the group down a lift to a point well below the waterline, the door opening to reveal a curved metal bulkhead that looked as if a flying saucer was wedged inside the hull.

York looked at Katya. 'The command module.' He tapped the shiny surface. 'Twenty-centimetre-thick titanium-reinforced steel. The entire pod can blow itself away from *Seaquest* and make off undetected, thanks to the same stealth technology we used for the escape sub.'

'I think of it as a giant ejection seat.' Costas beamed. 'Like the command module on the old *Saturn* moon rockets.'

'Just as long as it doesn't send us into space,' Katya said.

York spoke into an intercom and the circular hatch swung

open. A subdued red light from the battery of control panels on the far side cast an eerie glow over the interior. They ducked through and he pulled the hatch shut behind them, spinning the central wheel until the locking arms were fully engaged.

Immediately in front, several crew were busily preparing small-arms ammunition, pressing rounds into magazines and assembling weapons. Katya walked over and picked up a rifle and magazine, expertly loading it and cocking the bolt.

'Enfield SA80 Mark 2,' she announced. 'British Army personal weapon. Thirty-round magazine, 5.56 millimetre. Bullpup design, handle in front of the magazine, versatile for confined spaces.' She peered over the sights. 'The infrared four-times scope is a nice feature, but give me the new Kalashnikov AK102 any day.' She removed the clip and checked the chamber was clear before replacing the weapon in the rack.

She looked rather incongruous still in the elegant black dress she wore to the conference, Jack mused, but clearly she had more than adequate skills to hold her own in a fight.

'You're some lady,' he said. 'First a world expert on ancient Greek scripts, now a military small-arms instructor.'

'Where I come from,' Katya responded, 'it's the second qualification that counts.'

As they made their way past the armoury, York glanced at Jack. 'We must decide our course of action now.'

Jack nodded.

York led them up a short flight of steps to a platform about five metres across. He motioned towards a semicircle of swivel chairs which faced a battery of workstations along one side.

'The bridge console,' he said to Katya. 'It serves as

command centre and a virtual-reality bridge, allowing us to navigate *Seaquest* using the surveillance and imaging systems topside.'

Above them a concave screen displayed a panoramic digital reproduction of the view from *Seaquest*'s bridge. The cameras were equipped with infrared and thermal imaging sensors, so even though it was dusk they could still make out the low shape of *Vultura* and the fading heat signature of its forward gun turret.

'Peter will review our security options.' York turned to Howe.

Peter Howe looked at the others ruefully. 'I won't beat about the bush. It's bad, really bad. We're up against a purpose-built warship armed to the teeth with the latest weaponry, able to outgun and outrun virtually any naval or coastguard vessel assigned to deal with this kind of menace.'

Jack turned to Katya. 'IMU policy is to rely on friendly nations in this kind of situation. The presence of warships and aircraft is often sufficiently intimidating even if they are outside territorial waters and legally unable to intervene.'

Howe tapped a key and the screen above them showed the Admiralty Chart of the Aegean.

'The Greeks can't arrest *Vultura*, or chase her off. Even among the Greek islands to the north she can find a route more than six nautical miles offshore, and the straits into the Black Sea are designated international waters. The Russians made sure of that. She has a clear run back to her home port in Abkhazia.'

He aimed a light pointer at their current position on the lower part of the map.

'By this evening the Hellenic Navy should have frigates positioned here, here and here.' He shone to the north and west of the submerged volcano. 'The nearest is just under six nautical miles south-east of Thera, almost within visual range of *Seaquest*. But they won't come any closer.'

'Why not?' Katya asked.

'A wonderful thing called politics.' Howe swivelled round to face them. 'We're in disputed waters. A few miles east are a group of uninhabited islets claimed by both the Greeks and the Turks. The dispute has led them to the brink of war. We've informed the Turks about *Vultura* but politics dictates that their focus be on the Greeks, not some renegade Kazakh. The presence of Greek warships near the zone is enough to put the Turkish Maritime Defence Command on high alert. An hour ago four Turkish Air Force F16s flew a perimeter sweep five miles to the east. The Greeks and Turks have always been friends of IMU, but now they're powerless to intervene.' Howe switched off the image and the screen reverted to the view outside *Seaquest*.

York stood up and paced between the seats, his hands clenched tightly behind his back. 'We could never take on *Vultura* and hope to win. We can't rely on outside help. Our only option is to accede to their demands, to leave immediately and relinquish the wreck. As captain I must put the safety of my crew first.'

'We could try negotiating,' Costas offered.

'Out of the question!' York slammed his hand down on the console, the strain of the last few hours suddenly showing. 'These people will only negotiate face to face and on their own ground. Whoever went to *Vultura* would instantly become a hostage. I will not risk the life of a single member of my crew in the hands of these thugs.'

'Let me try.'

They all stared at Katya, her face set impassively.

'I'm your only option,' she said quietly. 'I'm a neutral party. Aslan would have nothing to gain from taking me hostage and everything to lose in his dealings with the Russian government.' She paused, her voice stronger. 'Women are respected among his people. And my family has influence. I can mention a few names that will be of great interest to him.'

There was a long silence while the others digested her words. Jack tried not to let his emotions get in the way as he turned over all the possibilities. He shrank from putting her in danger, but he knew she was right. A look at her expression confirmed he had little choice.

'All right.' He stood up. 'I invited Katya along, so this is my call. Open a secure channel and patch me through to *Vultura*.'

6

Jack raised his binoculars and levelled them at the far-off speckle that was the only point of reference between sea and sky. Even though it was now dark he could make out every detail of the distant vessel, the optical enhancer intensifying the available light to give an image as clear as day. He could just read the Cyrillic letters below the bow.

Vultura. How very appropriate, he thought. She was exactly that, a hideous scavenger lurking around the kill zone until the time was right to pounce and devour the fruits of others' labour.

Tom York stood beside him. 'Project 911,' he said, following Jack's gaze. 'The Russians call them escort ships, the equivalent of corvettes and frigates in NATO code. This is the latest, produced after the events of 2001 for anti-terrorist patrolling. About the same as our *Sea*-class vessels but sleeker. The machinery's in another league altogether. Two GT diesel gas turbines producing 52,000 hp for a cruising speed of 36 knots. Turbojet-boosters capable of hydrofoil speeds of 60 knots, almost as fast as a light aircraft. *Vultura* is one of half a dozen decommissioned when the Russian Navy went through its latest downsizing. The Oslo Treaty requires the Russian Federation to sell surplus warships only to governments recognized by the UN, so this one must have been picked up in some shady deal even before it left the shipyard.'

Jack trained his binoculars on the pods on either side of *Vultura*'s stern, then shifted slightly to take in the forward turret with its barrel trained directly at them.

York noticed his movement. 'Tulamahzavod 130 mm automatic cannon. Computerised GPS ranging that makes adjustments instantaneously on impact. Capable of firing a uranium-depleted armour-piercing shell that would punch a hole through *Seaquest*'s command module at twenty miles.'

They were standing on *Seaquest*'s helipad, the cool breeze gently ruffling the IMU flag at the stern. They had watched anxiously as Katya, now dressed more appropriately in an IMU jumpsuit, drove one of *Seaquest*'s Zodiacs into the darkness, the twin 90 hp outboards powering her over to *Vultura* in a matter of minutes. Before she descended the ladder, Jack had quietly taken her aside, running one last time over the operation of the Zodiac and reiterating York and Howe's briefing on her possible course of action if everything went badly wrong.

She had only been gone for twenty minutes and already the waiting seemed interminable. Costas decided to call a teleconference with Dillen and Hiebermeyer to occupy Jack's mind more productively, and the two men went into the navigation room behind *Seaquest*'s bridge.

Costas tapped a command and the monitor in front of them came to life, revealing two figures as clearly as if they had been sitting on the opposite side of the table. Jack shifted closer to Costas so their image would be similarly projected. They would miss Katya's expertise but a teleconference seemed the obvious way to conclude the proceedings. Dillen and Hiebermeyer had stayed on in Alexandria to await news from *Seaquest*, and Costas had already filled them in on the threat posed by *Vultura*.

'Professor. Maurice. Greetings.'

'Good to see you again, Jack,' Dillen said. 'I'd like to start where we left off, with these symbols.'

At the touch of a key they could call up a set of images that had been scanned in earlier. In the lower right-hand corner of the monitor they were currently viewing Costas' own triumphant discovery, the remarkable golden disc from the Minoan wreck. The strange symbols on the surface had been digitally enhanced so they could study them more closely.

Hiebermeyer leaned forward. 'You said you'd seen that central device before, Jack.'

'Yes. And those symbols running round the edge, the little heads and paddles and so on. I suddenly realized where as we were flying out of Alexandria. The Phaistos discs.'

Costas looked on questioningly as Jack called up an image of two pottery discs, both seemingly identical and covered by a spiralling band of miniature symbols. One symbol looked remarkably like the device on the papyrus and the gold disc. The rest looked otherworldly, especially the little heads with hooked noses and Mohican haircuts.

'Aztec?' Costas hazarded.

'Nice try, but no,' Jack replied. 'Much closer to home. Minoan Crete.'

'The disc on the left was found near the palace of Phaistos almost a hundred years ago.' Dillen clicked on the screen as he spoke, the projector flashing up a view of a wide stone forecourt overlooking a plain with snow-capped mountains in the background. After a moment the image reverted to the discs. 'It's clay, about sixteen centimetres across, and the symbols were impressed on both sides. Many are identical, stamped with the same die.'

Dillen enlarged the right-hand disc. 'This one came up with the French excavations last year.'

'Date?' Hiebermeyer demanded.

'The palace was abandoned in the sixteenth century BC, following the eruption of Thera. Unlike Knossos, it was never reoccupied. So the discs may have been lost about the same time as your shipwreck.'

'But they could date earlier,' Jack suggested.

'Much earlier.' Dillen's voice had a now-familiar edge of excitement. 'Costas, what do you know about thermo-luminescence dating?'

Costas looked perplexed but replied enthusiastically. 'If you bury mineral crystals they gradually absorb radioactive isotopes from the surrounding material until they're at the same level. If you then heat the mineral the trapped electrons are emitted as thermoluminescence.' Costas began to guess where the question was leading. 'When you fire pottery it emits stored TL, setting its TL clock back to zero. Bury it and the pottery begins to reabsorb isotopes at a set rate. If you know this rate as well as the TL level of the surrounding sediment you can date the clay by heating it and measuring the TL emission.'

'How precisely?' Dillen asked.

'The latest refinements in optically stimulated lumines-cence allow us to go back half a million years,' Costas replied. 'That's the date for burnt hearth material from the earliest Neanderthal sites in Europe. For kiln-fired pottery, which first appears in the fifth millennium BC in the Near East, combined TL-OSL can date a sherd to within a few hundred years if the conditions are right.'

Costas had built up a formidable expertise in archaeological science since joining IMU, fuelled by his conviction that most of the questions Jack posed about the distant past would one day be resolved by hard science.

'The second disc, the one discovered last year, was fired.' Dillen picked up a sheet of paper as he spoke. 'A fragment was sent to the Oxford Thermoluminescence Laboratory for analysis, using a new strontium technique which can fix the date of firing with even greater accuracy. I've just had the results.'

The others looked on expectantly.

'Give or take a hundred years, that disc was fired in 5500 BC.'

There was a collective gasp of astonishment.

'Impossible,' snorted Hiebermeyer.

'That's a little earlier than our wreck,' Costas exclaimed.

'Just four thousand years earlier,' Jack said quietly.

'Two and a half millennia before the palace at Knossos.' Hiebermeyer was still shaking his head. 'Only a few centuries after the first farmers arrived on Crete. And if that's writing, then it's the earliest known by two thousand years. Near Eastern cuneiform and Egyptian hieroglyphics don't appear until the late fourth millennium BC.'

'It seems incredible,' Dillen replied. 'But you'll soon see why I'm convinced it is true.'

Jack and Costas watched the screen intently as Dillen

loaded a CD-ROM into his laptop and linked it to the multimedia projector. The picture of the pottery discs was replaced by the symbols arranged as a column, each one fronting groups clustered together like words. They could see he had been applying similar techniques of analysis to those he had used to study the Greek script on the papyrus.

Jack reactivated the teleconference module and they were once again face to face with Dillen and Hiebermeyer two hundred miles away in Alexandria.

'Those are the symbols from the Phaistos discs,' Jack said.

'Correct.' Dillen tapped a key and the two discs reappeared, this time in the lower left-hand corner. 'The thing that has most baffled scholars is that the discs are virtually identical, except in one crucial respect.' He moved a cursor to highlight various features. 'On one side, what I call the obverse, both discs have exactly one hundred and twenty-three symbols. Both are segmented into thirty-one groupings, each comprising anywhere from two to seven symbols. The menu, if you like, is the same, comprising forty-five different symbols. And the frequency is identical. So the Mohican head occurs thirteen times, the marching man six times, the flayed oxhide eleven times, and so on. It's a similar story on the reverse, except with thirty words and one hundred and eighteen symbols.'

'But the order and groupings are different,' Jack pointed out.

'Precisely. Look at the first disc. Walking man plus tree, three times. Sun disc plus Mohican head, eight times. And twice the entire sequence of arrow, baton, paddle, boat, oxhide and human head. None of these groupings occur on the second disc.'

'Bizarre,' Costas murmured.

'I believe the discs were kept together as a pair, one legible and the other meaningless. Whoever did this was trying to suggest that the type, number and frequency of the symbols were what was important, not their associations. It was a ruse, a way of diverting attention from the grouping of the symbols, of dissuading the curious from seeking meaning in the sequence.'

'But surely there is meaning in this,' Costas cut in impatiently. He clicked on his mouse to highlight combinations on the first disc. 'Boat beside paddle. Walking man. Mohican man always looking in the same direction. Sheaf of corn. The circular symbol, presumably the sun, in about half the groupings. It's some kind of journey, maybe not a real one but a journey through the year, showing the cycle of the seasons.'

Dillen smiled. 'Precisely the line taken by scholars who believe the first disc contains a message, that it was not just decorative. It does seem to offer more sense than the second disc, more logic in the sequence of images.'

'But?'

'But that may be part of the ruse. The creator of the first disc may have deliberately paired symbols which seem to belong together, like paddle and boat, in the hope that people would attempt to decipher the disc in just this way.'

'But surely paddle and boat do go together,' Costas protested.

'Only if you assume they're pictograms, in which case paddle means paddle, boat means boat. Paddle and boat together mean going by water, seafaring, movement.'

'Pictograms were the first form of writing,' Hiebermeyer added. 'But even the earliest Egyptian hieroglyphs were not all pictograms.'

'A symbol can also be a phonogram, where the object represents a sound, not a thing or an action,' Dillen continued. 'In English we might use a paddle to represent the letter P, or the syllable *pa*.'

Costas slowly nodded. 'So you mean the symbols on the discs could be a kind of alphabet?'

'Yes, though not in the strict sense of the word. The earliest version of our alphabet was the north Semitic precursor of the Phoenician alphabet of the second millennium BC. The innovative feature was a different symbol for each of the main vowel and consonant sounds. Earlier systems tended to be syllabic, each symbol representing a vowel and a consonant. That's how we interpret the Linear A writing of the Minoans and the Linear B of the Mycenaeans.' Dillen tapped a key and the screen reverted to the image of the golden disc. 'Which brings us to your wreck find.'

He magnified the image to show the mysterious symbol deeply impressed in the centre of the gold disc. After a pause it was joined by another image, an irregular black slab covered with three separate bands of finely-spaced writing.

'The Rosetta Stone?' Hiebermeyer looked baffled.

'As you know, Napoleon's army of conquest in Egypt in 1798 included a legion of scholars and draughtsmen. This was their most sensational discovery, found near ancient Saïs on the Rosetta branch of the Nile.' Dillen highlighted each section of text in turn, beginning at the top. 'Egyptian hieroglyphics. Egyptian demotic. Hellenistic Greek. Twenty years later a philologist named Champollion realized these were translations of the same narrative, a trilingual decree issued by Ptolemy V in 196 BC when the Greeks controlled Egypt. Champollion used his knowledge of ancient Greek to translate the other two texts. The Rosetta Stone was the key to deciphering hieroglyphics.' Dillen tapped a key and the stone disappeared, the screen again reverting to the image of the golden disc.

'Ignore that device in the centre for the moment and concentrate on the symbols round the edge.' He highlighted each of the three bands in turn, from outer to inner. 'Mycenaean Linear B. Minoan Linear A. The Phaistos symbols.'

Jack had already guessed as much, but the confirmation still made his heart pound with excitement.

'Gentlemen, we have our very own Rosetta Stone.'

Over the next few minutes Dillen explained that the Mycenaeans who took over Crete following the eruption of Thera originally had no script of their own, and instead had borrowed Linear A symbols from Minoan seafarers who had traded with mainland Greece. Their script, Linear B, was brilliantly deciphered soon after the Second World War as an early version of Greek. But the language of the Minoans had remained a mystery until earlier that year, when the largest ever cache of Linear A tablets had been discovered at Knossos. By great good fortune several of the tablets proved to be bilingual with Linear B. Now the gold disc offered the extraordinary possibility of deciphering the symbols of the Phaistos discs as well.

'There are no Phaistos symbols from Knossos and there's no bilingual text for them,' Dillen continued. 'I'd assumed it would be a lost language, one quite distinct from Minoan or from Mycenaean Greek.'

The others listened without interruption as Dillen worked methodically through the Linear A and Linear B symbols on the gold disc, showing their consistency with other examples of writing from Bronze Age Crete. He had arranged all of the symbols in rows and columns to study the concordance.

'I began with the first of the Phaistos discs, the one found a hundred years ago,' Dillen said. 'Like you I thought this one most likely to be intelligible.'

He tapped the keyboard and all thirty-one groups of symbols from the obverse appeared with the phonetic translation beneath them.

'Here it is, reading from the centre outward following the direction of the walking man and the face symbols, as logic would seem to dictate.'

Jack quickly scanned the lines. 'I don't recognize any Linear words or see any of the familiar combinations of syllables.'

'I'm afraid you're right.' Dillen tapped the keys again and another thirty-one groupings appeared in the lower part of the screen. 'Here it is back to front, spiralling from the edge to the centre. It's the same story. Absolutely nothing.'

The screen went blank and there was a brief silence.

'And the second disc?' Jack asked.

Dillen's expression gave little away, only the hint of a smile betraying his excitement. He tapped the keys and repeated the exercise.

'Here it is, spiralling outwards.'

Jack's heart sank as he again saw nothing recognizable in the words. Then he began to see pairings that looked oddly familiar.

'There's something here but it's not quite right.'

Dillen allowed him a moment more to stare at the screen. 'Back to front,' he prompted.

Jack peered at the screen again and suddenly slammed his hand down on the table. 'Of course!'

Dillen could contain himself no longer and smiled broadly as he tapped one final time and the sequence appeared in reverse order. There was a sharp intake of breath as Jack saw at once what they were looking at.

'Extraordinary,' he murmured. 'That disc dates more than two thousand years before the Bronze Age even began. Yet it's the language of Linear A, the language of Crete at the time of our shipwreck.' He could scarcely believe what he was saying. 'It's *Minoan*.'

At that moment the intercom crackled on *Seaquest* and broke the spell.

'Jack. Come on deck at once. There's activity on *Vultura*.' There was no mistaking the urgency in Tom York's tones.

Jack leapt to his feet without a word and bounded onto the bridge, Costas following close behind. Within seconds both men stood beside York and Howe, their gaze directed towards the distant glimmer of lights on the horizon.

In the sea ahead was a faint disturbance, a swirl of spray that quickly became recognizable as *Seaquest*'s Zodiac. Soon they could make out Katya at the wheel, her long hair flowing in the wind. Jack grasped the rail and momentarily shut his eyes, the anxieties of the last few hours suddenly replaced by a flood of relief. Thank God she was all right.

Costas looked at his friend with affection. He knew his friend too well, that Jack's entire emotional being was fast becoming wrapped up in their quest.

As the boat drew alongside and the outboards powered down, the air was filled with a new sound, the muffled roar of distant diesels. Jack snatched up the night scope and trained it on the horizon. The grey shape of *Vultura* filled the image, its hull low and menacing. Suddenly a surge of white appeared at the stern, a billowing arc made brilliant by the phosphorescence stirred up by the engines. Slowly, lazily, like an awakening beast with nothing to fear, *Vultura* turned in a wide arc and roared off into the darkness, its wake lingering like a rocket's exhaust long after the vessel had been swallowed up by the night.

Jack lowered the scope and looked at the figure who had just scrambled over the side. She smiled and gave a quick wave. Jack spoke under his breath, his words only audible to Costas beside him.

'Katya, you are an angel.'

7

The helicopter swooped low over the coastal mountains of western Turkey, its rotor reverberating in the deep bays that indented the shoreline. To the east the rosy aura of dawn revealed the rugged contours of the Anatolian Plateau, and across the Aegean the ghostly forms of islands could just be seen through the morning mist.

Jack eased back on the Lynx's control column and flipped on the autopilot. The helicopter would unerringly follow the course he had plotted into its navigational computer, bringing them to its programmed destination almost five hundred nautical miles north-east.

A familiar voice came over the intercom.

'Something I don't understand about our gold disc,' Costas

said. 'I'm assuming it was made about 1600 BC, shortly before the shipwreck. Yet the only parallel for those symbols in the outer band dates four thousand years earlier, on the second Phaistos disc from Crete.'

Katya joined in. 'It's astonishing that the language of Bronze Age Crete was already spoken by the first Neolithic colonists on the island. Professor Dillen's decipherment will revolutionize our picture of the origins of Greek civilization.'

Jack was still elated by Katya's success in defusing the confrontation with *Vultura* the evening before. Their deliverance had been little short of a miracle and he knew it. She said she had shown Aslan pictures of the Roman wreck Jack had dived on the week before and convinced him that all they had found were pottery amphoras, that the wreck was not worthy of his attention and *Seaquest* was only there to test new mapping equipment.

Jack was convinced there was more to it than this, more than Katya was willing or able to say. He had grilled her but she had remained tight-lipped. He knew only too well the shady world of deal and counter-deal, mafia trade-offs and bribery in which citizens of the former Soviet Union were forced to operate. Katya could clearly hold her own in this world.

The gnawing anxiety that had underlain the teleconference while she was away had transformed into an enormous zest to continue. On her return Katya had refused to rest and had joined Jack and Costas as they pored over the wreck plan and the next stage of the excavation far into the night, their enthusiasm driving them forward now they knew the project could carry on unhindered.

It was only her assurance that *Vultura* would not return that had persuaded Jack to undertake this morning's flight. It was to have been a routine visit, a scheduled inspection of *Seaquest*'s sister ship *Sea Venture* in the Black Sea, but had now been given special impetus by reports of a startling discovery off the north coast of Turkey.

'What neither of you know,' Jack said, 'is that we now have an independent date for the gold disc. It was emailed through while you were asleep.' He handed a slip of paper to Costas in the co-pilot's seat. After a moment there was a whoop of delight.

'Hydration dating! They've done it!' Costas, always more at home with the certainties of science than theories which never seemed to reach any firm conclusions, was in his element. 'It's a technique refined at IMU,' he explained to Katya. 'Certain minerals absorb a minute amount of water on their surface over time. This hydration rind develops afresh on surfaces that have been chipped or formed by man, so can be used to date stone and metal artefacts.'

'The classic example is obsidian,' Jack added. 'The glassy volcanic stone found in the Aegean only on the island of Melos. Obsidian tools from hunter-gatherer sites on mainland Greece have been hydration dated to 12,000 BC, the final phase of the Ice Age. It's the earliest evidence for maritime trade in the ancient world.'

'Hydration dating of gold has only been possible using very high precision equipment,' Costas said. 'IMU has taken the lead in VHP research because of the number of times we find gold.'

'What is the date?' Katya demanded.

'The three bands of symbols were impressed in the middle of the second millennium BC. The estimate is 1600 BC, plus or minus a hundred years.'

'That fits with the wreck date,' Katya said.

'It could hardly be much earlier,' Jack pointed out. 'The inner band is Mycenaean Linear B, which was only developed about that time.'

'But that was only the date of the symbols, the date when they were punched in the metal. It comes from the hydration rind on the symbols themselves.' Costas spoke with barely suppressed excitement. 'The disc itself is older. Much older. And that central symbol was in the original mould. Any guesses?' He hardly paused. 'It dates from *6000 BC*.'

By now it was a sparkling summer morning, their view extending unimpeded in every direction. They were flying over the north-west promontory of Turkey towards the Dardanelles, the narrow channel dividing Europe from Asia. To the east it widened into the Sea of Marmara before narrowing into the Bosporus, the strait leading to the Black Sea.

Jack made a slight adjustment to the autopilot and peered over Costas' shoulder. Gallipoli was clearly visible, the great finger of land jutting into the Aegean that defined the northern shore of the Dardanelles. Immediately below lay the plain of Hissarlik, site of fabled Troy. They were at a vortex of history, a place where sea and land narrowed to funnel huge movements of people from south to north and east to west, from the time of the earliest hominids to the rise of Islam. The tranquil scene belied the bloody conflicts this had spawned, from the siege of Troy to the slaughter at Gallipoli three thousand years later during the First World War.

To Jack and Costas this was no land of ghosts but familiar territory which brought back a warm glow of achievement. It was here they had carried out their first excavation together when they had been stationed at the NATO base at Izmir. A farmer had ploughed up some blackened timbers and fragments of bronze armour between the present coast and the ruins of Troy. Their excavation had shown the site to be the silted-up shoreline of the Bronze Age, and revealed the charred remains of a line of war-galleys burnt in a huge conflagration around 1150 BC.

It had been a sensational discovery, the first-ever artefacts from the Trojan War itself, a revelation which made scholars look afresh at legends once dismissed as half-truths. For Jack it was a turning point, the experience that rekindled his passion for archaeology and the unsolved mysteries of the past.

'OK. Let me get this straight.' Costas was trying to tie together the extraordinary revelations of the last few days into some kind of coherent whole. 'First a papyrus is found in Egypt which shows that Plato was not making up the Atlantis legend. It was dictated to a Greek named Solon by an Egyptian priest around 580 BC. The story was almost immeasurably ancient, dating back thousands of years to before the time of the Pharaohs.'

'The papyrus also shows Plato's story is a muddle,' Jack prompted.

'The account never reached the outside world because it was stolen and lost. What survived was garbled, a conflation of the end of the Minoans in the mid-second millennium BC with what Solon could remember of Atlantis. His confusion persuaded scholars to equate the Atlantis story with the eruption of Thera and the destruction of the palaces on Crete.'

'It was the only plausible interpretation,' Jack said.

'We now know Atlantis was some kind of citadel, not a continent or an island. It was located on a waterfront, with a wide valley and high mountains inland. It was somehow surmounted by a bull symbol. Several days' journey from it was a cataract, and between the cataract and Egypt lay a sea filled with islands. Some time between seven and eight thousand years ago it vanished beneath the sea.'

'And now we have this extraordinary riddle from the discs,' Katya said.

'The link between the papyrus and the discs is that symbol. It's exactly the same, like the letter H with four arms on either side.'

'I think we can safely call it the Atlantis symbol,' Katya asserted.

'It's the only one that has no concordance with a Linear A or Linear B sign,' Jack said. 'It may be a logogram representing Atlantis itself, like the bull of Minoan Knossos or the owl of classical Athens.'

'One thing that puzzles me,' said Costas, 'is why the clay discs and the gold disc were made at all. Maurice Hiebermeyer said that sacred knowledge was passed down by word of mouth from high priest to high priest to ensure it remained uncorrupted, to keep it secret. So why did they need a decoder in the form of these discs?'

'I have a theory about that,' said Jack.

A red warning light flashed on the instrument panel. He switched the controls to manual and engaged the two auxiliary fuel tanks, necessary for the long flight. After reverting to autopilot he pressed a CD-ROM into the console and folded down a miniature screen from the cockpit ceiling. It showed a gaudy procession of longboats leaving a town, the inhabitants peering out from elaborately tiered seaside dwellings.

'The famous marine fresco, found in the 1960s in the Admiral's House at Akrotiri on Thera. Usually interpreted as a ceremonial occasion, perhaps the consecration of a new high priest.'

He tapped a key and the image changed to an aerial photograph showing layers of ruinous walls and balustrades protruding from a cliff face.

'The earthquake that damaged the Parthenon last year also dislodged the cliff face on the shore of Paleo Kameni, "Old Burnt", the second biggest islet in the Thera group. It exposed the remains of what looks like a cliff-top monastery. Much of what we know about Minoan religion comes from so-called peak sanctuaries, sacred enclosures on the hilltops and mountains of Crete. We now believe the island of Thera was the greatest peak sanctuary of them all.'

'The home of the gods, the entrance to the underworld,' Costas offered.

'Something like that,' Jack replied. 'The peak sanctuary itself was blown to smithereens when Thera erupted. But there was also a religious community, one buried under ash and pumice beyond the caldera.'

'And your theory about the discs?' Costas prompted.

'I'm coming to that,' said Jack. 'First let's consider our shipwreck. The best guess is it was caused before the eruption of Thera, sunk in a shockwave before the main blast.'

The other two murmured in agreement.

'I now believe she was more than just a wealthy merchantman. Think of the cargo. Gold chalices and necklaces. Gold and ivory statues, some almost life-sized. Libation altars carved out of rare Egyptian porphyry. The bull's head rhyton. Vastly more wealth than would normally be entrusted to a single cargo.'

'What are you suggesting?' Costas asked.

'I think we've found the treasury of the high priests of Thera, the most sacred repository of Bronze Age civilization. I believe the discs were the most coveted possessions of the high priests. The gold disc was the oldest, brought out only for the most sacred ceremonies, and originally had no markings other than the central symbol. The ancient clay disc, the older of the two Phaistos discs, was a record tablet rather than a revered object. It contained a key to knowledge, but was written in ancient symbols only the priests could decipher. Following the warning earthquake, fearful of impending apocalypse, the high priest ordered these symbols to be stamped round the edge of the gold disc. They were a lexicon, a concordance of the ancient symbols on the clay disc with the prevailing Linear A and B scripts. Any literate Minoan would realize the syllabic groupings were an ancestral version of their own language.'

'So it was an insurance policy,' Katya suggested. 'A code book for reading the clay disc in case the priests should all perish.'

'Yes.' Jack turned towards her. 'Along with the magnificent bull's head rhyton, the divers came up with a bundle of ebony and ivory rods exquisitely carved with images of the great mother goddess. We believe they were the sacred staffs of the Minoans, ritual accoutrements like the staffs of bishops and cardinals. I think they accompanied the high priest himself as he fled the island sanctuary.'

'And the Phaistos discs?'

'At the same time as having the symbols stamped on the gold disc, the high priest ordered a replica to be made of the ancient clay disc, one which appeared to contain a similar text but was in fact meaningless. As Professor Dillen said, the replica was a way of putting outsiders off seeking too much meaning in the symbols. Only the priests would know the significance of the text and have access to the concordance on the golden disc.'

'How did they come to be at Phaistos?' Costas demanded.

'I believe they were originally in the same repository as the golden disc, in the same temple storeroom on the island of Thera,' Jack said. 'The high priest sent them in an earlier shipment which reached Crete safely. Phaistos would have seemed an obvious refuge, high above the sea and protected from the volcano by Mount Ida to the north.'

'And a religious centre,' added Katya.

'Next to the palace is Hagia Triadha, a complex of ruins which has long perplexed archaeologists. It's where both the discs were discovered a hundred years apart. We now think it was a kind of seminary, a training college for priests who would then be despatched to the peak sanctuaries.'

'But Phaistos and Hagia Triadha were both destroyed at the time of the eruption,' Katya interjected. 'Levelled by an earthquake and never reoccupied, the discs buried in the ruins only days after they arrived from Thera.'

'I have one final question,' said Costas. 'How did the high priest of the temple of Saïs in the Nile Delta come to know of Atlantis almost a thousand years after the eruption of Thera and the loss of these discs?'

'I believe the Egyptians knew the story from the same source, far back in prehistory, that it survived separately in each civilization. It was sacred, passed down scrupulously without embellishment or emendation, as shown by the identical details of the Atlantis symbol on both the papyrus and the discs.'

'We have Solon the Lawmaker to thank for the connection,' Katya said. 'If he hadn't fastidiously copied that symbol beside the Greek word Atlantis we might not be here.'

'The Phaistos discs were worthless, made of pottery,' Costas mused, 'of value only for the symbols. But the disc from the wreck is solid unalloyed gold, maybe the biggest ingot to survive from prehistory.' He turned in his seat and looked keenly at Jack. 'My hunch is there's more to this than meets the eye. I think our golden paperweight will somehow unlock an even greater mystery.'

★

They had passed the Sea of Marmara and were flying over the Bosporus. The clear air of the Aegean had transformed into a haze of smog from the sprawl of Istanbul. They could just distinguish the Golden Horn, the inlet where Greek colonists founded Byzantium in the seventh century BC. Beside it a forest of minarets poked up out of the morning mist. On the promontory they could make out the palace of Topkapi, once the very symbol of oriental decadence but now one of the finest archaeological museums in the world. Near the seafront were the great walls of Constantinople, the capital of the Byzantine Empire, which kept Rome alive in the east until the city fell to the Turks in 1453.

'It's one of my favourite cities,' Jack said. 'Once you find your way around, it's got the richest history you can imagine.'

'When this is over I'd like you to take me there,' Katya said.

Ahead lay the Black Sea, the broad sweep of coast on either side of the Bosporus seemingly extending to infinity. The GPS showed the final leg of their journey due east to a position some ten nautical miles north of the Turkish port of Trabzon. Jack opened the IMU channel on the VHF relayer and engaged the scrambler, punching in a routine position fix for the crew of *Sea Venture*.

Moments later a blue light flashed on the lower right-hand corner of the screen above the central console.

'Incoming email,' Costas said.

Jack double-clicked the mouse and waited while the address appeared.

'It's from Professor Dillen. Let's hope it's his translation of the Phaistos disc.'

Katya leaned forward from the back seat and they waited in hushed anticipation. Soon all the words were visible on the screen.

My dear Jack,

Since our teleconference last night I have worked flat out to complete the translation. Much has depended on the co-operation of colleagues around the world. The Linear A archive found at Knossos last year was parcelled out to many different scholars for study, and you know how protective academics can be of their unpublished data – remember the trouble we had accessing the Dead Sea Scrolls when we began our search for Sodom and Gomorrah. Fortunately most scholars of Minoan epigraphy are former students of mine.

Only the obverse of the second disc was meaningful. The attempt to conceal the true text was even more extensive than we thought.

Our mysterious symbol occurs twice and I have simply translated it as Atlantis.

Here it is:

Beneath the sign of the bull lies the outstretched eagle god. (At) his tail (here is) golden-walled Atlantis, the great golden door of the (citadel?). (His) wingtips touch the rising and the setting of the sun. (At the) rising of the sun (here is) the mountain of fire and metal. (Here is) the hall of the high priests [Throne room? Audience chamber?]. Above (here is) Atlantis. (Here is) the mother goddess. (Here is) the place (of) the gods (and) the storeroom (of) knowledge.

I do not yet know what to make of this. Is it a riddle? Maurice and I are eager to know what you think.

Yours ever,
James Dillen

They read the translation several times in silence. Costas was the first to speak, his mind as ever seeking practicality where others saw only mystery.

'This is no riddle. It's a treasure map.'

8

'Jack! Welcome aboard!'

The voice was raised above the din of the Rolls-Royce Gem turboshafts as they powered down. Jack had just stepped out onto the inflatable skid landing gear, a modification of the usual fixed-wheel naval configuration that allowed the IMU helicopters to land on water. He hurried over to shake Malcolm Macleod's outstretched hand, his tall frame stooped low as the rotor shuddered to a halt. Costas and Katya followed close behind. As they made their way below, several of the crew scurried round the Lynx, securing it to the deck, and began offloading gearbags from the cargo bay.

Sea Venture differed from *Seaquest* only in the range of equipment suited to her role as IMU's chief deep-sea research vessel. She had recently conducted the first manned submersible survey of the Mariana Trench in the western Pacific. Her present role in the Black Sea had begun as a routine sedimentological analysis but had now taken on a startling new dimension.

'Follow me to the bridge console.'

Malcolm Macleod led them below the same dome-shaped screen they had viewed on *Seaquest*. Macleod was Jack's counterpart in the department of oceanography, a man whose expertise Jack had come greatly to respect through their many collaborative projects around the world.

The burly, red-haired Scotsman sat down in the operator's chair beside the console.

'Welcome to *Sea Venture*. I trust your inspection can wait until I show you what we've found.'

Jack nodded. 'Go on.'

'Do you know about the Messinian salinity crisis?'

Jack and Costas nodded but Katya looked perplexed.

'OK. For the benefit of our new colleague.' Macleod smiled at Katya. 'Named after deposits found near the Strait of Messina in Sicily. In the early 1970s the deep-sea drilling ship *Glomar Challenger* took core samples across the Mediterranean. Beneath the sea floor they found a huge layer of compacted evaporates, in places three kilometres thick. It formed during the late Miocene, the most recent geological era before our own, around five and a half million years ago.'

'Evaporates?' Katya asked.

'Mainly halite, common rock salt, the stuff left when seawater evaporates. Above and below it are marls, normal marine sediments of clay and calcium carbonate. The salt layer formed at the same time across the Mediterranean.'

'What does this mean?'

'It means the Mediterranean evaporated.'

Katya looked incredulous. 'The Mediterranean evaporated? All of it?'

Macleod nodded. 'The trigger was a huge drop in atmospheric temperature, a far colder spell than our recent Ice Age. The polar ice trapped a vast amount of the world's oceans, causing the sea level to fall as much as five hundred metres. The Mediterranean was sealed off and began to dry up, eventually leaving only brackish mire in the deepest basins.'

'Like the Dead Sea,' Katya suggested.

'Even more saline, in fact barely liquid at all. Too salty for most life, hence the paucity of fossils. Large areas became desert.'

'When did it fill up again?'

'About two hundred thousand years later. It would have been a dramatic process, a result of massive melt at the Poles. The first trickles from the Atlantic would have become a torrent, the biggest waterfall ever, a hundred times bigger than Niagara, carving the Strait of Gibraltar down to its present depth.'

'How is this relevant to the Black Sea?' Katya asked.

'The Messinian salinity crisis is an established scientific fact.' Macleod looked across keenly at Jack. 'It will help you believe the unbelievable, which is what I'm going to tell you next.'

They gathered behind *Sea Venture*'s remote operated vehicle station on the far side of the console. Macleod invited Katya to sit behind the screen and showed her how to use the joystick.

'Think of it as a flight simulator. Use the joystick to fly it any way you want, up or down, sideways or backwards. Speed control is the dial on the left-hand side.'

Macleod put his hand on Katya's and executed a full clockwise circle, pulling it round at maximum depression. The wide-format video screen remained pitch-black but the direction indicator spun through 360 degrees. The depth gauge read 135 metres, and a set of GPS co-ordinates showed the ROV's position with an accuracy deviation of less than half a metre.

Macleod pulled the stick back to its default alignment.

'A freefall spin followed by a perfect recovery.' He grinned at Jack, who well remembered their ROV dogfights when they had trained together at the IMU deep-sea equipment facility off Bermuda.

'ROVs have been used extensively by scientific teams for a couple of decades now,' Macleod explained. 'But over the last few years the technology has become increasingly refined. For exploratory survey we use AUVs, autonomous operated vehicles, which have multitask sensor packages including video and side-scan sonar. Once a target is identified we deploy direct-control ROVs. The IMU Mark 7 we're operating here is not much larger than a briefcase, small enough to penetrate a sub-sea vent.'

'You can turn one of these babies on a dime,' Costas added. 'And the Doppler radio-pulse control means it can go fifteen nautical miles horizontally or straight down to the deepest abyss.'

'Nearly there,' Macleod interrupted. 'Activating flood-lights.'

He depressed the joystick, flipping several switches on the console panel as he did so. Suddenly the screen came to life, the inky blackness replaced by a brilliant shimmer of speckles.

'Silt,' Macleod explained. 'Our lights reflecting off particles disturbed in the water.'

They began to make out something more substantial, a

shadowy background which gradually came into clearer view. It was the sea floor, a bleak, featureless expanse of grey. Macleod switched on the ROV's terrain-contour radar which showed the seabed sloping down on a 30-degree gradient from the south.

'Depth 148 metres.'

A strange tower-like structure suddenly hove into view and Macleod halted the ROV a few metres away.

'Another of Costas' ingenious contraptions. A remote-operated excavator, capable of drilling cores a hundred metres below the seabed or airlifting huge volumes of sediment.' With his free hand Macleod reached into a box beside his seat. 'And this is what we found just below the sea floor.'

He passed Katya a shiny black object the size of his fist. She weighed it in her hand and cast a quizzical look.

'A beach pebble?'

'Worn smooth on the seashore. All along this gradient we've found evidence of an ancient coastline, one hundred and fifty metres deep and ten nautical miles from shore. Even more astonishing is its date. It's one of the most remarkable discoveries we've ever made.'

Macleod punched in a set of GPS co-ordinates and the image on the screen began to move, the floodlit sea floor showing little change as the ROV kept to the same depth contour.

'I've put it on autopilot. Fifteen minutes to target.'

Katya handed back the blackened beach pebble. 'Could this be associated with the Messinian salinity crisis?'

'We certainly would have put it before the arrival of humans – or rather, hominids – in this region two million years ago.'

'But?'

'But we would have been wrong. Wildly wrong. Submerged

shorelines are hardly unusual in our line of work but this one's big news. Follow me and I'll show you.'

Macleod downloaded a computer-generated isometric map of the Black Sea and the Bosporus.

'The relationship between the Mediterranean and the Black Sea is a kind of microcosm of the Atlantic and the Mediterranean,' he explained. 'The Bosporus is only about one hundred metres deep. Any lowering of the Mediterranean below that depth and it becomes a land bridge, cutting off the Black Sea. These were the conditions that allowed the first hominids in Europe to cross over from Asia.' He moved the cursor to highlight three river systems leading into the sea.

'When the Bosporus was a land bridge, evaporation caused the Black Sea to lower, just like the Mediterranean in the salinity crisis. But the Black Sea was replenished by river inflow, from the Danube, the Dnieper and the Don. A median was reached where the rate of evaporation equalled the rate of inflow, and from then on the change was in salinity, with the Black Sea eventually becoming a vast freshwater lake.'

He punched a key and the computer began to simulate the events he had been describing, showing the Bosporus becoming dry and the Black Sea lowering to a point about 150 metres below present sea level and 50 metres below the floor of the Bosporus, where its level was maintained by inflow from the rivers.

He swivelled round and looked at the others.

'Now for the surprise. This is not an image from the early Pleistocene, from the depths of the Ice Age. What you're looking at is the Black Sea less than ten thousand years ago.'

Katya looked dumbfounded. 'You mean *after* the Ice Age?'

Macleod nodded vigorously. 'The most recent glaciation peaked about twenty thousand years ago. We believe the Black Sea was cut off some time before that and had already dropped to the hundred and fifty metre contour. Our beach was the seashore for the next twelve thousand years.'

'Then what happened?'

'It recapitulates the Messinian salinity crisis. The glaciers melt, the Mediterranean rises, water cascades over the Bosporus. The immediate cause may have been a retreat phase some seven thousand years ago in the West Antarctic Ice Sheet. We believe it took only a year for the Black Sea to reach its present level. At full flow almost twenty cubic kilometres poured in daily, resulting in a rise of up to forty centimetres a day or two to three metres a week.'

Jack pointed at the lower part of the map. 'Could you give us a close-up of this?'

'Certainly.' Macleod tapped a sequence and the screen zoomed in on the coast of northern Turkey. The isometric terrain mapper continued to depict the topography of the land before the inundation.

Jack edged forward as he spoke. 'We're currently eleven nautical miles off the north coast of Turkey, say eighteen kilometres, and the depth of the sea below us is about one hundred and fifty metres. A constant gradient to the present seashore would mean a rise of about ten metres for every kilometre and a half inland, say a ratio of one to one hundred and fifty. That's a pretty shallow slope, hardly noticeable. If the sea rose as quickly as you indicate then we're looking at three or four hundred metres being flooded inland every week, say fifty metres a day.'

'Or even more,' Macleod said. 'Before the inundation, much of what lies beneath us was only a few metres above sea level, with a sharper gradient close to the present shoreline as you begin to ascend the Anatolian Plateau. Within weeks huge areas would have been swamped.'

Jack looked at the map in silence for a few moments. 'We're

talking about the early Neolithic, the first period of farming,' he mused. 'What would conditions have been like here?'

Macleod beamed. 'I've had our palaeoclimatologists working overtime on that one. They've run a series of simulations with all possible variables to reconstruct the environment between the end of the Pleistocene and the inundation.'

'And?'

'They believe this was the most fertile region in the entire Near East.'

Katya let out a low whistle. 'It could be an entirely new tapestry of human history. A strip of coast twenty kilometres wide, hundreds of kilometres long, in one of the key areas for the development of civilization. And never before explored by archaeologists.'

Macleod was twitching with excitement. 'And now the reason you're here. It's time to return to the ROV monitor.'

The seabed was now more undulating, with occasional rocky outcrops and furrowed depressions where there had once been ravines and river valleys. The depth gauge showed the ROV was over the submerged land surface, some fifteen metres shallower and a kilometre inland from the ancient shoreline. The GPS co-ordinates were beginning to converge with the target figures programmed in by Macleod.

'The Black Sea should be an archaeologists' paradise,' Jack said. 'The upper hundred metres are low in salt, a relic of the freshwater lake and a result of river inflow. Marine borers such as the shipworm *Teredo navalis* require a more saline environment, so ancient timbers can survive here in pristine condition. It's always been a dream of mine to find a trireme, an ancient oared warship.'

'But it's a biologist's nightmare,' Macleod countered. 'Below a hundred metres it's poisoned with hydrogen sulphide, a result of the chemical alteration of seawater as bacteria use it to digest the huge quantities of organic matter that come in with the rivers. And the abyssal depths are even worse. When the high-saline waters of the Mediterranean cascaded over the Bosporus they sank almost two thousand metres to the deepest part of the sea. It's still there, a stagnant layer two hundred metres thick, unable to support any life. One of the world's most noxious environments.'

'At the Izmir NATO base I interrogated a submariner who had defected from the Soviet Black Sea Fleet,' Costas murmured. 'An engineer who had worked on their top-secret deep-sea probes. He claimed to have seen shipwrecks standing proud of the seabed with their rigging intact. He showed me a picture where you could even make out human corpses, a jumble of spectral forms encased in brine. It's one of the spookiest things I've ever seen.'

'Almost as remarkable as this.'

A red light flashed in the lower right corner of the screen as the GPS fix converged. Almost simultaneously the seabed transformed into a scene so extraordinary it took their breath away. Directly in front of the ROV the floodlight reflected off a complex of low-set buildings, their flat roofs merging into each other like an Indian pueblo. Ladders connected lower and upper rooms. Everything was shrouded in a ghostly layer of silt like the ash from a volcanic eruption. It was a haunting and desolate image, yet one which made their hearts race with excitement.

'Fantastic,' Jack exclaimed. 'Can we take a closer look?'

'I'll put us where we were when I called you yesterday.'

Macleod switched to manual and jetted the ROV towards an entrance in one of the rooftops. By gingerly feathering the joystick he moved inside, slowly panning the camera round the walls. They were decorated with moulded designs just visible in the gloom, long-necked ungulates, ibexes perhaps, as well as lions and tigers bounding along with outstretched limbs.

'Hydraulic mortar,' Costas murmured.

'What?' Jack asked distractedly.

'It's the only way those walls can have survived underwater. The mixture must include a hydraulic binding agent. They had access to volcanic dust.'

At the far end of the submerged room was a form instantly recognizable to any student of prehistory. It was the U-shape of a bull's horns, a larger than life carving embedded in a wide plinth like an altar.

'It's early Neolithic. No question about it.' Jack was ebullient, his attention completely focused on the extraordinary images in front of them. 'This is a household shrine, exactly like one excavated more than thirty years ago at Çatal Hüyük.'

'Where?' Costas enquired.

'Central Turkey, on the Konya Plain about four hundred kilometres south of here. Possibly the earliest town in the world, a farming community established ten thousand years ago at the dawn of agriculture. A tightly packed conglomeration of mud-brick buildings with timber frames just like these.'

'A unique site,' Katya said.

'Until now. This changes everything.'

'There's more,' said Macleod. 'Much more. The sonar shows anomalies like this along the ancient coast as far as we've surveyed, about thirty kilometres either way. They occur every couple of kilometres and each one is undoubtedly another village or homestead.'

'Amazing.' Jack's mind was racing. 'This land must have been incredibly productive, supporting a population far larger than the fertile crescent of Mesopotamia and the Levant.' He looked at Macleod, a wide grin on his face. 'For an expert on deep-sea hydrothermal vents you've done a pretty good day's work.'

9

Sea Venture cut a white-flecked swath as she made her way south from her position above the submerged ancient shoreline. The sky was clear but the sea was a dark and forbidding contrast to the deep blue of the Mediterranean. Ahead loomed the forested slopes of northern Turkey and the crest of the Anatolian Plateau, which marked the beginning of the uplands of Asia Minor.

As soon as the ROV had been recovered, *Sea Venture* had made maximum headway for the IMU supply base at Trabzon, the Black Sea port whose whitewashed buildings nestled against the shoreline to the south. Katya was enjoying her first chance to relax since arriving in Alexandria three days previously, her long hair blowing in the breeze as she stripped down to a bathing costume that left little to the imagination. Beside her on deck Jack was finding it hard to concentrate as he talked to Costas and Macleod.

Costas had been advising Macleod on the best way to map the sunken Neolithic village, drawing on their success with photogrammetry at the Minoan wreck. They had agreed that *Seaquest* would join *Sea Venture* in the Black Sea as soon as possible; her equipment and expertise were essential for a full investigation. Another vessel had already been despatched from Carthage to assist at the wreck site and it would now take over from *Seaquest*.

'If the sea was rising up to forty centimetres a day after the Bosporus was breached,' Costas said, his voice raised against the wind, 'then it would have been pretty obvious to the coastal population. After a few days they'd have guessed the long-term prognosis was not good.'

'Right,' Macleod agreed. 'The Neolithic village is ten metres higher than the ancient shoreline. They would have had about a month to get out. That would explain the absence of artefacts in the rooms we saw.'

'Could this be the Biblical flood?' Costas ventured.

'Virtually every civilization has a flood myth, but most can be related to river floods rather than some oceanic deluge,' Jack said. 'Catastrophic river floods were more likely early on, before people learned to build embankments and channels to control the waters.'

'That's always seemed the most likely basis for the Epic of Gilgamesh,' Katya said. 'A flood story written on twelve clay tablets about 2000 BC, discovered in the ruins of Nineveh in Iraq. Gilgamesh was a Sumerian king of Uruk on the Euphrates, a place first settled in the late sixth millennium BC.'

'The Biblical flood may have had a different origin,' Macleod added. 'IMU has surveyed the Mediterranean coast of Israel and found evidence for human activity dating back to the end of the Ice Age, to the time of the great melt twelve thousand years ago. Five kilometres offshore we found stone tools and shell middens where Palaeolithic hunter-gatherers ranged before it was submerged.'

'You're suggesting the Israelites of the Old Testament retained some memory of these events?' Costas asked.

'Oral tradition can survive thousands of years, especially in a tightly knit society. But some of our displaced farmers from the Black Sea could also have settled in Israel.'

'Remember Noah's Ark,' Jack said. 'A huge ship built after warnings of a flood. Breeding pairs of every animal. Think of our Black Sea farmers. The sea would have been their main escape route and they would have taken as many of their animals as possible, in breeding pairs to start up new populations.'

'I thought they didn't have big boats that early on,' Costas said.

'Neolithic shipwrights could build longboats able to carry several tons of cargo. The first farmers on Cyprus had giant aurochs, the ancestor of today's cattle, as well as pigs and deer. None of these species were indigenous and they can only have been brought by boat. That was around 9000 BC. The same thing probably happened on Crete a thousand years later.'

Costas scratched his chin thoughtfully. 'So the story of Noah might contain a kernel of truth, not one huge vessel but many smaller vessels carrying farmers and livestock from the Black Sea.'

Jack nodded. 'It's a very compelling idea.'

Sea Venture's engines powered down as she made for the harbour entrance at Trabzon. Beside the eastern quay they could see the grey silhouettes of two *Dogan*-class FPB-57 fast attack craft, part of the Turkish Navy's response to the increasing scourge of smuggling on the Black Sea. The Turks had taken an uncompromising view, striking hard and fast and shooting to kill. Jack felt reassured by the sight, knowing his contacts in the Turkish Navy would ensure a swift response should they encounter any trouble in territorial waters.

They were standing by the railing on the upper deck as *Sea Venture* edged towards the western quay. Costas peered up at the densely wooded slopes above the town.

'Where did they go after the flood? They wouldn't have been able to farm up there.'

'They would have needed to go a long way inland,' Jack agreed. 'And this was a large population, tens of thousands at least, to judge by the number of settlements we saw on the sonar read-out.'

'So they split up.'

'It may have been an organized exodus, orchestrated by a central authority to ensure the greatest chance of finding suitable new lands for the entire population. Some went south over that ridge, some east, some west. Malcolm mentioned Israel. There are other obvious destinations.'

Costas spoke excitedly. 'The early civilizations. Egypt. Mesopotamia. The Indus Valley. Crete.'

'It is not so far-fetched.' The words came from Katya, who had sat up and was now fully absorbed in the discussion. 'One of the most striking features about the history of language is that much of it stems from a common root. Across Europe, Russia, the Middle East, the Indian subcontinent, most of the languages spoken today have one origin.'

'Indo-European,' Costas offered.

'An ancient mother tongue which many linguists already thought came from the Black Sea region. We can reconstruct its vocabulary from words held in common by later languages, such as Sanscrit *pitar*, Latin *pater* and German *vater*, the origin of English *father*.'

'What about words for agriculture?' Costas asked.

'The vocabulary shows they ploughed the land, wore woollen clothing and worked leather. They had domesticated animals including oxen, pigs and sheep. They had complex social structures and wealth differentiation. They worshipped a great mother goddess.'

'What are you suggesting?'

'Many of us already believe Indo-European expansion went hand in hand with the spread of agriculture, a gradual process over many years. I now suggest it was the result of one migration. Our Black Sea farmers were the original Indo-Europeans.'

Jack balanced a sketchpad and pencil on the railing and quickly drew an outline map of the ancient world.

'Here's a hypothesis,' he said. 'Our Indo-Europeans leave their homeland on the Black Sea coast.' He drew a sweeping arrow east from their present position. 'One group goes towards the Caucasus, modern Georgia. Some of them travel overland to the Zagros Mountains, eventually reaching the Indus Valley in Pakistan.'

'They would have seen Mount Ararat soon after striking inland,' Macleod asserted. 'It would have been an awesome sight, much loftier than any of the mountains they knew. It may have become fixed in folklore as the place where they finally realized they had escaped the flood.'

Jack marked another arrow on the map. 'A second group heads south over the Anatolian Plateau to Mesopotamia, settling on the banks of the Tigris and Euphrates.'

'And another north-west to the Danube,' Costas suggested.

Jack slashed a third arrow across the map. 'Some settle there, others use the river system to reach the heartland of Europe.'

Macleod spoke excitedly. 'Britain became an island at the end of the Ice Age, when the North Sea flooded. But these people had the technology to get across. Were they the first farmers in Britain, the ancestors of the people who built Stonehenge?'

'The Celtic language of Britain was Indo-European,' Katya added.

Jack drew an arrow west which branched in different directions like an overhanging tree. 'And the final group, perhaps the most significant, paddle west and portage past the Bosporus, then re-embark and set off across the Aegean. Some settle in Greece and Crete, some in Israel and Egypt, some as far away as Italy and Spain.'

'The Bosporus would have been an awesome sight,' Costas mused. 'Something that remained in the collective memory like Mount Ararat for the eastern group, hence the cataract of Bos mentioned on the disc.'

Katya stared intently at Jack. 'It fits beautifully with the linguistic evidence,' she said. 'There are more than forty ancient languages with Indo-European roots.'

Jack nodded and looked down at his map. 'Professor Dillen tells me the Minoan language of Linear A and the Phaistos symbols is the closest we have to the Indo-European mother tongue. Crete may have seen the greatest survival of Indo-European culture.'

Sea Venture was now drawing alongside the quay at Trabzon. Several crew had jumped the narrowing gap and were busy laying hawser lines to secure the vessel. A small group were gathered on the dockside, Turkish officials and staff from IMU's supply depot who were keen to hear about the latest discoveries. Among them was the handsome figure of Mustafa Alközen, a former Turkish naval officer who was IMU's chief representative in the country. Jack and Costas waved across at their old friend, happy to renew a partnership which had begun when they were stationed together at the Izmir base and he had joined them to excavate the galleys of the Trojan War.

Costas turned back and looked at Macleod. 'I have one final question.'

'Fire away.'

'The date.'

Macleod grinned broadly and tapped a map case he was holding. 'I was wondering when you'd ask that.'

He took out three large photographs and passed them over. They were stills from the ROV camera, the depth and co-ordinates imprinted in the lower right-hand corner. They showed a large wooden frame with stacks of logs alongside.

'It looks like a building site,' said Costas.

'We came across it yesterday beside the house with the shrine. New rooms were being added at the time the village was abandoned.' Macleod pointed to one stack of wood on the sea floor. 'We used the ROV's water jet to clear away the silt. They're recently felled trunks, the bark still firmly in place and sap on the surface.'

He opened his case and took out a clear plastic tube about half a metre long. It contained a thin wooden rod.

'The ROV has a hollow drill which can extract samples up to two metres long from timber and other compacted materials.'

The honey-coloured grain was remarkably well preserved, as if it had just come from a living tree. Macleod passed it to Costas who saw at once what he was driving at.

'Dendrochronology.'

'You got it. There's a continuous tree-ring sequence for Asia Minor from 8500 BC to the present day. We bored into the heart of the log and found fifty-four rings, enough for dating.'

'And?'

'In *Sea Venture*'s lab we have a scanner which matches the baseline sequences in a matter of seconds.'

Jack looked questioningly at Macleod, who was enjoying milking the drama for all it was worth.

'You're the archaeologist,' Macleod said. 'What's your estimate?'

Jack played along. 'Soon after the end of the Ice Age but long enough ago for the Mediterranean to have reached the level of the Bosporus. I'd say eighth, maybe seventh millennium BC.'

Macleod leaned on the railing and looked intently at Jack. The others waited with bated breath.

'Close, but not close enough. That tree was felled in 5545 BC, give or take a year.'

Costas looked incredulous. 'Impossible! That's way too late!'

'It's corroborated by all the other tree-ring dates from the site. It seems we underestimated by a millennium the time it took the Mediterranean to rise to its present level.'

'Most linguists place the Indo-Europeans between 6000 and 5000 BC,' Katya exclaimed. 'It all falls into place perfectly.'

Jack and Costas gripped the rail as *Sea Venture*'s gangway was secured to the quayside below them. After so many adventures together they shared the same hunches, could second-guess the other's thoughts. Yet they could scarcely believe where they were leading, a possibility so fantastic their minds rebelled until the power of logic became overwhelming.

'That date,' Costas said quietly. 'We've seen it before.'

Jack's voice held total conviction as he leaned towards Macleod. 'I can tell you about these Indo-Europeans. They had a great citadel by the sea, a storeroom of knowledge entered by great golden doors.'

'What are you talking about?'

Jack paused and then spoke quietly. 'Atlantis.'

'Jack, my friend! Good to see you.'

The deep voice came from a figure on the quayside, his dark features offset by chinos and a white shirt bearing the IMU logo.

Jack reached out and shook hands with Mustafa Alközen as he and Costas stepped off the gangway onto the quayside. As they looked over the modern town towards the ruined citadel it was hard to imagine this had once been the capital of the Kingdom of Trebizond, the medieval offshoot of Byzantium renowned for its splendour and decadence. From earliest times the city had flourished as a hub of trade between east and west, a tradition now darkly continued in the flood of black marketeers who had arrived since the fall of the Soviet Union and provided a haven for smugglers and agents of organized crime in the east.

Malcolm Macleod had gone ahead to deal with the crowd of officials and journalists who had gathered as *Sea Venture* came in. They had agreed that his briefing on the Neolithic village discovery should be deliberately vague until they had carried out more exploration. They knew unscrupulous eyes would already be monitoring their work by satellite, and they were wary of giving away more than the minimum needed to satisfy the journalists. Fortunately the site lay eleven nautical miles offshore, just within territorial waters. Already the Turkish Navy fast attack craft moored on the opposite side of the harbour had been detailed to maintain round-the-clock vigilance until the investigations were complete and the site had been accorded special protection status by the Turkish government.

'Mustafa, meet our new colleague. Dr Katya Svetlanova.'

Katya had slipped a dress over her swimsuit and was carrying a palm computer and documents case. She shook the proffered hand and smiled up at Mustafa.

'Dr Svetlanova. Jack told me on the radio about your formidable expertise. It is my pleasure.'

Jack and Mustafa walked ahead of the other two as they made their way towards the IMU depot at the end of the quay. Jack talked quietly and intensely, filling Mustafa in on all the events since the discovery of the papyrus. He had decided to take advantage of *Sea Venture*'s revictualling stop to tap into the Turk's unique expertise and bring him into the small fold of people who knew about the papyrus and the discs.

Just before entering the low-set concrete building, Jack handed over a notepad which the other man passed to his secretary as they reached the door. It contained a wish list of archaeological and diving equipment from the IMU store which Jack had compiled in the final minutes before disembarking from *Sea Venture*.

They were joined by Katya and Costas in front of a large steel door. After Mustafa tapped in a security code, the door swung open and he led them through a succession of laboratories and repair shops. At the far end they entered a room lined with wooden cabinets with a table in the centre.

'The chart room,' Mustafa explained to Katya. 'It doubles as our operational headquarters. Please be seated.'

He opened a drawer and extracted a chart of the Aegean and southern Black Sea region, encompassing the Turkish coast all the way to its eastern border with the Republic of Georgia. He spread it out and clipped it to the table. From a small drawer underneath, he extracted a set of navigational dividers and cartographic rulers, placing them side by side as Katya set up her computer.

After a few moments she looked up. 'I'm ready.'

They had agreed that Katya should give the translation of the papyrus while they tried to make sense of it on the chart.

She read slowly from the screen. '*Through the islands until the sea narrows.*'

'This clearly refers to the Aegean archipelago from the viewpoint of Egypt,' Jack said. 'The Aegean has more than fifteen hundred islands in a confined area. On a clear day north of Crete you can't sail anywhere without having at least one island in view.'

'So the narrows must be the Dardanelles,' Costas asserted.

'What clinches it is the next passage.' The three men looked expectantly at Katya. '*Past the Cataract of Bos.*'

Jack was suddenly animated. 'It should have been glaringly obvious. The Bosporus, the entrance to the Black Sea.'

Costas turned to Katya, his voice edged with incredulity. 'Could our word Bosporus be that ancient?'

'It dates back at least two and a half thousand years, to the time of the earliest Greek geographical writings. But it's probably thousands of years older. *Bos* is Indo-European for *bull.*'

'Strait of the Bull,' Costas mused. 'This may be a long shot, but I'm thinking of the bull symbols in that Neolithic house and from Minoan Crete. They're quite abstract, showing the bull's horns as a kind of saddle, a bit like a Japanese headrest. That would have been precisely the appearance of the Bosporus from the Black Sea before the flood, a great saddle gouged into a ridge high above the sea.'

Jack looked at his friend appreciatively. 'You never cease to amaze me. That's the best idea I've heard for a long time.'

Costas warmed to his theme. 'To people who worshipped the bull the sight of all that water cascading through the horns must have seemed portentous, a sign from the gods.'

Jack nodded and turned to Katya. 'So we're in the Black Sea. What next?'

'And then twenty dromoi along the southern shore.'

Jack leaned forward. 'On the face of it we have a problem. There are some records of voyage times in the Black Sea during the Roman period. One of them starts here, at what the Romans called the Maeotic Lake.' He pointed to the Sea of Azov, the lagoon beside the Crimean Peninsula. 'From there it took eleven days to get to Rhodes. Only four days were spent on the Black Sea.'

Mustafa looked pensively at the map. 'So a twenty-day voyage from the Bosporus, twenty *dromoi* or runs, would take us beyond the eastern littoral of the Black Sea.'

Costas looked crestfallen. 'Maybe the early boats were slower.'

'The opposite,' said Jack. 'Paddled longboats would have been faster than sailing ships, less subject to the vagaries of the winds.'

'And the inflow during the flood would have created a strong easterly current,' Mustafa said glumly. 'Enough to propel a ship to the far shore in only a few days. I'm afraid Atlantis is off the map in more ways than one.'

A crushing sense of disappointment pervaded the room. Suddenly Atlantis seemed as far away as it had ever been, a story consigned to the annals of myth and fable.

'There is a solution,' Jack said slowly. 'The Egyptian account is not based on their own experience. If so, they would never have described the Bosporus as a cataract, since the Mediterranean and Black Sea had equalized long before the Egyptians began to explore that far north. Instead, their source was the account handed down from the Black Sea migrants, telling of their voyage *from* Atlantis. The Egyptians simply reversed it.'

'Of course!' Mustafa was excited again. '*From* Atlantis means against the current. In describing the route *to* Atlantis, the Egyptians used the same voyage times they had been told for the outward journey. They could never have guessed there would be a significant difference between the two.'

Jack looked pointedly at Mustafa. 'What we need is some way of estimating the speed of the current, of calculating the headway a Neolithic boat would have made against the flow. That should give us the distance for each day's run and the measure from the Bosporus to a point of embarkation twenty days back.'

Mustafa straightened up and replied confidently, 'You've come to the right place.'

10

The sun was setting over the shoreline to the west as the group reassembled in the chart room. For three hours Mustafa had been hunched over a cluster of computer screens in an annexe and only ten minutes before had called to announce he was ready. They were joined by Malcolm Macleod, who had scheduled a press conference to announce the Neolithic village discovery when the Navy FAC boat was in position over the site the following morning.

Costas was the first to pull up a chair. The others clustered round as he eagerly scanned the console.

'What've you got?'

Mustafa replied without taking his eyes off the central screen. 'A few glitches in the navigation software which I

127

had to iron out, but the whole thing comes together very nicely.'

They had first collaborated with Mustafa when he was a lieutenant-commander in charge of the Computer-Aided Navigation Research and Development unit at the Izmir NATO base. After leaving the Turkish Navy and completing an archaeology PhD he had specialized in the application of CAN technology to scientific use. Over the past year he had worked with Costas on an innovative software package for calculating the effect of wind and current on navigation in antiquity. Regarded as one of the finest minds in the field, he was also a formidable station chief who had more than proved his worth when IMU had operated in Turkish waters before.

He tapped the keyboard and the image of a boat appeared on the central screen. 'This is what Jack and I came up with.'

'It's based on Neolithic timbers dug up last year at the mouth of the Danube,' Jack explained. 'Ours is an open boat, about twenty-five metres long and three metres in beam. Rowing only became widespread at the end of the Bronze Age, so it's got fifteen paddlers on either side. It could take two oxen, as we've depicted here, several pairs of smaller animals such as pigs and deer, about two dozen women and children and a relief crew of paddlers.'

'You're sure they had no sails?' Macleod asked.

Jack nodded. 'Sailing was an early Bronze Age invention on the Nile, where boats could float to the delta and then sail back upstream with the prevailing northerly wind. The Egyptians may in fact have introduced sailing to the Aegean, where paddling was actually a better way of getting round the islands.'

'The program indicates the vessel would make six knots in dead calm,' Mustafa said. 'That's six nautical miles per hour, about seven statute miles.'

'They would have needed daylight to beach their vessel, tend to their animals and set up camp,' Jack said. 'And the reverse in the mornings.'

'We now know the exodus took place in late spring or early summer,' Macleod revealed. 'We ran our high-resolution sub-bottom profiler over an area of one square kilometre next to the Neolithic village. The silt concealed a perfectly preserved field system complete with plough furrows and irrigation ditches. The palaeoenvironmental lab has just completed their analysis of core samples we took from the ROV. They show the crop was grain. Einkorn wheat, *Triticum monococcum* to be precise, sown about two months prior to the inundation.'

'Grain is usually sown in these latitudes in April or May,' Jack remarked.

'Correct. We're talking June or July, around two months after the Bosporus was breached.'

'Six knots means forty-eight nautical miles over an eight-hour run,' Mustafa continued. 'That assumes a relief crew as well as water and provisions and a working day of eight hours. In placid seas our boat would have made it along the southern shore in a little over eleven days.' He tapped a key eleven times, advancing the miniature representation of the boat along an isometric map of the Black Sea. 'This is where the CAN program really comes into play.'

He tapped again and the simulation subtly transformed. The sea became ruffled, and the level dropped to show the Bosporus as a waterfall.

'Here we are in the summer of 5545 BC, about two months after the flood began.'

He repositioned the boat near the Bosporus.

'The first variable is wind. The prevailing summer winds are from the north. Ships sailing west might only have made serious headway once they reached Sinope, midway along the southern shore where the coast begins to trend west-south-west. Before that, coming up the coast west-north-west, they would have needed oars.'

'How different was the climate?' Katya asked.

'The main fluctuations today are caused by the North Atlantic Oscillation,' Mustafa replied. 'In a warm phase, low atmospheric pressure over the North Pole causes strong westerlies which keep Arctic air in the north, meaning the Mediterranean and Black Sea are hot and dry. In a cold phase, Arctic air flows south, including the northerlies over the Black Sea. Basically it's windier and wetter.'

'And in antiquity?'

'We think the early Holocene, the first few thousand years after the great melt, would have corresponded more closely to a cold phase. It was less arid than today with a good deal more precipitation. The southern Black Sea would have been an optimal place for the development of agriculture.'

'And the effect on navigation?' Jack asked.

'Stronger northerlies and westerlies by twenty to thirty per cent. I've fed these in and come up with a best-fit prediction for each fifty nautical mile sector of the coast two months into the flood, including the effect of wind on water movement.'

'Your second variable must be the flood itself.'

'We're looking at ten cubic miles of seawater pouring in every day for eighteen months, then a gradual fall-off over the next six months until equilibrium is reached. The exodus took place during the period of maximum inflow.'

He tapped the keyboard and a sequence of figures appeared on the right-hand screen.

'This shows the speed of the current east from the Bosporus. It diminishes from twelve knots at the waterfall to just under two knots in the most easterly sector, more than five hundred miles away.'

Costas joined in. 'If they were only making six knots, our Neolithic farmers, they would never have reached the Bosporus.'

Mustafa nodded. 'I can even predict where they made final landfall, thirty miles east where the current became too strong. From here they would have portaged up the Asiatic shore of the Bosporus to the Dardanelles. The current through the straits would also have been very strong, so I doubt whether they would have re-embarked before reaching the Aegean.'

'That would have been a hell of a portage,' said Macleod. 'Almost two hundred nautical miles.'

'They probably disassembled the hulls and used yoked oxen to pull the timbers on sledges,' Jack replied. 'Most early planked boats were joined by sewing the timbers together with cord, allowing the hulls to be easily dismantled.'

'Perhaps those who went east really did leave their vessels at Mount Ararat,' Katya mused. 'They could have disassembled the timbers and hauled them to the point where it was clear they weren't going to need them again, unlike the western group who were probably always within sight of the sea during their portage.'

Costas was peering at the Dardanelles. 'They could even have set off from the hill of Hissarlik. Some of our farmers may have stayed on to become the first Trojans.'

Costas' words brought home again the enormity of their discovery, and for a moment they were overwhelmed by a sense of awe. Carefully, methodically they had been piecing together a jigsaw which had confounded scholars for generations, uncovering a framework which was no longer in the realm of speculation. They were not simply building up one corner of the puzzle but had begun to rewrite history on a grand scale. Yet the source was so embedded in fantasy it still seemed a fable, a revelation whose truth they could hardly bring themselves to acknowledge.

Jack turned to Mustafa. 'How far is twenty *dromoi* in these conditions?'

Mustafa pointed to the right-hand screen. 'We work backwards from the point of disembarkation near the Bosporus. In the final day they only made half a knot against the current and wind, meaning a run of no more than four miles.' He tapped a key and the boat moved slightly east.

'Then the distances are progressively greater, until we reach the run past Sinope where they covered thirty miles.' He tapped twelve times and the boat hopped halfway back along the Black Sea coast. 'Then it becomes slightly more arduous for a few days as they head north-west against the prevailing wind.'

'That's fifteen runs,' said Jack. 'Where do the final five take us?'

Mustafa tapped five more times and the boat ended up in the south-eastern corner of the Black Sea, exactly on the predicted contour of the coast before the flood.

'Bingo,' Jack said.

After printing out the CAN data Mustafa led the others into a partitioned area adjacent to the chart room. He dimmed the lights and arranged several chairs around a central console the size of a kitchen table. He flipped a switch and the surface lit up.

'A holographic light table,' Mustafa explained. 'The latest in bathymetric representation. It can model a three-dimensional image of any area of seabed for which we have survey data, from entire ocean floors to sectors only a couple of metres across. Archaeological sites, for example.'

He tapped a command and the table erupted in colour. It was an underwater excavation, brilliantly clear with every detail sharply delineated. A mass of sediment had been cleared away to reveal rows of pottery vats and metal ingots lying across a keel, with timbers projecting on either side. The hull was cradled in a gully above a precipitous slope, great tongues of rock disappearing down either side where lava had once flowed.

'The Minoan wreck as it looked ten minutes ago. Jack asked me to have it relayed through so he could monitor progress. Once we have this equipment fully online we'll truly enter the age of remote fieldwork, able to direct excavations without ever getting wet.'

In the old days huge efforts were required to plan underwater sites, the measurements being taken painstakingly by hand. Now all this was eliminated by the use of digital photogrammetry, a sophisticated mapping package which utilized a remote operated vehicle to take images wired directly to *Seaquest*. In a ten-minute sweep over the wreck that morning the ROV had collected more data than an entire excavation in the past. As well as the hologram, the data were fed into a laser projector which constructed a latex model of the site in *Seaquest*'s conference room, modifications continuously being made as the excavators stripped off artefacts and sediment. The innovative system was another reason to be thankful to Efram Jacobovich, IMU's founding benefactor, who had put the expertise of his giant software company entirely at their disposal.

Jack had spent several hours scrutinizing the hologram that afternoon during a teleconference with the excavation team. But for the others it was a breathtaking sight, as if they had suddenly been transported to the seabed of the Aegean eight hundred nautical miles away. It showed the remarkable progress made in the twenty-four hours since they had flown off by helicopter. The team had removed most of the overburden and sent another trove of artefacts to the safety of the Carthage museum. Under a layer of pottery amphoras filled with ritual incense was a hull far better preserved than Jack had dared imagine, its mortise-and-tenon joints as crisp and clear as if they had been chiselled yesterday.

Mustafa tapped again. 'And now the Black Sea.'

The wreck disintegrated into a kaleidoscope of colours from which a model of the Black Sea took shape. In the centre was the abyssal plain, the toxic netherworld almost 2,200 metres deep. Around the edge were the coastal shallows which sloped off more gently than most parts of the Mediterranean.

He tapped another key to highlight the line of the coast before the flood.

'Our target area.'

A pinprick of light appeared in the far south-eastern corner.

'Forty-two degrees north latitude, forty-two degrees east longitude. That's as precise as we can get with our distance calculation from the Bosporus.'

'That's a pretty big area,' Costas cautioned. 'A nautical mile is one minute of latitude, a degree sixty minutes. That's three hundred and sixty square miles.'

'Remember we're looking for a coastal site,' Jack said. 'If we follow the ancient coastline on the landward side we should eventually reach our target.'

'The closer we can pinpoint it now, the better,' Mustafa said. 'According to the bathymetry the ancient coastline in this sector is at least thirty miles offshore, well beyond territorial waters. It'll become pretty obvious we're searching along a particular contour. There are going to be prying eyes about.'

There was a murmur from the others as the implications

became depressingly apparent. The map showed how dangerously close they would be to the far shore of the Black Sea, a modern-day Barbary Coast where east met west in a new and sinister fashion.

'I'm intrigued by this feature.' Macleod pointed to an irregularity in the sea floor, a ridge about five kilometres long, parallel to the ancient shoreline. On the seaward side was a narrow chasm which dropped below five hundred metres, an anomaly where the average gradient did not reach this depth for another thirty miles offshore. 'It's the only upstanding feature for miles around. If I was going to build a citadel I'd want a commanding position. This is an obvious place.'

'But the final passage from the papyrus talks about salt lakes,' Costas said.

Katya took her cue and read from the palm computer.

'Then you reach the citadel. And there below lies a vast golden plain, the deep basins, the salt lakes, as far as the eye can see.'

'That's the image I have of the Mediterranean during the Messinian salinity crisis,' Costas commented. 'Stagnant brine lakes, like the southern Dead Sea today.'

'I think I have an explanation.' Mustafa tapped the keyboard and the hologram transformed to a close-up of the south-eastern sector. 'With the sea level lowered one hundred and fifty metres, much of the area inland from that ridge was only just dry, a metre or two above the ancient shoreline. Large areas were actually a few metres below sea level. As the level dropped to its lowest, towards the end of the Pleistocene, it would have left salt lakes in those depressions. They were shallow and would have evaporated quickly, leaving immense salt pans. They'd have been visible from an elevated position some distance away as they wouldn't have supported any vegetation.'

'And let's remember how important salt was,' Jack said. 'It

was a vital preservative, a major trade commodity in its own right. The early Romans flourished because they controlled the salt pans at the mouth of the Tiber, and we may be looking at a similar story here thousands of years earlier.'

Costas spoke thoughtfully. '*Golden plain* could mean fields of wheat and barley, a rich prairie of cultivated grain with the mountains of Anatolia in the background. It was the "mountain-girt plain" of Plato's account.'

'You've got it,' said Mustafa.

'Am I right in thinking part of the ridge is above water today?' Costas was peering at the geomorphology on the hologram.

'It's the top of a small volcano. The ridge is part of the zone of seismic disturbance along the Asiatic plate that extends west to the north Anatolian fault. The volcano's not entirely dormant but hasn't erupted in recorded history. The caldera is about a kilometre in diameter and rises three hundred metres above sea level.'

'What's its name?'

'Doesn't have one,' Macleod answered. 'It's been disputed territory ever since the Crimean War of 1853 to '56 between Ottoman Turkey and Tsarist Russia. It's in international waters but lies almost exactly off the border between Turkey and Georgia.'

'The area's been a no-go zone for a long time,' Mustafa continued. 'Just months before the collapse of the Soviet Union in 1991 a nuclear sub went down somewhere near here in mysterious circumstances.' The others were intrigued, and Mustafa carried on cautiously. 'It was never found, but the search operation led to shots being exchanged between Turkish and Soviet warships. It was a potential global flashpoint, given Turkey's NATO affiliations. Both sides agreed to back off and the confrontation was hushed up, but as a result there's been hardly any hydrographic research in this area.'

'Sounds like we're on our own again,' Costas said glumly. 'Friendly countries on either side but powerless to intervene.'

'We're doing what we can,' Mustafa said. 'The 1992 Black Sea economic co-operation agreement led to the establishment of Blackseafor, the Black Sea naval co-operation task group. It's still more gesture than substance, and most Turkish maritime interdiction has continued to be unilateral. But at least the basis for intervention exists. There's also a glimmer of hope on the scientific side. The Turkish National Oceanographic Commission is considering an offer from the Georgian Academy of Sciences to collaborate on a survey that would include that island.'

'But no hope of a protection force,' Costas said.

'Nothing pre-emptive. The situation's way too delicate. The ball's in our court.'

The sun had set and the forested slopes behind the lights of Trabzon were shrouded in darkness. Jack and Katya were walking slowly along the pebbly beach, the crunch of their footsteps joining the sound of the waves as they gently lapped the shore.

Earlier they had attended a gathering at the residence of the vice-admiral in command of Blackseafor, and the lingering scent of pine needles from the outdoor reception followed them into the night. They had left the eastern jetty far behind. Jack was still wearing his dinner jacket but had loosened his collar and removed his tie, pocketing it along with the Distinguished Service Cross he had reluctantly worn for the occasion.

Katya was wearing a shimmering black gown. She had

loosened her hair and removed her shoes to walk barefoot in the surf.

'You look stunning.'

'You don't look so bad yourself.' Katya gazed up at Jack and smiled, gently touching his arm. 'I think we've come far enough now.'

They walked up the beach and sat together on a slab of rock overlooking the sea. The rising moon cast a sparkling light on the water, the waves dancing and shimmering in front of them. Above the northern horizon was a band of pitch-darkness, a storm front rolling down from the Russian steppes. A chill breeze brought early intimation of an unseasonal change that would alter the face of the sea over the coming days.

Jack drew up his legs and folded his arms over his knees, his eyes fixed on the horizon. 'This is always the most intensive time, when you know a great discovery is within your grasp. Any delay is frustrating.'

Katya smiled at him again. 'You've done all you can.'

They had been discussing arrangements for joining *Seaquest* the next day. Before the reception Jack had spoken to Tom York on the IMU secure channel. By now *Seaquest* would be making her way at top speed towards the Bosporus, having left the wreck excavation in the safe hands of the support vessel. By the time of their projected rendezvous by helicopter the next morning, *Seaquest* would be in the Black Sea. They were anxious to join her as soon as possible to ensure the equipment was fully prepared.

Katya was facing away from him and seemed preoccupied.

'You don't share my excitement.'

When she replied her words confirmed Jack's sense that something was troubling her.

'To you in the west people like Aslan are faceless, like the enemies of the Cold War,' she said. 'But to me they're real people, real flesh and blood. Monsters who have made my home an uncharted wasteland of violence and greed. To know it you must live there, a world of terror and anarchy the west hasn't seen since the Middle Ages. The years of suppression have fuelled a feeding frenzy where the only pretence at control is provided by gangsters and warlords.' Her voice was filled with emotion as she looked out to sea. 'And these are my people. I am one of them.'

'One with the will and strength to fight it.' Jack was drawn irresistibly to her dark silhouette as she sat framed against the lowering horizon.

'It's my world we're about to enter, and I don't know if I can protect you.' She turned to face him, her eyes fathomless as she stared into his. 'But of course I share your incredible excitement.'

They drew together and kissed, at first gently and then long and passionately. Jack was suddenly overwhelmed by desire as he felt her body against his. He eased the gown off her shoulders and pulled her closer.

11

'Holding steady on three-one-fiver degrees. Depth sixty-five metres, ascent rate one metre per second. We should be seeing the surface soon.'

Jack peered through the Plexiglas dome to his left. Despite the gloom he could just make out Costas beneath an identical dome some fifteen metres away, his head seemingly disembodied in the eerie glow cast by the instrument panels. As they rose higher the submersible came into clearer view. The dome capped a yellow man-sized pod, the casing angled forward so the pilot could sit comfortably. Below were pontoon-like ballast tanks, and behind was the housing for the battery which powered a dozen vectored water jets positioned around an external frame. Two pincer-like robotic arms gave the submersible the appearance of a giant scarab beetle.

'There she is now.'

Jack looked up and saw the silhouette of *Seaquest* twenty metres above. He adjusted the water ballast discharge to slow his ascent and looked again at Costas, who was manoeuvring alongside in preparation for surfacing.

Costas beamed at his friend. 'Mission accomplished.'

Costas had every reason to be pleased with himself. They had just concluded the sea trials of Aquapod IV, the latest one-man submersible his team had designed for IMU. It had a maximum operational depth of fifteen hundred metres, almost twice the previous marque. The hypercharged lithium-anode battery had a life of fifty hours at an optimal cruising speed of three knots. Their one-hour dive that morning to the bottom of the Black Sea had shown the equipment was well up to the task ahead, an exploration along the line of the ancient coast further east than they had ever gone before.

'*Seaquest*, this is Aquapod Alpha. We are coming in safe and sound. Over.'

They could already see the four divers waiting just below the surface to guide them in. With ten metres to go they stopped to lock the Aquapods together, a standard procedure to prevent them crashing into each other in rough seas. While Jack remained stationary, Costas gingerly manoeuvred until the locking pinions aligned. With the flick of a switch he fired four metal rods through the cleats on the outer frame.

'Locking secured. Haul us in.'

The divers quickly descended and attached the lifting harness. Jack and Costas switched to standby and disengaged the balance adjustors which kept them horizontal. As the divers swam away to safety positions the winch operator smoothly drew the submersibles up into the hull.

They broke surface inside a floodlit chamber the size of a small aircraft hangar. *Seaquest* was equipped with a fully internalized docking berth, a useful feature when the weather was too rough for operations from deck or they wished to remain concealed. The hull had opened up like the bomb doors on a giant aircraft. As the two sections closed, Jack and Costas unlocked the domes which also served as entry canopies. A platform slid under them and rose like the elevator on an aircraft carrier, locking tight once the last of the water had drained off.

Tom York was on hand to greet the two men as they clambered out.

'Successful trial, I trust?'

Jack was the first to drop on deck. He spoke quickly as he stripped off his survival suit.

'No problems to report. We'll use the Aquapods for our reconnaissance this afternoon. The robotic arms will need to be replaced by the digital videocamera and floodlight pods.'

'It's being done as we speak.'

Jack glanced round and saw the maintenance crew already hard at work on the submersibles. Costas was hunched over the battery recharging unit deep in conversation with one of the technicians. Jack smiled to himself as he saw that his friend had neglected to remove his headset in his enthusiasm to discuss the submersible's performance with his engineering team.

Jack spoke to York as he strode forward and stowed his suit in one of the lockers that lined the chamber.

'We have an hour before *Seaquest* is in position. It's a chance to review our options one last time. I'd like all personnel in the bridge console at eleven hundred hours.'

Twenty minutes later they stood in front of a semicircle of men and women inside *Seaquest*'s command module. York had engaged the automated navigation and surveillance system, activating the virtual bridge which allowed the ship to be operated from the console beside Jack. The hemispherical screen above them displayed a panoramic view of the sea, its choppy grey surface an ominous portent of the storm which had been brewing in the north over the past twenty-four hours.

Jack folded his arms and addressed the group.

'We're a skeleton crew, and our job is going to be that much more demanding. I'm not going to beat about the bush. We face a real risk, probably a greater one than we have ever faced before.'

After joining *Seaquest* by helicopter the day before, Jack had decided to reduce the complement to the minimum. The entire crew had volunteered, but he had refused to endanger the lives of scientists whose job would only really begin once they had made a discovery. In addition to the deck and engineering officers, he had selected the most experienced weapons technicians, including several ex-Special Forces men Jack had known since the Navy.

'What can we expect in the way of outside backing?'

The question came from Katya, who was standing among the crew wearing a standard-issue blue jumpsuit with the IMU shoulder flash. Jack had tried to persuade her to leave with the others when *Sea Venture* came out to meet them as they passed Trabzon, but she had insisted her linguistic expertise would be vital for any inscriptions they might find. In truth Jack knew from their long hours together the night before that she would not leave him now, that they had a bond that could not be broken and she shared his sense of responsibility for *Seaquest* and her crew as they sailed ever further into the danger zone.

'I'll let our security chief answer that one.'

Peter Howe stepped out and took Jack's place.

'The bad news is we'll be in international waters, beyond the twelve-mile limit agreed in a 1973 protocol between the USSR and Turkey. The good news is Georgia and Turkey signed a Coast Security Co-operative Agreement in 1998 and have agreed to provide back-up in the event of a major discovery. The pretext would be the memorandum of understanding they've just signed with UN ratification to carry out collaborative geological research on that volcanic island. They would be acting under the provisions of international law.'

He stepped back and looked up at the Admiralty Chart of the eastern Black Sea above the console.

'The problem is they'll only help if Russian suspicions can be allayed about that submarine last heard of somewhere near here in 1991. Any hint of other nations involved in a search and they'll go ballistic. Literally. And there are other concerns. Since the early nineties the Russians have actively participated in the Abkhazian civil war, ostensibly as a stabilization force but in reality to draw the region back to Moscow. Their main interest is oil. In 1999 their monopoly on Caspian Sea output was threatened by the first pipeline to bypass Russia, from Baku in Azerbaijan to Supsa on the Georgian coast near Abkhazia. The Russians would do anything to prevent further western investment even if it means anarchy and civil war.' Howe turned to face the assembled group.

'We've told the Russian embassy we're carrying out a hydrographic survey under joint contract to the Turkish and Georgian governments. They seem to have bought it. But if they saw warships converging on the spot, they'd assume we were on to the sub. The Russian bear may have lost most of her claws but she still has the biggest fleet in the region.

Relations between Ankara and Moscow are already at rock bottom because of the narcotics trade. There would be an ugly international incident at least, very possibly a shooting war which could quickly escalate to engulf this part of the world.'

'A small point of interest,' Costas interjected. 'I didn't think Georgia had a navy.'

'That's another problem,' York replied glumly. 'The Georgians inherited virtually nothing of the Soviet Black Sea Fleet. They have a Ukrainian-built Project 206MP fast attack craft and a decommissioned US Coastguard cutter transferred through the US Excess Defense Articles Program. But don't get your hopes up. The FAC has no missiles because there are no storage and testing facilities. And the cutter has a single fifty-calibre machine gun.'

'That's not the real Georgian Navy.'

They all turned towards Katya.

'The real Georgian Navy is hidden away along the coast to the north,' she said. 'It is the navy of the warlords, men from central Asia who use Abkhazia to access the rich pickings of the Black Sea and Mediterranean. These are the ones to fear, my friends, not the Russians. I speak from personal experience.'

Katya was listened to with great respect by the crew. Her stature in their eyes was unassailable, since she had single-handedly defused the stand-off in the Aegean two days before.

'And the Turkish Navy?' Costas looked hopefully towards Mustafa, who had come on board from *Sea Venture* the previous day.

'We have a strong Black Sea presence,' the Turk replied. 'But we're badly overstretched in the war against smuggling. To support *Seaquest* the Turkish Navy would need to transfer units up from the Aegean. We cannot redeploy in advance because any change in our Black Sea fleet would excite immediate suspicion from the Russians. My government will only take the risk if a major discovery is confirmed.'

'So we're on our own.'

'I fear so.'

In the brief lull that followed, York despatched two of the crew topside, the rising wind threatening gear that needed lashing to the deck. Jack quickly interjected to focus discussion on the matter to hand, the urgency of his tone reflecting the short time now available until *Seaquest* arrived on site.

'We must be sure we hit the right spot first time. You can be certain we're under satellite surveillance right now, under the eyes of people who will not buy the story of hydrographic research for long.'

One of the ex-Navy men put up a hand. 'Excuse me, sir, but what exactly is it we're after?'

Jack moved aside to let the crew see the computer screen in the front of the console. 'Mustafa, I'll let you explain how we got here.'

Mustafa called up the isometric image of the Black Sea and swiftly ran through their interpretation of the papyrus text, advancing the boat along the shoreline until it reached the south-eastern sector. Now they had left their final port of call, Jack had decided to take the crew of *Seaquest* fully into his confidence. Those who had not yet heard the details stood mesmerized; even the veterans were transfixed by the immensity of a find that seemed to loom so fabulously out of the mists of legend.

'We reach target point by following the 150-metre depth contour, the shoreline before the flood. It swings out to sea as we move east from Trabzon. At present *Seaquest* is just over twelve nautical miles offshore but we'll gradually head further out as we go east.'

He tapped a key and the image transformed to a close-up map.

'This is our best-fit scenario for Atlantis. It's an area of seabed twenty nautical miles long by five miles wide. The 150-metre depth contour runs along the north side, so what we're looking at here was all dry land. If we lower the sea level to that contour, we get some idea of its appearance before the flood.'

The image transformed to show an inland plain leading to a ridge along the coast several kilometres long. Beyond it was the volcano.

'There's not much detail because there's so little bathymetric data for this area. But we're convinced the site must be either the ridge or the volcano. The ridge rises a hundred metres above the ancient shoreline. The trouble is, there's no acropolis, no outcrop for a citadel. The papyrus is difficult to understand without it.'

'The volcano is the outstanding landmark,' Howe observed. 'The north-west side forms a series of terraced platforms before it reaches a cliff. A citadel at this point would have been impressively situated, with views for miles on either side. You can imagine a town spreading along the lower slopes beside the seashore.'

'Defence was probably a factor, though not an overriding one if there were no other nearby city states,' Jack asserted. 'The only threat might have been marauding bands of hunter-gatherers, a last residue from the Ice Age, but they would have been few in number. Finding high ground was mainly about avoiding floodplains and marshland.'

'What about volcanic activity?' York asked.

'No significant eruption for well over a million years,'

Mustafa replied. 'What you see today is occasional vental activity, geysers of gas and steam that spew out as pressure inside the core periodically builds up.'

They looked up at the virtual-reality screen where they could now just make out the island on the horizon. It was the peak of the volcano that had remained above water after the inundation. The wisps of steam rising from its summit seemed to join the grey and lowering sky, the leading edge of the storm that was rolling in from the north with alarming speed.

Jack spoke again. 'In antiquity seismic events were almost invariably viewed as signs from the gods. A volcano with low-key activity could have become a focus for ritual observance, perhaps one of the original motivations for settling at this spot. In such a fertile region I'd expect both the volcano and the ridge to be occupied. But we must choose between the two. We may not have the chance to stake a second claim before unwelcome visitors arrive. We've got twenty minutes before *Seaquest* is over that ridge. I welcome any suggestions.'

There was another brief hiatus while Jack conferred with York. They made several adjustments on the navigational console and scrolled through the radar surveillance images. As the two men turned back towards the assembled crew, Katya produced her palm computer and tapped in a sequence of commands.

'Either place would fit the text,' she said. 'Both the ridge and the volcano overlooked a wide valley to the south with distant mountains and salt lakes in between.'

'Does the papyrus tell us anything more that might help?' one of the crew asked.

'Not really.' Katya peered at the text again and shook her head. 'The final fragments of writing seem to refer to the interior of the citadel.'

'There is something else.'

They all looked at Costas, who had been staring intently at the image of the island as it became larger and more clearly defined. He drew his gaze away and turned to Katya.

'Give us that first phrase after reaching Atlantis.'

Katya tapped a command and read from the screen.

'*Under the sign of the bull.*'

They all looked questioningly at Costas.

'You're familiar with the rooftop bar in the Maritime Museum at Carthage.'

There was a general murmur of assent.

'The view across the Bay of Tunis to the east, the evening sun splashing its rosy light on the sea, the twin mountain peaks of Ba'al Qarnain piercing the sky in the background.'

They all nodded.

'Well, perhaps fewer of you will be so familiar with the view first thing in the morning. The midsummer sun rises directly over the saddle between the peaks. To the Phoenicians this was a holy mountain, sacred to the sky god. Ba'al Qarnain means Two-Horned Lord.' He turned to Jack. 'I believe *sign of the bull* refers to the profile of that island.'

They all looked up at the looming landmass on the screen.

'I'm puzzled,' Howe cut in. 'From where we are the island doesn't look anything like that.'

'Try another direction,' Costas said. 'We're looking south-east. What about the view from the shoreline, from below the volcano where a settlement would have been?'

Mustafa quickly tapped the keyboard to reorientate the view from the north-east, increasing the magnification as he did so to bring the viewpoint down to the ancient shoreline beneath the volcano.

There was a gasp of astonishment as the image locked into place. Above them loomed two peaks separated by a deep saddle.

Costas looked at the screen triumphantly. 'There, ladies and gentlemen, are our bull's horns.'

Jack grinned broadly at his friend. 'I knew you'd do something useful eventually.' He turned to York.

'I think we have our answer. Lay in a course for that island at maximum speed.'

12

The twin floodlights on either side of the Aquapods cast a brilliant swath of illumination on the seabed, the beams angled inward to converge five metres below. The light reflected off millions of particles of suspended silt as if they were passing through endless veils of speckly haze. Isolated rocky outcrops reared up and disappeared behind as they pressed on at maximum speed. To the left the bottom dropped off sharply into the abyss, the desolate grey of the sea floor sliding into a forbidding blackness devoid of all life.

The intercom crackled.

'Jack, this is *Seaquest*. Do you read me? Over.'

'We read you loud and clear.'

'The drone has got something.' York's voice was edged with excitement. 'You should reach its position in about five hundred metres by maintaining your present trajectory. I'm sending the co-ordinates so you can program in a fix.'

Earlier that day, the island had loomed out of the horizon like some mythical apparition. Just before *Seaquest* arrived, the sea had gone dead calm, an eerie lull that seemed to draw up its vapours in a ghostly pall. As the wind picked up again and curled the mist towards the barren shore, they felt like explorers who had chanced upon some lost world. With its lack of vegetation and sheer rock the island seemed old beyond belief, a craggy wasteland reduced by time and weather to its bare essence. Yet if their instincts were right, it was here that all the hopes and potential of mankind had first taken root.

They had brought *Seaquest* to a halt two nautical miles west of the island. For a reconnaissance towards its submerged slopes they had used a sonar drone rather than the ROV, which was limited to visual survey. For three hours now there had been nothing unusual in the sonar readout, and they had made the decision to deploy the Aquapods as well. Speed was now paramount.

Jack gave a thumbs-up to Costas, who was hugging the seabed at the 140 metre contour. They could sense each other's excitement, a thrill of anticipation that needed no exchange of words. From the moment of the telephone call when Hiebermeyer first uttered that word from the papyrus, Jack had known they would be propelled to some greater revelation. All through the painstaking process of translation and decipherment he had felt supremely confident that this was the one, that the stars were all in alignment this time. Yet the pace of events since they cracked the code had left little time for reflection. Only days before he had been elated beyond belief by the Minoan wreck. Now they were on the cusp of one of the greatest archaeological discoveries of all time.

The Aquapods slowed to a crawl and they continued in silence, each man aware of the other through their Plexiglas domes as the yellow pods inched forward a few metres apart in the gloom.

Moments later a vista of spectral shapes began to materialize out of the haze. They had studied the images of the Neolithic village off Trabzon in anticipation of this moment. But nothing could have prepared them for the reality of entering a place which had been lost to the world for almost eight thousand years.

Suddenly it was happening.

'Slow down.' Jack spoke with bated breath. 'Take a look at that.'

What had seemed strangely regular undulations in the seabed took on a new form as Jack fired a blast from his water jet to clear away the sediment. As it settled they could see the gaping mouths of a pair of huge pottery jars, buried upright side by side between low retaining walls. Another blast revealed a second pair of jars, and identical undulations continued upslope as far as they could see.

'It's a storehouse, probably for grain,' Jack said. 'They're just like the *pithoi* at Knossos. Only four thousand years older.'

Suddenly a larger shape appeared before them, completely blocking their way ahead. For a moment it seemed as if they had come to the edge of the world. They were at the base of an enormous cliff extending on the same line in either direction, its sheer wall broken by ledges and fissures like a quarry face. Then they saw curious rectangular patches of pitch blackness, some at regular intervals on the same level.

They realized with amazement what they were looking at.

It was a huge conglomeration of walls and flat roofs, broken by windows and entranceways, all shrouded in a blanket of silt. It was like the Neolithic village but on a gigantic scale. The buildings rose four or five storeys, the highest blocks reached by terraces of rooftop platforms linked by stairways and ladders.

They halted their Aquapods and gazed in awe, forcing their minds to register an image that seemed more fantasy than fact.

'It's like some huge condominium,' Costas marvelled.

Jack shut his eyes hard and then opened them again, disbelief turning to wonder as the silt stirred up by the Aquapods began to settle and reveal the unmistakable signs of human endeavour all round them.

'People got about on the rooftops, through those hatches.' His heart was thumping, his mouth was dry, but he forced himself to speak in the dispassionate tones of a professional archaeologist. 'My guess is each of these blocks housed an extended family. As the group got larger they built upwards, adding timber-framed mud-brick storeys.'

As they ascended they could see the blocks were riddled by a maze of alleyways, astonishingly reminiscent of the medieval bazaars of the Middle East.

'It must have bustled with crafts and trade,' Jack said. 'There's no way these people were just farmers. They were expert potters and carpenters and metalworkers.'

He paused, staring through the Plexiglas at what looked like a ground-floor shopfront.

'Someone in this place made that gold disc.'

For several minutes they passed over more flat-roofed

highrises, the dark windows staring at them like sightless eyes caught in the glare of their floodlights. About five hundred metres due east from the storehouse the conglomeration came to an abrupt end. In the murk ahead they could make out another complex, perhaps twenty metres away, and below them a space wider and more regular than the alleyways.

'It's a road,' Jack said. 'It must go down to the ancient seafront. Let's go inland and then resume our original course.'

They veered south and followed the road gently upslope. Two hundred metres on, it was bisected by another road running east-west. They turned and followed it due east, the Aquapods maintaining an altitude of twenty metres to avoid the mass of buildings on either side.

'Extraordinary,' Jack said. 'These blocks are separated by a regular grid of streets, the earliest by thousands of years.'

'Someone planned this place.'

Tutankhamun's tomb, the palace of Knossos, the fabled walls of Troy, all the hallowed discoveries of archaeology suddenly seemed pedestrian and mundane, mere stepping stones to the marvels that now lay before them.

'Atlantis,' Costas breathed. 'A few days ago I didn't even believe it existed.' He looked across at the figure in the other Plexiglas dome. 'A little thanks would be appreciated.'

Jack grinned in spite of his preoccupation with the fabulous images around them.

'OK. You pointed us in the right direction. I owe you a large gin and tonic.'

'That's what I got last time.'

'A lifetime's supply then.'

'Done.'

A moment later the buildings on either side suddenly

disappeared and the sea floor dropped away out of sight. Fifty metres on, there was still nothing except a haze of suspended silt.

'My depth sounder shows the sea floor has dropped almost twenty metres below the level of the road,' Jack exclaimed. 'I suggest we descend and backtrack to the point where the buildings disappeared.'

They vented their water ballast until the lights revealed the sea floor. It was level and featureless, unlike the undulating surface they had traversed on their way towards the western edge of the city.

A few minutes later they had returned to the point where they last saw structures. In front of them the sea floor rose abruptly at a 45-degree angle until it reached the base of the buildings and the end of the road above.

Costas moved his Aquapod forward until its ballast tanks rested on the floor just before it angled upwards. He directed a long blast from his water jet at the slope and then drew back to Jack's position.

'Just as I thought.'

The silt cleared to reveal a stepped terrace like the seating in a theatre. Between the floor and the beginning of the terrace was a vertical wall three metres high.

'This was hewn out of living rock,' Costas said. 'It's tufa, isn't it? The same dark stone used in ancient Rome. Lightweight but tough, easily quarried but an excellent load-bearer.'

'But we haven't seen any masonry buildings,' Jack protested.

'There must be some pretty massive structures some-where.'

Jack was looking closely at the features in front of them. 'This is more than just a quarry. Let's follow those terraces and see where they take us.'

Twenty minutes later they had traversed three sides of a vast sunken courtyard almost a kilometre long and half a kilometre wide. Whereas the road layout respected the line of the ancient coast, running parallel and at right angles to it, the courtyard was aligned off to the south-east. They had skirted it clockwise and were now at the south-eastern boundary opposite their starting point. Above them buildings and the road resumed exactly as they appeared on the other side of the courtyard.

'It looks like a stadium,' Costas murmured. 'I remember you saying those palace courtyards in Crete were for bull-baiting, for sacrifices and other rituals.'

'The Minoan courtyards were smaller,' Jack replied. 'Even the arena of the Colosseum in Rome is only eighty metres across. This is huge.' He thought for a moment. 'It's just a hunch, but before we continue along the road I'd like to see across the middle of this space.'

Inside his dome Costas nodded in agreement.

They set out across the courtyard due west. After about 150 metres, they came to a halt. Ahead of them was a mass of silt-covered stone, its shape irregular and quite unlike the courtyard boundary.

Costas fired his water jet at the rock face, shrouding his dome in silt. After a few moments his voice came over the intercom.

'It's an outcrop left standing when the rest was quarried out.'

Jack was slowly traversing south-east along a spur which extended twenty metres from the main mass. It terminated in a rounded ledge about two metres high and five metres across. Costas followed as Jack gently cleaned the surface with his water jet, blowing away silt to reveal the bare rock.

They stared transfixed by the shape that emerged, their minds unable to acknowledge what lay before them.

'My God.'

'It's . . .' Jack faltered.

'It's a *paw*,' Costas whispered.

'A lion's paw.' Jack quickly regained his composure. 'This must be a gigantic statue, at least a hundred metres long and thirty metres high.'

'Are you thinking what I'm thinking?'

'A *sphinx*.'

For a moment the two men stared at each other through their domes in stupefied silence. Eventually Costas' voice crackled over the intercom.

'Seems incredible but anything's possible in this place. Whatever's up there is a long way off our entry route and we wouldn't have seen it. I'm going to check it out.'

Jack remained stationary while Costas floated upwards, gradually receding until all that was left was a diminishing halo of light. Just as that too seemed about to disappear, it came to an abrupt halt some thirty metres above the sea floor.

Jack waited anxiously for Costas to report. After more than a minute he could restrain himself no longer.

'What can you see?'

The voice that came through seemed strangely suppressed.

'Remind me. A sphinx has a lion's body and a human head. Right?'

'Right.'

'Try this for a variant.'

Costas flicked his floodlights to full beam. The image that appeared high above was awesome and terrifying, the stuff of nightmares. It was as if a flash of lightning on a stormy night had revealed a huge beast towering over them, its features silhouetted in a spectral sheen that burst forth between rolling banks of clouds.

Jack stared up transfixed, scarcely able to register an image for which all their experience, all their years of exploration and extraordinary discovery, could provide no preparation.

It was an immense bull's head, its huge horns sweeping up into the darkness beyond the arc of light, its snout half open as if it were about to lower its head and paw the ground before the onslaught.

After what seemed an eternity, Costas angled his Aquapod forward and panned the light down the neck of the beast, showing where it became a lion's body.

'It's carved from the living rock, basalt by the look of it,' he said. 'The horns extend at least ten metres above the buildings. This must once have been a jutting ridge of lava that flowed down to the sea.'

He was descending more rapidly now and soon reached Jack.

'It's facing the volcano,' he continued. 'That explains the strange alignment of the courtyard. It respects the orientation of the twin peaks rather than the line of the coast, which would have been a more practical benchmark for the street layout.'

Jack quickly latched on to the significance of Costas' words.

'And the rising sun would have shone directly between the horns and the two peaks,' he said. 'It must have been a sight even the ancients could scarcely have imagined in their wildest fantasies about the lost world of Atlantis.'

The two Aquapods rose slowly together over the parapet, their water jets kicking up a storm of silt as they powered away from the floor of the courtyard. The rearing form of the giant bull-sphinx was swallowed in the darkness behind them, but the image of the colossal head with its curved horns high above remained etched in their minds.

The south-eastern perimeter was higher than the rest, rising at least ten metres vertically.

'It's a stairway,' said Jack. 'A grand entrance into the courtyard.'

The two Aquapods veered off to either side, Jack to the left and Costas to the right. Soon each appeared to the other as no more than a distant smudge of yellow in the gloom. At the top was a wide roadway, which their water jets revealed had a lustrous white surface.

'It looks like marble pavement.'

'I had no idea people quarried stone this early.' Costas was already amazed by the scale of stone extraction in the courtyard, and now here was evidence for masonry. 'I thought quarrying didn't begin until the Egyptians.'

'Stone Age hunters dug for flint to make tools, but this is the earliest evidence for precision-cut building stone. It predates the first Egyptian quarries by at least two thousand years.'

They continued silently onwards, neither able to comprehend the enormity of their find. Churned-up phosphorescence billowed behind them like vapour trails. The road followed the same orientation as the courtyard, leading from the ferocious gaze of the bull-sphinx directly towards the foot of the volcano.

'I can see structures to my right,' Costas announced. 'Pedestals, pillars, columns. I'm just passing one that's square-sided, about two metres across. It towers way up out of sight. It looks like an obelisk.'

'I'm getting the same,' Jack said. 'They're laid out symmetrically, just like the Egyptian temple precincts at Luxor and Karnak.'

The floodlights revealed a succession of ghostly forms on

either side of the processional way, the shapes looming into view and then disappearing like phantasms glimpsed in a swirling sandstorm. They saw altars and plinths, animal-headed statues and the carved limbs of creatures too bizarre to make out. Both men began to feel unnerved, as if they were being lured by these beckoning sentinels into a world beyond their experience.

'It's like the entrance to Hades,' Costas murmured.

They ran the gauntlet between the eerie lines of statues, a lurking, brooding presence that seemed to reproach them for trespassing in a domain that had been theirs alone for millennia.

Moments later the pall lifted as the roadway abruptly terminated at two large structures divided by a central passageway. It was about ten metres wide, less than half the width of the roadway, and had shallow steps like those which led up from the courtyard.

'I can see squared blocks, each four or five metres long and maybe two metres high.' Costas was suddenly elated. 'This is where all the quarried stone went!' He stopped just inside the passageway and used his water jet to blow silt from the base of the wall. He angled his light so it shone up the structure.

Jack was about ten metres from Costas and could see his face in the dome as he looked across.

'My turn for a recce.'

Jack vented water and began to rise, but rather than receding gradually upwards, he abruptly vanished over a rim not far above.

Several long minutes later his voice crackled over the intercom.

'Costas. Do you read me? This is incredible.'

'What is it?'

There was a pause. 'Think of the most outstanding monuments of ancient Egypt.' Jack's Aquapod reappeared as he descended back into the passageway.

'Not a pyramid.'

'You've got it.'

'But pyramids have sloping sides. These are vertical.'

'What you're looking at is the base of a massive terrace,' Jack explained. 'About ten metres above us it turns into a platform ten metres wide. Above that there's another terrace with the same dimensions, then another, and so on. I went along the entire length of this side and could see the terrace continuing on the south-east side. It's the same basic design as the first Egyptian pyramids, the stepped pyramids of the early third millennium BC.'

'How big is it?'

'That's the difference. This is huge, more like the Great Pyramid at Giza. I'd estimate one hundred and fifty metres across the base and eighty metres high, more than halfway to sea level. It's incredible. This must rank as the oldest and largest masonry edifice in the world.'

'And on my side?'

'Identical. A pair of giant pyramids marking the end of the processional way. Beyond this I'd expect some form of temple or a mortuary complex, maybe cut into the side of the volcano.'

Costas activated the navigational monitor which rose like a fighter pilot's gunsight in front of him. Jack looked down as the radio-pulse modem flashed the same image to his screen.

'A recently declassified hydrographic chart,' Costas explained. 'Made by a British survey vessel taking manual soundings following the Allied defeat of Ottoman Turkey at the end of the First World War. Unfortunately the

Royal Navy only had a limited window before the Turkish Republic acquired control and the Soviet build-up closed the door on the Black Sea. It's the most detailed we've got, but at 1 to 50,000 it only shows broad contours of bathymetry.'

'What's your point?'

'Take a look at the island.' Costas tapped a command for a close-up view. 'The only irregular features large enough to appear in the survey were those two underwater mounts up against the north-west side of the island. Strangely symmetrical, aren't they?'

'The pyramids!' Jack's face broke into a broad grin. 'So much for our detective work. Atlantis has been marked on a chart for more than eighty years.'

They eased along the centre of the passageway, the looming pyramids with their massive, perfectly joined masonry just visible through the gloom on either side. As Jack had estimated, they passed the far corners after 150 metres. The steps continued ahead into the darkness.

The only sound as they crept forward was the whirring of the water jets as they maintained a constant altitude a metre above the sea floor.

'Look out!'

There was a sudden commotion and a muffled curse. For a split second Costas' attention had been diverted and he had collided with an obstacle dead ahead.

'You OK?' Jack had been trailing five metres behind but now drew up abreast, his face full of concern as he peered through the whirlwind of silt.

'No obvious damage,' Costas responded. 'Luckily we were only going at a snail's pace.'

He ran a routine diagnostic on his robotic arm and floodlight array before powering back a few metres.

'Number one driving rule, always look where you're going,' Jack told him.

'Thanks for the advice.'

'So what was it?'

They strained to see through the silt. The disturbance had reduced visibility to less than a metre, but as the sediment settled they began to make out a curious shape directly in front of them.

'It looks like an outsized bathroom mirror,' Costas said.

It was a huge disc, perhaps five metres in diameter, standing on a pedestal about two metres high.

'Let's check for inscriptions,' Jack suggested. 'You blow away the silt and I'll hover above to see if anything shows up.'

Costas unclamped a metallic glove from his instrument panel, inserted his left arm and flexed his fingers. The robotic arm at the front of the Aquapod exactly mimicked his movements. He angled the arm down to the water jet nozzles protruding from the undercarriage and selected a pencil-sized tube. After activating the jet, he began cleaning methodically from the centre of the disc outwards, tracing ever increasing circles on the rock.

'It's a fine-grained stone.' The voice came from the halo of yellow that was all Jack could see of Costas in the silt below. 'Granite or brecchia, similar to Egyptian porphyry. Only this has greenish flecks like the *lapis lacedaemonia* of Sparta. It must have been a local marble submerged by the flood.'

'Can you see any inscriptions?'

'There are some linear grooves.'

Costas jetted gently back to hover alongside Jack. As the silt settled, the entire pattern was revealed.

Jack let out a whoop of joy. 'Yes!'

With geometric precision the mason had carved a complex of horizontal and vertical grooves on the polished surface. In the centre was a symbol like the letter H, with a vertical line hanging from the crossbar and the sides extending in a row of short horizontal lines like the end of a garden rake.

Jack reached with his free hand into his suit and triumphantly held up a polymer copy of the gold disc for Costas to see. It was an exact replica made by laser in the Carthage Museum where the original was now safely under lock and key in the museum vault. The copy had reached *Sea Venture* by helicopter shortly before their own arrival.

'Brought this along just in case,' Jack said.

'*Atlantis.*' Costas beamed at Jack.

'This must mark the entrance.' Jack was elated but looked determinedly at his friend. 'We must press on. We've already over-extended our recce time and *Seaquest* will be waiting for us to re-establish contact.'

They accelerated and swooped round either side of the stone disc, but almost immediately slowed down as they confronted a sharp incline in the slope. The passageway narrowed to a steep stairway not much wider than the two Aquapods. As they began to ascend they could just make out the vertiginous rocky slopes of the volcano on either side.

Costas elevated his floodlights and peered intently ahead, mindful of his collision a few minutes before. After they had risen only a few steps he said, 'There's something strange here.'

Jack was concentrating on a series of carved animal heads that lined his side of the stairway. They seemed to be processing upwards, drawing him on, and were identically carved beside each step. At first they looked like the snarling lions of Sumerian and Egyptian art, but as he peered closer he was astonished to see they had huge incisors like the sabre-toothed tigers of the Ice Age. So much to wonder at, so much to take in, he thought.

'What is it?' he asked.

Costas' voice was puzzled. 'It's incredibly dark above us, almost pitch black. We've risen to a depth of one hundred metres and should be getting more vestigial sunlight. It should be getting lighter, not darker. It must be some kind of overhang. I suggest we . . . Stop!' he suddenly yelled.

The Aquapods came to a halt only inches away from the obstruction.

'Christ.' Costas forcefully exhaled. 'Almost did it again.'

The two men stared in open-mouthed astonishment. Above them loomed a colossal shape that extended on either side as far as they could see. It cut directly across the staircase, blocking their progress and concealing any entrance that might lie beyond.

'My God,' Jack exclaimed. 'I can see rivets. *It's a shipwreck.*'

His mind reeled as it rushed from deepest antiquity to the modern world, to an intrusion that seemed almost blasphemous after all they had seen.

'It must have wedged between the pyramids and the volcano.'

'Just what we need,' Jack said resignedly. 'Probably First or Second World War. There are plenty of uncharted ships sunk by U-boats all over the Black Sea.'

'I've got a bad feeling about this.' Costas had been edging his Aquapod up the curve of the hull. 'See you in a moment.'

He powered off to the left almost out of sight and then swung round and returned without pausing, his floodlights angled up against the dark mass. Jack wondered how much damage had been done, how much precious time was going to be needed to get over this unwelcome new obstacle.

'Well, what is it?'

Costas drew up alongside and spoke slowly, his tone a mixture of apprehension and high excitement.

'You can forget Atlantis for a while. We've just found ourselves a Russian nuclear submarine.'

13

'It's an *Akula*-class SSN, a nuclear-powered attack submarine. I have no doubt this is *Kazbek*, the boat that went missing in this sector in 1991.' York hunched over the screens on *Seaquest*'s bridge console, his eyes flickering between the sonar image they had just acquired from an ROV run over the wreck and a set of specifications downloaded from IMU's database on naval vessels of the former Soviet bloc.

Jack and Costas had arrived back in the Aquapods less than an hour before and had gone straight into conference with York and Howe. The storm that had been brewing up in the northern sky all morning was now making its presence felt, and Howe had activated the water ballast trimming system to keep the ship stable. It was an ominous development that heightened Jack's anxiety about getting back underwater with maximum urgency, and all available hands were now huddled round the console as they attempted to troubleshoot the sinister presence that was blocking their way on the seabed.

'*Akula* is the NATO designation, Russian for shark. *Kazbek* is named after the highest mountain in the central Caucasus.' Katya walked over to the console, handing Jack a coffee with a smile. 'The Soviet designation was Project 971.'

'How can you possibly know all this?'

The question came from a scientist named Lanowski who had joined *Seaquest* in Trabzon, a lank-haired man with pebble glasses who was eyeing Katya with evident disdain.

'Before studying for my doctorate I completed my national service as an analyst in the submarine warfare division of the Intelligence Directorate of the Soviet Navy.'

The scientist fiddled with his glasses and was silent.

'We considered these the best all-purpose attack submarines, the equivalent of the American *Los Angeles* class,' she added. '*Kazbek* was laid down at Komsomolsk-on-Amur in 1988 and commissioned in early 1991. Only one reactor, contrary to western intelligence assessments. Four 650 millimetre and six 533 millimetre launch tubes for multiple weapons, including cruise missiles.'

'But it has no nuclear warheads,' York said firmly. 'This is not an SSBN, a ballistic missile boat. What puzzles me is why the Russians were so fanatical about keeping the loss a secret. Most of the technology had been familiar to us since the type first appeared in the mid-eighties. Just before I left the Royal Navy I participated in a Strategic Arms Reduction Treaty visit to the Northern Fleet sub base at Yagel'naya near Murmansk where we were given a guided tour of the latest *Akula*. We saw everything except the reactor room and the tactical operations centre.'

'An IMU team decommissioned an *Akula I* during the Vladivostok clean-up two years ago,' Costas added. 'I personally dismembered it bit by bit.'

One of the crew spoke up. 'What happened to *Kazbek*? Reactor malfunction?'

'That's what we feared at the time.' Mustafa Alközen stepped out to address the group. 'A meltdown would have precipitated a massive radiation leak, killing the crew and irradiating the sea for miles around. Yet the Turkish early-warning monitors detected no abnormal radiation in territorial waters.'

'A reactor failure anyway rarely results in meltdown,' York said. 'More often it actually reduces radiation emission. And it's not the end of the road. If the core can't be reactivated there are always the auxiliary diesels as back-up.'

'What we're about to see may answer the question.' Costas directed their attention to the video monitor above the console, where images taken from his Aquapod on the seabed had been downloaded. He aimed a remote control and fast-forwarded through a series of extraordinary scenes of the bull-sphinx and the pyramids until the shapes became less distinct. He stilled the video at a mass of tangled metal, the wreckage outlined in a halo of yellow where the floodlights reflected off sediment suspended in the water.

'The stern,' Costas said simply. 'The propeller, or what's left of it. The seven blades are intact but it's sheared off at the shaft. That mess in the foreground is the lower stabilizer fin, and the distinctive high aft fin of the *Akula* class is visible above it.'

'Must have been a hell of an impact,' a crewman said.

'We checked out the eastern pyramid just before we surfaced,' Costas continued. 'There's extensive damage to the masonry at the corner opposite the volcano. Our guess is the sub was making south-west at its maximum speed of over thirty knots and detected these structures too late for evasive action. They avoided a head-on collision by swerving to port but in doing so crashed the stern into the pyramid, with the results you can see. The sub carried on for another hundred metres until its bow jammed into a cleft just ahead of the ancient stairway. It sank upright between the pyramid and the volcano.'

'Incredible,' York said. 'It would have been sheer madness to travel at speed so close to an island so poorly charted.'

'Something went badly wrong,' Costas agreed.

'As far as we can tell there were no survivors,' York continued. 'Yet even at a hundred metres the crew would have stood a chance using the Soviet version of the Steinke-hood life jacket and breathing apparatus. Even a single floating corpse would have been detected by satellite monitors from the miniature radio transmitter incorporated in the hood. Why didn't they eject a SLOT buoy, a submarine-launched one-way transmitter? The hull's even more baffling. You say the damage is external and there's no evidence the casing was breached. Why didn't they blow the ballast tanks? The *Akula* is double-hulled, with three times the reserve buoyancy of a single-hulled boat.'

'All good questions.' Jack moved out of the shadows where he had been quietly listening. 'And we may well find answers. But we must stick to our objective. Time is running out fast.'

He moved in front of the group beside Costas and scanned the faces intently.

'We're here to find the heart of Atlantis, not to restart the

Cold War. We believe the text is leading us inside that volcano, up the processional way from the bull-sphinx towards some kind of sanctuary. The stairway continues under the submarine but not beyond it. We checked.'

He put his hands on his hips.

'Our objective lies beneath a metal cylinder one hundred and eight metres long, weighing nine thousand tons. We have to assume the ballast tanks can't be vented. Even if we had the equipment to shift the submarine, our activities would be obvious on the surface and the Russians would be on to us like a shot. Any attempt to get outside help and we'd lose the initiative. Atlantis would become a free-for-all for Aslan and his band of looters. The images of the site you've just seen would be our last.'

He paused and spoke slowly.

'We have only one option. We're going to have to get inside and cut our way through to the rock face.'

'Depth seventy-five metres and dropping. We should be entering visible range now.'

Katya peered through the Plexiglas porthole to her left. What at first seemed impenetrable gloom gradually revealed itself as a seascape of massive shapes and shadows. The dark hull of the sunken submarine suddenly loomed ahead in all its awesome magnitude.

Costas pulled back on the steering column and turned to his co-pilot. 'Jack, get ready with the landing gear. Prepare for a jolt.'

Katya was sitting beside two crewmen and a mass of equipment in the central fuselage of the DSRV-4, the deep submergence rescue vehicle which was standard on all IMU *Sea*-class vessels. The floor in front held a universal coupling which could be mated with the escape hatch of virtually any submarine, allowing trapped sailors to be removed in batches of eight or ten. The crewmen had been making final adjustments to the generic docking collar to fit the Russian SSN.

Twenty minutes earlier they had glimpsed their last of *Seaquest* as her wavering silhouette receded in the turbulent waters above.

'Coming about 180 degrees due south. Making my depth 95 metres.'

There was a dull thump as they came to rest on the submarine's forward casing. Ahead of them rose the bulk of the conning tower, the periscope and antenna array just visible in the floodlight above the dark portholes of the bridge. For the first time they could appreciate the immense size of the submarine, almost twice the tonnage of *Seaquest* and as long as a football pitch.

Costas looked over at Jack. 'The *Akula* class was the quietest sub the Soviets ever designed. It's got an anechoic coating, thin tiles of rubber on the outer casing designed to absorb active sonar pulses. That's why we didn't make a bigger bang when we landed. It also makes it easier to grip the casing using the hydraulic suction cups on our landing gear.'

He eased the control stick forward and the DSRV bounced a few metres closer to the fin. As he dropped down again the entrance to the escape trunk came into view.

'Just as York suspected. The trunk's closed and sealed. Any attempt at escape and it would have been open.'

Costas had calculated that the ancient stairway would be under the torpedo room near the nose cone, making the forward escape hatch their nearest access point. Katya had explained that even in a low-level emergency the bulkheads would have automatically sealed off the reactor from the forward operational area, leaving no way of accessing the torpedo room from the aft hatch.

'Gently as she goes.'

Costas had been using the digital navigational display to align the DSRV with its objective. A moment later there was a satisfying thud as the docking ring settled over the escape hatch. He switched off the navigational array and flipped up four handles on either side of the joystick, bringing the DSRV down flush with the deck and engaging the stabilizing legs with their suction feet.

'Have soft seal. Docking secured.'

He undid his seatbelt and craned round to address Katya and the two crewmen.

'Let's rehearse the drill one last time. The deep-penetration sonar on the ROV suggests the forward part of the submarine remains watertight. The rest we're unsure about because the reactor and other machinery fills much of the internal space, but it could also be dry.'

He crawled towards the coupling array, Jack following closely behind.

'Directly beneath us is the forward escape trunk,' he continued. 'In a wet escape crewmen climb into the chamber and don their rebreathers. The lower hatch closes, the trunk fills up and the crewmen escape through the upper hatch.'

'And a dry escape?' Katya asked.

'The DSRV couples directly with the outer escape hatch,' Costas replied. 'In the modified *Akula I* the hatch is set two metres into the hull, creating an additional outer chamber which acts as a safety measure for the rescue crew. With our own hatch shut we can couple with the hull, open the casing hatch, pump the outer chamber dry and open the escape hatch two metres below with a robotic arm. We then use the DSRV's external sensor array to test the interior environment without actually exposing ourselves to it.'

Costas nodded at the crewmen and they set about securing the seal. After manually locking the ring they crawled to the aft part of the submersible and sat side by side at a small console. With the flick of a switch the covering over the hatch in front of Katya retracted into the DSRV's hull casing, revealing a concave Plexiglas dome which lit up as a floodlight activated and the crewmen set about decoupling the submarine's hatch. A few moments later there was a sharp hiss as the seawater inside the chamber was pumped out and replaced with air from one of the DSRV's external high-pressure cylinders.

'Chamber evacuated and equalized,' one of the crewmen said. 'Activating robotic arm now.'

Katya squeezed in between Costas and Jack for a better view. Below them they could see a thin tube terminating in a grapple-like device, its movement controlled by one of the crewmen using a small joystick and navigation screen.

'It works by pressure differential,' Costas explained. 'We've filled the chamber with air at ambient barometric pressure, the same as inside the DSRV. We hook that arm to the hatch, ratchet it up to exert some pull, then slowly decrease the pressure in the chamber until it's lower than the submarine. Then bingo, it springs open.'

They watched as the robotic arm disengaged the safety lock and clenched the central handle, the shaft straightening as tension was applied. The crewman at the far end of the console was concentrating on a screen which gave him a close-up view of the casing.

'Pressure one bar. Reducing now.' He cracked open a valve on a pipe above him and activated an extractor pump which drew air out of the chamber.

'Point nine five bar. Point nine zero. Point eight five. Point eight zero. Now!'

As he snapped the valve shut they could see the hatch waft up as if it were riding a wave. The arm automatically retracted and pulled the hatch taut against the side of the chamber. They could see through into the bowels of the submarine, the floodlight dancing off piping and bulkheads in the passageway below.

'Pressure point seven nine five bar.'

'About what I expected.' Costas looked at the crewmen. 'Give me full environmental specs before we compensate.'

A sensor array incorporating a gas spectrometer, a Geiger counter and a radiation dose meter was lowered into view from the external pod.

'Radiation dose zero point six millirems per hour, less than you get in an airliner. General toxicity level moderate, with no indication of significant gas or chemical leakage. High ammonia content probably due to organic decay. Oxygen eight point two per cent, nitrogen seventy per cent, carbon dioxide twenty-two per cent, carbon monoxide zero point eight per cent, a little risky for prolonged exposure. Temperature plus two degrees Celsius.'

'Thanks, Andy.' Costas looked wryly at Jack. 'Stepping in there now would be like landing on top of Everest in tropical kit with a mouthful of rotten eggs.'

'Wonderful,' Jack said. 'Why is it this kind of thing always happens when you take the lead?'

Costas grinned and looked back at the console. 'Andy, compensate to ambient using pure oxygen and engage CO_2 scrubbers.'

There was a sharp hiss as the DSRV began to bleed oxygen into the hatch from its external gas cylinders.

'The *Akula* class has its own scrubbers,' Katya said. 'If we could activate them they'd do the job for us. There's also a unit that breaks down seawater to release oxygen. These subs can stay down for months at a time with air that's cleaner and better oxygenated than on the surface.'

Costas wiped the sweat from his brow and looked at her. 'It would take too long. The battery which powered those systems would have depleted within a few months of the auxiliary diesel shutting down, and I'd prefer to save the DSRV battery for reactivating the emergency lighting. Our own scrubber incorporates carbon monoxide and hydrogen burners as well as a range of chemical filters.'

A voice broke in from the console. 'We've reached ambient pressure. In ten minutes the scrubbing cycle will be complete.'

'Right,' said Costas. 'Time to kit up.'

They wore close-fitting E-suits, all-environment shells of Kevlar-reinforced crushed neoprene which were an amalgam of the latest diving drysuits with US Navý SEALS chemical and biological warfare gear. Wrapped round their calves were flexible silicon fins which could be pulled down over their feet underwater.

Costas quickly briefed them as he clipped on his straps. 'We should be able to breathe safely but I suggest we wear full-face masks anyway, as the regulators will moisturize and warm up the air as well as filter out residual impurities. There's a supplemental oxygen feed which kicks in as soon as the sensor detects atmospheric depletion.'

The mask was a silicon-enriched helmet which conformed closely to the shape of the face. After finalizing his own gear, Jack helped Katya don her self-contained life support system, a streamlined polypropylene backpack which contained a compact oxygen rebreather, a multi-stage regulator and a triple set of titanium-reinforced cylinders pumped up to eight hundred times barometric pressure. The IMU cylinders were ultralight and slimline, weighing less than a single old-fashioned scuba set and ergonomically designed so they were hardly aware of the extra bulk.

On their wrists micro-consoles displayed full environmental data as well as computations for a range of breathing mixtures from the helium, oxygen and air in the cylinders. The gas was mixed automatically, the computer taking account of depth, dive profile, temperature and even individual physiology.

'The intercom should allow us to communicate with the DSRV,' Costas said. 'Switch it on when you activate the SCLS system just before we go in.'

After they had double-checked each other, Jack took down a 9-millimetre Beretta 92FS from a shelf above the hatch. He slammed a fifteen-round magazine into the butt and sealed the pistol in a waterproof holster with a spare magazine on his chest.

'Standard equipment.' He glanced reassuringly at Katya, remembering their conversation the night before about the risks involved. 'You can never be too safe in this game.'

'Dr Howard. Urgent message from *Seaquest*.'

'Put it on audio.' Jack snapped open his visor and took the mike from the crewman. 'This is Howard. Over.'

'Jack, this is Tom.' The voice was crackling with static. 'That weather front has finally hit us. Violent electrical storms, visibility down to fifty metres. Storm force ten and rising. Far worse than I feared. I cannot hold present position so close to the island. I repeat, I cannot hold present position. Over.'

The urgency in his voice was absolutely clear despite the disturbance.

Jack clicked the reply button. 'What's the forecast? Over.'

'One of the biggest fronts ever recorded at this time of year. Your chance to abort is now. Over.'

The DSRV was too large to be deployed through *Seaquest*'s inner berth and instead had been swung out over the stern davits. The experience had given them a sharp appreciation of the perils of returning in rough seas.

'What's the alternative? Over.'

'You'd be on your own for twenty-four hours. I intend to take *Seaquest* north twenty nautical miles behind the front and then follow it back south. Over.'

'There's no way the DSRV could follow *Seaquest* that far underwater,' Costas muttered. 'The battery's designed for life support during rescue operations and would only power us a couple of miles before draining.'

Jack paused before raising the mike. 'Tom, give us a moment. Over.'

In the brief silence Jack looked at the others and received a nod from each of them. Andy and Ben were IMU veterans, Andy a submersibles specialist who was Costas' chief technician and Ben a former Royal Marine who had served in the Special Boat Section before joining Peter Howe's security department. Both men would follow Jack anywhere and were deeply committed to the goals of IMU.

Jack felt a surge of adrenalin as he saw the response was unanimous and without reservation. They had come too far to let their target slip from their grasp. By now *Seaquest*'s movements would have excited interest among their adversaries, men who would eliminate them without a moment's hesitation if they stood in their way. They knew this was their only chance.

Jack picked up the mike again.

'We are staying. I repeat, we are staying. We'll turn the

weather to our advantage. I assume no hostile vessels will be able to get near either. We'll need the time you're away to get through the sub. Over.'

'I understand.' The voice was barely discernible through the static. 'Retract your radio buoy and only use it in an emergency as it'll be picked up by every receiver for miles around. Wait for us to contact you. The best of luck to you all. *Seaquest* out.'

For a moment the only sound was the low hum of the CO_2 scrubbers and the whirr of the electric motor used to pull in the radio buoy.

'Ten minutes are up.' Ben said from the console. 'You're good to go.'

'Right. Let's get this show on the road.'

Andy slid over and unlocked the docking clamp. The hatch opened outwards with no resistance, the pressure inside the DSRV and the submarine now equalized.

Costas swung his legs over and found the rungs of the ladder on the inside wall. He started to raise his mask and then paused.

'One final thing.'

Jack and Katya looked at him.

'This is no *Marie Celeste*. The *Kazbek* had a full complement of seventy-three men when she went down. There may be some pretty grim sights in there.'

'We'll head forward through the passageway. The bulkhead behind us seals off the reactor compartment.'

Costas stepped off the final rung of the ladder in the escape trunk and swung round, his headlamp throwing a wavering beam into the heart of the submarine. Jack followed close behind, his tall frame bent nearly double as he reached back to offer Katya a hand. She cast a final glance up at the crewmen peering down from the DSRV before ducking through the hatch behind the two men.

'What's the white stuff?' she asked.

Everywhere they looked a pale encrustation covered the surface like icing. Katya rubbed her glove along a railing, causing the substance to sprinkle off like snow and revealing the shiny metal beneath.

'It's a precipitate,' Costas replied. 'Probably the result of an ionization reaction between the metal and the increased levels of carbon dioxide after the scrubbers shut down.'

The ghostly lustre only added to the sense that this was a place utterly cut off, so far removed from the images outside that the ancient city seemed to belong to another kind of dream world.

They advanced slowly along a raised gangway into an open space obscured by darkness. A few steps inside, Costas stopped below an electrical box set between the piping above their heads. He delved into his tool belt for a miniature pneumatic cleaner attached to a CO_2 cartridge and used it to blow away precipitate from a socket. After plugging in a cord he had trailed from the DSRV, an orange indicator light flashed above the panel.

'Hey presto. It still works after all these years. And we all thought Soviet technology was so inferior.' He looked at Katya. 'No offence intended.'

'None taken.'

A few moments later the fluorescent lighting came on, its first pulses surging like distant lightning. As they switched off their headlamps a bizarre world came into view, a jumble of consoles and equipment shrouded in mottled white. It was as if they were in an ice cave, an impression enhanced by the blue lighting and the clouds of exhalation that issued from their masks into the frigid air.

'This is the control room attack centre,' said Costas. 'There should be some clue here to what happened.'

They made their way cautiously to the end of the gangway and down a short flight of steps. On the deck lay a pile of Kalashnikov rifles, the familiar banana-shaped magazines jutting out in front of the stairway. Jack picked one up as Katya looked on.

'Special Forces issue, with folding stock,' she commented. 'AK-74M, the 5.45 millimetre derivative of the AK-47. With the worsening political situation the Soviet General Staff's Intelligence Directorate put naval *spetsialnoe naznachenie* – special purpose – troops on some nuclear submarines. Better known by their acronym *spetsnaz*. The GRU were terrified of defection or insurrection and the *spetsnaz* were directly answerable to them rather than the captain.'

'But their weapons wou:'' ~ rmally be locked away in the armoury,' Jack pointed out. 'And there's something else strange here.' He snapped off the magazine and pulled back the bolt. 'The magazine's half empty and there's a round in the chamber. This gun's been fired.'

A quick check revealed that the other weapons were in a similar state. Below the assault rifles they could see a jumble of handguns, empty magazines and spent cartridge cases.

'It looks like someone cleaned up after a battle.'

'That's exactly what happened.' Costas spoke from the centre of the room. 'Take a look around you.'

In the middle was a command chair flanked by two columns housing the periscope arrays. Set into the walls around the dais were consoles for weapons and navigation control, which made up the operational heart of the vessel.

Everywhere they looked was destruction. Computer monitors had been reduced to jagged holes of broken glass, their innards spewed out in a jumble of wires and circuit boards. Both periscopes had been smashed beyond recognition, the mangled eyepieces hanging off at crazy angles. The chart table had been violently ripped apart, the jagged gouges running across its surface the unmistakable result of automatic rifle fire.

'The ship control station is shot to hell.' Costas was surveying the wreckage at the far corner of the room. 'Now I see why they couldn't move.'

'Where are they?' Katya demanded. 'The crew?'

'There were survivors.' Costas paused. 'Someone stashed those weapons, and I'd guess there were bodies which have been disposed of somewhere.'

'Wherever they camped out, it wasn't here,' said Jack. 'I suggest we move on to the accommodation quarters.'

Katya led them along the walkway towards the forward compartments of the submarine. Once again they plunged into darkness, the auxiliary electrical system only providing emergency lighting in the main compartments. As they inched forward, Jack and Costas could just make out Katya's silhouette as she felt for the handrail and fumbled for the switch on her headlamp.

There was a sudden clatter and an ear-piercing shriek. Jack and Costas leapt forward. Katya was slumped in the passageway.

Jack knelt over her and checked her regulator. His face was drawn with concern as he looked into her eyes.

She was mumbling incoherently in Russian. After a moment she raised herself on one elbow and the two men helped her to her feet. She spoke falteringly.

'I've had a . . . shock, that's all. I've just seen . . .'

Her voice faded away as she raised her arm and pointed in the direction of the sonar room at the end of the corridor.

Jack switched on his headlamp. What it revealed was an image of horror, a spectre drawn from the worst nightmare. Looming out of the darkness was the white-shrouded form of a hanging man, the arms dangling like some ghoulish puppet, the face lolling and grotesque as it leered through long-dead eyes.

It was the very apparition of death, the guardian of a tomb where no living being belonged. Jack suddenly felt chilled to the bone.

Katya recovered herself and straightened. Cautiously the three of them edged into the room. The body was wearing the dark serge of a Soviet naval officer and was suspended by the neck from a wire noose. The floor was strewn with discarded food cartons and other debris.

'His name was Sergei Vassilyevich Kuznetsov.' Katya was reading from a diary she'd found on the table behind the corpse. 'Captain, Second Rank, Soviet Navy. Order of the Red Star for services to state security. He was the *Kazbek*'s *zampolit*, the *zamestitel' komandira po politicheskoi chasti*, the deputy commander for political affairs. Responsible for overseeing political reliability and ensuring the captain carried out his orders.'

'A KGB stooge,' Costas said.

'I can think of a few captains I knew in the Black Sea Fleet who would not be displeased by this sight.' She read on. 'He spent his final days right here. The active sonar had been disabled so he couldn't send a signal. But he monitored the passive radar pulse wave detector for any sign of surface vessels in the vicinity.' She turned a page.

'My God. The final entry is for December 25th, 1991. By coincidence the last day the Red Flag flew over the Kremlin.'

She looked up at Jack and Costas, her eyes wide. 'The sub went down on June 17th that year, which means this man was alive in here for more than six months!'

They looked in horrified fascination at the corpse.

'It's possible,' Costas said eventually. 'Physically, that is. The battery could have sustained the CO_2 scrubbers and the electrolysis desalination machine that extracts oxygen from seawater. And there was evidently plenty to eat and drink.' He surveyed the scatter of empty vodka bottles among the rubbish on the floor. 'Psychologically is another matter. How anyone could remain sane in these conditions is beyond me.'

'The diary's full of political rhetoric, the kind of empty communist propaganda we had drummed into us like religion,' Katya said. 'Only the most fanatical party members were chosen as political officers, the equivalent of the Nazi Gestapo.'

'Something very odd went on here,' Jack murmured. 'I can't believe in six months he found no way of signalling the surface. He could have manually ejected a buoy through a torpedo tube or discharged floating waste. It doesn't make sense.'

'Listen to this.' Katya's voice betrayed a dawning realization as she flicked from page to page, pausing occasionally to scan an entry. She lingered for a moment and then began to translate.

I am the chosen one. I have buried my comrades with full military honours. They sacrificed their lives for the Motherland. Their strength gives me strength. Long live the Revolution! She looked up.

'What does it mean?' Costas asked.

'According to this diary, there were twelve of them. Five days after the sinking they selected one man to survive. The rest took cyanide tablets. Their bodies were weighted and ejected through the torpedo tubes.'

'Had they given up all hope?' Costas sounded incredulous.

'They were determined beyond reason that the submarine should not fall into NATO hands. They were prepared to destroy the vessel if any would-be rescuer turned out to be hostile.'

'I can almost see the logic,' Costas said. 'You only need one man to detonate charges. One man uses less food and air, so the submarine can be guarded that much longer. Everyone else is worse than redundant, a drain on precious resources. They must have chosen the man least likely to crack up.'

Jack knelt down beside the empty bottles and shook his head. 'There must be more to it than that. It still doesn't add up.'

'Their world was about to collapse,' Costas said. 'Diehards like these may have convinced themselves they were a last bastion of communism, a final bulwark against the west.'

They looked at Katya.

'We all knew the end was near,' she said, 'and some refused to accept it. But they did not put madmen in nuclear submarines.'

One question had been nagging at them since they first saw the dangling corpse, and Costas finally spoke up.

'What happened to the rest of the crew?'

Katya was reading another part of the diary, a look of increasing incredulity on her face as she began to piece it together.

'It's as we suspected in naval intelligence at the time, only worse,' she said. 'This was a renegade boat. Her captain, Yevgeni Mikhailovich Antonov, set out on a routine patrol from the Black Sea Fleet submarine base at Sevastopol. He disappeared south without ever making contact again.'

'He could never have hoped to get out of the Black Sea

without being detected,' Costas said. 'The Turks maintain a one hundred per cent sonar blanket over the Bosporus.'

'I don't believe that was his intention. I believe he was heading to a rendezvous, perhaps at this island.'

'It seems a strange time to defect,' Jack remarked. 'Right at the end of the Cold War, the collapse of the Soviet Union in sight. Any astute naval officer would have seen it coming. It would have made more sense simply to hang on and wait.'

'Antonov was a brilliant submariner but also a maverick. He hated the Americans so much he was deemed too risky for ballistic missile boats. I do not think this was a defection.'

Jack was still troubled. 'He must have had something to offer someone, something to make it worthwhile.'

'Does the diary say what happened to him?' Costas asked.

Katya read before looking up again. 'Our friend the *zampolit* got to know what was afoot several hours before the sinking. He rallied the *spetsnaz* team and confronted the captain in the control room. Antonov had already issued sidearms to his officers but they were no match for assault rifles. After a bloody battle they forced the captain and the surviving crew to surrender, but not before the sub had run out of control and crashed into the sea floor.'

'What did they do with the captain?'

'Before the confrontation Kuznetsov sealed off the engineering compartment and reversed the extractor fans to pump in the carbon monoxide collected in the scrubbers. The engineers would have been dead before they knew what was happening. As for Antonov and his men, they were forced back behind the escape trunk and sealed in the reactor compartment.'

'Death by slow irradiation. It could have taken days, even weeks.' Costas stared at the mummified face, a hideous sentinel that seemed duty-bound even in death. He looked as if he wanted to drive his fist into the shrivelled head. 'You deserved your end, you sadistic bastard.'

14

'This is a ship of the dead. The sooner we get out of here the better.' Katya snapped shut the diary and led them out of the sonar room past the dangling corpse. She avoided a final glance at the body, its ghastly visage already seared into her mind.

'Headlamps on all the time now,' Costas ordered. 'We must assume he rigged this boat to blow.'

After a few steps he held up his hand.

'That's the weapons loading hatch above us,' he said. 'We should be able to take the chute directly down to the torpedo room. It's an open elevator shaft but has a rung ladder on the inside.'

They moved to the edge of the shaft directly below the

hatch. Just as Costas was about to step onto the upper rung, he paused and eyed one of the pipes that led from the sonar room down the chute. He brushed away the encrustation from a slight ridge that ran the length of the pipe, revealing a pair of red-coated wires taped to the metal.

'Wait here.'

He worked his way back towards the sonar room, occasionally stopping to flick away encrustation. He briefly disappeared behind the dangling corpse and then made his way back.

'Just as I suspected,' he said. 'The wires lead back to a switch which has been duct-taped to the console. It's an SPDT switch, a single-pole double-throw device which can actuate a current and control two different circuits. My guess is the wires go down to the torpedo room where our friend has activated a pair of warheads. The explosion would blow this boat into bite-sized chunks, and us with it.'

Costas led the way, tracing the wires down the chute, and the other two cautiously followed. The encrustation softened the reverberations of their feet to a dull echo that thudded ominously through the shaft. Halfway down they paused to peer through a hatch into the officers' wardroom, their headlamps revealing another scene of disarray with bedding and packages strewn over the floor.

Moments later Costas reached the base of the chute.

'Good. The emergency lighting works here as well.'

The compartment beyond was filled with tightly-packed racks, only a narrow aisle allowing access to the far end. It had been designed so that weapons could be lowered down the chute directly into the holding racks and be fed by automated gantry to the launch tubes.

'A normal complement on a Project 971U would be thirty weapons,' Katya said. 'Up to twelve SS-N-21 Sampson cruise missiles and an assortment of anti-ship missiles. But the largest warheads will probably be on the torpedoes.'

Costas followed the wires into a tight passageway between the racks to the left of the central aisle. After a few moments on his hands and knees, he stood up with a triumphant gleam in his eye.

'Bingo. It's those two cradles directly in front of you. A pair of 65-76 Kit torpedoes. The largest torpedoes ever built, almost eleven metres long. Each packs 450 kilograms of HE, enough to punch through a titanium-armoured pressure hull. But it should be a simple matter to deactivate the warheads and remove the wires.'

'Since when have you been an expert on defusing Russian torpedoes?' Jack asked doubtfully.

'Every time I try something new it seems to work. You should know that by now.' Costas' demeanour suddenly turned serious. 'We have no choice. The fuses are electromagnetic, and there's going to be decay in the circuitry after so many years in this environment. They're probably dangerously unstable as they are, and our equipment will disturb the electromagnetic field. It's a problem we can't bypass.'

'OK, you win.' Jack looked at Katya, who nodded in agreement. 'We've come this far. Let's do it.'

Costas lay on his back in the confined space between the racks and pushed his way in feet first until his head came to rest a quarter of the way down the torpedoes. He lifted his visor for a moment and wrinkled his nose as he took his first breath inside the submarine without the benefit of the SCLS filter.

The other two came up alongside, Jack in the narrow walkway to the left and Katya in the wider central aisle. They could see Costas' upturned face on the deck between the torpedoes. He wriggled towards the torpedo beside Jack until his head was nearly beneath it.

'We're in luck. They have a screw-off plug in the outer casing which allows the warheads to be armed manually in the event of electronic failure. The plug on this one has been opened and the wire goes inside. I should be able to reach in and switch off the fuse, and then cut the wire.' Costas rolled over sideways and inspected the other torpedo. 'Same on this one.'

'Remember these things are volatile,' Katya cautioned. 'They're not electric like most torpedoes but run on kerosene and hydrogen peroxide. The submarine *Kursk* was destroyed in the Barents Sea in 2000 by the explosion of leaked hydrogen peroxide from a 65–76 torpedo, one of these.'

Costas grimaced and nodded. He rolled back and lay motionless between the two racks, his headlamp shining directly upwards.

'What's the delay?' Jack demanded.

'I'm putting myself in our friend's position. If he and his buddies were so fanatical about protecting this sub they must have had a contingency in case they all died. They must have assumed the wreck would eventually be found. My hunch is he booby-trapped this detonator. It's too simple as it is.'

'What do you suggest?'

'There's one obvious possibility.' Costas reached down to his tool belt and pulled out a device the size of a pocket calculator. They could just make out the green glow of a digital LCD screen as he activated the sensor. He raised the device to the wire that ran between the torpedoes just above his head and carefully attached it using a miniature alligator clip.

'Christ. Just as I thought.'

'What is it?'

'This is a volt-amp meter. It's giving a positive reading of fifteen milliamps. This wire is live.'

'What does that mean?' Jack asked.

'It means the wiring must be hooked up to a battery outlet. The sub's main lead-acid batteries probably still have enough stored voltage to produce a current at this low amperage. The wiring must be a continuous loop from the positive to the negative poles of the battery, with the switch in the sonar room forming the actuator and the two warhead fuses the link. Setting it up would have been risky but they must have calculated the amperage would be too weak to detonate the warheads. The key is the electrical surge if anyone tries to remove the wires. Disconnect the warhead fuse activator and you have an instantaneous surge. Flip the switch in the sonar room and you get the same thing. There's no circuit breaker to cut off the current. We'd be atomized before I'd taken my fingers off the wire.'

Jack let out a long exhalation and sat back against the walkway. 'So what do we do now?'

'It's direct current, so the charge flow will be one way. If I cut the negative, there'll be a surge and we're gone. If I cut the positive, everything should go dead and we'll be safe.'

'Which is which?'

Costas rolled his head to the right and looked ruefully through the narrow space at Jack. 'Our friend might still have the last laugh. With such low amperage there's no way of telling.'

Jack lay back on the walkway and closed his eyes. After a moment Costas spoke again.

'To ignite a bomb with an electrical surge, the flashpoint needs to be in direct contact with the explosive materials in the detonator or main charge. They would need to have opened up the warhead to introduce the outflow wire. There's more room to manoeuvre on Katya's side so I suggest that's where it's attached. That would make the wire to my left the positive one.'

Costas turned towards Katya and pushed as far as he could against the torpedo, extending his left arm under the rack until he touched the wire that emerged from the warhead. He dropped his hand to the deck and began scrabbling around in the encrustation.

'I can feel wire.'

Katya uncovered more and pulled it taut as far back as the weapons loading chute. She hurried over and peered up the ladder before returning.

'It goes back to the switch,' she announced.

'Right. I'm convinced.' Costas withdrew his arm and reached into his belt for a compact multi-tool, pulling it open to form a pair of high-precision wire-cutters. The rubber in his E-suit glove would provide insulation against electric shock, though if that happened he would not live long enough to care.

He tilted his head back towards Jack.

'You're with me on this one?'

'I'm with you.'

Costas resumed his position of a moment before, his left hand now holding the cutters directly beneath the wire where it hung in a shallow arc from the plughole in the warhead housing.

For a few seconds he lay motionless. The only sound was the steady drip of condensation and the shallow rasp of breathing from their respirators. Katya and Jack stared at each other beneath the torpedo rack.

Costas was sweating behind his mask and snapped it open with his right hand for a clearer view. He pulled off his glove between his knees and wiped his brow before staring determinedly at the wire.

Katya shut her eyes tight in the split second it took Costas to lock the cutter's blades on the wire. He squeezed hard and there was a loud snap.

Then silence.

All three of them held their breath for what seemed an eternity. Then Costas let out a long sigh and slumped on the deck. After a pause he holstered his multi-tool and reconnected his visor and respirator. He tilted his head towards Jack with a twinkle in his eye.

'See? No problem.'

Jack had the thousand-yard stare of a man who had looked death in the face once too often. He shifted his gaze to Costas and managed a half-smile.

'No problem.'

15

At the entrance to the weapons bay Costas extracted another gadget from his belt, a yellow box the size of a cellphone. He flipped open the lid to reveal a small LCD screen which glowed dull green.

'Global positioning system,' he announced. 'This should do the trick.'

'How can it work here?' Katya asked.

A series of figures flashed on the screen.

'That box is our speciality, a combined underwater acoustic GPS receiver and navigation computer,' Jack said. 'Inside the sub we can't send out acoustic waves so we have no access to GPS. Instead we downloaded the specs for this class of sub from the IMU database and mated it with a series of GPS fixes we took via surface buoys outside the submarine on our Aquapod recce this morning. The computer should allow us to navigate inside as if we were using GPS.'

'Got it,' Costas announced. 'In the Aquapod I took a fix where the stairway disappeared under the submarine. It's on the port side of the torpedo room. Bearing two hundred and forty-one degrees from our present position, seven point six metres ahead and two metres down. That puts us beyond the weapons racks just ahead of the port-side ballast tank.'

As Costas began to look for a way through the crowded racks, Katya reached out and held his arm.

'Before we go there's something you should see.'

She pointed towards the central aisle in the weapons bay just beyond the spot where they had lain in mortal fear only minutes before.

'That aisle should be unobstructed to allow the gantry to sling the weapons off the racks and ferry them to the tubes. But it's blocked.'

It should have been glaringly obvious, but they had been so focused on the booby trap they had failed to take in the rest of the room.

'It's a pair of stacked crates.' Costas eased himself into the narrow space on the left-hand side between the crates and the weapons racks, his head just protruding over the uppermost box.

'There are two more behind. And another two beyond that.' Costas' voice was muffled as he slid further along. 'Six altogether, each about four metres long by one and a half metres across. They must have been hoisted down the chute and jigged into place using the torpedo harness.'

'Are they weapons crates?' Jack asked.

Costas re-emerged and shook off the white precipitate clinging to him. 'They're too short for a torpedo or missile and too wide to be tube-launched. We'd need to open one up, but we don't have the equipment or the time.'

'There are some markings.' Katya was squatting down in front of the lower crate and rubbing vigorously at the encrustation. It fell away to reveal a metallic surface with impressed figures in two separate clusters. 'Soviet Defence Ministry encodings.' She pointed at the uppermost group of symbols. 'These are weapons all right.'

Her hand moved to the other group which she inspected more closely.

'Electro . . .' She faltered. 'Electrochimpribor.'

They were beginning to think the unthinkable.

'Combine Electrochimpribor,' Katya said quietly. 'Otherwise known as Plant 418, the main Soviet thermonuclear weapons assembly site.'

Costas slumped heavily against the torpedo rack. 'Holy Mother of God. These are nukes. Each of these crates is just about the right size for an SLBM warhead.'

'Type SS-N-20 Sturgeon, to be precise.' Katya stood up and faced the two men. 'Each one is five times more powerful than the Hiroshima bomb. There are six crates, ten warheads in each.' She paused and stared at the crates. 'The authorities went to elaborate lengths to keep the loss of this submarine a secret. Afterwards there were a number of perplexing disappearances, especially from *Kazbek*'s home port of Sevastopol. I now believe they were victims of an old-fashioned Stalinist purge. The executions went unnoticed in the momentous events of that year.'

'Are you suggesting these nukes were stolen?' Costas asked incredulously.

'The Soviet military was deeply disillusioned after the Afghan war in the 1980s. The navy had begun to disintegrate with ships laid up and crews idle. Pay was dismal or non-existent. More intelligence was sold to the west during the final few years of the Soviet Union than during the height of the Cold War.'

'How does Antonov fit in?' Costas asked.

'He was a man who could be harnessed to good effect but was dangerous when the reins were loosened. He hated *glasnost* and *perestroika* and came to despise the regime for its collusion with the west. This looks like his ultimate act of defiance.'

'If the regime could no longer hit at the west then he could,' Costas murmured.

'And his crew would follow him anywhere, especially with the lure of prize money.'

'Where would he be taking these?'

'Saddam Hussein in Iraq. The Taliban in Afghanistan. Hamas in Syria. The North Koreans. This was 1991, remember.'

'There must have been a middleman,' Jack said.

'The vultures were already circling, even before the collapse of the Soviet Union,' Katya replied bleakly.

'I underestimated our friend the political officer,' Costas said quietly. 'He may have been a fanatic, but he may also have saved humanity from its worst catastrophe.'

'It's not over yet.' Jack straightened. 'Somewhere out there is a dissatisfied customer, someone who has been watching and waiting over the years. And his potential clients now are far worse than ever before; they're terrorists driven only by hate.'

The blue glow from the submarine's emergency lighting barely penetrated the gloom at the forward end of the torpedo room. Costas switched his headlamp to full beam before leading the way through the maze of weapons racks towards the co-ordinates indicated by his transceiver. Jack and Katya followed close behind, their survival suits taking on an increasingly spectral hue as they brushed against the white encrustation which clung to every surface of the submarine's interior. After squeezing through a final passage they crouched in single file on a narrow walkway flush with the hull casing.

Costas braced himself with his back against the casing. He hooked his fingers through one of the metre-long floor grates.

'Here goes.'

He rocked forward and heaved with all his strength. Seconds later the grate relented with a metallic shriek and a shower of precipitate. Jack crawled forward to help shift it aside, leaving Costas space to swing his legs over and peer into the darkness below. He lowered himself until only his helmet was visible below the walkway.

'I'm on the floor above the bilges,' he announced. 'This is as far down as you can go without wading in toxic soup.' He took the GPS unit from his pocket.

Jack stepped over the hole to let Katya move up to the edge. All three headlamps now shone at the flickering green display.

'Bingo.' Costas looked up from the screen and stared at the casing less than an arm's length away. 'I'm five metres above the point where the steps disappeared under the submarine. We're bang on target.'

'How does the casing look?' Jack asked.

'We're in luck. For most of its length *Kazbek* has a double skin, an inner pressure casing and an outer hydrodynamic hull separated by twenty centimetres of rubber. It provides better acoustic insulation and space for a ballast tank. But just before the nose cone it reverts to single thickness to allow more internal space as the casing tapers.'

Katya leaned forward. 'There's something I don't fully understand.'

'Fire away.'

'Between us and that rock face lies a twenty-centimetre-thick wall of metal. How do we get through?'

Costas craned his neck up to look at Katya. He had left his visor open since defusing the warheads and the mixture of sweat-streaked grime and white precipitate looked like some bizarre war paint.

'Light amplification by stimulated emission of radiation.'

Katya paused. 'Laser?'

'You got it.'

At that moment there was a metallic clatter behind them. Before leaving the weapons bay Costas had radioed Ben and Andy in the DSRV with instructions on how to reach the torpedo room. The two men had taken the perimeter walkway and now appeared fully kitted up in E-suits and festooned with gearbags.

'We'll need a bigger opening,' Costas said to the men. 'Then come down and join me.'

Jack and Katya prised out two more grates so the men could lower themselves to the bilge floor. As soon as they had settled in the confined space, they unzipped the bags and began assembling the apparatus inside.

Costas chalked a circle about a metre in diameter on the hull casing, using a tape measure as a crude compass. He moved aside as the two crewmen lifted the apparatus into place. It looked like a scaled-down lunar module, a cluster of articulated legs extending from a polyhedral central unit the size of a desktop PC. Ben held the unit in front of the GPS fix while Andy positioned the legs round the chalked circle. After a quick inspection he flipped a switch and the suction pads sealed against the hull. At the same time a cluster of rods sprang through each joint to lock the apparatus into one unyielding mass.

Ben extended a telescopic tube from both sides of the unit, one end to the centre of the chalked circle and the other to the dark recess below the metal grating of the floor. To the left of the unit was an open-topped three-sided box about half a metre across. Above the tube was a sighting device and below it a handle and trigger.

After a quick check Ben plugged in a cable they had trailed from the DSRV. The LCD screen behind the unit came to life and booted through a series of read-outs before settling on a blank display peppered with program icons.

'Good work, guys,' Costas said. 'Now let's get this baby into action.'

He tapped in a series of commands, his eyes darting between keyboard and screen. After the program finalized, he leaned forward and pressed his right eye against the viewfinder, making small adjustments to the tube alignment using a pair of joysticks on either side.

Less than five minutes after the power had been connected he rocked back and looked up at Jack.

'We're ready.'

'Fire away.'

Costas grasped the handle with the trigger. As he pulled it a cathode-ray tube above the keyboard began to flash amber.

'T minus sixty seconds.'

The light transformed to continuous green.

'Good to go,' Costas announced.

'Time frame?' Jack demanded.

'Two minutes. We could slice through the casing like butter but the drain on the DSRV's batteries would be intolerable. Even what we're doing will stretch our safety margins if we're planning to use the DSRV to return to *Seaquest*.' Costas looked up at Katya, his face a picture of suppressed excitement.

'What you're looking at is a far-infrared sealed gas semiconductor laser,' he explained. 'Hook this baby up to the DSRV's two seven hundred amp silver-zinc batteries and you have a ten kilowatt ten point six micron beam. That's enough to give the Klingons pause for thought.'

Jack grunted impatiently as Costas checked the timer and flicked a switch on the keyboard.

'The viewfinder is a positioning device which allows us to fire the beam perpendicular to the fix on the hull,' he continued. 'The laser is currently burning a hole in the casing one centimetre in diameter. I've just fired in a one-way valve which allows us to extrude material while keeping seawater out.'

'In theory,' Jack retorted.

'Nothing wrong with a cold shower.'

The module began emitting a low warning sound. Costas resumed his position behind the screen and began running a series of diagnostics. After a pause he placed his right hand round the handle.

'The beam automatically shut off five millimetres before completion. I'm reactivating now.'

He squeezed the trigger and remained motionless. After a few moments the green light suddenly reverted to flashing amber. Costas peered down the viewfinder, the sweat from his forehead dripping over the tube. He leaned back and relaxed.

'The plug held. We're through.'

Costas moved aside to let Ben take his place at the console. Together they finished assembling the open-topped box to the left of the unit. Within it a lattice of lines glowed a luminous green like the stage backdrop of a miniature theatre.

'Ben's had more practice,' Costas said. 'Some of the software is so new I didn't have a chance to play with it before we left for the wreck excavation.'

'You mean you haven't tried this before?' Katya asked.

'Has to be a first time for everything.'

Katya closed her eyes momentarily. For all the high technology and military-style planning, it seemed that IMU operations, including defusing booby traps, ran on a wing and a prayer.

'Here's where this baby comes into her own,' Costas enthused. 'This is one of the most sophisticated multi-task lasers ever produced. Watch that box.'

The dull green luminosity transformed into a shimmer of tiny particles which pulsated every few seconds. Each surge left an image of increasing complexity, the lines progressively more concrete. After about a minute the image had become three-dimensional. It was as if someone had pressed glowing green putty inside to create a miniature grotto.

'A hologram!' Katya exclaimed.

'Correct.' Costas remained glued to the image. 'Phase two was the insertion of a low-energy ultraviolet laser through the hole in the casing, a mapping device which reproduces the image as a hologram in the box. You can adjust the laser so it only reflects off material of a particular density, in this case the vesicular basalt of the volcano.'

Jack looked at Katya. 'We use it to replicate artefacts,' he said. 'The mapping data are transferred to a high-intensity infrared laser which can cut virtually any material with an accuracy tolerance of one micron, less than a particle of dust.'

'It produced the synthetic polymer copy of the gold disc from the Minoan shipwreck.'

Jack nodded. 'IMU also developed the hardware needed

to reproduce the Elgin Marbles for the Parthenon in Athens.'

Costas leaned over the console. 'OK, Ben. Maximum resolution.'

The surge of green pulsating up and down began to sharpen features which had appeared in outline moments before. They could make out the bulbous outcrops of basalt, a wall of lava formed millennia before the first hominids reached these shores.

It was Katya who first noticed the regularities at the base of the image.

'I can see steps!' she exclaimed.

They watched as the horizontal lines took on an unmistakable shape. The final half-dozen steps leading up from the cliff face terminated in a platform five metres wide. Above it a rocky overhang reached out as far as the submarine, completely sealing off the platform.

Ben began the final countdown with each pulse of the laser. 'Ninety-seven . . . ninety-eight . . . ninety-nine . . . one hundred. Resolution complete.'

All eyes focused on the dark recess in the centre of the image. What at first seemed an opaque haze gradually resolved itself into a rectilinear niche four metres high and three metres wide. It was at the rear of the platform behind the stairs and had clearly been hewn out of the rock.

As the scanner retracted, the niche came into clear view. In the centre they could make out a vertical groove from floor to ceiling. Horizontal grooves extended along the upper and lower edges. Each panel was adorned with the unmistakable U shape of the bull's horns.

Costas let out a low whistle as Katya leaned forward to see.

Jack rummaged in his front pocket and pulled out a crumpled piece of paper. He quietly read out Dillen's translation: '*The great golden door of the citadel.*'

Costas looked up at his friend and saw the familiar fire of excitement.

'I can't vouch for the gold,' Jack said. 'But I can tell you one thing. We've found the gateway to Atlantis.'

16

Jack watched Katya on the other side of the walkway. She was leaning over the gap talking to Costas, her contorted position emphasizing the narrow confines between the weapons racks and the hull casing. The bobbing dance of their headlamps seemed to magnify the sepulchral gloom around them. There should at least be the groan of ageing bulkheads, the signs of fallibility that gave life to any hull. He had to remind himself that *Kazbek* had been laid down less than two decades previously and still had the integrity to withstand many times the current water pressure. It seemed at odds with the ghostly interior, with the shroud of precipitate that looked as if it had built up over eons like the secretions of a limestone cave.

As his gaze strayed into the dark recess beyond, Jack felt a sudden tightening, a jolt of primeval fear he was powerless to control.

He could not let this happen to him again.

Not here. Not now.

He forced his gaze away from the interior towards the activity below. For a moment he closed his eyes and clenched his jaw as he summoned all his strength to fight the nightmare grip of claustrophobia. The anxiety of the last hours had left him vulnerable, had opened a chink in his armour.

He would have to be careful.

Just as his breathing was settling, Costas glanced up at him and gestured at the holographic display with its virtual-reality image of the cliff face. It was mesmerizing proof they were exactly on target.

'Phase three is to get through the hull to that entranceway,' he said to Katya.

'A piece of cake, as you would say.'

'Just wait and see.'

There was a sudden hiss like water escaping through a radiator valve.

'There's a five-metre gap between the submarine's casing and the cliff,' Costas explained. 'We need to create something like an escape tunnel.' He pointed to a cylinder attached to the unit. 'That's full of a liquefied silicate, electromagnetic hydrosilicate 4, or EH-4. We call it magic sludge. That hissing is the sound of it being forced by gas pressure through the hole we've just made onto the outside of the casing, where it's congealing like jelly.'

He stopped to peer at a percentile display on the screen. As the figure reached one hundred the hissing abruptly ceased.

'OK, Andy. Extrusion complete.'

Andy closed the valve and clamped on a second cylinder.

Costas turned back to Katya. 'In simple terms, we're making an inflatable chamber, effectively creating an extension of the submarine's casing out of the silicate.'

'The magic sludge.'

'Yes. That's where Lanowski comes in.'

'Oh.' Katya grimaced as she remembered the new arrival from Trabzon, the ill-kempt figure who refused to believe she could possibly know anything about submarines.

'Maybe not the ideal dinner-party companion,' Costas said. 'But a brilliant polycompounds engineer. We poached him from MIT when the US Department of Defense contracted IMU to find a way of preserving the Second World War wrecks at Pearl Harbor. He discovered a hydraulic sealant which can triple the strength of metal hull remains, extract damaging sea salts from old iron and inhibit corrosion. We're using it for a different purpose here, of course. Lanowski discovered it's also an exceptional binding agent for certain crystalline minerals.'

'How do you blow it into a bubble?' Katya asked.

'That's the ingenious part.'

While they were talking, Ben and Andy had been busy assembling another component of the laser unit. Around the chalked circle they had placed a ring of small devices, each one secured to the casing by a suction cup activated by a vacuum gun. Wires fanned inwards to a control panel beside the console.

'Those are diodes.' Costas pointed at the devices. 'Solid-state semiconductors. Each one contains a solenoid coil which acts like a bar magnet if you pass a current through it. The cable from the DSRV plugs into the control panel and connects to those wires. We've been using the cable to charge up a reserve battery so we can operate independently if necessary. Either way we've got enough voltage to propagate a directional beam of electromagnetic radiation right through the hull casing.'

Costas moved aside in the increasingly cramped space to allow the crewmen to assume positions behind the control panel.

'The extruded mixture is suspended in liquid carbon dioxide, CO_2 hydrate,' he explained. 'The solution's denser than seawater and the pressure at this depth keeps it from breaking up into droplets. The anechoic coating on the submarine is like sandpaper and should keep the mixture from flowing off.'

The two crewmen had called up a version of the holographic image on the computer monitor. Andy was reading off co-ordinates while Ben tapped the figures on the keyboard, each input producing a small red cross-hair on the screen. The cross-hairs began to describe an irregular circle round the doorway.

'Lanowski worked out a way of using crystalline nanotechnology to grow a magnetic lattice through the solution,' Costas went on. 'At the moment the mixture is like liquefied fibreglass, with millions of tiny filaments compressed against each other. Add a blast of electromagnetic radiation and they lock together as a rock-hard mesh in the direction of the pulse.'

'Like reinforced concrete,' Katya said.

'A fair analogy. Only for its weight and density our stuff is about a hundred times stronger than any other construction material known.'

The cross-hatches became a continuous circle and a green light flashed on the control bar below. Andy slid off the seat and Costas took his place in front of the holographic box.

'OK.' Costas straightened up. 'Let's do it.'

Ben flipped a switch on the diode transistor panel. There

was a low humming and the light surrounding the image began to pulsate. The percentile counter sped through to one hundred and flashed green.

'We're in business.' Costas glanced at Katya, his face flushed with excitement. 'We've just fired a 140-volt electromagnetic current through the diodes, magnetizing the EH-4 into a ring which was then projected as a one-centimetre thick membrane to the co-ordinates represented by the cross-hairs. The chamber's cone-shaped, with the wide end encompassing the entire rock platform.' He tapped the keyboard. 'The current binds the membrane to the casing as a continuous solid mass. The probe showed the basalt has a high degree of magnetism, so the current was able to lock into the rock despite the irregularities of the surface.'

Andy disengaged the wires that led from the diodes to the transistor panel.

'Now that the initial surge has gone through we only need two wires to maintain the charge,' Costas said. 'Removing the rest allows us to access the casing and complete the final stage.'

'Cutting through the hull?' Katya asked.

He nodded. 'First we need to drain the compartment. Andy's about to activate a vacuum which will suck the water out through the hole and dump it into the sub. The bilges can take another metre. This boat's not going anywhere anyway.'

'Not yet,' Jack said. He had been silently watching the proceedings from the walkway, the E-suits and the laser contraption like a scene from science-fiction. His thoughts were dominated by the nuclear horror it was their duty to prevent.

'Ready to activate pump,' said Ben.

Costas flicked the switch and the hum of the transformer was drowned out by the whine of an electric motor. Seconds later they could hear the spray of water being ejected into the darkness below.

'We're simultaneously injecting air at atmospheric pressure,' Costas said. 'The membrane's strong enough to prevent the chamber from imploding under the weight of the seawater.'

The spray abruptly ceased and Andy gestured towards the screen. 'We're dry,' he announced. 'Initiating phase four.'

Jack leaned down and peered intently at the holographic box for any changes in the appearance of the cliff face. The pulsating image showed the scanner had reactivated and was relaying data to the holographic converter.

'The rock-cut door seems to be holding,' he said.

Costas glanced at the hologram. 'The probe is detecting fine leakage along the jamb. It's exactly as we predicted.'

'We modelled this scenario last night on *Seaquest*,' Jack explained. 'We assumed the stairs would lead to some kind of doorway. We also assumed that seawater would have worked its way through and flooded whatever lies beyond. The fact that the door didn't spring open under the weight of the water inside shows there's a rock-cut jamb that prevents it from opening outwards. There's very little marine growth as the hydrogen sulphide in the water eats away any calcite secretions.'

There was a sudden sound of spray beneath them as the vacuum pump automatically kicked in to expel the puddle of water that had begun to accumulate at the far end of the chamber.

'There must also be some kind of locking device,' Jack murmured. 'If this really is the way to the heart of Atlantis then they must have gone to great lengths to keep out unwanted visitors.'

'Either way, we're going in wet,' Costas replied.

Katya looked bewildered. 'Going in wet?'

'Our only way of getting beyond those doors,' Costas explained. 'We'll walk out dry but then we'll need to seal the hull and flood the chamber. If the doors hinge inwards we'll need to equalize the pressure against the weight of water on the other side. Once inside we're going to be underwater until we reach sea level.'

Ben and Andy were making final adjustments to a robotic arm which they had extended from the central unit to a point just above the chalked circle. After they double-checked its position Ben slid a locking pin through while Andy sat behind the console and tapped in a sequence of commands.

Costas leaned over to inspect the device before addressing the other two.

'That arm's an extension of the laser we used to bore the hole in the casing. It pivots clockwise on a central axis and should slice through the hull with ease. Fortunately the *Akula*-class was made of steel, not titanium.'

'How will the hatch keep from imploding inwards when the chamber fills with water?' Katya asked.

'The cut's angled outwards so the hatch will only open into the chamber and will reseat with water pressure once we're gone.'

Andy swivelled round to face Costas. 'All systems go. Ready to activate final phase.'

Costas gripped the edge of the walkway and surveyed the equipment one last time.

'Engage.'

Katya watched in fascination as the laser began to describe a clockwise arc on the submarine's casing, the manipulator arm pivoting round the central unit like an outsized draughtsman's compass. The cut was only a few millimetres wide and followed the line of the circle chalked by Costas round the GPS fix. After the beam had traversed the first quadrant, Ben positioned a small metallic tube against the cut. With a deft movement he cracked a miniature CO_2 cylinder at the back which punched a magnetic strip through to the exterior, creating a hinge so the hatch would swing back against the membrane of the chamber wall.

'Fifteen minutes to go,' Costas said. 'Time to kit up.'

Jack lent a hand as Costas hauled himself up onto the walkway.

'The moment the hatch is shut there's no safety net. Our lives depend on our equipment and each other.'

Slowly, methodically, he double-checked the self-contained life support equipment they had donned in the DSRV. After calibrating the decompression computer on his left wrist he inspected the sealings on Katya's E-suit.

'The Kevlar mesh has good resistance to rock and metal,' he said. 'The rubber sealings divide the suit into a number of compartments, so a leak doesn't mean you'll get completely flooded. Even so we're going to have to be careful. At almost one hundred metres we're below the deepest thermocline and the temperature will only be a couple of degrees Celsius, as cold as the Atlantic.'

After getting Jack to cast an eye over his equipment Costas disengaged a small console from his left shoulder. It had a digital LCD display and was connected to the manifold on his backpack.

'When that chamber floods we'll be subject to the pressure of the surrounding seawater, almost ten atmospheres,' he explained. 'That happens to be the same depth as the Minoan wreck, so we're using our tried and tested trimix formula. Any deeper will stretch the envelope for oxygen toxicity. We badly need that passageway to go up and not down.'

'What about decompression sickness?' Katya asked.

'Shouldn't be a problem.' Costas snapped the console back on its retainer. 'At this depth the trimix is mainly helium and oxygen. The nitrogen increases as we ascend, the regulator automatically adjusting the mixture as the pressure decreases. Unless we linger too long we should only need a few brief decompression stops to let the excess gas dissipate from our bloodstreams as we go up.'

'We'll be going up,' Jack asserted. 'My guess is this will lead to some kind of peak sanctuary.'

'That makes sense geologically,' Costas said. 'It would have been a Herculean task to bore horizontally through layers of compacted basalt. They would have run into vents and even the magma chimney. It would have been easier to tunnel upwards along the line of the lava flow, at about the angle of the stairway.'

'Well, we already know these people were brilliant engineers.' Katya spoke as she fine-tuned her two-way VHF receiver to the same frequency as the other two. 'They could quarry an area the size of a football pitch, build pyramids more impressive than anything in ancient Egypt. I don't think tunnelling would have posed any great obstacle for them.' She reinstalled the communications console on her helmet. 'We should expect the unexpected.'

The only noise was the low hum of the generator as the laser worked past the halfway point. Unlike the ragged cut of an oxyacetylene torch the edge was as smooth as if it had been tooled by high-precision machinery. The steady advance of the manipulator arm seemed to count down the final minutes before they would step into the unknown.

Just as the laser was entering the final quadrant, there was a sudden vibration. It was as if an earth tremor had shaken the entire submarine. It was followed by a dull thump and muffled clanging noise, then an ominous silence.

'Engage reserve battery!' Costas ordered.

'Already done. No break detected in the current.'

The electrical hum resumed as Andy yanked out the cord leading back to the DSRV and scanned the screen for faults.

'What the hell was that?' Jack demanded.

'It came through the hull casing,' Andy replied. 'I can't source it.'

'Not forward,' Ben asserted. 'We're only a few metres from the bow cowling and would know about any impact there. It must be aft, maybe just this side of the bulkhead sealing the reactor chamber.'

Costas looked grimly at Jack. 'We have to assume the DSRV has been compromised.'

'What do you mean, *compromised*?' Katya demanded.

'I mean we've got visitors.'

Jack pulled back the slide on his Beretta and checked that a round had been chambered. After satisfying himself, he let the slide spring forward to close the receiver and gently eased the hammer to the safety position. He would be able to empty the fifteen 9 millimetre Parabellum rounds within seconds should the need arise.

'I don't understand,' Katya said. 'Is it our people?'

'Impossible,' Costas said. 'The storm will be raging until dawn tomorrow, another twelve hours from now. *Seaquest* is at least ten nautical miles north. That's too far for an Aquapod insertion, and in this weather there's no way the helicopter could get low enough to drop divers close to the site.'

'If they were IMU divers they'd have made contact by now, even just tapping Morse on the casing,' Ben said.

Katya still seemed mystified. 'How could *Seaquest* have missed them? They must have arrived before the storm began, yet the monitors showed no surface craft within a fifteen-mile radius.'

'In these conditions satellite surveillance is next to useless, but *Seaquest*'s radar should have picked up any surface anomaly in this sector.' Costas paused, his fingers drumming against the railing. 'There is one possibility.' He looked at Jack. 'A vessel could already have been in position on the far side of the volcano, hove in too close for its radar signature to be distinguishable. A submersible launched from there could have found *Kazbek* and mated with the DSRV, allowing an assault team to enter the escape trunk.'

'That would account for the noise,' Ben ventured.

'Already in position?' Katya wasn't convinced. 'How could they already be in position behind the island? No one else has the Atlantis text, no one else has the expertise to translate and interpret the directions.' She looked at the men. 'I fear for the safety of *Seaquest*.'

Jack held Katya's gaze a moment longer than the others. In that split second he sensed something was amiss, that she was withholding more than just the apprehension they were all trying to suppress. Just as he was about to question her, another jolt rattled the submarine and ended all room for speculation. He thrust the Beretta into the holster on his chest.

'Costas, you're here with Andy. That hatch may be our only escape route. Ben, you're with me.'

'I'm coming too.' Katya spoke matter-of-factly. 'We'll need all the firepower we can muster. *Akula* submarines carry a reserve armoury in the wardroom on the deck above us. I know the location.'

There was no time for argument. They quickly stripped off their SCLS backpacks and propped them against the casing.

Jack spoke as they crouched together on the walkway. 'These people haven't come to dig up ancient relics. They'll assume we've found their prize and are cut off from surface communication. Eliminate us and they can complete the transaction that went so badly wrong all those years ago. This is no longer just about Atlantis. Five metres away are enough nukes to end western civilization.'

As Katya stepped onto the first rung of the ladder leading to the deck above, she leaned aside to avoid the flurry of white precipitate dislodged by Jack's ascent. After cautiously climbing a dozen rungs she tapped his leg, at the same time signalling to Ben who was following behind.

'This is it,' she whispered.

They had reached the level above the torpedo room where they had seen the crew's quarters on their way down less than an hour before. Katya stepped through the hatch and pushed aside the debris scattered around the entrance. Jack followed close behind and Ben a moment later. As they huddled together in the gloom, Jack reached over and switched on Katya's headlamp.

'It's on the lowest setting,' he whispered. 'It should be OK as long as you don't shine into the chute where it might reflect into the alleyway above us.'

Katya traversed the narrow beam across to the far side of the room. Beyond a pair of mess tables a hatch was ajar. She gestured for them to remain put and made her way across the floor, taking care to avoid any noise and keeping the beam fixed ahead. As she crouched through the hatch, Ben leaned back into the chute to listen for any sound above.

After several minutes of tense silence Katya reappeared, her headlamp switched off to avoid shining into the chute. As she made her way towards them they could see she was festooned with equipment.

'An AKS-74U,' she whispered. 'Also a nine-millimetre Makarov pistol, same as the Walther PPK. The weapons locker had mostly been emptied and this is all I could find. There's also a box of ammunition.'

'This will do nicely.' Ben unslung the weapon from Katya's shoulder. The AKS-74U had similar dimensions to the Heckler & Koch MP5, the familiar arm of police in the west, but unlike most submachine guns it chambered a high velocity 5.45 millimetre rifle round. The engineers at the Kalashnikov Arms Design Bureau had perfected a sound suppressor which did not compromise muzzle velocity and developed an expansion chamber which made the weapon more manageable on automatic than any other firearm of similar calibre.

There was another muffled sound far away in the bowels of the submarine. Jack raised his head in alarm and they all strained to listen. What at first seemed a distant metallic clatter became steadily more distinct, a succession of dull thuds that continued for twenty seconds and then ceased.

'Footsteps,' Jack whispered. 'In the level above us back towards the escape trunk. My guess is our friends are in the control room. We must intercept them before they reach the loading chute.'

Jack and Katya each took a Kalashnikov magazine and quickly pressed in rounds from the ammunition box. Katya passed her magazine to Ben, who placed it with the remaining loose rounds in a pouch on his belt. He attached the other magazine to the weapon, pulled back the bolt and flicked the selector to safety. Katya cocked the Makarov and slid it under the tool belt on her waist.

'Right,' Jack whispered. 'We move.'

It seemed an eternity since they had stumbled on the horrifying spectre at the entrance to the sonar room. As they reached the final rungs of the ladder, Jack felt thankful for the darkness that concealed them from the sentinel's baleful gaze.

He reached down to help Katya up. Seconds later all three of them stood with weapons at the ready. Through the passageway aft they could see the glow of the emergency lighting in the control room.

Jack led them in single file along the left side of the passageway with the Beretta extended. Just before the entrance he froze and raised one arm in warning. Katya huddled behind him while Ben seemed to melt into the darkness on the other side.

From her restricted viewpoint all Katya could see was the mass of disarticulated machinery and smashed consoles. The shroud of precipitate lent a two-dimensional quality to the scene, as if they were viewing a painting too abstract to register any separate shapes or textures.

She suddenly saw why Jack had stopped. Beside the twisted remains of the periscope a ghostly figure disengaged from the background, the form only discernible when it moved. As it advanced towards them it was clear the figure was oblivious of their presence.

There was a deafening crack from Jack's Beretta. Through the storm of white that shook from the walls she watched the figure stagger back against the periscope housing and drop awkwardly to the deck. Jack fired five more times in quick succession, each round sending up a hail of bullet fragments that shrieked and rattled around the room.

Katya was stunned by the ferocity of the noise. To her horror she saw the figure slowly raise itself and level the Uzi submachine gun it was carrying towards the passageway. She could clearly make out the pockmarks where Jack's bullets had bounced harmlessly off its Kevlar exoskeleton. Their opponent opened up with his Uzi, a savage ripping noise that sent bullets whining down the passageway and sparking off the machinery behind them.

From out of the darkness to the side came a staccato burst from Ben's AKS-74U, the noise through the silencer less ear-rending than the Beretta but the effect more deadly. The rounds slammed into the advancing figure and hurled him back against the periscope housing, the bullets from his Uzi tracing a wild arc on the ceiling. Each impact punched him with the force of a jackhammer, his limbs jolting in a crazy rag-doll dance. As the Kevlar shredded, his torso slumped forward at a grotesque angle where his spine had been blown out of his back. He was dead before he hit the ground.

Another automatic weapon from somewhere in the far recess of the room added to the shattering din. The reverberations sent a tremor through the submarine, the concussions sucking the air as the bullets snapped past.

Jack crouched down and rocked on the balls of his feet like a sprinter before a race.

'Covering fire!'

Ben emptied the remainder of his magazine into the room as Jack broke cover and ran towards the central dais, the Beretta blasting into the space beyond the periscope array where the other gunfire originated. There was a scream and a clatter followed by retreating footsteps. Katya ran out behind Jack, her ears ringing from the gunfire. They were quickly joined by Ben and the three of them crouched side by side against the smashed base of the periscope housing.

'How many more?' Ben asked.

'Two, maybe three. We got one of them. If we can hold them in the passageway that'll limit their field of fire.'

The two men ejected their magazines and reloaded. While Ben pressed the loose rounds from his pouch into the magazine, Katya looked at the scene of carnage beside them.

It was a sickening sight. Amid a slew of congealing blood and spent Uzi casings the man's body sat bizarrely angled, his torso bent double and his head resting face down. The bullets had torn apart his breathing pack, the cylinders and regulator array splattered with fragments of bone and flesh. In the space below was a ragged hole where his heart and lungs had been. A ruptured hose from his oxygen regulator had blown into the cavity, producing a bloody froth that hissed and bubbled in a grotesque parody of the man's final breaths.

Katya knelt down and lifted the man's head. She shuddered and quickly let go. Jack felt sure she recognized him. He reached over to put a hand on her shoulder and she turned round.

'There has been enough death in this boat.' She suddenly looked tired. 'Now is the time to end it.'

Before Jack could stop her she stood up and raised both arms in surrender. She stepped into the gap between the periscopes.

'My name is Katya Svetlanova.' She spoke loudly in Russian, the words resonating through the chamber.

There was an immediate commotion and the sound of muffled conversation. At length a male voice responded in a dialect neither Jack nor Ben recognized. Katya lowered her arms and began a heated dialogue which lasted several minutes. She seemed in complete command of the situation, her voice exuding authority and confidence, whereas the man was wavering and deferential. After a final curt sentence she slumped down and shoved the pistol into her belt.

'He's a Kazakh,' she said. 'I told him we'd booby-trapped the passageways between here and the torpedo room. I said we'd only negotiate face to face with their leader. That won't happen, but it'll buy us time while they work out their next move.'

Jack looked at her. She had twice been instrumental in averting disaster, first by preventing an attack by *Vultura* in the

Aegean and now by negotiating with the gunmen. It seemed that as long as she was present, their adversaries would keep their distance and bide their time.

'Those men,' he said. 'I'm assuming they're our friends from *Vultura*.'

'You are correct,' she replied quietly. 'And they are utterly ruthless.'

'What do we do now?' Ben asked.

There was a dull thumping noise from far off in the submarine.

'There's your answer,' Jack replied. It was a pre-arranged signal from Costas that the operation to cut through the hull was complete. Jack got up and led the other two out of the control room, skirting round the slick of blood still seeping out of the corpse by the dais. As they retreated down the corridor, Jack glanced back one last time at the wreckage of the room to make sure they were not being followed.

They left Ben squatting in the shadows beside the top of the loading chute. He had signalled his intention and waved Jack and Katya on. With only a magazine and a half at his disposal the odds were stacked against him, but Jack knew if it came to a showdown every round would find its mark.

It took only a few minutes for Jack and Katya to traverse the now familiar route down the chute and round the edge of the torpedo room. As they reached the opening in the grating, they wordlessly donned the SCLS packs they had left there, checking each other's straps and activating the regulator consoles.

They knew what they had to do. There was nothing to be gained from lingering with Ben and Andy, a siege that could have only one outcome. Their defence rested on the potency of Katya's threat and as soon as that failed their numbers would make no difference. This was their only chance, their only hope of reaching help while the storm raged overhead.

The stakes were terrifyingly high.

As they lowered themselves onto the bilge floor they could see Costas had already shut his visor and sealed his helmet. They quickly followed suit, but not before Katya handed her pistol to Andy at the console.

'You may have more need of this than me,' she said.

Andy nodded appreciatively and holstered the weapon before turning back to the screen. While Jack quickly recounted the stand-off in the control room, Costas finished retracting the telescopic arm. The laser had cut a perfect circle a metre and a half wide in the hull casing.

'It pivots on the hinge we inserted,' Andy said. 'All I need to do now is reduce the air pressure in the chamber and it should spring outward like a hatch.'

They looked with mixed emotions at the casing, apprehensive about the perils awaiting them yet drawn by the overpowering excitement of a lost world beyond their wildest imaginings.

'OK,' said Costas. 'Let's do it.'

17

Costas crouched through, careful to avoid the razor-sharp rim where the laser had cut into the casing. He reached forward to test the strength of the magnetized membrane and then turned to help Katya and Jack. Once they were safely through, he heaved the hatch shut, fearful that a tear in the membrane would cause uncontrollable flooding in the submarine. The flush join where the hatch closed was testament to the microsurgical precision of the laser.

Although the membrane was translucent there was scarcely any natural light at this depth, and it was further blocked by the rocky overhang which extended all the way to the submarine and cut them off from the sea outside.

When they activated their headlamps, all around them the

light reflected off the crystalline lattice of the membrane, producing a brilliant shimmer of white. Ahead of them the cliff face seemed startlingly unfamiliar, the monochrome green of the hologram giving little sense of its lustrous surface. It was as if they were looking at an old-fashioned sepia photograph, a hazy border framing the tinted image of some long-lost grotto.

They walked slowly forward, their posture becoming upright as the tunnel widened. The membrane was rock-hard and provided a sure grip despite the trickle of water that ran down from the platform ahead. About eight metres in, they reached the point where the membrane had bonded magnetically with the cliff face. Costas led the way onto the stairs and crouched down to inspect the surface.

'Almost total absence of marine encrustation, not even algae. I've never seen a sea more dead than this one. If we took off our helmets this place would reek of rotten eggs from the hydrogen sulphide in the water.'

He joggled the volume setting on his communications console and looked over to make sure the others could hear. Jack murmured in acknowledgement but was preoccupied by the image in front of him. He and Katya stood side by side only a few metres from the darkness at the rear of the platform.

As Costas joined them, his headlamp added further definition to the scene. Directly in front was a rectilinear rock-cut niche about twice their height and three times as wide. It was recessed about three metres into the cliff face and had been polished to an immaculate finish. On the back wall was the image that had transfixed them on the hologram, the outline of a great double door.

Katya was the first to state the obvious, her voice taut with excitement.

'It's *gold*!'

As their beams converged they were nearly blinded by the glare. Katya cautiously trained her headlamp on the lower edge below the brilliant shimmer.

'Gold-plated, I'd guess,' Costas said matter-of-factly. 'Beaten and burnished and then attached to stone slabs underneath. There was plenty of river gold in the Caucasus at this period but it would have stretched the resource to make these solid gold. They would have been too soft anyway.'

Through the chink round the edge a fine sheen of water sprayed out from the cavity beyond. The light from their headlamps refracted into a myriad tiny rainbows, a kaleidoscopic halo that added to the dazzling effect of the gold.

'They're butted against a sill, a low jamb in the rock all round the edge.' Costas was peering at the lower right-hand corner. 'That's what's keeping the doors from bursting out on us. They're designed to open inwards as we thought.'

He stood back and turned to Jack. 'We need to flood this chamber to equalize the water pressure on both sides of the door. Are we ready?'

The other two nodded and adjusted their regulator consoles, changing their breathing gas from compressed air to the trimix necessary to survive almost one hundred metres below sea level. Katya swayed slightly, feeling a rush of light-headedness as the unfamiliar mixture came online. Costas reached over to steady her.

'You'll get used to it,' he said. 'It'll clear your head for all those inscriptions you're going to translate.'

Katya and Jack checked each other's cylinder pressures before giving the OK signal to Costas, who slid back along the membrane to the submarine. After activating his own regulator he gave a succession of sharp raps on the casing with his multi-tool. Seconds later a violent jet of water burst through the hole in the centre of the hatch, slamming into the cliff with the force of a water cannon. Andy had reversed the high-pressure pump and drawn the water up from the bilges through a filtration device to cleanse it of toxins and solid matter.

They flattened themselves against the wall to avoid the blast of water that thundered past them. As it rebounded off the rock and began to soak them, Jack gasped in pain.

'What is it?' Katya demanded. 'Are you all right?'

'It's nothing.'

Jack's posture said exactly the opposite, his body contorted as he held himself against the rock. It was only as the water welled up around their legs that he slowly straightened himself, his rasping breath clearly audible through the intercom.

'It was during our little showdown.' His tone belied his agony. 'I took a hit on the right side when we rushed the room. I didn't say anything because there was nothing to be done. The bullet penetrated the Kevlar so I've got a leaky chamber. The water's cold. It'll pass.'

The reality was more serious. Even though it was only a low-velocity Uzi round, the bullet had fractured a rib and left a penetrating flesh wound. He had already lost a lot of blood and he knew he would soon be running on borrowed time. The rush of water had staunched the bleeding and was numbing the pain, but the rent in his suit was worse than he had intimated. In the near-freezing conditions it would only be a matter of time before his core temperature dropped to danger level.

As he tried to control his breathing he felt a sudden wave of dizziness, a sure sign of oxygen depletion. His body's craving for nourishment after losing so much blood was not being satisfied. He began to hyperventilate.

Not again.

He went rigid as the water seethed up and enveloped him. He felt a clawing need for space as the gap above the water diminished, a rising fear as claustrophobia began to take hold.

He desperately needed to convince himself it was physiological, a natural reaction as his body struggled to adjust, not blind panic.

Relax. Let it go.

His breathing was coming in ragged gulps as he knelt on the floor, his arms hanging and his head bowed as the noise of his regulator was drowned out by the seething cauldron around him. He was only just conscious of Katya and Costas in front, seemingly oblivious of him, their bodies swathed in white water as they watched the surface level rise.

He closed his eyes.

A surge of water suddenly pushed him back, encircling his body as if he were in the vortex of a whirlpool. On either side it seemed to caress him as the weight in front pressed down hard, a cloying mass that pinned him against the membrane.

He opened his eyes onto horror.

All he could see was a hideous visage pressed up against him, its eyeless sockets and leering grin rebounding like a demented puppet, its ghostly arms flapping as it tried to encircle him in a deathly embrace. With each surge the water clouded with flecks of white and grey that seemed to detach from the apparition like snow.

Jack was powerless to resist, caught in a nightmare of paralysis with no escape. It bore down on him relentlessly, overwhelmingly.

He stopped breathing, his mouth frozen in mid-scream.

It was a hallucination.

His rational mind told him he was in the grip of narcosis. *The man they had killed in the gun battle. The hanging corpse in the sonar room.* It was the ghosts of the submarine, wraiths who had stayed on to haunt them.

He closed his eyes tight, all his reserves fighting the slide into darkness.

In a flash he was back in the mineshaft five months ago, in the place of his nemesis. Once again he felt the shock as the gas surged up the shaft and slammed him against the beam, severing his air supply and extinguishing all light. The choking suffocation in the pitch darkness before Costas found him and buddy-breathed him back to life. The horror as the second surge blew him out of Costas' grasp and towards the surface. The hours in the recompression chamber, hours of crushing exhaustion punctuated by moments of sheer terror as consciousness sent him back to the instant of panic over and over again. It had been the experience all divers dread, the one that shatters the confidence built up precariously over the years, toppling him into a world where all the controls, all the parameters, had to be painstakingly rebuilt from scratch.

And now it was happening again.

'Jack! Look at me. Everything's all right. It's gone.'

Costas stared into Jack's wide-open eyes and gripped him by the shoulders. As the noise of the water jet subsided and he began to hear his exhaust again, Jack heaved a shuddering breath and began to relax.

It was Costas. He was still in the chamber.

'It must have been one of the bodies Kuznetsov ejected from the torpedo tube. Got lodged in the rock niche and was then blown out by the water jet. Not a pretty sight.' Costas gestured towards the white-flecked form now wafting in the water towards the submarine's casing, its torso obscenely mangled where Costas had punched it aside, causing the adiposed tissue that still clung to the skeleton to disintegrate.

Instead of revulsion Jack felt an enormous elation, the exhilaration of the survivor who has faced oblivion and beaten it. The rush of adrenalin would propel him through whatever lay ahead of them.

Katya had been blown back by the force of the water against the membrane and had been oblivious to his panic. Jack looked up at her and spoke hoarsely through the intercom, his breath still coming in ragged bursts.

'My turn for a shock, that's all.'

She could never know the demons that had haunted him, the force that had beckoned him on and nearly spelled the end for him.

The swirling maelstrom ended and the water attained a limpid clarity soon after the turbulence had ceased. Costas' eyes remained locked on Jack's until he could see he had fully relaxed. After a moment Costas reached down and undid the velcro straps that held Jack's fins to his legs, pulling the silicon blades over his feet and snapping them in place.

Jack rolled over and watched the bubbles from his exhaust coalesce into little pools of translucence that wobbled and shimmered into each other on the ceiling of the membrane. He felt his cylinder pack scrape along the bottom and quickly injected a blast of air into his suit to achieve neutral buoyancy.

Costas swam from the casing towards the rock face. As he reached it an incomprehensible high-pitched noise filled their earphones. Jack found himself shaking uncontrollably, the terror of the last few minutes having transformed into delirious relief.

'Hey, Mickey Mouse,' he said. 'I think you should activate your voice modulator.'

The combination of extreme pressure and helium distorted the voice to a comical degree, and IMU had developed a compensating device to avoid precisely the response Jack was finding so difficult to control.

'My apologies. I'll try again.' Costas turned a dial on the side of his visor. He found a best-fit frequency and switched to automatic, ensuring the modulator would respond to changes in pressure and gas make-up as their depth altered.

'Andy has relaxed the magnetization to make the membrane semi-flexible, allowing the ambient pressure of the sea to pass through into this space and match the pressure of the water behind that door. It's 9.8 bar, almost 100 metres. At this depth the trimix only gives us half an hour.'

With their headlamps reduced to half-beam to limit the reflection, they could make out more features of the entranceway. On each panel was the magnificent bull's horn symbol which had been visible in the hologram, life-size forms, beaten in gold, which stood out in low relief.

Costas extracted another contraption from his tool belt.

'Something I knocked up in the geophysics lab at IMU,' he said. 'Ground penetrating radar, generating broadband electromagnetic waves to reveal subsurface images. We call them acoustic flashlights. The GPR signal only goes five metres but should tell us whether there's solid obstruction on the other side.'

He extended the transducer antenna and swam to and fro along the base of the entranceway, eventually coming to rest beside the crack between the doors.

'It's clear,' he announced. 'No resistance after half a metre, which must be the thickness of the doors. I looked closely along the lower jamb and there's nothing that should cause us trouble.'

'Metallic corrosion?' Katya enquired.

'Gold doesn't corrode perceptibly in seawater.'

Costas replaced the unit in his belt and arched his fingers

over the sill below the doors. He pulled his body back and forth a few times then rested.

'Here goes,' he said.

In a sudden frenzy of finning he rocketed himself forward, bringing the full force of his body to bear on the door. He continued heaving for a few moments before settling down exhausted. The doors seemed like solid rock, the two-metre high outline mere etchings on the cliff face.

'Nothing doing,' he gasped bleakly.

'Wait. Look at this.'

Jack had been hovering a metre above and had been enveloped in a sheen of bubbles from Costas' exhaust. His eye had been caught by a curious feature refracted through the turbulence, an anomaly too small to have been picked up by the hologram laser.

It looked like a shallow, saucer-sized depression centred between the two sets of bull's horns. The crack between the doors was concealed beneath it, making it seem like a seal stamped into the metal after they had been shut for the last time.

Katya moved up beside him and reached out to touch it.

'It feels crystalline,' she said. 'It's complex, lots of right angles and flat planes.'

The crystal was immaculate, so nearly flawless it was almost invisible. The movement of Katya's hand as she traced the shape looked like the gesticulations of a mime artist. It was only when they dimmed their headlamps that a form began to emerge, the light refracting like a prism to reveal lines and angles.

When Jack moved, the lines suddenly coalesced into a familiar shape.

'My God,' he breathed. 'The Atlantis symbol!'

For a moment they stared in amazement, the trials of the

last few hours suddenly fallen away as they were sucked back into the extraordinary excitement of discovery.

'In the Aquapods we saw the symbol carved into a roundel in front of the pyramids,' Jack said. 'It would seem consistent to have it here as well.'

'Yes,' said Katya. 'A sort of talisman to proclaim the sanctity of the place.'

Costas pressed his visor against the crystal. 'The carving's incredible,' he murmured. 'Most silica compounds wouldn't last this long in seawater with such high sulphur content without forming a reaction patina.'

Jack's mind was racing as he stared at the door. Suddenly he grunted and pulled out an oblong package which he had wedged in beside the Beretta.

'I brought along a little talisman of my own.'

He unwrapped the copy of the gold disc from the Minoan wreck. As he turned it over to reveal the symbol, the light from his headlamp danced off the surface.

'Behold the key to Atlantis,' he said jubilantly.

Costas erupted with excitement. 'Of course!' He took the disc from Jack and held it up. 'The convex shape exactly matches the concavity on the door. The symbol on the disc is in reverse, pressed into the metal, whereas the crystal is a mirror image in obverse. The disc should fit like a key into a lock.'

'I had a hunch it might prove useful,' Jack said.

'That door isn't going to budge an inch,' Costas said. 'This could be our only chance.'

Jack finned upwards a few strokes until he was directly in front of the symbol on the door, Katya immediately to his left.

'Only one way to find out,' he said.

18

As Jack aligned the disc with the door the crystal seemed to be pulling him in, as if some primeval force were drawing together two halves of a whole which destiny had kept apart for too long. And sure enough, the disc mated with the crystal and slid smoothly inwards until it was flush with the doors.

'Bingo,' he said quietly.

He placed his palm on the disc and kicked hard with his fins to bring pressure to bear. Abruptly the disc sank inwards and spun rapidly clockwise, the motion causing the water to corkscrew like the wake from a propeller. As it stopped turning there was a low grinding noise, the disc disengaged and the doors swung ajar.

There was little resistance as Jack pushed the doors wide.

Their view was momentarily obscured by the sheen of turbulence where ice-cold water inside mingled with the seawater around them. Jack sucked in his breath to conceal a spasm of pain, a stabbing sensation where the tear in his suit had exposed his chest to the freezing water. The other two saw his agony but knew he would rebuff their sympathy.

Costas had floated over the sill and was examining the mechanism revealed in the edge of the door.

'Fascinating,' he murmured. 'The door was held by a granite beam like a crossbar, in two lengths scarfed together. The upper surface has been carved into ridges and furrows like a cog. The crystal was embedded in a stone cylinder with matching ridges. When Jack pressed the disc, the cogs engaged.'

Costas prised the disc from the crystal and passed it to Jack for safekeeping.

'How did it spin on its own?' Katya asked.

'The ends of the beam are weighted, probably inside cavities adjacent to the jambs. When the cog was engaged, the weights pulled the two lengths apart, spinning the cylinder.'

'To onlookers the automation would have seemed miraculous, the work of the gods,' Jack said.

'An impressive piece of engineering.'

'Simplicity of purpose, economy of design, durability of materials.' Costas grinned at them through his visor. 'It would have won first prize hands down in the student competition at MIT when I was there.'

They turned their headlamps on full beam. The water ahead was crystal clear, free from contaminants in the thousands of years since it first seeped through the cracks in the doorway.

The light sparkled off the rock walls as their beams traversed from side to side. They were looking into a rectangular chamber the size of the torpedo room in the submarine. Immediately in front was a massive pedestal hewn from the living rock.

'It's an altar!' Jack exclaimed. 'You can see the channels where the blood spilled down the stairs outside.'

'Human sacrifice?' Costas queried.

'It has a long history among the Semitic peoples of the Near East,' Katya said. 'Think of Abraham and Isaac in the Old Testament.'

'But never on a mass scale,' Jack countered. 'The story of Abraham and Isaac is powerful precisely because it's exceptional. The Minoans also sacrificed humans, but the only evidence is a peak sanctuary near Knossos where an earthquake toppled the temple in mid-ritual and preserved the skeleton. It was probably only ever performed in relation to catastrophes like the eruption of Thera.'

They were finning towards the pedestal in the centre of the chamber, their beams converging on the edge of the sacrificial platform. As the top came into view they were confronted by an image almost too fantastic to comprehend, a spectre that vanished like a genie as soon as they came close to it.

'Did you see what I saw?' Katya breathed.

'Extraordinary,' Costas murmured. 'The bones must have disintegrated thousands of years ago, but in the stillness the calcium salts remained where they fell. The slightest disturbance and it disappeared like a puff of smoke.'

For a split second they had seen a recumbent bull, its giant shape reduced to an imprint of white streaks like a faded photographic negative. In the corners of the table they could make out holes where its limbs had been tied down before the sacrifice, the rope long since disappeared as the seawater rose and took the carcass in its icy embrace.

Jack picked up a dagger lying on one side of the table. The

stone handle was incised with a fearsome beast, half bull, half eagle.

'There's your answer,' he said softly. 'The courtyard with the colossal statue by the shoreline was the world's first bullfighting arena. The doomed animals were led up the processional way between the pyramids and then driven up the stairs to this slab. It would have been a spectacular site, overlooking the entire city on the plain below, the sacrifice perhaps timed to coincide with the first flash of sunlight overhead through the twin peaks of the volcano to the horns of the bull-sphinx in the courtyard far below. The whole city must have come to a standstill.'

He paused and looked at the other two solemnly through his visor. 'We've just borne witness to the final sacrifice, the last desperate attempt by the priests to repel the rising seas before the doors to this chamber were locked shut for all time.'

They finned over the altar and headed towards a yawning black hole in the rear of the chamber. The shimmer grew more intense as they swam forward, the light from their headlamps sparkling off the walls as if they were billowing curtains of crystal and gold.

'*Golden-walled Atlantis*,' Jack said quietly.

Just before they reached the portal, Costas veered off to the right, his beam reduced to a narrow orb as he closed in on the wall.

'It's iron pyrites, fool's gold.' His voice was hushed in awe. 'The crystals are so large and close-set they look like gold plate until you get close up.'

'But the island's volcanic, made of igneous rock,' Katya said.

'Mainly basalt,' Costas agreed. 'Molten magma that cooled too quickly for mineral crystals to form. The basalt between the cliff and the ancient shoreline was low in silica so cooled slowly as it flowed out over the limestone substrate. Further up it formed from acidic lava rich in silica that solidified as soon as it hit the surface. In the Aquapods we saw fissures of obsidian, the black volcanic glass that forms when rhyolitic lava is quickly chilled.'

'Obsidian blades were the sharpest known until the development of high-carbon steel in the Middle Ages,' Jack said. 'That dagger was obsidian.'

Costas came towards them along the back wall. 'Incredible,' he mused. 'Obsidian for tools, tufa for masonry, volcanic dust for mortar, salt for food preservation. Not to mention the richest farmland anywhere and a sea teeming with fish. These people had it all.'

'What about the granite in the doors?' Katya persisted.

'Also igneous,' Costas replied. 'But it's not the result of volcanic eruption. It's an intrusive rock that forms deep in the earth's crust as the magma slowly cools, producing crystalline structures dominated by feldspar and quartz. It's called plutonic after the Greek god of the underworld. It was thrust upwards by plate tectonics.'

'That explains another resource,' Jack interjected. 'The pressure also metamorphosed seabed limestone into marble, providing fine-grained stone for those sculptures outside. There must be outcrops lower down these slopes and on that ridge to the west.'

'We're inside a composite volcano,' Costas continued. 'A combination cinder cone and shield volcano, the lava interlayered with pyroclastic ash and rock. Think Mount Saint Helens, Vesuvius, Thera. Instead of building up behind a plug and erupting explosively the magma wells up through a folded outcrop of plutonic rock and solidifies as a basaltic shield, an event repeated every time the pressure builds up. My guess is that the deeper reaches of this rock are a seething cauldron of gas and lava that force their way through fissures to leave a honeycomb of passageways and caverns. Deep down this volcano is literally riddled with rivers of fire.'

'And the fool's gold?' Katya asked.

'An unusually dense node of iron forced up with the granite. Slow cooling deep in the earth's crust formed huge crystals. They're fabulous, a unique discovery.'

They turned back for one last look at the world they were leaving. In their headlamps the water was suffused with colour, the light sparkling off the rock in a shimmer of gold.

'This chamber is a geologist's dream,' Costas murmured reverentially. 'Polish it up and you've got a spectacle that would dazzle any onlooker. To the priests it must have seemed a godsend. An awesome complement to the pyrotechnics of the volcano itself.'

Beyond the silhouette of the altar they could just make out the casing of the submarine at the end of the tunnel. It was a reminder of the sinister enemy that barred their way back to the world above, that their only hope of rescue for Ben and Andy lay in the pitch-blackness ahead.

Before confronting the forbidding darkness of the portal, Costas finned back to the centre of the chamber. He extracted an item from his tool belt and swam round the altar before returning, an orange tape reeling out of a spool on his backpack.

'It's something I thought of when you were telling us of legends that hark back to conflict between the Mycenaeans and Minoans in the Bronze Age,' he explained. 'When Theseus arrived at Knossos to kill the Minotaur he was given a ball of thread by Ariadne to guide him through the labyrinth. Under this rock we have no access to GPS and can only navigate by dead-reckoning with compass and depth gauge. Ariadne's thread may be the only safety line we've got.'

★

Jack led the way out of the sacrificial chamber and through the portal, his headlamp trained on the tunnel ahead. After about ten metres the passageway narrowed and curved off to the right. He paused to let the other two draw up on either side of him, the space just wide enough to accommodate them line abreast.

They were alone in the deathly stillness of a place no human had entered since the dawn of civilization. Jack experienced a familiar surge of excitement, the burst of adrenalin briefly alleviating the debilitating effects of his wound and urging him on into the unknown.

The passageway began to snake along in alternating curves, each bend seeming to exaggerate the distance from the entrance. The experience was strangely disorientating, as if the ancient architects of this world had known the unsettling effect the absence of straight lines had on the human sense of direction.

They paused while Costas paid out the final length of tape and attached a fresh spool to his back. In the narrow confines, their lamps cast a brilliant light on the walls around them, the surface lustrous as if it had been kept polished over the millennia.

Jack finned a few metres ahead and noticed an aberration in the wall.

'I've got markings.'

The other two quickly swam up to join him.

'Man-made,' Costas asserted. 'Chiselled into the rock. They're just like the cartouches around those precursor hieroglyphics Hiebermeyer found on that ancient stone in the temple where Solon visited the high priest.'

Hundreds of nearly identical markings were aligned in twenty horizontal registers that extended beyond the next curve in the passageway. Each marking comprised a symbol surrounded by an oval border, the cartouche Costas had referred to. The symbols within the cartouches were rectilinear, each with a vertical stem and containing varying numbers and arrangements of horizontal bars branching off to either side.

'They look like runes,' Costas said.

'Impossible,' Katya retorted. 'Runes derive from the Etruscan and Latin alphabets, from contact with the Mediterranean during the classical period. Six thousand years too late for us.'

The other two withdrew to allow her more space. She scanned one of the registers close up, then pushed away for a wider view.

'I don't believe this is an alphabet at all,' she said. 'In an alphabet there's a direct correspondence between graphemes and phonemes, between the symbol and the unit of sound. Most alphabets have twenty to thirty symbols and few languages have more than forty significant sounds. There are too many permutations here, in the number and location of the horizontal bars. Conversely there aren't enough for these to be logograms, where the symbol represents a word, as in Chinese.'

'Syllabic?' Costas suggested.

Katya shook her head. 'The symbols on the Phaistos discs are syllabic phonograms. There's no way the Atlanteans would have developed two syllabic systems to be used in a sacred context.'

'Prepare to be amazed.' Costas' voice was loud and clear on the intercom even though he had disappeared round the next curve in the passageway. The other two swam towards him, their lights converging as they followed his gaze.

The symbols ended abruptly at a vertical line incised from

floor to ceiling. Beyond it was a magnificent bull, its outline carved in bas-relief. It was life-sized, its enormous head with curved horns facing them, its massive body resting on a platform, its legs splayed. The eyes had been deeply carved to show the iris and were preternaturally wide, as if the beast had been caught in a moment of primordial fear.

'Of course,' Katya suddenly exclaimed. 'They're numerical!'

Jack immediately understood. 'This is the sacrificial ritual in the entrance chamber,' he enthused. 'The symbols must be a tally, a record of each sacrifice.'

'They're even arranged *boustrophēdon*.' Katya glanced at Costas. 'As you know from modern Greek, *bous* means ox and *strophos* turning. "As the ox turns when ploughing a field", in alternate directions. Like snakes and ladders.' She pointed to the way the line framing each cartouche looped round to the one below.

Costas swivelled round to address Jack, his eyes gleaming with excitement.

'When would sacrifices have taken place?'

'Events associated with the harvest and the seasons. Summer and winter solstices, the coming of spring, thanksgiving for crops.'

'The lunar cycle?' Costas prompted.

'Very possibly,' Jack replied. 'The interval between full moons was probably the first exact measurement of time ever made. The difference between the lunar and solar year really mattered to people dependent on knowing where they were in the crop cycle. The synodic cycle, the lunar cycle, falls short of the solar year by eleven days, so an additional month is intercalated every three or four years. Celestial observations to measure the difference were probably carried out at the Minoan peak sanctuaries. I'll bet there's an observatory here as well.'

Costas pointed to a curious set of symbols directly above the bull.

'That's why I ask,' he said.

What had at first seemed an abstract embellishment suddenly took on new meaning. Immediately above the animal's spine was a roundel about two palm widths across. On either side a succession of mirror images fanned out symmetrically, first a half-roundel, then a quarter-roundel and finally a single curved line.

'Behold the lunar cycle,' Costas proclaimed. 'New moon, quarter moon, half moon, full moon, then the same in reverse.'

'The gold disc,' Jack said softly. 'It was a lunar symbol. The obverse represents the full moon, the elliptical profile depicts the moon as it passes through its monthly cycle.'

He did not need to take out the disc for them to know he was right, that the lentoid shape exactly matched the concave depression of the roundel carved in the rock above them.

Costas swam a few metres to the left of the bull, the mass of wall carvings laid out in front of him like some exotic eastern carpet.

'The maximum number of bars on the right-hand side of each stem is six, and often the slashes continue up the left side as well. The fact that there are sometimes seven on that side almost killed my theory.'

'Which is?' Jack asked.

They could hear Costas draw a deep breath from his regulator. 'Each cartouche represents a year, each horizontal bar a month. You go up the right side first, then up the left. January's lower right, December's upper left.'

Jack was swimming along the wall above Costas where most of the cartouches contained the maximum number of lines.

'Of course,' he exclaimed. 'Those with the extra line contain thirteen altogether. They must represent years with the extra month in the lunar calendar. Look at the sequence here. The leap month occurs alternately every three and four cartouches, exactly what you'd need to keep the lunar year in step with the solar cycle.'

'How do you account for the missing months?' Katya had sunk to the floor and was examining the lower cartouches. Some contained only the vertical line, and others only one or two bars at seemingly random points on either side.

'Most sacrifices are propitiatory, right? They're carried out in the hope of a return, some sign of favour from the gods. Where better than an active volcano? Magma outflows, seismic tremors, even rainbows caused by gas and steam.'

'So a sacrifice was always carried out at the beginning of the lunar month.' Katya had immediately followed Costas' drift. 'If a sign was observed before the next new moon then a line was carved. If not then no marking.'

'Exactly,' Costas said. 'The central part in front of Jack has many symbols, pretty well every month for twenty-five or thirty years. Then there are long periods with few symbols. My guess is we'd see a comparable pattern of volatility for this type of volcano, with several decades of activity alternating with similar periods of near dormancy. We're not talking spectacular eruptions but more like a cauldron bubbling over before slowly filling up again.'

'To judge by the marking, the last sacrifice was in May or June, precisely the time of year for the flood indicated by the pollen analyses from Trabzon,' said Katya. 'For several years before there are no markings at all. In their last ever sacrifice it looks like they got lucky.'

'They needed it,' Costas said wryly.

They stared at the final symbol, a hastily gouged marking

that contrasted starkly with the careful incisions of previous years. They could scarcely imagine the terror of the people as they faced unimaginable catastrophe, desperately seeking some sign of hope before abandoning a homeland where they had prospered since history began.

Jack finned back to the opposite wall so he could take in most of the symbols at a glance.

'There are about fifteen hundred cartouches altogether,' he calculated. 'Working back from a flood date of 5545 BC, that takes us to the eighth millennium BC. It's incredible. Fifteen hundred years of continuous use, uninterrupted by war or natural disaster, a time when there were enough animals for a bull sacrifice every month. Atlantis did not spring up overnight.'

'Remember we're only looking at a record of events since the passageway was enlarged,' Costas cautioned. 'This was originally a volcanic fissure accessible from outside. I'll bet this place was visited long before the first sacrifice.'

'We need to move,' Jack said. 'We don't know what lies ahead.'

The bull carving assumed a sinuous, elongated shape as it curved round the final bend in the wall. As they passed the tail, the passageway straightened and continued without deviation as far as their lights could penetrate. On either side niches were carved into the rock, each one a shallow bowl inside a recessed overhang like a miniature wayside shrine.

'For torches or candles, probably of tallow, animal fat,' Jack observed.

'Good to know those bull carcasses were put to some use,' Costas said.

They forged ahead. After about fifteen metres the passageway ended abruptly at three entranceways, two set obliquely on either side of the centre one. The passages beyond seemed to recede identically into the pitch darkness of the volcano's core.

'Another test,' Costas said bleakly.

'Not the central passageway,' Jack said. 'It's too obvious.'

Katya was peering through the right-hand entrance and the other two gravitated towards her. They crowded together at the sill and nodded wordlessly to each other. Katya pulled herself forward and took the lead. The passageway was only wide enough for two of them side by side and barely high enough to hover upright.

It continued unswervingly for twenty metres, the smooth walls giving nothing away. The gap between Katya and the other two increased as Costas stopped to add another reel to the tape that trailed behind him while Jack waited for him. He put his gloved hand to the rent on his side.

He grimaced. 'The water, it's warmer. I can feel it.'

Neither Costas nor Katya had any sense of the outside temperature in their E-suits, and until now they had seen no reason to monitor the thermometers on their consoles.

'I've got a bad feeling about this,' Costas said. 'There must be a volcanic vent that's boiling it up. We need to get out of here.'

They suddenly realized Katya was not responding. As Jack anxiously swam forward, the reason became apparent. His earphones crackled with a crescendo of static that would have drowned out any reception.

'Localized electromagnetic field.' Costas' voice became clearer as he swam alongside. 'Some kind of lodestone in the rock, a concentrated mineral extrusion like the fool's gold in the entrance chamber.'

A curve to the right showed where Katya had disappeared from view. They finned rapidly, their attention fully focused on the darkness ahead. As they rounded the bend the walls changed from a lustrous polish to the rough-hewn appearance of a quarry face. The view ahead blurred and wavered like a mirage.

'It's scalding,' Jack gasped. 'I can't go any further.'

They had passed beyond the manmade walls and were now surrounded by the jagged contours of a volcanic fissure. Katya suddenly appeared through the murk like a phantasm in a desert storm and in that split second they sensed some dark force beyond, some denizen of the deep hurtling towards them with inexorable intent.

'Go!' Katya screamed. 'Back to the passageway!'

Jack reached out towards her but was thrown back by an enormous surge he was powerless to resist. All they could do was try desperately to avoid the serrated edges of the lava as they tumbled through the water at terrifying speed. Before they knew it they were back within the smooth walls of the passageway. An immense tremor left them shocked and dazed almost ten metres in from the fissure.

Katya was hyperventilating and fighting to control her breathing. Jack swam over to her and checked her equipment. For a moment, a fleeting moment, he remembered his own fear, but he firmly parcelled it away in his mind, determined that it had burned its last and was now extinguished.

'I think that was the wrong way,' she panted.

Costas righted himself and swam back a few metres to splice the tape which had been severed by the force that had nearly annihilated them. They had re-entered the zone of magnetic disturbance and his voice crackled over the intercom.

'A phreatic explosion. Happens when water hits molten lava. Cooks off like gunpowder.' He paused to catch his breath, his sentences punctuated by deep pulls on his regulator. 'And this fissure's like a gun barrel. If it hadn't blown through a vent somewhere behind us we'd be the latest addition to the sacrificial tally.'

They quickly returned to the three entranceways. They avoided the central one, continuing to trust Jack's instinct. As they approached the left-hand entranceway, Jack sank to the floor, suddenly overcome by a wave of nausea as his body struggled to cope with the change from searing heat to the frigid waters of the passageway.

'I'm all right,' he gasped. 'Just give me a moment.'

Costas looked at him with concern and then followed Katya to the sill of the doorway. She had still not recovered from the shock and her voice was tense.

'Your turn to lead,' she said. 'I want to stay beside Jack.'

19

The left-hand tunnel angled abruptly downwards, the walls constricting further and funnelling them into the bowels of the volcano. The image fuelled the turmoil in Jack's system as he battled his wound. Now he also had to cope with the debilitating effects of increased pressure as they sank into the icy blackness of the tunnel.

'I can see steps chiselled out below,' Costas announced. 'We'll have to pray it levels out soon. Another ten metres and we're gone.'

Costas anxiously monitored his depth gauge as they descended, their automatic buoyancy compensators bleeding enough air into their suits to keep them from plummeting. After a few metres the drop increased alarmingly. For a moment Jack and Katya could see nothing, their vision obscured by the cloud of bubbles from Costas' exhaust as he sank directly beneath them.

'It's all right,' his voice came up. 'I can see a floor.'

The steps below turned to footholds as the face became vertical. Jack sank down the final few metres and landed on his knees. Katya followed.

'One hundred and sixteen metres,' Costas muttered. 'That's it for this trimix solution. Another few metres and the regulators would have aborted.'

There was no response from the other two and Costas anxiously scanned their faces for signs of nitrogen narcosis. As his eyes grew accustomed to the surroundings he realized why they were silent. The claustrophobic confines of the tunnel had given way to a vast magma chamber, its fiery contents long since dissipated to leave an elongated cavity like the hall of a medieval castle. The analogy seemed particularly apt as Costas looked back at their point of entry. The tunnel above gaped like the chute of an ancient chimney, the rock face below spreading into a recess like a baronial fireplace.

The chamber seemed an entirely natural phenomenon, its nave-like shape the result of titanic forces in the earth's crust rather than any human agency. As Costas' mind adjusted to the size of the room he began to see swirling patterns in the basalt on either side, a tumult of twisted shapes as if a cascading river of lava had frozen in mid-flow. Suddenly he saw what had captivated the other two. It was as if he had been presented with a brain-teaser and his mind had intuitively focused on the forms of the geology. As soon as he recognized the alternative, a fantastic scene revealed itself before his eyes. The walls were covered with a spectacular menagerie of animals painted and incised into the rock, their forms respecting the contours of the chamber and taking advantage of natural patterns in the basalt. Some were life-sized, others larger than life, but all were rendered in a highly naturalistic style that made their identification easy.

At a glance Costas could make out rhinoceros, bison, deer, horses, huge cats and bulls. There were hundreds of them, some standing alone but most in overlapping groups, image after image piled on top of each other like a reused canvas. The effect was startlingly three-dimensional, and combined with the mildly hallucinogenic effect of the nitrogen, they seemed to Costas to be alive, a mass of slavering beasts surging towards him like some wayward mirage.

'Incredible.' Jack finally broke the silence, his voice hushed with awe. 'The hall of the ancestors.'

Costas shook away the phantom image and looked questioningly at his friend.

'You hinted at it,' Jack explained. 'That there were people here long before those first bull sacrifices. Well, here's your evidence. These paintings are from the Upper Palaeolithic, the final period of the Old Stone Age when people hunted big game along the edge of the glaciers. We've just swum back thousands of years to the first explosion of human artistic creativity, thirty-five to twelve thousand years ago.'

'How can you be sure?'

'Look at the species.'

They finned in line abreast towards the centre of the gallery, the exhaust from their breathing rising in great shrouds of silver towards the ceiling. Everywhere they aimed their headlamps, new marvels of ancient art appeared. Despite the urgent need to press on, they were drawn by the enormity of what they were seeing.

'There are no domesticates,' Katya ventured. 'No cows, sheep, pigs. And some of these look like extinct species to me.'

'Exactly,' Jack said, his excitement evident. 'Ice Age

megafauna, outsized mammals that died out at the end of the Pleistocene ten thousand years ago. You can even identify the subspecies. This is amazing. The bulls, for example, are not modern cattle but aurochs, *Bos primigenius*, a type of wild ox ancestral to domestic cattle which had disappeared in this region by the Neolithic. The rhino is the woolly rhinoceros, another extinct type that stood more than two metres tall. They looked like oversized musk ox, the only relic of Pleistocene megafauna to survive today.'

As they progressed further, an immense form came into view on the left-hand wall, its torso a natural bulge in the rock. It stood almost three times their height and had huge, sweeping tusks at least six metres long.

'A woolly mammoth!' Jack exclaimed. 'Mammoths became extinct south of the Caucasus during the last interglacial, when it became too warm for them this far south. Either these artists ranged incredibly widely, up to the edge of the glaciers on the northern steppes, or we're looking at a painting at least forty thousand years old.'

'I thought Palaeolithic cave paintings were only found in western Europe,' Katya murmured.

'Mainly in the Pyrenees and the Dordogne, most famously at Altamira and Lascaux. These are the only ones east of Italy, the first proof that European hunter-gatherers reached the shores of western Asia.'

'I take it these paintings had some kind of religious significance,' Costas said. 'An animal cult, the worship of animal spirits?'

'At the dawn of art many of these representations would have had a magical quality,' Jack affirmed. 'Especially if they were the work of shamans or medicine men, people who sought out places like this where their images would seem most awesome.'

'Or medicine women,' Katya interjected. 'Many hunter-gatherer societies were matriarchal and worshipped a mother goddess. The women didn't just rear children and pick berries.'

Another colossal image came into view, this time a giant male aurochs. It was mirrored by an identical image on the opposite wall, a unique arrangement that made them stand out like fearsome sentinels confronting anyone advancing through the gallery. They were crouched forward on heavily muscled forelegs and were in a state of high sexual arousal.

'They look like the sacrificial bull in the passageway,' Costas observed. 'And the posture's the same as the giant bull-sphinx in the courtyard.'

Jack was grappling with the implications of their discovery. 'By the time of the flood most of these animals would have been mythical beasts of the past, the mammoth and rhinoceros being like the sphinx or griffon to later cultures. The one thread of continuity was the bull. For prehistoric hunters the rampant aurochs was the most powerful symbol of potency. For early farmers oxen were crucial as draught animals, and cattle for meat, milk and hides.'

'Are you saying the Neolithic people of Atlantis worshipped images that were already thirty thousand years old?' Costas asked incredulously.

'Not all the paintings are likely to be that old,' Jack replied. 'Most galleries of cave art are not homogeneous, but represent episodic accumulations over long periods with older paintings being retouched or replaced. But even the most recent additions, from the very end of the Ice Age, must be at least twelve thousand years old, more than five thousand years before the end of Atlantis.'

'As far back for the people of Atlantis as the Bronze Age is for us,' Katya said.

'In early societies art generally survived only if it continued to have cultural or religious significance,' Jack asserted. 'Up to this point all of the passageways have been squared and polished, yet the custodians of Atlantis deliberately left this chamber unaltered. These paintings were venerated as ancestral images.'

He finned over and inspected the mammoth's immense haunch, careful not to disturb the pigments which had survived so long in the frigid stillness of the water.

'I knew Atlantis would hold extraordinary surprises,' he said. 'But I never expected to find the first clear link between the beliefs of early *Homo sapiens* and our Neolithic ancestors, a cult of the bull that has existed since the dawn of time.' He gently pushed off, still looking at the awesome image of the mammoth. 'Or to discover the earliest work of art anywhere in the world.'

They were now more than thirty metres from the entrance chute and halfway through the gallery. Above them the rock towered like a great cathedral, the ceiling a billowing vault of lava frozen in mid-flow as it surged down the walls. As the figures of the aurochs receded, more clusters of animals came into view, in places so dense they seemed like herds stampeding them head on.

'At Lascaux there are six hundred paintings and twelve thousand etchings,' Jack murmured. 'Here there must be three or four times that number. It's sensational. It's like stumbling across a prehistoric Louvre.'

He and Katya were so absorbed by the astonishing scenes on either side they failed to register the far end of the chamber. Costas alerted them, having swum ahead anxiously after consulting his dive computer.

'Look in front of you,' he said.

The end of the gallery was now less than ten metres away.

As their headlamps played across the rock, they could see it was devoid of paintings, its surface smoothed and polished like the earlier passageways. But then they began to trace the outline of a carving. It was immense, extending at least fifteen metres across the entire wall.

Costas' beam joined theirs and the image became complete.

'It's a bird of prey,' Katya exclaimed.

'*The outstretched eagle god*,' Jack said softly.

The carving was in the same bas-relief as the sacrificial bull in the passageway. It looked remarkably similar to the imperial eagles of ancient Mesopotamia or Rome, its head arched stiffly to the right and its eye staring haughtily over a sharply downturned beak. But instead of extending outwards, the wings were angled up to the corners of the chamber. It was as if the bird was about to fall on its prey, its talons stretched almost to the floor.

'It's later than the paintings,' Jack said. 'Palaeolithic hunters didn't have the tools to carve basalt like this. It must be contemporary with the bull carving, from the Neolithic.'

As their lights illuminated the fearsome talons they realized the eagle was poised over a series of dark entranceways along the base of the wall. There were four altogether, one under each wingtip and one under each set of talons.

'It looks as if we've got four choices,' Jack said.

They scanned the wall urgently for clues, aware that their time at this depth was running perilously short. They had left the submarine almost half an hour before. After they had swum the length of the wall inspecting each doorway in turn, they came together at the centre.

'They're identical,' Katya said despondently. 'It is going to be the luck of the draw again.'

'Wait a moment.' Costas was staring at the image above

them, its wingtips almost lost in the cavernous heights of the chamber. 'That shape. I've seen it somewhere before.'

The other two followed Costas' gaze. Katya suddenly drew in her breath sharply.

'The Atlantis symbol!'

Costas was jubilant. 'The shoulders and wings are the central H of the symbol. The legs are the lower spoke. The Atlantis symbol is an outstretched eagle!'

Jack excitedly produced the disc so they could see the rectilinear device impressed in the surface, an image so familiar yet until now inscrutable in its form.

'Maybe it's like the Egyptian *ankh* symbol,' Katya said. 'The hieroglyph of a cross with a loop above it that meant life force.'

'When I saw the sacrificial tally in the passageway I began to think the Atlantis symbol was more than just a key, that it was also a numerical device,' Costas said. 'Maybe a binary code, using horizontal and vertical lines for 0 and 1, or a calculator for relating the solar and lunar cycles. But now it looks as if it's simply a representation of the sacred eagle, an abstraction which could easily be copied on different materials because of its straight lines. Yet even so . . .'

'It may contain some kind of message,' Jack interjected.

'A map?'

Jack swam over to Katya. 'Can you call up Dillen's translation of the Phaistos disc?'

She swiftly detached her palm computer in its waterproof housing from her shoulder. After a few moments a paragraph began to scroll on the screen.

Beneath the sign of the bull lies the outstretched eagle god. At his tail here is golden-walled Atlantis, the great golden door of the citadel. His wingtips touch the rising and the setting of the sun. At the rising of the sun here is the mountain of fire and crystal. Here is the hall of the high priests . . .

'Stop there.' Jack turned to Costas. 'What's our bearing?'

Costas had second-guessed his friend and was already consulting his compass. 'Taking into account likely magnetic variability in the rock, I'd say this wall is oriented almost exactly east-west.'

'Right.' Jack quickly marshalled his thoughts. '*Sign of the bull* refers to this volcano, to the twin peaks. *The outstretched eagle god* is this image above us, the wings aligned precisely to the rising and setting sun. The *hall of the high priests* is at the rising sun. That means the eastern doorway, beneath the left wingtip.'

Costas was nodding, his eyes fixed on the symbol. 'There's more to it than that.' He took the disc from Jack, tracing the lines as he spoke. 'Imagine this is a map, not a scaled representation but a diagram like a subway plan. The vertical line corresponding to the legs of the eagle is the passage leading from the door in the cliff face. These two lines halfway up the eagle's leg are our dead-end alleys, just beyond the bull carving. We're now at the heart of the symbol, the point from which the wings extend left and right.'

'So the two doorways in front of us lead to the neck and head of the eagle,' Jack said. 'And the text on the disc has a double message, telling us not only to take the eastern door but also to follow the passageways beyond to a point corresponding with the left wingtip.'

'So where do all the other passageways lead?' Katya asked.

'My guess is most of them form a complex of tunnels and galleries like this one. Imagine a subterranean monastery, complete with cult rooms, living quarters for priests and retainers, kitchens and food storage areas, scriptoria and workshops. The Palaeolithic hunters who first came here may have noticed the symmetrical layout, a freak of nature that could be conceived as a spread-eagle pattern. Later rock-cutting may have regularized the pattern even further.'

'Unfortunately we have no time for exploration.' Costas had finned alongside Jack and was viewing his contents gauge with alarm. 'The gunshot wound and exposure have aggravated your breathing rate. You're almost down to the emergency reserve. You have enough trimix to get back to the submarine but no more. It's your call.'

Jack's reply was unhesitating. As long as their besiegers were in place there was no way back through the submarine. Their only chance was to find a way through the maze of tunnels to the surface.

'We go on.'

Costas looked at his friend and nodded wordlessly. Katya reached out and gripped Jack's arm. They swam towards the left-hand doorway, casting a final glance at the cavern behind them. As their beams danced across the undulating surface the animals looked distorted and elongated, as if they had reared up and were straining to follow them, a fantastic cavalcade set to burst forth from the depths of the Ice Age.

As he reached the corner, Costas paused to fit another reel of tape. Then he swam forward to face the forbidding darkness of the passageway, Jack and Katya poised on either side of him.

'Right,' he said. 'Follow me.'

20

'Theseus, this is Ariadne. Theseus, this is Ariadne. Do you read me? Over.'

Tom York repeated the message he had relayed continuously for the past half-hour, using the code names he had agreed with Jack and the others before they departed for the submarine in the DSRV. He clicked off the mike and replaced it on the VHF receiver beside the radar console. It was now early morning and *Seaquest* was almost back at her original position, having shadowed the storm as it rolled towards the southern shore of the Black Sea. Even though it was almost twelve hours since they had parted ways, he was not unduly concerned. It may have taken some time to penetrate the submarine, and Costas' laser contraption was untested. They may have decided against deploying the radio buoy from the DSRV until the surface conditions were less tumultuous.

Earlier, through IMU's link to GCHQ Cheltenham, the UK communications and intelligence-gathering head-quarters, he had determined that one of the new-generation digital terrain-mapping satellites was due overhead within the hour. They were at the edge of its purview and the window would only be five minutes, but they should get a high-resolution image of the island if the cloud lifted enough to allow an unimpeded view from the six hundred kilometre orbit trajectory. Even with visual obstruction the infrared thermal sensors would provide a detailed image, one which would be dominated by intense radiation from the volcano but might pick up the signatures of individual humans if they were far enough away from the core.

'Captain, land ahoy. South-south-west, off the starboard bow.'

With the coming of dawn he and the helmsman had moved from the virtual bridge in the command module to the deckhouse topside. As the vessel pitched and rolled he gripped the handrail and peered out through the rain-lashed window, surveying the battened-down equipment on the foredeck that had survived the onslaught. The dull light of dawn revealed a restless sea, its ragged surface crested with dying whitecaps. The horizon steadily retreated as the pall of sea fog dissipated and the sun's rays burned through.

'Range three thousand metres,' York estimated. 'Reduce your speed to one quarter and bring us round to bearing seven-five degrees.'

The crewman checked the laser distance-finder while York confirmed the GPS fix and leaned over the Admiralty Chart beside the compass binnacle. A few moments later the island came dramatically into view, its glistening surface rising to a near perfect cone.

'My God!' the crewman exclaimed. 'It's erupting!'

York replaced his dividers and snatched up a pair of binoculars. The umbrella shrouding the island was not just sea mist but a plume discharging from the volcano itself. As the cloud base rose, the plume stretched skywards like a ribbon, its upper reaches wavering to and fro before streaming south with the wind. In the middle was a truncated rainbow, a vivid streak of colour that flickered luminously as the sun broke through.

York kept his glasses trained on the spectacle for a full minute.

'I don't think so,' he replied. 'There's no particulate matter. I've seen this before, in the Vanuatu Islands in the South Pacific. Rainwater saturates the porous upper layers of ash and vaporizes when it comes into contact with magma, causing a plume that rises for hours after the clouds have cleared. But I've never seen one quite like this. The vapour appears to have been channelled into a single chimney, producing a column that looks no more than twenty metres wide.'

'If this happened in ancient times it must have seemed awesome, a supernatural event,' the crewman ventured.

'I wish Jack could see this.' York looked pensively at the waves. 'It lends credence to his theory that the mountain was sacred, a place of worship like those Minoan peak sanctuaries. It would have seemed the very home of the gods.'

York raised his binoculars again to scan the volcano where it sloped down in front of them. The surface appeared desolate and lifeless, the scorched ash of the cone giving way to a barren tumult of basalt below. About halfway down he saw a line of dark patches above rectilinear features that looked like platforms or balconies. He closed his eyes briefly against the sunlight, looked again, then grunted. He put the binoculars down and walked over to the high-resolution telescope beside the binnacle, only to be interrupted by a voice at the door.

'That's quite a sight. I assume it's water vapour.' Peter Howe stepped onto the bridge. He was wearing green rubber boots, brown corduroys and a white roll-neck sweater, and was carrying two steaming mugs.

'You look like something out of the Battle of the Atlantic,' York said.

'Battle of the Black Sea, more like. That was a hell of a night.' Howe passed over a mug and slumped on the helmsman's seat. His face was unshaven and lined with fatigue, the tiredness accentuating his New Zealand drawl. 'I know you kept us out of the eye of the storm but we still had our work cut out stopping the gear from rolling. We nearly lost the escape sub.'

They had retrieved the submersible soon after despatching the DSRV, its passengers safely delivered to *Sea Venture* some thirty nautical miles west. Even though they had secured the craft inside the internal bay it had bounced off its pivots during the night, nearly causing a massive weight displacement that would have been fatal for the ship and crew. If the efforts of Howe and his team had failed, they would have had no recourse but to ditch the sub, a move that might have saved *Seaquest* but would have cut off their only emergency escape route.

'We're only a skeleton crew of twelve,' Howe continued. 'My people have been working flat out through the night. What's our status?'

York looked at the SATNAV monitor and watched their co-ordinates converge with the GPS fix where they had launched the DSRV the day before. The storm had almost abated, the sea had reduced to a moderate swell and the morning sunlight shimmered off the glassy surface of the island. It was going to be a perfect summer's day.

'If we still haven't heard from Jack in six hours' time I'm sending in the divers. Meanwhile, you can stand down the crew for the next watch so they can have a well-earned rest. I'll call reveille at twelve hundred hours.'

'And our guardian angels?'

'Same time frame. If there's no contact we'll transmit emergency status notification at twelve hundred hours.'

Their guardian angels were the naval task force, which was their ultimate back-up. Already a Turkish frigate and FAC flotilla had passed through the Bosporus and was steaming full speed in their direction, and in Trabzon a flight of Seahawk helicopters with elements of the Turkish Special Forces Amphibious Marine Brigade was in advanced readiness. Mustafa Alközen and a team of high-ranking Turkish diplomats had flown to the Georgian capital Tbilisi to ensure that any intervention was a fully collaborative effort between the two nations.

'Right.' Howe spoke with obvious relief. 'I'm going to check the forward gun turret and then catch some shut-eye myself. See you at noon.'

York nodded and moved to the binnacle. Twenty minutes ago the helmsman had reported a huge cleft in the seabed, a previously uncharted tectonic fault ten kilometres long and over five hundred metres deep. He had watched as the depth-finder charted their progress from the canyon up to the line of the ancient shoreline 150 metres deep. They had now reached their rendezvous position and were hove to one and a half nautical miles north-north-west of the island, almost exactly the spot where Jack and Costas had first seen the ancient city from the Aquapods the day before.

York looked towards the island, the twin peaks and saddle

now clearly visible where the caldera had collapsed eons ago. He stood still, in awe at what might lie below. It was almost beyond belief that the waters in front of him concealed the greatest wonder of the ancient world, a city that pre-dated all others by thousands of years and contained towering pyramids, colossal statues and multi-storeyed tenements, a community more advanced than any other in prehistory. And to cap it all somewhere below lay the sinister form of a Soviet nuclear submarine, something he had spent half a lifetime training to destroy.

A voice crackled over the radio. '*Seaquest*, this is *Sea Venture*. Do you read me? Over.'

York grabbed the mike and spoke excitedly. 'Macleod, this is *Seaquest*. Relay your co-ordinates. Over.'

'We're still trapped in Trabzon by the storm.' The voice was wavering and distorted, the effect of 100 miles of electrical mayhem. 'But Mustafa's managed to tap into a satellite. It's hot-wired for heat imagery. It should be streaming in now.'

York swivelled to get a closer look at the screen on the navigation console, moving alongside the crewman who had the helm. A flickering sheen of colour resolved itself into a rocky landscape and then fragmented into a mosaic of pixels.

'You're looking at the central part of the island.' Macleod's voice was barely audible. 'The eastern shore is at the top. We've only got a few moments before we lose the satellite.'

The upper half of the screen remained obscure but another sweep of the scanner revealed a vivid image at the centre. Beside the jagged contusions of lava lay the edge of a wide platform, a radius of evenly spaced stones just visible to the left. To the right was the unmistakable outline of a rock-cut stairway.

'Yes!' The crewman punched the air. 'They made it!'

York eagerly followed his gaze. Two red blotches detached

from the stairway and were clearly moving. A third appeared from the haze of pixels at the top of the screen.

'Strange.' York was uneasy. 'They're moving up from the direction of the shoreline, yet Jack was convinced the underground passage would land them near the top of the volcano. And they should have made radio contact as soon as they reached the surface.'

As if on cue his worst suspicions were confirmed. A fourth and then a fifth figure emerged into view, fanned out on either side of the stairway.

'Christ,' the crewman exclaimed. 'Not ours.'

The image disintegrated and the crackle of the radio became continuous. The crewman's head jerked towards a warning light on the adjacent screen.

'Sir, you should see this.'

The monitor displayed the circular sweep of a military-specification Racal Decca TM1226 surface-search and navigation radar.

'There's a contact detaching itself from the east side of the island. I can't be sure until the image clarifies, but I'd say we're looking at a warship the size of a frigate, maybe a large FAC.'

Just then there was a terrific shriek overhead and the two men were thrown violently back. York picked himself up and ran to the starboard wing just in time to see a plume of spray erupt five hundred metres off the bow. At the same moment they heard a distant crack of gunfire, the sound reverberating off the island and rolling towards them in the clear morning air.

'All systems down, I repeat, all systems down,' the crewman shouted. 'Radar, radio, computers. Everything's dead.'

York lurched back into the deckhouse and quickly looked around. Through the door to the navigation room he could see his monitor was blank. The lighting and VHF radio in the bridge were out, along with the GPS receiver and all other LCD displays. He immediately pulled down the handle on the clockwork klaxon and flipped open the lid on the voice tube that led to all quarters of the ship.

'Now hear this,' he bellowed above the alarm. 'Red alert. Red alert. We are under attack. All electronics are down. I repeat, all electronics are down. Major Howe report to the bridge at once. All other crew assemble in the internal bay and prepare to deploy the escape sub *Neptune II*.' He snapped the lid shut and looked across at the helmsman, his face grim and drawn. 'An E-bomb.'

The other man nodded knowingly. The gravest addition in recent years to the terrorist arsenal had been electromagnetic bombs, magnetically charged shells that emitted a multimillion watt microwave pulse when they exploded. The most powerful made a lightning bolt seem like a lightbulb, and could disable all electric power, computers and telecommunications within their radius.

'Time for you to join the others, Mike,' York ordered the helmsman. 'The reserve battery packs in the sub and the command module are protected from electromagnetic interference so should still be operable. Peter and I will stay as long as possible and depart in the module if necessary. It's imperative that you reach Turkish territorial waters before transmitting your position. The call code is "Ariadne needs Guardian Angel" on the secure IMU channel. As senior crewman you have my authority.'

'Aye, sir. And good luck, Captain.'

'And to you too.'

As the crewman clattered hurriedly down the ladder, York focused his binoculars on the eastern extremity of the island. Seconds later a low form slipped out from behind the rocks, its raking prow as menacing as a shark's snout. In the pellucid morning light every feature seemed accentuated, from the gun turret in front of the sleek superstructure to the fanjet nacelles on the stern.

He knew it could only be *Vultura*. Apart from the US and Britain, only the Russians had developed electromagnetic pulse artillery shells. During the most recent Gulf conflict Russia's studied neutrality had led a number of diehard cold warriors to suggest she had secretly supplied the insurgents with weapons. Now York had confirmation of what many had suspected, that the shells were part of an illegal traffic from the old Soviet arsenals that reached terrorists by way of the criminal underworld. Aslan was probably not the only warlord to retain some of the prized hardware for his personal use.

As York zipped up his survival suit, Howe came bounding up the ladder. He was already half into a white flash-resistant overall and passed another to York. The two men quickly kitted up and each took a helmet from a bin under the console, the Kevlar domes incorporating bulbous ear-protectors and shatterproof retractable visors.

'This is it, then,' Howe said.

'God be with us.'

The two men slid down the ladder to the deck. Behind the superstructure the helipad lay empty, the Lynx having flown off to Trabzon as soon as the storm brewed up.

'The automated firing system will be useless without electronics,' Howe said. 'But I put the pod on manual when I last checked it so we should be able to crank it up by hand.'

Their only hope was surprise. *Vultura* would not know they carried fixed armament; the weapons pod was retracted during *Seaquest*'s normal operations. Aslan's intent was undoubtedly to board and plunder and then dispose of the ship at his leisure. They had little power to affect the fate of *Seaquest* but they might exact a small price in return. With *Vultura*'s gun trained on them, they knew their first shot would unleash hell, a furious onslaught the vessel was not built to withstand.

Together the two men crouched in the middle of the foredeck and heaved up a circular hatch. Below them lay the dull grey of the turret armour, the Breda twin 40 millimetre barrels elevated from the compact mounting in the centre.

Howe dropped down to the gunner's platform behind the breech mechanism and looked up at York. 'We need to be ready to fire as soon as we raise the turret and acquire the target. We're going to have to do this the old-fashioned way. I'm gun layer and you're forward observer.'

The weapon would normally have been operational from *Seaquest*'s bridge, the range-finding provided by a Bofors 9LV 200 Mark 2 tracking radar and 9LV 228 fire-control system. As it was, York did not even have use of the hand-held laser rangefinder and had to rely entirely on his navigational skills. Fortunately he remembered the distance from the rendezvous co-ordinates to the eastern tip of the island, where *Vultura* was now exposed broadside on.

'Range three thousand three hundred metres.' York raised his arms as a crude sighting aid, his right arm held out at forty-five degrees from *Seaquest*'s bow and his left arm at *Vultura*'s stern. 'Azimuth two hundred and forty degrees on our axis.'

Howe repeated the instructions and spun the wheel beside the gunner's seat until the barrels were aligned on *Vultura*. He swiftly calculated the angle of elevation, moving a ratchet on the semicircular metal compass so the barrels would fall on the trajectory as they raised the turret.

'Barometric pressure and humidity normal, wind speed

negligible. No need for compensation at this range.'

York lowered himself to the floor beside Howe to help with the ammunition. The belt feeds from the hold magazine were empty since the ship had not been prepared for battle before the attack, and in any case did not operate without electronics. Instead they began extracting shells from reserve lockers on either side of the turret interior.

'We'll have to use the manual feed,' Howe said. 'High explosive for the left barrel, armour-piercing for the right, five rounds each. I doubt whether we'll have the opportunity for more. We'll use the HE for rangefinding because the impact is more visible and then switch to solid shot.'

York began stacking the five-kilo shells in the racks above the receivers, red-tipped to the left and blue-tipped to the right. When he had finished, Howe sat in the gunner's seat and pulled back the bolt on each barrel to chamber a round.

'Bloody frustrating having only ten shells for a gun that fires four hundred and fifty rounds per minute,' Howe observed nonchalantly. 'Maybe the gods of Atlantis will smile on us.'

The two men pulled down their safety visors. York eased his body into the narrow space in front of the wheel controlling barrel elevation while Howe grasped the manual override that raised and lowered the turret. After giving the wheel an experimental turn he looked at York.

'Ready to elevate?'

York gave a thumbs-up.

'Now!'

As the turret rose and the barrels depressed, York felt a surge of adrenalin course through him. He had faced hostile action many times, but always from the detached position of a bridge or control room. Now he was about to engage an enemy in mortal combat behind the cold metal of a gun. For the first time he knew what it felt like for the men crouched behind the cannons of Nelson's *Victory* or inside the mighty turrets of dreadnoughts at Jutland or the North Cape. Their survival was in the balance, the odds stacked heavily against them faced with *Vultura*'s 130 millimetre gun with its state-of-the-art GPS-linked ranging system.

The pod rose above the deck and the silhouette of *Vultura* came into view. As York watched the barrels drop to the pre-set mark and lock into place, he slammed shut the handle on the elevation wheel and raised his right arm.

'On my mark!'

Howe flipped up the safety and curled his finger round the trigger.

'Fire!'

There was an ear-splitting crack and the left-hand barrel recoiled violently on its springs. York snatched up his binoculars and followed the trajectory of the shell as it screamed through the air. A few moments later a fountain of spray erupted just to the right of *Vultura*.

'Twenty degrees left,' York yelled.

Howe spun the azimuth wheel and locked the carriage in place.

'Fire!'

There was another jarring report and jet of flame from the left-hand barrel. The gas blowback instantaneously ejected the spent casing and chambered a new round.

'Hit!' York shouted. 'Armour-piercing, five rounds rapid!'

He had seen the red flash where the explosive had detonated against metal and sent a spray of splinters over *Vultura*'s stern. Their hope now was that solid shot would disable the ship's propulsion system, wreaking damage on the turbofan boosters that gave *Vultura* more speed than almost any other surface vessel.

'Fire!'

Howe pulled the right-hand trigger and held it down. With a noise like a giant jackhammer the gun blasted off the five-round burst at full cyclic rate, the magazine emptying in under a second and the spent cases flying from the breech with each recoil.

Even before the reverberation had ceased there was a sickening crash towards the stern of *Seaquest* and a massive vibration through the deck. The two men watched in horror as the ship took half a dozen direct hits just above the waterline. At this range the powerful Nitrex propellant meant *Vultura* could fire at a virtually level trajectory, the uranium-depleted AP rounds raking *Seaquest* from stern to midships. It was as if she had been skewered by a giant pitchfork, each shell punching effortlessly through the bulkheads and emerging from the other side in a jet of fire and debris.

'They'll go for the bridge next,' York yelled. 'Then it'll be us.'

While *Seaquest* heaved and groaned, York trained his binoculars on *Vultura*'s stern. Puffs of smoke were showing where she had been hit. A movement caught his attention and he shifted the binoculars down. A rigid-hulled inflatable was planing towards them, its twin outboards churning a wide V-shaped wake. Inside it he could see a group of crouching figures. It was already past the halfway point and closing fast.

'Enemy RIB approaching, range eight hundred metres,' he cried. 'Depressing barrels to minimum elevation. Engage over open sights!'

York frantically spun the elevation wheel while Howe flipped up the metallic viewfinder in front of the gunner's seat. Just as his hand closed on the left-hand trigger, there was a deafening crash that threw both men to the floor. With a sound like a thousand smashing windows, a hail of metal splinters ricocheted off the turret armour. One of them sliced deep into York's leg and drenched his overalls with blood. Seconds later two further explosions swept the deck and a searing concussion marked another armour-piercing projectile as it ploughed through the deckhouse and crashed in the sea off the starboard bow.

York hauled himself to his feet, his ears ringing furiously and his left leg useless, and stared at the gaping hole where the bridge had been. For a man wedded to the sea it was an appalling sight, as if he were helplessly watching the woman he loved in her death throes, sightless, beyond speech, her face destroyed.

'Let's get those bastards.' His voice was cold and steady despite the pain.

'Aye, aye, sir.'

Howe was back in the gunner's seat with the RIB in his sights as it hurtled towards them less than two hundred metres away. With the barrels at maximum depression he blasted off the remaining HE rounds at one-second intervals. The first fell short but raised the pontoons until they caught the wind and seemed to take off. The second passed under the keel and blew the RIB entirely out of the water, the stern careening up so they could see the six wetsuited men clinging desperately to the floorboards. The third exploded against the transom, igniting the fuel supply and vaporizing the boat and its occupants in a fireball of carnage that rolled towards them at frightening speed.

The two men had no time for elation. The end when it came was as violent and merciless as they could have foreseen.

As the first burning fragments of the RIB hit the turret, they felt a gigantic ripple course beneath their feet. Rivets burst out and the metal twisted grotesquely from one side of the deck to the other. A moment later another shell blasted the turret off its mounting and blew them towards the starboard railing.

They were enveloped in a holocaust of fire, a burning vortex that hurled them into a narrowing void.

As York fought oblivion he caught a final glimpse of *Seaquest*, a pyre of destruction yet still miraculously afloat, a ship ravaged beyond recognition yet as defiant as the volcano that loomed impassively behind.

21

As they plunged into the forbidding darkness of the tunnel beneath the eagle's left wing tip, they could see the walls had been smoothed and polished like the previous passageways. For the first few metres beyond the hall of the ancestors, Costas led the way, but soon it widened and Jack and Katya were able to swim alongside. After about ten metres the floor became a shallow stairway, the worn steps progressing upwards at a steady gradient as far as their lights could penetrate.

'The gods are with us this time,' Costas said. 'Another few minutes at this depth and we'd have been here permanently.'

As they ascended the slope, they conserved energy by using their buoyancy compensators for lift. The walls were carved with a continuous frieze of life-sized bulls, their sinuous forms startlingly reminiscent of Minoan bull paintings on Crete. They seemed to glower and stomp on either side as they processed upwards.

Just as Jack's breathing rate was beginning to stabilize his computer gave an audible warning that he was about to go on reserve. He sensed a momentary tightening in his regulator as the emergency supply kicked in and then it flowed freely again.

'As we ascend and the pressure reduces you'll get more volume from the reserve supply,' Costas assured him. 'If you run out we can always buddy-breathe.'

'Great.' Jack grimaced through his visor before concentrating on maintaining his buoyancy just above neutral.

For the next few minutes the only sound was the exhalation of bubbles as they gradually rose up the passageway. After about a hundred metres Costas signalled them to halt.

'We're now seventy metres below sea level,' he announced. 'My computer says we need a five-minute decompression stop. Even though we've mainly been on helium and oxygen, we've still absorbed a lot of nitrogen. We need to off-gas.'

Despite the stabbing pain in his side, Jack made a conscious effort not to hyperventilate. He sank exhausted to the stairs and reached for the disc.

'Time for some map reading,' he said.

The other two dropped down beside him as he rotated the disc until the symbol was aligned in the direction of the passageway.

'If our decipherment is correct we're here, along the left shoulder of the eagle,' Costas pointed out. 'We can't have much further to go along this route. We're getting close to the cliff face.'

'When this passageway ends we make a right turn,' Katya said. 'Then all the way along the wing of the eagle until the final turning to the left, and then to the eastern tip.'

'If we're heading to the caldera we need to rise about a hundred metres and go four hundred metres south, on a gradient of thirty degrees. At some point we'll break sea level but still be underground.'

'What happens if the passage goes down?' Katya enquired.

'We get boiled alive,' Costas said bluntly. 'The core is a seething mass of molten lava and scorching gas. Even going up we may find our way barred by lava that's flowed out since the flood.'

Their timers simultaneously sounded a five-minute alarm to show the stop was over. Jack returned the disc to his pocket and stiffly pushed off from the stairway.

'We have no choice,' he said. 'Let's pray that Ben and Andy are still holding out. We're their only lifeline.'

As they passed above the sixty-metre mark their regulators began to replace helium with nitrogen as the main inert gas. Soon their breathing mixture would differ from atmospheric air only in the enriched oxygen that was injected during the final few metres to scrub their bloodstreams of any excess nitrogen.

Costas led the way as the stairway began to constrict into a narrow tunnel. After a final step it veered right, apparently following a natural fissure, before regaining its original course and promptly depositing them at the entrance to another cavern.

'Here's our intersection, bang on target.'

Their headlamps revealed a chamber about ten metres long by five metres wide, with doorways on all four sides. The decompression stop had briefly revitalized Jack and he swam forward for a closer look. In the centre was an oblong table flanked by pedestals set about two metres from each corner. The table was hewn from the rock and had a raised rim like the upturned lid of a sarcophagus. The pedestals were free-standing basins like the fonts of medieval churches.

'There are no runnels for blood and it would have been impossible to bring a large animal this far into the mountain,' he said. 'Sacrifices tended to be public affairs and whatever went on here could only have been attended by a select few.'

'An ablution table, for ritual purification?' Costas suggested.

Katya finned over to the doorway opposite their point of entry. She peered into the corridor beyond and briefly switched off her headlamp.

'I can see light,' she said. 'It's barely discernible, but there are four separate pools evenly spaced.'

Jack and Costas swam over. They too could see faint smudges of hazy green.

'We're only fifty metres below sea level and a few metres inside the cliff face.' Costas flicked his light back on as he spoke. 'It's early morning outside, so there should be some vestigial light at this depth.'

'The corridor corresponds with one of the parallel lines jutting out from the wing of the eagle,' Jack said. 'I'll bet they're accommodation quarters, with windows and balconies overlooking the pyramids. Just like the Minoan complex on the cliffs of Thera, a magnificent location which served the monastic ideal yet also dominated the population on the coast below.'

'We could get out through one of those windows,' Katya suggested.

'Not a chance,' Costas said. 'They look like ventilation shafts, probably less than a metre wide. And we don't have time to explore. Our map's held true so far and I vote we follow it.'

Just then a vibration coursed through them, a blurring of

the water that made Jack suddenly fear he was about to black out. It was followed by further vibrations and then a series of dull hammering noises, each one preceding a muffled sound like breaking glass a long distance off. There was no way of telling the direction the sound was coming from.

'The submarine!' Katya exclaimed.

'It's too distinct, too contained,' Costas said. 'Any explosion in the *Kazbek* and we wouldn't be here talking about it.'

'I've heard that sound before.' Jack was looking at Costas, his anger palpable even through the visor. 'I think it's the vibration of shells tearing through a hull. There's a gun battle raging on the surface above us.'

'Whatever it is, we need to find a way out now,' Costas urged. 'Come on.'

They finned towards the entrance that marked the right-hand turn indicated by the symbol. After passing the basins, Costas paused to check his compass bearing.

'Due south,' he announced. 'All we do now is follow this route as far as it goes and then turn left.'

Katya was approaching the entranceway a few metres ahead of the other two. She suddenly halted.

'Look up,' she said excitedly.

Above the entranceway was a huge lintel carved out of the rock. The front was deeply scored with symbols, some occupying the full half-metre height of the slab. They were separated into two groups of four, each group surrounded by an incised boundary like a hieroglyphic cartouche.

There was no mistaking what they were.

'The sheaf of corn. The paddle. The half-moon. And those Mohican heads,' Katya said.

'It's the final proof,' Jack murmured. 'The Phaistos disc, the golden disc from the wreck. Both of them came from this place. We're looking at the sacred script of Atlantis.'

'What does it mean?' Costas asked.

Katya was already consulting her palm computer. She and Dillen had programmed in a concordance which matched each of the Atlantis symbols with its syllabic equivalent in Linear A, providing a best-fit translation from the Minoan vocabulary so far deciphered.

'*Ti-ka-ti-re, ka-ka-me-re.*' Katya slowly enunciated the sounds, her Russian inflection giving a slight burr to the final syllables of each word.

She scrolled through alphabetically, Jack and Costas watching the flickering words as they appeared on the LCD display.

'They're both in the Minoan lexicon,' she announced. '*Ti-ka-ti* means route or direction. *Ka-ka-me* means dead or death. The suffix *re* means to or of. So it translates as "the route of death", "the way of death".'

They peered up at the inscription above their heads, the symbols standing out as crisp as if they had been carved only days before.

'That doesn't sound too promising,' Costas said glumly.

Jack winced and the other two looked at him with renewed anxiety. He summoned up his remaining energy and powered ahead into the passageway.

'This should be the last leg. Follow me.'

Costas lingered for a moment to tie the final spool of tape to his backpack. All he could see of the other two was the turbulence in their wake; the passageway sloped up at a shallow angle. As he finned after them the reassuring glimmer of their headlamps appeared further up the tunnel.

'Keep your ascent rate below five seconds per metre,' he instructed. 'Our time in that chamber counts as another decompression stop, and with this gradient we shouldn't need to halt again before reaching the surface.'

The floor was rough as if deliberately left unfinished to provide a better grip. On either side were parallel grooves like the ruts in ancient cartways. Suddenly they were at the entrance to another chamber, the walls falling away into pitch darkness yet the ramp continuing upwards.

It was a cavernous space that dwarfed even the hall of the ancestors. All around them were undulating folds of rock that seemed to ripple as they panned their headlamps back and forth. The sides plummeted into a yawning chasm, the sheer drop broken only by gnarled contusions of lava that punctuated the walls like knots in old oak. Everywhere they looked were twisted rivers of lava, testament to the colossal forces that blasted through the chamber from the molten core of the earth.

'The core of the volcano must only be a couple of hundred metres south,' Costas said. 'Magma and gas punched through the compacted ash of the cone to leave gaping holes and then solidify. The result is this giant honeycomb effect, an expanded hollow core intermeshed with a lattice of basalt formations.'

They peered through the crystal-clear water and the ramp revealed itself as a giant causeway, an immense spine of rock that spanned the space as far as they could see. To the left their headlamps played over another massive dyke, followed by another one an equal distance beyond, both projecting at right angles from the central spine and merging with the wall of the chamber.

It was Costas who pointed out the obvious, the reason why the geometry seemed so strangely familiar.

'The central spine is the upper wing on the symbol. The dykes are two of the projections to the left. We're on the home stretch.'

'It must have seemed awesome to the first people who

reached this chamber,' Jack said. 'My guess is the other side of the core also has basalt intrusions radiating outwards where the magma followed fissures to the surface. If the pattern's symmetrical it's easy to see how it acquired magical qualities. It was the image of their sacred eagle god.'

Katya was transfixed by the spectacular cascades of rock around them. The causeway was like the final bridge to a subterranean stronghold, an ultimate test of nerve that would leave anyone brave enough to venture across it exposed above a moat of fire.

She could just make out entrances in the wall at the end of the two branching ramps. Directly ahead she could see the distant shimmer of a rock wall a hundred metres away, its dimensions concealed in the darkness. She shuddered as she remembered the grim epithet over the entrance into the chamber.

Costas began to swim determinedly along the causeway. 'Jack's only got a few minutes of air left. Time to find the surface.'

Jack and Katya swam on either side of Costas above the ruts which continued from the passageway. Just after they passed the junction with the first causeway to the left, another feature came into view, a depression midway along the central spine that had been invisible from the entrance.

As they neared the feature a remarkable scene unfolded before their eyes. The indentation extended the full five-metre width of the causeway and an equivalent distance across. It was about two metres deep and reached by steps on either side. Overlooking the canyon to the right was a bull's horn sculpture with the characteristic vertical sides and sweeping interior curve. An identical carving rose up just to the left of centre, and perched between was a massive slab.

The horns had been carved out of the rock, their tips almost reaching the level of the causeway, whereas the slab was a lustrous white marble similar to the stone they had seen worked into fantastic animal shapes beside the processional way outside.

As they sank down for a closer look they could see the slab was tilted out a metre over the void.

'Of course,' Jack cried. 'That inscription. Not "the way of death" but "the way of the dead". Ever since we first saw Atlantis I've been wondering where the cemeteries were. Now we know. That last room was a mortuary, a preparation chamber. And this is where they disposed of their dead.'

Even Costas was momentarily diverted from the urgency of their escape and swam over to peer down the chasm. He flicked on his high-intensity halogen beam for a few seconds, aware that only a brief burst could deplete his battery reserve.

'They chose the right spot,' he concurred. 'The lava down there's jagged, the quick-drying type, and fills the ravine as a solidified torrent. Seven thousand years ago that could well have been an active duct. Molten lava simmers away at 1100 degrees Celsius, hot enough to melt a car, so you've got a ready-made crematorium.'

Katya was inspecting the steps leading down to the platform.

'This must be where they brought the bodies before placing them on the slab for their final journey,' she surmised. 'The ruts on the ramp are two metres apart, just right for a bier. They must have been worn down by the feet of pallbearers over countless thousands of funerary processions.'

Jack was staring into the depths of the chasm, all his imagination marshalled to conjure up an image of the ritual last performed at this spot millennia before. He had excavated many ancient burial sites, the dead often telling a better story than the detritus of the living, and he had expected their greatest discovery to be a rich necropolis. Now he knew the only mortal remains of the people of Atlantis were encoded within themselves, in the genes of those intrepid seafarers who had escaped the flood and spread the seeds of civilization.

'So this is the underworld of the ancients,' he said, his breath short. 'And the Styx was no placid backwater but a burning river of fire.'

'Old Charon the boatman would have taken a raincheck on this one,' Costas said. 'It looks like the gates of hell to me. Let's get out of here before we wake up the god of this place and he reactivates the furnace.'

As they finned up the final section of the ramp, Jack was gasping. His ragged breathing was audible and Katya turned towards him in alarm. Costas had stayed close by and now pulled his friend to a halt.

'Time to buddy-breathe,' he said.

After fumbling briefly behind his backpack he produced a vulcanized hose which he pushed into an outlet on Jack's manifold. He opened the valve a few turns and there was a hiss as the two systems equalized.

'Thanks.' Jack's breathing was suddenly easier.

'We've got a problem,' Costas announced.

Jack had been concentrating on his breathing but now looked up at the rock face looming in front of them.

'A lava plug,' he said bleakly.

About five metres ahead the ledge terminated at the north-eastern extremity of the chamber. They could just make out an entrance, as wide as the walkway and capped by a lintel. But these features were obscured by a giant clot of solidified lava, an ugly eruption that had oozed into the chasm and left only a small aperture near the top.

Costas turned to Jack. 'We're only eight metres below sea

level, within the ten-metre safety margin for oxygen toxicity, so while we're working this one out we may as well cleanse our systems.'

He switched his and Katya's computers to manual override and cranked open the oxygen valves on their manifolds. Then he and Jack swam in tandem to the hole and peered into the space beyond.

'The lava tube must have broken through the basalt into the passageway some time after the flood,' Costas said. 'The aperture is the result of a gas blowout. If we're lucky there'll be a cavity all the way through.'

Jack pulled himself into the jagged slit so his head and shoulders disappeared. Beyond the constriction he could see the cavity opening out like a ventilation duct, the walls mottled with igneous contusions where the gas had exploded through the cooling lava with the force of a jet afterburner.

'There's no way we'll get through with our equipment on,' he said. 'After the blowout the lava must have expanded as it solidified, narrowing the first few metres to a tunnel barely wide enough for Katya, let alone me or you.'

They knew what they had to do. Jack began to unbuckle his cylinder harness.

'It makes sense for me to go first. You and Katya both still have your reserve. And I'm the one who can free-dive to forty metres.'

'Not with a bullet hole in your side.'

'Let me blast some oxygen into the tunnel,' Jack replied. 'I can see undulations in the ceiling that might trap pockets of gas and provide a safety stop.'

Costas paused, instinctively reluctant to expel any of their dwindling supply, but he saw the sense in Jack's words. He detached a regulator second stage from his backpack and passed it over. With his long reach Jack extended the hose as far as he could into the fissure and pressed the purge valve. There was a thunderous roar as the oxygen erupted into the space and cascaded like white water along the upper surface of the rock.

Costas watched intently as the readout on his contents gauge dropped below fifty bar and the reserve warning began to flash.

'Enough!' he said.

Jack released the purge and placed the regulator just inside the lip of the aperture. As he eased off his backpack and wedged it in a fold in the lava, Costas detached the tape from his back and tied it to Jack's upper arm.

'Standard rope signals,' he instructed. 'One pull means OK. Two pulls means you want another blast of oxygen. Continuous pulls means you're through and it's safe for us to follow.'

Jack nodded as he checked to make sure the reel was clear. He would be cut off from the intercom as he would need to retract his visor to access air pockets in the tunnel. He released the safety lock on his helmet and looked across at Costas, who had just confirmed on his computer that they had satisfied decompression requirements.

'Ready.'

'Transfer to regulator.'

As Costas disengaged the umbilical, Jack shut his eyes tight and flipped back his helmet, at the same time shoving the regulator second stage in his mouth and extracting the face mask kept in a side pocket for emergency use. He pressed it to his face and blew through his nose to clear the water, remaining still for a few moments to let his breathing rate subside as the shock of the cold wore off.

After unclipping a hand-held torch, Jack drew himself up to the aperture, Costas following close behind to ensure the hose was not stretched taut. As Jack grasped the lintel he felt an indentation where the lava had folded over the rock surface. His fingers traced the form of a symbol cut deep into the basalt.

He turned towards Katya and gesticulated excitedly. She gave an exaggerated nod before returning her gaze to him, clearly more concerned by his chances of making it through the tunnel.

Jack turned back and relaxed completely, his body suspended from the lintel and his eyes closed. Using the technique of a free diver he breathed slowly and deeply to saturate his body with oxygen. After about a minute he gave the OK signal to Costas and placed his hand over the regulator. He took five quick breaths then spat it out and launched himself forward in a frenzy of bubbles.

Costas reached out to grasp the tape which was their precious lifeline. As it began to slip through his fingers he spoke quietly under his breath.

'Good luck, my friend. We need it.'

22

For the first few metres Jack had to claw his way through the narrow confines of the tunnel where the lava had sagged over the entrance. He could feel his suit rip as he squeezed past the razor-sharp knots of lava. He glanced back to make sure the tape was undamaged and then set off rapidly down the tunnel, his arms extended forward and the torch shining directly ahead.

As he rocketed along he could sense the gradual incline where the lava flow conformed to the rising angle of the passageway. He flipped over and saw pools of luminosity on the ceiling where the oxygen from Costas' regulator had collected. Almost exactly a minute after taking his last breath he popped his head into a pool that filled a fissure in the lava.

He took three breaths in rapid succession, at the same time checking his depth gauge and breaking out a Cyalume chemical lightstick to leave floating in the bubble as a beacon for the others to follow.

'Three metres below sea level,' he said to himself. 'A piece of cake.'

He ducked down and pushed off again into the passageway. Almost immediately it forked. He guessed that one passage would lead to safety and the other would follow the vent where the lava had blown through from the core. It was a life or death decision which would determine the fate of the other two.

After checking his compass Jack swam resolutely up the left-hand passage, exhaling slightly to prevent his lungs from rupturing as the pressure decreased. A shimmering lens of iridescence appeared before him, a surface too wide to be a pool of oxygen caught against the ceiling of the tunnel.

His lungs began to spasm as he scraped with increasing desperation through the narrowing folds of rock. As he pushed beyond the lava and broke surface he almost crashed his head against the rock ceiling. He gasped repeatedly then staggered out of the water. He had reached sea level but was still deep within the volcano, the passageway ahead showing no sign of an exit as it continued to rise.

It had only been three minutes since he had left Costas and Katya but it seemed an eternity. As he fought unconsciousness he focused all his energies on the orange tape that emerged behind him, pulling again and again until it slackened in his hands and he lay still.

There was a huge eruption of spray as Costas hove into view, his body welling out like a surfacing whale. Katya followed seconds later and immediately began inspecting Jack's wound, her face etched with concern as she saw the crust of blood which had oozed through the gash in his suit.

Costas ripped off his mask and breathed heavily, his dark hair matted to his forehead and his face puffed and red.

'Remind me to diet,' he panted. 'I had a spot of bother with that final section.'

He struggled to the edge of the pool and kicked off his fins. Jack had recovered enough to raise himself on his elbows and was unscrewing the beam projector on his flashlight so the exposed bulb would cast a shadowy candlelight around them.

'Join the club,' he replied. 'I feel like I've been through a meat grinder.'

Their voices sounded rich and resonant after so long on the intercom. Jack eased himself further up the slope and flinched with pain.

'I stowed Katya's backpack just inside the tunnel,' Costas said. 'There's enough trimix left for two of us to buddy-breathe back to the submarine in case we need it. I also tied the end of the tape to the lightstick in that air pocket. If we have to go back we just remember to turn right at that fork.'

The water was peppered with tiny bubbles fizzing to the surface. They stared at it as they caught their breath.

'That's odd,' Costas said. 'Looks like more than just the remains of oxygen from the regulator. Must be some kind of gas discharge from that volcanic vent.'

Now they were all safely out they were able to look around their new environment. Up the slope was another rectilinear rock-cut passageway leading inexorably upwards, yet the view was oddly different.

'It's algae,' Costas said. 'There must be just enough natural light for photosynthesis. We must be closer to the outside than I thought.'

Now that the commotion in the pool had died down, they could hear the steady sound of dripping.

'Rainwater,' Costas said. 'The volcano will be saturated after the storm. There'll be a vapour plume the size of a nuclear explosion.'

'At least *Seaquest* should have no trouble finding us.' Jack's words were laboured as he raised himself to his knees. The rush of oxygen had sustained him through the tunnel but now his body was working overtime to flush the remaining nitrogen. He staggered as he stood up, careful to avoid the slippery patches where the rainwater spattered around them. He knew his trial was not over yet. He had beaten the clock on his air supply but would now have to face much greater pain without the numbing frigidity of the water.

Jack saw the looks of concern. 'I'll be all right. Costas, you take point.'

Just as she was about to move, Katya glanced at Jack.

'Oh, I almost forgot.'

Her olive skin and sleek black hair glistened as the water trickled off it.

'That inscription on the lintel,' she said. 'I had a look while we were waiting for you to get through. The first symbol was the Mohican head, the syllable *at.* I'm certain the second symbol was the sheaf of corn, *al* or *la.* I have no doubt the complete inscription reads *Atlantis.* It's our final waymarker.'

Jack nodded, too groggy to speak.

They began to make their way up the slope. Now that they had discarded their breathing apparatus they no longer had the headlamps which formed part of the helmet assembly. The hand-held torches were designed as emergency strobe beacons, and using them continuously quickly drained the batteries. As they worked their way up the slope, the lights began to waver and fade in unison.

'Time for chemical illumination,' Costas said.

They pocketed their torches and Costas and Katya cracked open their lightsticks. Combined with the faint beginnings of natural light, the sticks produced an unearthly aura, a glow chillingly reminiscent of the emergency lighting they had activated in the submarine's shattered control room.

'Keep close together,' Costas warned. 'These things may last for hours but they barely light up the floor. We don't know what to expect.'

As they rounded a bend in the passage, the acrid odour which had irritated their nostrils since surfacing suddenly became indescribably foul. A warm draught carried with it the sickly-sweet smell of decay, as if the dead of Atlantis were still putrefying in their sepulchre far below.

'Sulphur dioxide,' Costas announced, his nose crinkling slightly. 'Unpleasant, but not toxic if we don't stick around for too long. There must be an active vent nearby.'

As they continued upwards they saw where another lava tube had broken through, gushing its contents like spilled concrete over the tunnel floor. The lava was jagged and brittle but did not restrict their passage like the previous flow. The hole where it emerged was rent with a honeycomb of cracks and fissures, the source of the unholy wind that intensified with every step of their approach.

'These two lava tubes we've encountered are relatively recent,' Costas said. 'They must have broken through since the flood, otherwise the priests would have had them cleaned out and the tunnel repaired.'

'There must have been similar eruptions during the time of Atlantis,' Katya said shakily. 'This place is far more active than geologists ever suspected. We're inside a time bomb.'

Jack had been fighting the pain, a pulverizing sensation that had grown as the numbing effect of the cold wore off. Now every breath was a vicious stab, every step an agonizing jolt that pushed him to the brink of collapse.

'You two go on. We must contact *Seaquest* as soon as possible. I'll follow when I can.'

'Not a chance.' Costas had never seen his friend concede defeat, and knew Jack would force himself on until he dropped, whatever the odds. 'I'll carry you on my back if it comes to it.'

Jack marshalled his remaining strength and slowly, agonizingly, followed the other two over the lava, picking his way carefully across the jagged formations. Progress was easier as the sloping floor became a series of shallow steps. About twenty metres beyond the lava, the passageway curved south, the dimensions gradually losing their regularity as the walls gave way to the natural shapes of a volcanic fissure. As the tunnel constricted further, they began to climb single file, with Costas in the lead.

'I can see light ahead,' he announced. 'This must be it.'

The elevation increased sharply and they soon found themselves scrambling on their hands and knees. As they approached the dim aura of light the algae made each step progressively more treacherous. Costas slithered over the final shelf and turned back to give Jack a hand.

They had come out beside a conduit some three metres wide by three metres deep, the sides smoothed by millennia of erosion. At the bottom was a shallow stream that seemed to plummet down a narrow canyon, the distant roar of water audible but their view completely obscured by a sheen of mist. To the right the conduit headed into the rock face with a glimmer of light beyond.

Costas peered at his console to check his altimeter.

'We calculated the height of the volcano before the flood at three hundred and fifty metres above sea level. We're now one hundred and thirty-five metres above present sea level, only about eighty metres below the tip of the cone.'

Having penetrated the volcano on the north side, they were now facing due west, the shape of the passageways reflecting the incline of the upper slopes. Ahead of them the dark mouth of the tunnel seemed set to plunge back into the labyrinth, yet it could only be a short stretch before they reached open air.

'Be careful,' Costas said. 'One wrong step and this chute will send us straight to hell.'

They had lost track of time since embarking in the DSRV from *Seaquest* the previous day. The jumble of rock was a twilight world of shadows and flickering shapes. As they negotiated a short flight of steps cut into the rock, the conduit became gloomier still, and they once again had to rely on the eerie glow from the lightsticks.

The tunnel followed the drift of the basalt, each successive layer clearly visible in the stratigraphy of the walls. The flow had undermined the gas-charged lava of the cone, the ash and cinders compressed like concrete with chunks of pumice and jagged scoriae embedded in the matrix. The higher they climbed, the more porous it became, with rainwater dripping through the clumps that protruded from the ceiling. The temperature was becoming noticeably warmer.

After about twenty metres the tunnel narrowed and funnelled the water flowing against them into a violent current. Jack stumbled sideways, his body suddenly convulsed with pain. Katya waded over to help him stay upright against the torrent which was now waist high. With agonizing slowness the two of them forced their way past the constriction while Costas forged ahead and disappeared into the veil of mist. As they staggered forward, the walls suddenly opened out again and the flow diminished to little more than a trickle. They rounded a corner and saw Costas standing motionless, his dripping form silhouetted against a background of opaque illumination.

'It's a huge skylight,' he announced excitedly. 'We must be just below the caldera.'

The opening far above was wide enough for faint daylight to reveal the awesome scale of the chamber in front of them. It was a vast rotunda, at least fifty metres across by fifty metres high, the walls rising to a circular aperture which framed the sky like a giant oculus. To Jack it was astonishingly reminiscent of the Pantheon in Rome, the ancient temple to all the gods, its soaring dome representing mastery over the heavens.

Even more breathtaking was the apparition in the centre. From skylight to floor was an immense column of swirling gas exactly the width of the oculus. It seemed to project the daylight straight down like a giant beam, a glowing pillar of pale light.

After gazing in awe for a moment they realized it was rocketing upwards at immense speed, giving the illusion that they themselves were hurtling inexorably downward into the fiery depths of the volcano. All their instincts told them there should be a deafening roar yet the chamber was eerily quiet.

'It's water vapour,' Costas finally exclaimed. 'So this is what happens to the rainwater that isn't channelled out. It must be like a blast furnace down there.'

The increasing heat they had felt during the ascent was emanating from the chimney in front of them.

They were standing on the outer edge of a wide platform that ran round the rotunda several metres above the central floor. Evenly spaced doorways, identical to the one they had just emerged from, had been cut into the rock all the way round the perimeter. Each one was topped with the now familiar symbols. Beyond the inside edge of the platform they could just make out the central dais of the chamber. Backing onto the vapour column were four stone seats, each in the shape of bull's horns and arranged at cardinal points of the compass. The one facing them was obscured by the platform but was clearly larger than the others, the tips of the horns reaching up towards the oculus.

'It must be some sort of throne room,' Costas said, awestruck. 'An audience chamber for the high priests.'

'The hall of the ancestors. The funerary chamber. And now the audience chamber,' Katya murmured. 'This must be our last staging post to the holy of holies.'

They had been in a state of constant high excitement, exhilarated by the thrill of discovery since leaving the submarine. Now as they confronted the very core of the volcano their exuberance was tempered with unease, as if they knew the ultimate revelation would not be yielded without a price. Even Costas faltered, reluctant to abandon the security of the tunnel and pitch himself forward into the unknown.

It was Jack who broke the spell and urged them on. He turned towards the other two, his face streaked with grime and his rugged features underscored by pain.

'This is where the text was leading us,' he said. 'The sanctuary of Atlantis is somewhere here.'

Without further ado he pushed himself forward and limped ahead, his willpower the only thing keeping him from buckling. Costas walked alongside and Katya immediately behind, her face set impassively as they made for the lip of the platform.

Just as the throne began to come into view over the edge of the platform, they were blinded by a beam of light. They instinctively cowered and shielded their eyes. Through the glare they made out two figures that materialized to right and left.

Just as suddenly the light disappeared. As their vision cleared, they saw that the two figures were clad in black just like their assailants in the submarine, and each carried a Heckler & Koch MP5 levelled menacingly from the hip. Jack and Costas raised their hands; they would have no chance of reaching their weapons before being cut down in a hail of bullets.

Ahead a flight of twelve shallow steps descended to the dais. A portable searchlight was aimed at them beside the stairs. A raised walkway led directly to the bull's horn sculpture whose tips they had seen above the platform edge. It was the ostentatious backing for a massive stone seat, more ornate than the others.

The seat was occupied.

'Dr Howard. A pleasure to meet you at last.'

Jack recognized the voice, the same drawling, guttural tone that had come over *Seaquest*'s radio from *Vultura* three days ago. He and Costas were pushed roughly down the stairs and the bloated form of Aslan came clearly into view. He was slouched on the throne, his feet planted firmly in front and his immense forearms draped over the sides. His pale and ageless face would have seemed almost like some priest of old were it not for the signs of rampant excess in his corpulent frame. With his billowing red robe and oriental features he seemed the epitome of an eastern despot, an image straight from the court of Genghis Khan, except for the thoroughly modern warriors on either side of him, each carrying a submachine gun.

Directly to Aslan's right stood a diminutive figure at odds with the rest of the entourage. It was a plain-featured woman wearing a drab grey overcoat, her hair pulled back in a bun.

'Olga Ivanovna Bortsev,' Katya hissed.

'Your research assistant has been most helpful,' Aslan boomed good-naturedly. 'Ever since she reported back to me I have kept your vessel under constant surveillance. I have been wanting to visit this island for a long time. Fortunately my men found a way up outside and into this chamber. It seems we arrived in the nick of time.' Suddenly his voice hardened. 'I am here to claim lost property.'

Costas could restrain himself no longer and lunged forward. He was immediately sent sprawling as the butt of a gun slammed into his stomach.

'Costas Demetrios Kazantzakis,' Aslan said with a sneer. 'A Greek.' He spat out the word contemptuously.

As Costas struggled to his feet, Aslan turned his attention to Katya, his dark eyes narrowing and the corners of his mouth betraying the hint of a smile.

'Katya Svetlanova. Or should I say Katya Petrovna Nazarbetov.'

Katya's look had changed to angry defiance. Jack felt his legs slip out from under him as his body finally gave in. Her reply seemed to come from somewhere else, from a shadowy netherworld disconnected from reality.

'*Father.*'

23

Ben shifted almost imperceptibly on his haunches, never once letting his eyes waver from the smudge of light that emanated from the control room at the far end of the passageway. He had held the same position for hour after hour, relieved only for short spells by Andy from the torpedo room below. With his body pressed against the casing and dusted with white precipitate he seemed almost a part of the submarine's fabric, little different from the macabre corpse of the *zampolit* hanging in the darkness only an arm's length behind.

Despite his E-suit the cold had crept insidiously into his body, and the fingers curled round the trigger guard of the AKSU had been numb for hours. Yet he knew how to compartmentalize pain, how to push away everything except what was needed to watch and wait. Years before he had learned that the true test of toughness was extreme endurance, the rare quality that had singled him out among all the other applicants for Special Forces.

He had taken his visor off and an acrid smell reached him before he sensed any movement.

'I managed to get up a brew.' Andy crept behind him and thrust a steaming mug under his face. 'Some foul Soviet muck.'

Ben grunted but cradled the coffee gratefully in his free hand. They had no food other than the high-energy bars in their emergency packs, but had found some sealed water bottles in the wardroom and had made sure they were well hydrated.

'Anything yet?' Andy asked.

Ben shook his head. It had been almost eighteen hours since Jack and the others had left, a full day since they had last seen sunlight. Their watches told them it was early evening, yet with no link to the outside world they had little sense of the passage of time. Ahead of them their opponents had noisily consolidated their position below the escape hatch, periods of activity and raised voices punctuated by long silences. For hours they had endured the moans and wails of a wounded man until a muffled gunshot had put an end to it. Half an hour before there had been an intense commotion which Ben knew was the enemy submersible docking with their own deep submergence rescue vehicle, and he had heard the clatter of footsteps down the entry hatch. He had tapped a prearranged signal for Andy to join him in expectation of the worst.

'Here we go.'

Suddenly a torch shone down the passage towards them. Despite the harsh brightness neither man flinched. Ben put down the mug and flipped off the safety catch on the AKSU, and Andy pulled out the Makarov and melted into the darkness on the other side of the bulkhead.

The man's voice that came down was hoarse and strained, the words half in English, half Russian.

'Crewmen of *Seaquest*. We wish to talk.'

Ben replied sharply in Russian. 'Come any closer and we will destroy the submarine.'

'That will not be necessary.' The words this time were English and came from a woman. Ben and Andy kept their eyes averted, aware that a moment's blindness in the torchlight could lose them their advantage. They could hear that she had advanced ahead of the man and stood only about five metres in front of them.

'You are pawns in other men's games. Come over to us and you will be richly rewarded. You may keep your weapons.' The woman's ingratiating tone made her accent seem even colder, harsher.

'I repeat,' Ben said. 'One step closer.'

'You await your friends.' There was a contemptuous laugh. 'Katya,' she spat out the word, 'is an irrelevance. But I had the pleasure of meeting Dr Howard in Alexandria. Most interesting on the location of Atlantis. And most enjoyable to make his acquaintance and that of Dr Kazantzakis again this morning.'

'You have been warned for the last time.'

'Your so-called friends are dead or captured. Your ship is destroyed. Nobody else knows the location of this submarine. Your enterprise is doomed. Join us and save your lives.'

Ben and Andy listened impassively, neither of them baulking or believing a word. Ben looked at Andy, then turned back.

'*Not a chance,*' he said.

★

Jack awoke with a start to the rays of morning sunlight playing across his face. He opened his eyes, looked round blearily, then shut them again. He must be dreaming, he thought. He was lying on his back in the middle of a king-sized bed on freshly laundered linen. The bed occupied one side of a cavernous room, its walls whitewashed and hung with half a dozen modernist paintings which all seemed vaguely familiar. Opposite him was a huge bay window, its tinted glass revealing a cloudless sky and a line of sun-bleached hills.

He began to raise himself and felt a stab of pain in his left side. He looked down and saw that a bandage covered his ribcage below a mass of bruising. Suddenly it all came back to him, their extraordinary adventure in the volcano, their final passage into the audience chamber, the image of Costas sprawled in agony and Katya standing beside him. He sat up with a jolt as he remembered her last word, his mind reeling in disbelief.

'Good morning, Dr Howard. Your host is awaiting you.'

Jack looked up and saw a demure man of indeterminate age standing at the door. He had the Mongoloid features of central Asia, yet his English accent was as immaculate as his manservant's uniform.

'Where am I?' Jack demanded gruffly.

'All in good time, sir. The bathroom?'

Jack looked in the direction the man had indicated. He knew there was little point in remonstrating and eased himself onto the richly hued mahogany floor. He padded into the bathroom, ignoring the jacuzzi and opting instead for the shower. He returned to find new clothes laid out for him, an Armani black roll-neck shirt, white slacks and Gucci leather shoes, all in his size. With his three-day stubble and weather-beaten features he felt at odds with designer clothing, but he was thankful to be out of the E-suit with its unpleasant lining of congealed blood and seawater.

He smoothed back his thick hair and spotted the manservant hovering discreetly outside the doorway.

'Right,' Jack said grimly. 'Let's find your lord and master.'

As he followed the man down an escalator, Jack realized that the room he had occupied was one of a number of self-contained pods dotted around the ravines and slopes of the hillside, all linked together by a nexus of tubular passageways that radiated out from a central hub rising from the valley floor.

The edifice they were now entering was a vast circular building capped by a gleaming white dome. As they approached, Jack saw that the exterior panels had been angled to catch the morning sun as it shone down the valley, and below stood another battery of solar panels next to a structure that looked like a generating station. The whole complex seemed bizarrely futuristic, like a mock-up for a lunar station yet more elaborate than anything NASA had ever devised.

The attendant closed the doors behind Jack and he stepped guardedly into the room. Nothing about the utilitarian exterior had prepared him for the scene inside. It was an exact replica of the Pantheon in Rome. The vast space had precisely the dimensions of the original, capacious enough to accommodate a sphere more than forty-three metres in diameter, larger even than the dome of St Peter's in the Vatican. From the opening far above, a shaft of sunlight lit up the coffered vaulting, its gilt surface illuminating the interior just as the original would have done in the second century AD.

Below the dome the walls of the rotunda were broken by a succession of deep niches and shallow recesses, each flanked by marble columns and capped by an elaborate entablature. The floor and walls were inlaid with exotic marbles from the Roman period. At a glance Jack could identify the Egyptian red porphyry favoured by the emperors, green *lapis lacedaemonis* from Sparta and the beautiful honey-coloured *giallo antico* of Tunisia.

To Jack, this was more than antiquarian whimsy on a grand scale. Instead of the catafalques of kings, the niches were filled with books and the recesses with paintings and sculpture. The huge apse beside Jack was an auditorium with rows of luxurious seats in front of a full-sized cinema screen, and computer workstations were dotted around the room. Directly opposite the apse was an immense window. It faced north; the distant ridge Jack had seen from his bedroom window here filled the view, with the sea to the left.

The most striking addition to the ancient scheme was in the very centre, an image at once supremely modern and completely in keeping with the Roman conception. It was a planetarium projector, gleaming on its pedestal like a sputnik. In antiquity the initiate could gaze upwards and see order triumphing over chaos; here, though, the fantasy was taken one step further, into a dangerous realm of hubris the ancients would never have dared enter. To project an image of the night sky inside the dome was the ultimate illusion of power, the fantasy of total control over the heavens themselves.

It was the playroom of a man of culture and scholarship, Jack reflected, of incalculable wealth and indolence, someone whose ego knew no bounds and who would always seek to dominate the world around him.

'My small conceit,' a voice boomed. 'Unfortunately I could not have the original so I built a copy. An improved version, you will agree. Now you understand why I felt so at home inside that chamber in the volcano.'

The remarkable acoustics meant the voice could have come from beside Jack, but in fact it emanated from a chair next to the window in the far wall. The chair swivelled round and Aslan came into view, his posture and red robe exactly as Jack remembered before he lost consciousness.

'I trust you enjoyed a comfortable night. My doctors attended to your injuries.' He gestured towards a low-set table in front of him. 'Breakfast?'

Jack remained where he was and scanned the room again. It had a second occupant, Olga Bortsev, Katya's research assistant. She was staring at him from one of the niches in front of a table covered with open folio volumes. Jack cast her a malevolent glare and she looked back at him defiantly.

'Where is Dr Kazantzakis?' he demanded.

'Ah yes, your friend Costas,' Aslan replied with a hollow laugh. 'You need not be concerned. He is alive if not kicking. He is assisting us on the island.'

Jack reluctantly made his way across the room. His body desperately craved replenishment. As he approached the table, two waiters appeared with drinks and sumptuous platters of food. Jack chose a seat at the far end from Aslan and settled down gingerly in the soft leather cushions.

'Where is Katya?' he asked.

Aslan ignored him.

'I trust you liked my paintings,' he said conversationally. 'I had your suite hung with some of my latest acquisitions. I understand your family has a special interest in cubist and expressionist art of the early twentieth century.'

Jack's grandfather had been a major patron of European artists in the years following the First World War, and the Howard Gallery was famous for its modernist paintings and sculpture.

'Some nice canvases,' Jack said drily. 'Picasso, "Woman With a Baby", 1938. Missing from the Museum of Modern Art in Paris since last year. And I see your collection is not restricted to paintings.' He gestured towards a glass case in one of the niches. Inside was an artefact instantly recognizable the world over as the Mask of Agamemnon, the greatest treasure from Bronze Age Mycenae. It normally resided in the National Museum of Athens, but like the Picasso had disappeared in a series of daring heists across Europe the previous summer. To Jack it was a symbol of nobility that mocked the arrogance of its grotesque new custodian.

'I was a professor of Islamic art, and that is where my heart lies,' Aslan said. 'But I do not restrict my collecting to the fourteen hundred years since Muhammad received the word of Allah. The glory of God shines through the art of all ages. He has blessed me with the gift to make a collection that truly reflects His glory. Allah be praised.'

'Playing God won't make you any friends in the Islamic world,' Jack said quietly. 'Not very devout to keep a collection that mimics God's creation.'

Aslan waved dismissively as his cellphone chirped. He removed it from a pouch on his chair and spoke in a guttural tongue Jack took to be his native Kazakh.

The food on the table looked appetizing and Jack took the opportunity to make the most of it.

'My apologies.' Aslan slipped the phone back into its pouch. 'Business before pleasure, I fear. A small matter of a delayed shipment to one of our valued customers. You know the story.'

Jack ignored this. 'I take it I am in Abkhazia,' he said.

'You are correct.' Aslan pressed a button and his chair swivelled towards a map of the Black Sea on the opposite wall. He aimed a laser pointer at a region of mountains and valleys

316

between Georgia and the Russian Caucasus. 'A matter of destiny. This coast was the summer residence of the Khans of the Golden Horde, the western Mongol empire based on the River Volga. I am a direct descendent of Genghis Khan and Tamburlaine the Great. History, Dr Howard, is repeating itself. Only I will not stop here. I will take up the sword where my ancestors faltered.'

Abkhazia, fiercely independent and tribal, was a tailor-made hideout for warlords and terrorists. Once an autonomous region within the Soviet Republic of Georgia, the collapse of the USSR in 1991 had precipitated bloody civil war and ethnic cleansing in which thousands had died. With the upsurge of Islamic extremism, fighting had again broken out, leaving the Georgian government no alternative but to give up all claims to the region. Since then Abkhazia had become one of the most anarchic places on earth, its ruling junta surviving on payouts from gangsters and jihadists who had arrived from all corners of the world and transformed the old Soviet resorts along the coast into their own private fiefdoms.

'The border of Abkhazia is one hundred and fifty kilometres north of the volcano,' Jack observed tersely. 'What do you propose to do with us now?'

Aslan's demeanour suddenly changed; his face contorted to a sneer and his hands gripped the armrests until the whites of his knuckles showed.

'You I will ransom.' Aslan's voice was a snarl, his rage seething. 'We will get a good price on your head from that Jew.' He spat out the final word with all the venom he could muster, his hatred a poisonous cocktail of anti-Semitism and envy for Efram Jacobovich's spectacular success as a financier and businessman.

'And the others?'

'The Greek will co-operate when I tell him you will be

tortured and beheaded if he does otherwise. He has a small task to perform for us. He will lead us back through the volcano to *Kazbek*.'

'And Katya?'

Another dark cloud passed over Aslan's face and his voice dropped to little more than a whisper.

'In the Aegean I decided to stand off when she said she would lead us to a greater treasure. I gave her two days but she failed to make contact. Fortunately Olga had already copied the ancient texts in Alexandria and had done her work. We knew you could only be heading here.'

'Where is Katya?' Jack tried to keep his voice controlled.

'She was a loving child.' Aslan's eyes appeared briefly to soften. 'Our holidays in the dacha were a joy before her mother's untimely death. Olga and I tried our best.'

He looked at Olga, who smiled ingratiatingly back at him from the table of folios. When he turned back to Jack his voice was suddenly shrill and harsh.

'My daughter has dishonoured me and her faith. I had no control over her education in the Soviet period, then she fled west and was corrupted. She had the effrontery to reject my patronymic and adopt her mother's name. I will keep her on *Vultura* and take her back to Kazakhstan where she will be treated according to sharia law.'

'You mean mutilated and enslaved,' Jack said icily.

'She will be cleansed of the vices of the flesh. After the rite of circumcision I will send her to a holy college for moral purification. Then I will find her a suitable husband, *insh'allah*. If God wills it.'

Aslan closed his eyes for a few moments to calm himself. Then he snapped his fingers and two attendants materialized to help him to his feet. He smoothed his red robe and arranged his hands over his paunch.

'Come.' He nodded towards the window. 'Let me show you before we get down to business.'

As Jack followed the huge shuffling figure, his eye was caught by another glass case mounted on a plinth beside the window. With a thrill he recognized two exquisite ivory plaques from the ancient Silk Road site of Begram, treasures thought lost for ever when the Taliban desecrated the Kabul museum during their reign of terror in Afghanistan. He paused to inspect the intricate carving on the plaques, imports from second-century AD Han China found in a palace storeroom alongside priceless Indian lacquer and rare masterworks of Roman glass and bronze. He was delighted that the hoard had survived yet dismayed to find the artefacts in this monument to ego. Jack believed passionately that revealing the past helped unify nations by celebrating the shared achievement of humankind. The more great works of art disappeared into the black hole of bank vaults and private galleries, the less that goal seemed attainable.

Aslan turned and noticed Jack's interest. He seemed to derive great pleasure from what he saw as Jack's envy.

'It is my compulsion, my passion, second only to my faith,' he wheezed. 'I look forward to selecting items from your museum in Carthage as part of your ransom. And some of the paintings in the Howard Gallery interest me very much.'

Aslan led Jack across the room to a convex window which swept round the rotunda. It was as if they were looking out from an airport control tower, an impression enhanced by the complex of runways that spread out across the valley floor below them.

Jack tried to ignore Aslan and concentrate on the view. The runways formed a giant L shape, the east-west tarmac below them skirting the south side of the valley and the north-south runway lying to the west where the perimeter hills were low.

Beside it a cluster of warehouse-sized buildings marked the terminal. Next to it was a helipad, three of its four roundels occupied, by a Hind E, a Havoc and a Kamov Ka-50 Werewolf. The Werewolf rivalled the American Apache in manoeuvrability and firepower. Any one of them could deliver a devastating attack on a patrol vessel or police helicopter brazen enough to confront Aslan's operations.

Jack's gaze moved to a series of dark openings on the far side of the valley beyond the end of the runway. They were aircraft shelters dug deep into the rocky slope. To his astonishment he realized the two grey shapes in front were Harrier jump jets, their noses peering out from camouflaged covers that would be invisible to satellite surveillance.

'You see my hardware is not limited to the former Soviet arsenal.' Aslan beamed. 'Recently your government foolishly disbanded the Royal Navy's Sea Harrier force. Officially they were all scrapped, but a former minister with an interest in the arms trade proved amenable to a deal. Fortunately I have no lack of trained personnel. Olga was a reserve pilot in the Soviet Air Force and recently made our first experimental flight.'

With increasing dismay Jack followed Aslan's gaze as he pressed a button on the balustrade and the bookcases to either side retracted to reveal the coastline. The ridges bordering the valley continued out to form a wide natural harbour. The spur nearest them abutted a massive concrete quay that angled northwards to conceal the bay from passing ships.

Aslan's latest vessel was a Russian Project 1154 *Neustrashimy*-class frigate, from the same stable as *Vultura* but with three times the displacement. It was in the final stages of refit with weapons and communications pods being hoisted aboard by dockside cranes. A distant shower of sparks showed welders hard at work on the extended helipad and jump jet platform.

Jack thought again about *Seaquest*. She should have been hove to above Atlantis after following the storm back south as it abated. He dared not mention her in case she had escaped detection, but it seemed inconceivable that she would not have been spotted once she was within radar range of *Vultura*. He remembered the distant gunfire he was sure they had heard in the mortuary chamber. He was beginning to fear the worst.

'We are nearly ready for our maiden voyage. You will be my guest of honour at the commissioning ceremony.' Aslan paused, his hands folded over his belly and his face set in gluttonous contentment. 'With my two ships I will be able to roam the high seas at will. Nothing will stand in my way.'

As Jack took one final look over the scene, the awesome magnitude of Aslan's power began to sink in. Where the valley narrowed to the east were firing ranges and structures that looked like mock-ups for urban warfare training. Between the terminal and the sea was another circular hub, this one festooned with satellite dishes and antenna arrays. Along the ridge were camouflaged surveillance stations, and on the beach were weapons emplacements among the palm and eucalyptus trees which were all that remained of the Communist Party resort that had once occupied the valley.

'You will now appreciate it is futile to attempt escape. To the east are the Caucasus Mountains, to the north and south is bandit country where no westerner would survive. I trust you will instead enjoy my hospitality. I look forward to having a companion with whom I can converse about art and archaeology.'

Aslan seemed suddenly overcome by euphoria, his arms raised and his face suffused with rapture.

'This is my *Kehlsteinhaus*, my Eagle's Nest,' he ranted. 'It is my holy temple and fortress. You will agree that the view is as beautiful as the Bavarian Alps?'

Jack replied quietly, his eyes still fixed on the valley below.

'During what you would call the Great Patriotic War my father was a Royal Air Force pathfinder pilot,' he said. 'In 1945 he had the privilege of leading the raid on the Obersalzberg at Berchtesgaden. Neither the Führer's villa nor SS headquarters proved quite so invulnerable as their creator had envisaged.' Jack turned and gazed unwaveringly into Aslan's jet-black eyes. 'And history, as you said, Professor Nazarbetov, has a nasty habit of repeating itself.'

24

There was little sensation of speed as the shuttle accelerated down one of the tubular passageways, the air pocket beneath cushioning it like a hovercraft. Jack and Aslan sat on opposite seats, the other man's girth occupying the entire width of the compartment. Jack guessed they had descended to the valley floor and were now approaching the central hub he had seen from the Pantheon room.

A few moments earlier they had stopped to pick up another passenger who now stood motionless between them. He was an immense bear of a man in a tight-fitting black overall, with sloping forehead, flattened nose and pig-like eyes that stared out blankly under a pronounced brow ridge.

'Allow me to introduce your bodyguard,' Aslan said good-naturedly. 'Vladimir Yurevich Dalmotov. A former *spetsnaz* commando, a veteran of the war in Afghanistan, who defected to the Chechen freedom fighters after his brother was executed for garrotting the officer who sent his platoon to their deaths in Grosny. After Chechnya he hired himself out to the al Qaeda holy warriors for the liberation of Abkhazia. I found him by following the trail of bodies. He believes in no god yet Allah forgives him.'

As the shuttle drew to a halt the door slid open and two attendants entered to help Aslan to his feet. Jack had been biding his time since guessing that Costas and Katya were still on the island. As Dalmotov hustled him out Jack noted he had an Uzi slung over his back but wore no body armour.

The space they stepped into was in stark contrast to the opiate splendour of the living quarters. It was a giant hangar, its door retracted to reveal the helipad Jack had seen earlier. On the tarmac was the bulky form of the Hind; a maintenance crew was scurrying around the airframe and a fuelling tender stood waiting.

'Our transport from the island last night,' Aslan said. 'Now about to fulfil the purpose for which it was built.'

The view outside was partly obscured by a flatbed truck parked next to the door. While they watched, a team of men began offloading crates and stacking them against the wall beside a rack of flight suits.

Dalmotov muttered something to Aslan and loped across. He picked up one of the crates and prised it open with his bare hands, extracting and slotting together the components it contained. Even before he raised it to test the sights, Jack had identified the Barrett M82A1, probably the most lethal sniper rifle in the world. It was chambered for the Browning Machine Gun BMG 50 calibre round or the Russian 12.7 millimetre equivalent, firing a high-velocity slug that could penetrate tank armour at five hundred metres or take a man's head off at three times that distance.

'My modest contribution to the jihad.' Aslan smiled widely. 'You must have spotted our sniper training school beyond the runway. Dalmotov is our chief instructor. Our clients include the Irish Republican Army's New Brigade as well as al Qaeda, and they have never been less than entirely satisfied.'

Jack recalled the spate of high-profile sniper attacks earlier that year, a new and devastating phase in the terrorists' war against the west.

While Dalmotov oversaw the assembly of the weapons, Jack followed Aslan to a warehouse on the opposite side of the hangar. Inside, crates were being hammered shut and audited by figures in maintenance overalls. As a forklift passed by, Jack caught sight of the word stencilled in red letters on the side. One of Jack's first assignments with military intelligence had been to intercept a freighter from Libya carrying identical crates. It was Semtex, the deadly plastic explosive from the Czech Republic used by the IRA in their campaign of terror in Britain.

'This is our main transit facility,' Aslan explained. 'Normally the bay is sealed off to contain biological and chemical weapons, but I have just routed our last batch by transport helicopter to another satisfied customer in the Middle East.' Aslan paused, his hands clasped over his belly and his fat thumbs slowly revolving. His eyes narrowed and he stared into the middle distance.

Jack was beginning to recognize the warning signs of Aslan's volatile temper.

'I do have one unhappy customer, someone whose patience has been sorely stretched since 1991. When we tracked *Seaquest* from Trabzon we knew there could be only one possible destination, the place Olga had pinpointed from her study of the ancient text. We made our way to the volcano under cover of darkness. You have provided me the perfect screen to go where politics had denied me access for years. In the past any visit to this island would have provoked an immediate military response. Now if the satellite picks up any activity they will assume it is you, a legitimate scientific project. This was to have been our rendezvous point with the Russians, if that fool Antonov had not sunk his submarine and my merchandise through his own incompetence.'

'Captain Antonov would have delivered his cargo,' Jack replied bleakly. 'There was a mutiny led by the political officer. It was probably the only good thing the KGB ever did.'

'And the nuclear warheads?' Aslan cut in sharply.

'We saw only conventional weapons,' Jack lied.

'Then why did my daughter threaten nuclear holocaust when she negotiated with my men?'

Jack was silent for a moment. Katya had not revealed this detail of her parley in the submarine's control room.

'My men will keep you out,' he replied quietly. 'Your fundamentalist friends are not the only ones willing to die for a cause.'

'They may decide otherwise once they hear the fate that awaits you and that Greek if they do not capitulate.' Aslan smiled humourlessly, his serenity briefly returned. 'I think you will find our next stop most interesting.'

They left the hangar by a different passageway, this time in an open-topped car on a conveyor belt. They were heading towards the central hub about a kilometre closer to the sea. After a five-minute journey they stepped onto an escalator that took them to a lift door. An attendant punched a key that took them to the highest level.

The scene was straight from a NASA space launch. The

room was identical in dimensions to the Pantheon but filled with a mass of computer and surveillance equipment. As they stepped out Jack saw they had ascended inside a drum that rose in the centre like a truncated column. It was like the arena of a latter-day amphitheatre, surrounded by concentric tiers of workstations that faced them in continuous ripples of colour. On the wall behind, giant screens displayed maps and televisual images. The whole complex seemed like *Seaquest*'s control module but on a massive scale, with enough monitoring and communications equipment to run a small war.

Aslan was helped into an electronic wheelchair by two assistants. The rows of shadowy figures hunched behind the monitors seemed scarcely to have noticed their arrival.

'I prefer the excitement of *Vultura*. More hands-on, you might say.' Aslan settled back in his chair. 'But here I can control all my operations simultaneously. From the command chair I can view any screen in the room without moving.'

An attendant who had been waiting nervously on the sidelines leaned over and whispered urgently in his ear. Aslan's face remained impassive but his fingers began drumming the arms of his wheelchair. Without saying a word he pressed a button on his wheelchair and shot off towards a console where a group of figures were congregating. Jack followed with Dalmotov close behind. As they neared the console Jack noted that the screens immediately to the right were security monitors, similar to the type used in the Carthage Museum showing interior views within the complex.

The figures silently parted to allow Aslan access to the screen. Jack moved up until he stood directly behind the wheelchair and the operator who was working the console keyboard. Dalmotov stood at his elbow.

'We've finally made the link,' the operator said in English. 'SATSURV should be coming online now.'

The man was of Asian appearance but wore jeans and a white shirt rather than the black overalls that were standard issue in the place. From his accent Jack guessed that he had been educated in Britain.

The operator looked first at Jack and then questioningly at Aslan. The big man nodded languidly, a gesture not of indifference but of supreme confidence that his guest would never be in a position to divulge anything he saw or heard.

A mosaic of pixels resolved into a view of the Black Sea, the south-eastern corner still partly obscured by cloud from the storm. The thermal imaging transformed the scene into a spectrum of colours, the coastline emerging clearly as the satellite picked up infrared radiation from below the cloud base. The operator traced out a small square and magnified it to fill the screen. He repeated the process until the screen was dominated by the island, the centre a shifting halo of pinks and yellows where the core was emitting strong heat radiation.

On the sea nearby was a sliver of colour that signified a surface vessel. The operator increased magnification until it filled the entire screen, the imagery now at sub-metric resolution. The vessel was dead in the water, the hull careened to port with the bow submerged and its starboard screw dangling above the smashed remains of the rudder.

To his horror Jack recognized *Seaquest*, her lines still clear despite the appalling damage. The heat radiation showed where armour-piercing shells had slammed into the hull and left gaping exit wounds like high-velocity rounds through a human body. Jack felt gripped by anger as he surveyed the destruction. He swung the wheelchair round and confronted Aslan.

'Where are my people?' he demanded.

'There do not appear to be any human heat signatures,' Aslan replied calmly. 'Two of your crew were foolish enough to engage *Vultura* in a firefight yesterday morning. A somewhat one-sided battle as you might imagine. We will shortly be sending the Hind to dispose of the wreckage.'

On *Seaquest*'s shattered foredeck Jack could see the gun turret deployed and elevated. The barrels were at a crazy angle, evidently the result of a direct hit. Jack knew that York and Howe would not have abandoned her without a fight. He silently prayed they had managed to escape afterwards with the rest of the crew in the submersible.

'They were scientists and sailors, not fanatics and thugs,' Jack said coldly.

Aslan shrugged and turned back to the screen.

It transformed to show another ship, this one hove close in to the island. As the image magnified, all eyes were glued on the stern. A group of figures could be seen dismantling two large tubes which showed irregular patterns of thermal radiation as if they had been on fire. Just as Jack realized he was looking at battle damage to *Vultura*, Aslan snapped his fingers and a hand gripped Jack's shoulder like a vice.

'Why was I not told?' Aslan screamed in rage. 'Why was this kept concealed from me?'

The room went silent and he pointed at Jack. 'He is not worthy of ransom. He will be liquidated like his crew. Get him out of my sight!'

Before being hustled away Jack made a quick mental note of the GPS co-ordinates on the SATSURV screen. As Dalmotov pushed him he pretended to trip up against the security monitors. Earlier he had recognized the approach passageway and the hangar entrance on the two nearest screens. As he stumbled against the control panel he pressed the pause key.

Other CCTV cameras would chart their progress, but with all eyes diverted to the image of *Vultura* there was a chance they might go unnoticed.

Ever since he had woken that morning Jack had been determined to act. He knew Aslan's moods were fickle, that the rage of his last outburst would again revert to apparent conviviality, but Jack had decided to gamble no more on the whims of a megalomaniac. The shocking image of *Seaquest* and the uncertain fate of her crew had hardened his resolve. He owed it to those who may have paid the ultimate price. And he knew the fate of both Costas and Katya lay in his hands.

His opportunity came as the shuttle was speeding them from the control hub back to the hangar. Just beyond the halfway point Dalmotov stepped forward to peer at the docking bay as it came into view. It was a momentary lapse in vigilance, a mistake he would never have made had his instincts not been blunted by being too long in Aslan's lair. With lightning speed Jack drew back his left fist and slammed it into Dalmotov's back, a crushing impact that threw Jack off balance and left him clutching his hand in pain.

It was a blow that would have killed any ordinary man. Jack had brought his full force to bear at a point just below the ribcage where the shock of an impact can stop the heart and diaphragm simultaneously. He watched in disbelief as Dalmotov remained immobile, his huge physique seemingly impervious. Then he muttered something unintelligible and sank to his knees. He remained upright for a few seconds, his legs shuffling feebly, then toppled forward and lay still.

Jack heaved the recumbent form out of sight of any surveillance camera. The docking bay was empty and the only figures he could see were on the helipad outside the hangar entrance. As the shuttle drew to a halt he stepped out and pressed the return button, sending the carriage and its unconscious occupant back in the direction of the control hub. He was buying precious time and knew every second must count.

Without hesitating he marched brazenly towards the helipad entrance, praying his confident gait would allay suspicion. He reached the rack of flight suits, selected the longest and pulled it on. He tightened the lifejacket and donned a helmet, closing the visor so his face was concealed.

He snatched a duffel bag and picked up one of the Barrett sniper rifles. He had observed Dalmotov assembling the weapon and quickly found the locking pin. He detached the stock from the receiver and slid them both into the bag. Stacked alongside were cartons labelled BMG, the 50 calibre Browning Machine Gun round. Jack took a handful of the massive 14 millimetre cartridges and shoved them in beside the weapon.

After zipping up the bag he continued resolutely towards the hangar entrance. Once there he squatted down to survey the scene while pretending to adjust an ankle strap. The tarmac was hot to the touch, the summer sun having burned away the rainwater from the night before. In the glare the buildings of the compound seemed scorched and over-burdened with heat like the surrounding hills.

He had already decided which helicopter to go for. The Werewolf was the most sophisticated, but was parked with the Havoc at the far edge of the heliport. The Hind was only twenty metres in front and being prepared for flight. It had been a workhorse of the Russian war machine and the snout with its stepped tandem cockpit exuded reliability.

He straightened up and walked over to a crew chief who was feeding a belt into the ammunition loading port.

'Priority orders,' Jack barked. 'The schedule has moved forward. I am to leave at once.'

His Russian was rusty and heavily accented, but he hoped it would pass muster in a place where many of the personnel were Kazakhs and Abkhazians.

The man looked surprised but not unduly taken aback.

'The weapons hardpoints are still empty and you have only four hundred rounds of 12.7, but otherwise we are ready to go. You are cleared to mount up and begin pre-flight checks.'

Jack slung the duffel bag over his shoulder and climbed through the starboard door. He ducked into the cockpit and manoeuvred into the pilot's seat. He stashed the bag out of the way. The controls did not look as if they would present too many problems; the overall configuration differed little from other military helicopters he had flown.

As he strapped himself in, Jack looked out through the canopy. Over the bulging Plexiglas of the gunner's nacelle he could see a group of fitters wheeling two flatbed trolleys, each laden with tube launchers for the Spiral radio-guided anti-armour missile. The Hind was being loaded up for the final assault on *Seaquest*. At the same moment he glimpsed two men in flight suits coming towards him from the hangar entrance, evidently the Hind's pilot and gunner. The instant he saw the crew chief pick up his cellphone and raise his eyes in alarm, Jack knew his cover was blown.

The giant five-blade rotor was already turning, the twin 2,200 horsepower Isotov TV3-117 turboshafts having been warmed up as part of the pre-flight routine. Jack scanned the dials and saw the tank was full and oil and hydraulic pressures were up to mark. He prayed fervently that Aslan's anti-aircraft defences had not yet been briefed to shoot down one of their own. He gripped the two control sticks, his left hand pulling hard on the collective and twisting the throttle and his right hand pushing the cyclic as far forward as it would go.

In seconds the beat of the rotor rose in a mighty crescendo and the Hind lurched into the air with its nose angled down. For a few agonizing moments there was no movement as it strained and bucked against the force of gravity, its efforts drummed out in a deafening cacophony that reverberated off the buildings around the helipad. As Jack skilfully feathered the pedals to keep the machine from sliding sideways he caught sight of a great bear of a man running out of the hangar and roughly pushing aside the two dazed airmen. Dalmotov did not even bother with his Uzi, knowing the 9 millimetre rounds would splatter harmlessly off the helicopter's armour plating. Instead he raised a much more lethal weapon he had grabbed on his way through the hangar.

The first 50 calibre BMG round smashed straight through the forward gunner's nacelle, a position Jack would have taken had he known the helicopter was dual-control. As the machine suddenly sprang forward, a second round hit somewhere aft, a jarring impact that swung the fuselage sideways and forced Jack to compensate with an extra burst to the tail rotor.

As he wrestled with the controls, the helicopter rose over the hangar and clattered with increasing speed towards the southern seawall. To his left he could see the futuristic complex of Aslan's hillside palace and to the right the sleek lines of the frigate. Moments later he crossed the perimeter and was over the open sea, the undercarriage skimming the waves as he kept low to minimize his radar profile. With the throttle at maximum and the cyclic jammed forward, he soon reached the helicopter's maximum sea-level speed of 335 kilometres per hour, a figure he was able to boost slightly after finding the switch that retracted the undercarriage. The shoreline was now receding rapidly to the east, and ahead lay only the cloudless morning sky merging into a blue-grey haze on the horizon.

Fifteen nautical miles out, Jack pressed the pedal that controlled the tail rotor and pushed the cyclic to the left, gently easing the helicopter round until the compass read 180 degrees due south. He had already worked out how to activate the radar and GPS unit and now programmed in the co-ordinates for the island he had memorized on *Seaquest* three days previously. The computer calculated the remaining distance at just under 150 kilometres, a flight time of half an hour at present velocity. Despite the high fuel consumption, Jack had decided to maintain low altitude and maximum throttle, the fuel tanks over this distance providing ample margin.

He activated the autopilot and opened the visor on his helmet. Without pausing he lifted the duffel bag and began to assemble the rifle. He knew he could not afford to let his guard down for one moment. Aslan would do all in his power to bring him back.

25

'Bring the helicopter to a standstill and await escort. Comply immediately or you will be destroyed. You will not be warned again.'

Jack had heard the voice only once before, cursing gutturally in Russian, but there was no mistaking Dalmotov's heavily accented delivery as it crackled through the intercom. Jack had kept the two-way radio on throughout the flight and had been expecting contact as soon as his pursuers came within range. For the past ten minutes he had been monitoring the radar screen as two red dots converged on him from the north, their speed and trajectory leaving no doubt they were the Havoc and Werewolf from Aslan's base.

He was only ten nautical miles north of the island, less than five minutes' flying time away. He had sacrificed maximum speed by keeping low over the waves to suppress his radar profile, a gamble that had nearly paid off. Despite its age the Hind was marginally faster and more powerful than the other two machines, but they had gained on him by flying at a higher altitude where there was less air resistance.

As well as a fixed 30 millimetre high-speed cannon and two twenty-round pods of 80 millimetre rockets the Havoc and Werewolf each carried a lethal combination of laser-guided air-to-air and anti-ship missiles, weapons Jack had seen in the loading bay. By contrast the hardpoints on the Hind's stub wings were empty, the only firepower coming from the trademark four-barrelled 12.7 millimetre machine gun in the chin turret. It was a potentially devastating weapon, a mass killer in the Afghan and Chechen wars, but in the absence of a gunner Jack could only operate it on a fixed trajectory over open sights. At a cyclic rate of 1,200 rounds per minute per barrel, the four one-hundred round belts of armour-piercing would only allow a five-second burst, enough to cause colossal destruction at short range but scarcely sufficient to take on two such formidable adversaries.

Jack knew the odds would be stacked hopelessly against him in a stand-off battle. His only chance would be a close-up engagement of the most brutal kind.

'OK, Dalmotov, you win this time,' Jack muttered grimly to himself as he eased back on the throttle and spun the helicopter round to face his enemy. 'But don't count on seeing home again.'

The three helicopters hovered in line abreast thirty metres above the waves, the downdraught churning up whirlwinds of spray. In the centre the Hind seemed conspicuously bulky, the other two machines having been designed for manoeuvrability and reduced battlefield visibility. To Jack's right the Mi-28 Havoc looked like a hungry jackal with its low-set cockpit and protuberent snout. To his left the Ka-50 Werewolf's trademark twin counter-rotating coaxial rotors seemed to magnify its potency yet reduce the airframe to insect-like proportions.

Through the bulletproof flat-screen glazing of the Werewolf, Jack could make out the glowering form of Dalmotov.

He instructed Jack to fly fifty metres ahead of his escorts. The clatter of the rotors increased to a reverberating din as the three machines tilted forward and began to fly north-east in close formation.

As ordered, Jack switched off the two-way radio that would have allowed him to alert outside help. After activating the autopilot he settled back and cradled the Barrett out of sight on his lap. Fully assembled it was almost a metre and a half long and weighed fourteen kilograms. He had been obliged to remove the ten-round magazine to keep the barrel concealed below the cowling. With his right hand he checked the receiver where he had chambered one of the massive 50 calibre BMG rounds. His window of opportunity was closing with each kilometre and he knew he must act soon.

His chance came earlier than expected. Five minutes on they suddenly encountered a thermal, a residual effect of the storm the night before. They bucked and swayed in a roller-coaster ride that seemed to ripple from the Hind to the other two. In the split second longer it took the others to adjust their controls, Jack decided to act. As another jolt of turbulence hit, he twisted the throttle back and pulled hard on the collective. Despite the cutback in engine power, the updraught was enough to provide lift with the rotor blades pitched to maximum. The Hind bounced twenty metres above its original course, then faltered and began to drop. The other two passed below as if in slow motion, their blades almost skimming the Hind's underbelly. Suddenly Jack was behind them. It was a classic manoeuvre of First World War dogfighting that was used to devastating effect by British Harriers against the faster Argentinian Mirages during the Falklands conflict.

With the muzzle of the rifle wedged below the left window, Jack decided to use the Hind's integral firepower against the machine to the right. He twisted the throttle to maximum and swerved sideways until the Havoc was in his sights. The entire manoeuvre had taken less than five seconds, scarcely time for the others to register his absence, let alone take evasive action.

As the Hind bounced into position fifty metres astern, Jack flipped open the safety cover on top of the cyclic and pressed the red fire button. The four guns in the chin turret erupted in an immense wall of noise, a staccato hammering that threw Jack forward with the recoil. Each barrel spewed out twenty rounds per second, the casings ejecting in a wide arc on either side. For five seconds multiple prongs of flame shot out from under the nose and a withering hail of fire poured towards his opponent.

At first the Havoc appeared to be absorbing the rounds as they punched through the rear plating of the fuselage. Then a gaping hole suddenly appeared from fore to aft as the bullets shredded everything in their path, and the cockpit and its occupant disintegrated in a geyser of carnage. As the Hind tipped upwards, the final torrent of bullets caught the Havoc's turboshaft assembly, severing the rotor which spun off like a demented boomerang. Seconds later the fuselage exploded in a giant fireball of aviation fuel and detonating ammunition.

Jack pulled hard on the collective and rose above the

doomed helicopter. He settled on a level trajectory with the Werewolf, its sinister form now thirty metres to his left and slightly ahead. Jack could see the pilot battling with the controls as the lighter airframe was buffeted by the thermals and the aftershock of the explosion. Dalmotov seemed frozen in disbelief, unable to accept what had happened, but Jack knew it would be momentary; he had only seconds before he lost his advantage.

He levelled the Barrett out of the window and fired. The bullet left with a mighty crack, the noise reverberating inside his earphones. He swore as he saw sparks fly off the Werewolf's upper fuselage and quickly chambered another round. This time he aimed to the right to compensate for the 200 kilometre per hour airflow. He fired just as Dalmotov jerked his head round to look at him.

Like most close-support helicopters, the Werewolf was well protected against ground attack, the armoured shield round the cockpit designed to withstand 20 millimetre cannon strikes. Its vulnerability lay in the upper fuselage and engine mounting, areas less susceptible to ground fire, where defensive plating was sacrificed to allow maximum armour to be concentrated round the crew compartment. The counter-rotating airfoil was both its strength and its weakness, producing a highly agile machine but requiring a shaft that protruded high above the fuselage to accommodate the two heads for the three-blade coaxial rotors.

The second round struck just below the lower rotor, smashing through the machinery and severing the control line. For a moment nothing happened and the helicopter continued forward with its nose down. Then it began to judder and reared up at a crazy angle. Jack could see Dalmotov frantically working the controls. Even from a distance he could tell the cyclic and collective were dysfunctional and there was no response from the pedals. Dalmotov reached up to pull a red handle that hung above his head.

The Werewolf was unique among battlefield helicopters in having a pilot ejection seat. The problem with helicopter ejection had always been the rotor above the cockpit, but Kamov had devised an ingenious system whereby the blades were discarded and the pilot's seat was blasted up to a safe altitude for the parachute to open.

From the moment he pulled the handle, Dalmotov must have sensed something was terribly wrong. Instead of ejecting, the rotor blades remained fixed while the explosive charges around the canopy detonated in quick succession. The canopy blasted into the rotor and was hurled into space, leaving the blades bent but operational. Seconds later the seat ejected in a belch of smoke. By hideous chance it was caught between the two sets of blades and tumbled madly like a Catherine wheel spurting fire. After two full revolutions every protruding part of Dalmotov's body had been sliced away, his helmeted head tossed out like a football. After a final spin the rotors spewed out what was left of their macabre cargo and it disappeared below in a plume of spray.

Jack watched dispassionately as the Werewolf executed a crazy dance in ever diminishing circles, the blades snapping off one by one under the increasing air pressure until the fuselage plummeted into the sea and exploded.

Without lingering any further, he veered south on his original course and twisted the throttle to maximum. Dalmotov would have relayed an automated Mayday and position fix, and the technicians in Aslan's control centre would be redirecting the SATSURV to the slick of oil and debris where the helicopters had gone down. The sight would only stoke Aslan's rage, already incandescent after the damage to *Vultura*. Jack knew any value he had as a hostage would now be eclipsed by Aslan's need to exact retribution.

To his alarm he saw the fuel gauge was flickering dangerously close to empty. When he had last checked ten minutes before, it had read three-quarters full, and there was no way the ensuing action could have expended half the tank. He remembered the hit aft from Dalmotov's sniper rifle as he left the helipad. If the bullet had struck a fuel line, the jolting as they passed through the thermal could have exacerbated the damage, severing the connection and causing massive fuel loss.

He had no time for confirmation. He cut back on the throttle to minimize fuel consumption and dropped to thirty metres. The distant form of the island appeared out of the morning haze, the twin peaks with their distinctive bull's horn shape just as he had first seen them from *Seaquest* three days before. His only hope now was that the Hind would last long enough to get him within swimming distance of the northern shore.

As the twin turboshafts began to splutter and gasp, Jack's view was momentarily obscured by a pall of black smoke. He recoiled from the smell, an acrid reek of cordite and burning plastic. Seconds later it cleared and he was confronted by the hulk of *Seaquest* less than two hundred metres in front of him.

The satellite images were no preparation for the shocking reality. IMU's premier research vessel was wallowing with her foredeck nearly awash, her superstructure smashed beyond recognition and her starboard side rent with cavernous holes where *Vultura*'s shells had splayed open the plating as they tore through. It seemed a miracle she was still afloat, but Jack could tell that the forward bulkheads would soon be breached and she would be dragged under.

The Hind barely hung in the air as it shuddered over the ravaged hulk. Almost immediately it began to descend, the rotor no longer able to provide lift. As the engine coughed out its death throes, Jack only just had time to act.

He quickly unbuckled his safety harness and jammed the cyclic forward as far as it would go. By tilting the helicopter down he raised the stub wings behind the compartment out of his way, but in so doing he had also aimed the machine to nose-dive. With only seconds to spare, he threw off his helmet, ducked behind the cockpit and hurled himself out, his legs tightly crossed and his arms pressed hard against his chest to prevent them from ripping upwards as he hit the water.

Without his helmet he reduced the risk of whiplash but even so the impact was bone-jarring. He sliced into the sea feet first and plummeted deep enough to feel the thermocline. He splayed his limbs to halt his descent. As he swam back towards the surface, he felt a stabbing pain where the wound in his side had torn open. Partway up there was a tremendous concussion that sent a shock wave coursing through the water. He broke surface and saw the burning remains of the Hind a short distance away, a scene of devastation that could easily have been his own funeral pyre.

He cracked the CO_2 cartridge on his lifejacket and made for *Seaquest*. He was suddenly overwhelmed by fatigue, the adrenalin rush having taken its toll on his already depleted reserves.

Seaquest was so far down on her bow that he was able to swim over the submerged forecastle and haul himself on the sloping deck in front of the gun emplacement. It was the scene of York and Howe's last stand the day before. After grimly surveying the scene, Jack stripped off his lifejacket and picked his way cautiously towards the remains of the deckhouse. Just before reaching the hatch into the hold, he lost his footing and fell heavily. He realized with dismay that he had slipped on congealed blood, a crimson splatter that trailed to the starboard side of the hull.

Jack knew there was nothing to be gained from dwelling on the final moments of his crew. He sank back for a moment's respite beside the hatch while he summoned all his remaining willpower and strength.

Almost too late he saw the helicopter out of the corner of his eye. It was far away, just off the corner of the island, and the sound of its rotor was drowned out by the noise of *Seaquest* breaking up. He knew from the vacant pad at the heliport that Aslan had a fourth attack helicopter, and he guessed this was a Kamov Ka-28 Helix flown off *Vultura*. He squinted into the morning sun and saw the helicopter low over the water, aimed directly at him. Jack had been at the receiving end of enough helicopter attacks to know what to expect, yet rarely had he felt so vulnerable.

There was a distant flash as a telltale halo dropped and began to enlarge with horrifying speed. It was a heavy anti-ship missile, probably one of the feared Exocet AM.39 warheads he had seen stockpiled at Aslan's headquarters. Jack hurled himself through the hatch and tumbled to the lower deck, literally falling into the command module. Just as he spun the locking wheel, there was an immense crash. He was thrown violently back against a bulkhead and the world went dark.

26

The door slammed behind Costas as he flew into the bulkhead. It was a jarring impact, the protruding ridge of metal taking him full in the chest and leaving him fighting for breath. The blindfold had been ripped off but all he could see was a crimson blur. He rolled back slightly, his whole body convulsed with pain, and slowly raised his arm to feel his face. His right eye was swollen and closed over, numb to the touch. He moved his fingers to his left eye and wiped away the sticky sheen before opening it. Gradually his focus improved. From where he was lying he could see whitewashed piping running along the bulkhead, the front stamped with symbols and letters he could just make out as Cyrillic.

He had no sense of time or place. His last clear memory had

been Jack collapsing inside the audience chamber. Then there was blackness, a hazy memory of movement and pain. He had come to strapped in a chair with a blinding light thrust in his face. Then hour after hour of torment, of screaming and agonizing blows. Always the same black-clad figures, always the same question shouted in broken English. *How did you get from the submarine?* He guessed he was on *Vultura*, but all powers of analysis had shut down as his mind focused on survival. Again and again he was hurled into this room, then dragged back just when he thought it was all over.

And now it was happening again. This time there had been no respite. The door crashed open and there was a violent blow to his back, forcing up a slurry of blood and vomit. He was hauled to his knees retching and coughing and the blindfold was yanked on again, so tight he could feel the blood squeezing out of his swollen eye socket. He thought he could never feel another type of pain, but this was it. He concentrated his whole being on his one lifeline, that he was taking the punishment and not Jack. He had to hold on whatever it took until *Seaquest* arrived and the discovery of the warheads was made known.

He came round face down on a table with his hands tied behind the chair he was sitting on. He had no idea how long he had been there and could only see a nauseating speckle of stars where the blindfold pressed against his eyes. Through the throbbing of his head he could hear voices, not those of his tormentors but a man and a woman's. Earlier he had gathered from snatches of overheard conversation that his captors were expecting the return of Aslan by helicopter from their headquarters complex. Even the worst of them seemed apprehensive. There had been some kind of crisis, a downed helicopter, an escaped prisoner. Costas prayed it was Jack.

The voices seemed to be some distance away, in a corridor or an adjoining room, but the woman's was raised in anger and he could hear them clearly. They switched from Russian to English and he realized it was Aslan and Katya.

'These are personal matters,' Aslan said. 'We will speak in English so my mujahedin do not hear this blasphemy.'

'Your mujahedin.' Katya's voice was full of contempt. 'Your mujahedin are jihadists. They fight for Allah, not Aslan.'

'I am their new prophet. Their loyalty is to Aslan.'

'Aslan.' Katya spat out the word with derision. 'Who is Aslan? Piotr Alexandrovich Nazarbetov. A failed professor from an obscure university with delusions of grandeur. You do not even wear the beard of a holy man. And remember I know about our Mongol heritage. Genghis Khan was an infidel who destroyed half the Muslim world. Someone ought to tell that to your holy warriors.'

'You forget yourself, my daughter.' The voice was icy.

'I remember what I had to learn as a child. He who will abide by the Koran will prosper, he who offends against it will get the sword. The faith does not allow the murder of innocents.' Her voice was a ragged sob. 'I know what you did to my mother.'

Aslan's heavy breathing sounded to Costas like a pressure cooker about to explode.

'Your mujahedin are biding their time,' Katya continued. 'They are using you until you become expendable. That submarine will be your tomb as well. All you have done by creating this terrorist sanctuary is hasten your own demise.'

'Silence!' The demented scream was followed by the sounds of a scuffle and something being dragged away. Moments later there were returning footsteps. They halted behind Costas. A pair of hands jerked his shoulders back against the chair.

'Your presence is polluting,' the voice hissed against his ear, still breathing heavily. 'You are about to make your final journey.'

Fingers snapped and two pairs of hands wrenched him upright. In his world of darkness he was unaware of the blow when it came, an instant of pain followed by merciful oblivion.

Jack seemed to be in a living nightmare. He saw only pitch-blackness, a darkness so complete it eclipsed all sensory points of reference. All around him was an immense rushing noise punctuated by creaks and groans. His mind struggled to make sense of the unimaginable. As he lay contorted against the bulkhead he felt oddly lightweight, his body almost levitating as if he were caught in the grip of some demonic fever.

He now knew what it felt like to be trapped inside the bowels of a sinking ship as it plunged into the abyss. His salvation was *Seaquest*'s command module, its fifteen-centimetre thick walls of titanium-reinforced steel protecting him from the crushing pressure that would by now have burst his eardrums and collapsed his skull. He could hear rending and buckling as the remaining air pockets imploded, a noise that would have spelled instant death had he failed to make it into the module in time.

All he could do now was brace himself against the inevitable. The fall seemed interminable, far longer than he had expected, and the noise increased in a shrieking crescendo like an approaching express train. The end when it came was as violent as it was unheralded. The hull crashed into the seabed with a sickening jolt, generating a G force that would have killed him had he not been crouched with his head in his arms. It took all his strength to keep from being thrown upwards as the hull rebounded, the surge accompanied by a horrific tearing sound. Then the wreckage settled and silence descended.

'Activate emergency lighting.'

Jack spoke to himself as he felt his body for further injury. His voice sounded strangely disembodied, its cadences absorbed by the soundproof panelling on the walls, yet it gave a measure of reality in a world that had lost all waymarkers.

As a diver Jack was used to orienting in utter darkness, and now he brought all his experience to bear. After his tumble through the hatch the missile impact had blown him past the weapons locker towards the control panels on the far side of the module. Fortunately *Seaquest* had come to rest upright. As he rose uncertainly to his feet he could sense the slant of the deck where the bow had ploughed into the seabed. He dropped back to his knees and felt his way across the floor, his intimate knowledge of the vessel he had helped design guiding him past the consoles that lined the interior.

He reached a fuse box in the wall to the left of the entry hatch and felt for the switch that connected the reserve battery in its protective lead housing to the main circuitry. His hand found the lever that activated the emergency lighting. Not for the first time that day he shut his eyes tight and prayed for luck.

To his relief the room was immediately bathed in fluorescent green. His eyes quickly adjusted and he turned round to survey the scene. The module was below the waterline, and the shells which had skewered *Seaquest* had passed through the hull above. The equipment and fixtures seemed shipshape and battened down, the module having been designed to survive precisely this kind of attack.

His first task was to disengage the module from the hull. He made his way unsteadily to the central dais. It seemed inconceivable that he had assembled the crew here for the briefing less than 48 hours before. He slumped heavily in the command chair and activated the control panel. The LCD monitor scrolled through a series of password requests before initiating the disengage sequence. After the third password a drawer sprang open and he took out a key which he slotted into the panel and turned clockwise. The electronic propulsion and atmosphere control systems would kick in as soon as the module was a safe distance from the wreckage.

Without *Seaquest*'s sensors, Jack would have no data on depth or local environment until the module was clear of the hull and had activated its own array. He guessed he had fallen into the chasm recorded by *Seaquest* to the north of the island, a gash ten kilometres long and half a kilometre wide that Costas had identified as a tectonic fault on the same line as the volcano. If so, he was mired in the dustbin of the south-eastern Black Sea, a collecting point for silt and a reservoir of brine from the Ice Age. With every passing minute the wreckage would be sinking further into a slurry of sediment more intractable than quicksand. Even if he managed to disengage, he might simply drive the module deeper into the ooze, entombing him with no hope of escape.

He strapped himself in and leaned back on the headrest. The computer gave him three chances to abort and each time he pressed *continue*. After the final sequence, a red warning triangle appeared with the word *disengaging* flashing in the centre. For an alarming moment the room reverted to darkness as the computer re-routed the circuitry to the internal battery pod.

A few seconds later the silence was broken by a dull staccato noise outside the casing to his left. Each muffled concussion represented a tiny explosive charge rigged to blow out the rivets in *Seaquest*'s hull and create an aperture large enough for the module to pass through. As the panel sheared off, the space surrounding the module filled with seawater and the bathymetric sensor came online. Jack swivelled towards the exit trajectory and braced himself as the water jets came to life, a low hum that increased in a crescendo as the engines bucked against the pivots that secured the module to the hull. A series of detonations erupted behind him as the module separated from its retaining bolts. Simultaneously the locking clamps retracted and he was thrown back violently in the seat, the compression as the saucer ejected equalling the multiple G force of a rocket launch.

The module had been designed to blast from a sinking ship beyond the suction vortex as the hull plummeted to the sea floor. Jack had experienced a simulation at IMU's deep-water test facility off Bermuda, when the saucer came to a halt a hundred metres away. Here, the G force was followed by an equally violent jolt in the opposite direction, the module stopping only a few metres beyond the wreckage.

He had pitched his head forward in the standard safety posture and his only injuries were a series of painful welts where the straps dug into his shoulders. After taking a deep breath he unbuckled the harness and swivelled towards the workstation, his right hand pushed against the control panel to stop him sliding forward where the module had angled into the seabed.

To the left was a smaller monitor for the display of bathymetric data. As the numbers began to flicker he saw the depth gauge read a staggering 750 metres below sea level, a full hundred metres below the official maximum operating depth of the module. The base of the fault was far deeper than they had imagined, more than half a kilometre below the submerged ancient shoreline.

Jack switched on the sound navigation and ranging system

and waited while the screen came to life. The active sonar transducer emitted a high-frequency narrow-band pulse beam in a 360 degree vertical sweep to give a profile of the sea floor and any suspended objects up to the surface. During *Seaquest*'s run over the canyon two days previously they had established that the fault lay north-south, so he fixed the sonar trajectory east-west to give a cross-section of his position within the defile.

The speed of the beam meant the entire profile was visible on the monitor at once. The mottled green on either side showed where the canyon walls rose some four hundred metres apart. Near the top were jagged protrusions that narrowed the profile further still. The canyon bore all the characteristics of a horizontal tear fault, caused by plates in the earth's crust wrenching apart rather than grinding sideways. It was a geological rarity that would have delighted Costas but was of more immediate concern to Jack because it compounded the gravity of his situation.

He realized his chances against surviving this far had been truly astronomical. If *Seaquest* had sunk only fifty metres west she would have impacted with the lip of the canyon, smashing him to oblivion well before the wreckage reached the sea floor far below.

He turned his attention to the base of the fault where the profiler showed a mass of light green, denoting hundreds of metres of sediment. Partway up was a horizontal line level with the apex of the sonar, a compacted layer which was the resting place for *Seaquest*. Above it a lighter scattering of colour denoting suspended sediment continued for at least twenty metres until the screen became clear, indicating open water.

Jack knew he was atop a drift of sediment at least as deep as the ocean above, immense quantities of silt derived from land run-off mixed with dead marine organisms, natural seabed clays, volcanic debris and brine from the Ice Age evaporation. It was continuously being added to by fallout from above and at any moment could swallow him up like quicksand. And if the quicksand did not get him, an avalanche could. The suspended silt above the wreckage was the result of a turbidity current. IMU scientists had monitored turbidity currents in the Atlantic cascading off the continental shelf at 100 kilometres an hour, carving out submarine canyons and depositing millions of tons of silt. Like snow avalanches, the shock wave from one could trigger another. If he was caught anywhere near an underwater displacement of such magnitude he would be doomed without hope of reprieve.

Even before he tried the engines he knew it was a forlorn hope. The erratic hum as he powered up the unit only confirmed that the water jets were clogged with silt and incapable of shifting the module from the grave it had dug itself. There was no way the IMU engineers could have anticipated that the first deployment of their brainchild would be under twenty metres of ooze at the bottom of an uncharted abyss.

His one remaining option was a double-lock chamber behind him that allowed divers to enter and exit. The casing above was enveloped in a swirling cloud of sediment which might still be sufficiently fluid for escape, though with each passing minute the chances were diminishing as more of the particulate matter came out of solution and buried the module ever deeper in a mass of compacted sediment.

After a final glance at the sonar profile to memorize its features, he made his way to the double-lock chamber. The retaining wheel turned easily and he stepped inside. There were two compartments, each little larger than a closet, the first an equipment storage and kitting-up room and the second the double-lock chamber itself. He pushed his way past a rack of E-suits and trimix regulators until he stood before a metallic monster that looked like something from a science-fiction B movie.

Once again Jack had reason to be grateful to Costas. With the command module as yet untested he had insisted on a one-atmosphere diving suit as a back-up, a measure Jack had only grudgingly accepted because of the extra time needed for installation. In the event he had helped to stow the suit inside the chamber so was closely familiar with the escape procedure they had devised.

He stepped onto the grid in front of the suit and unlocked the coupling ring, pivoting the helmet forward and exposing the control panel inside. After satisfying himself that all systems were operational, he disconnected the belts that secured it to the bulkhead and scanned the exterior to make sure the joints were all fully sealed.

Officially designated Autonomous Deep Sea Anthropod, the suit had more in common with submersibles like the Aquapod than conventional scuba equipment. The Mark 5 ADSA allowed solo penetrations to ocean depths in excess of four hundred metres. The life support system was a rebreather which injected oxygen while scrubbing carbon dioxide from exhaled air to provide safe breathing gas for up to forty-eight hours. Like earlier suits, the ADSA was pressure resistant with liquid-filled joints and an all-metal carapace, though the material used was titanium-reinforced high-tensile steel which gave an unprecedented pressure rating of 2000 metres water depth.

The ADSA exemplified the great strides made by IMU in deep submersible technology. An ultrasonic multi-directional sonar fed a three-dimensional moving image into a snap-down headset, providing a virtual-reality navigation system in zero visibility. For mid-water mobility the suit was equipped with a computerized variable-buoyancy device and a vectored-thrust water-jet pack, a combination that gave the versatility of an astronaut on a space walk but without the need for a grounding tether.

After uncoupling the suit Jack stepped back into the main compartment and quickly backtracked to the weapons locker. From the top shelf he took a Beretta 9 millimetre handgun to replace the one confiscated by Aslan and shoved it into his flight suit. He then uncoupled an SA80-A2 assault rifle and grabbed three magazines. After slinging the rifle he extracted two small packages of Semtex plastic explosive, normally used for underwater demolition work, and two briefcase-sized boxes each containing a mesh of bubble mines and a detonator transceiver.

Back in the double-lock chamber he hooked the boxes to a pair of carabiners on the front of the ADSA and secured them with a retaining strap. He reached over and slid the rifle and magazines into a pouch under the control panel, the bull-pup SA80 fitting easily inside. After closing the hatch to the chamber and spinning the locking wheel he ascended the metal ladder and clambered into the suit. It was surprisingly spacious, providing room for him to withdraw his hands from the metal arms and operate the console controls. Despite its half-ton weight he was able to flex the leg joints and open and close the pincer-like hands. After checking the oxygen supply, he shut the dome and locked the neck seal, his body now encased in a self-contained life support system and the world outside the viewports suddenly remote and dispensable.

He was about to leave *Seaquest* for the last time. There was no chance for reflection, only an utter determination that her loss should not be in vain. Any sadness would come later.

He switched on the low-intensity interior lighting, adjusted the thermostat to 20 degrees Celsius and activated the sensor array. After checking the buoyancy and propulsion controls he extended the right-hand pincer against a switch on the door. The fluorescent lighting dimmed and water began to spray down. As the turgid liquid rose above the viewports, Jack felt the damp patch where the blood had oozed from his gunshot wound of the day before. He tried to steady his nerves.

'One small step for a man,' he muttered. 'One giant step for mankind.'

When the hatch opened and the elevator raised him above the module, Jack was engulfed in darkness, a black infinity which seemed to imprison him with no hope of escape. He activated the floodlights.

The view was like nothing he had seen before. It was a world lacking all standard points of reference, one where the normal dimensions of space and shape seemed to continuously fold in on each other. The beam lit up luminous clouds of silt that swirled in all directions, slow-motion whirl-pools that undulated like a multitude of miniature galaxies. He extended the manipulator arms and watched the silt separate into tendrils and streamers, shapes that soon gathered themselves together again and disappeared. In the harsh glare it seemed deathly white, like a pall of volcanic ash, the beam reflecting off particles a hundred times finer than beach sand.

Jack knew with utter certainty that he was the only living being ever to have penetrated this world. Some of the suspended sediment was biogenic, derived from diatoms and other organisms that had fallen from above, but unlike the abyssal plains of the Atlantic or the Pacific, the depths of the Black Sea lacked even microscopic life. He truly was in an underworld, a lifeless vacuum unparalleled anywhere else on earth.

For a moment it seemed as if the swirling mass would materialize as ghostly faces of long-dead mariners fated to dance a macabre jig for all eternity with the ebb and flow of the silt. Jack forced his mind to concentrate on the task at hand. The sediment was settling much faster than he had anticipated, the particles compacting with the glutinous density of mud in a tidal flat. Already it had buried the top of the command module and was creeping alarmingly up the legs of the ADSA. He had only seconds to act before it became an immovable sarcophagus on the seabed.

He engaged the buoyancy compensator and filled the reservoir on his back with air, quickly reducing the suit to neutral. As the readout turned to positive he pushed the joystick and twisted the throttle. With a lurch he moved upward, the sediment cascading past with increasing rapidity. He switched off the water jet to avoid clogging the intake and continued his ascent using buoyancy alone. For what seemed an eternity he rose through an unrelenting maelstrom. Then almost thirty metres above the wreckage he was free of it. He rose another twenty metres before neutralizing his buoyancy and angling his lights down towards the ooze that now entombed the wreckage of *Seaquest*.

The scene was impossible to fix to any kind of reality. It was like a satellite image of a vast tropical storm, the eddies of sediment swirling slowly like giant cyclones. He half expected to see flashes of light from electrical storms raging beneath.

He turned his attention to the sonar scanner he had activated moments before. The circular screen revealed the trench-like profile of the chasm, its features more sharply accentuated now the sensor array was clear of silt. He called up the NAVSURV program and tapped in the grid co-ordinates he had memorized for *Seaquest*'s final surface position and the north shore of the island. With known reference co-ordinates NAVSURV could plot present position, lay in a best-fit course and make continuous modifications as the terrain unfolded on the sonar display.

He flipped on the autopilot and watched as the computer fed data into the propulsion and buoyancy units. As the program finalized, he extracted the headset from its housing and pulled down the visor. The headset was hard-wired to the computer via a flexicord umbilical but still allowed complete freedom of movement, the visor acting as a see-through screen so he could still monitor the viewports.

He activated a control and the visor came to life. His view was filtered through a pale green lattice that changed in shape with every movement of his head. Like a pilot in a flight simulator, he was seeing a virtual-reality image of the topography around him, a three-dimensional version of the sonar display. The softly hued lines were a reassurance that he was not trapped in some eternal nightmare, that this was a finite world with boundaries that could be surmounted if his luck continued to hold.

As the water jets fired up and he began to move forward, Jack saw that the metallic joints of the arms had turned a vivid yellow. He remembered why the depths of the Black Sea were so utterly sterile. It was hydrogen sulphide, a byproduct of bacteria decomposing organic matter that flowed in with the rivers. He was mired in a vat of poison bigger than the world's entire chemical weapons arsenal, a reeking brew that would destroy his sense of smell at the first whiff and kill him with one breath.

The ADSA had been designed to the latest specifications for chemical and biological exposure as well as extreme pressure environments. But Jack knew it was only a matter of time before sulphur corrosion ate through a joint where the metal was exposed. Even a tiny ingression would prove deadly. He felt a cold wave of certainty pass through him, a sure knowledge he was trespassing in a world where even the dead were unwanted.

After a final systems check he gripped the throttle and stared grimly into the void in front of him.

'Right,' he muttered. 'Time to revisit old friends.'

Less than five minutes after emerging from the silt storm Jack had reached the western wall of the canyon. The three-dimensional lattice projected on his visor melded precisely with the contours of the rock face now visible ahead, a colossal precipice that reared four hundred metres above him. As he panned the light over the wall he saw that the rock was as stark as a freshly hewn quarry face, its surface untouched by marine growth since titanic forces had rent the sea floor a million years before.

He powered the transverse stern thruster and brought the ADSA round on a southerly course parallel to the rock face. Twenty metres below him the sediment maelstrom seemed to seethe and boil, a forbidding netherworld halfway between liquid and solid that lapped the wall of the canyon. By maintaining a constant altitude above the slope he was steadily climbing, the depth gauge registering a rise of almost a hundred metres in his first half-kilometre along the canyon wall.

As the gradient angled more sharply, a sector of the canyon floor appeared that was entirely denuded of sediment. Jack guessed it was an area where sediment had accumulated and then avalanched down the slope. He knew this was a danger zone; any disturbance could dislodge sediment further up the slope and engulf him.

The exposed sea floor was covered in a bizarre accretion, a crystalline mass stained a sickly yellow by the hydrogen sulphide that poisoned the water. He bled the buoyancy reservoir and sank down, at the same time extending a vacuum probe to sample the accretion. Moments later the results flashed up on the screen. It was sodium chloride, common salt. He was looking at fallout from the evaporation thousands of years before, at the vast bed of brine that had precipitated into the abyss when the Bosporus had sealed off the Black Sea during the Ice Age. The canyon Jack had christened the Atlantis Rift would have been a sump for the entire south-eastern sector of the sea.

As he jetted forward, the carpet of brine became patchy and gave way to a contorted landscape of shadowy shapes. It was a lava field, a jumble of frozen pirouettes where magma had welled up and solidified as it met the frigid water.

His view was interrupted by an opaque haze that shimmered like a diaphanous veil. The external temperature gauge soared to a horrifying 350 degrees Celsius, hot enough to melt lead. He barely registered the change before he was jolted violently forward and the ADSA spiralled out of control towards the canyon floor. On impulse he switched off the thrusters just as the ADSA bounced and then came to rest face down, the forward battery pod immobilized between folds of lava and the visor pressed against a jagged eruption of rock.

Jack raised himself on all fours inside the ADSA and crouched low over the control panel. He saw with relief that the LCD screens were still functioning. Once again he had been incredibly lucky. If there had been significant damage he would probably have been dead by now, the external pressure of several tons per square inch bearing down on any weakness and guaranteeing a swift if hideous end.

He put a mental block on the nightmarish world outside and concentrated on extricating himself from the lava folds. The propulsion unit would be of little use as it was mounted on the back and only provided lateral and transverse thrust. He would have to use the buoyancy compensator. The manual override was operated from a two-way trigger on the joystick, backward pressure bleeding air in and forward pressure venting it.

After bracing himself, he squeezed hard. He could hear the burst of air entering the reservoir and watched the dial creep up to maximum capacity. To his dismay there was absolutely no movement. He emptied the reservoir and filled it again, with the same result. He knew he could not repeat the procedure without depleting the air supply beyond safety margins.

His only fallback was to wrest the ADSA physically from the seabed. So far he had only been deploying the ADSA in submersible mode but it was also a true inner-space suit, designed for the underwater equivalent of moon walking. Despite its cumbersome appearance, it was highly mobile, its thirty-kilogramme submerged weight allowing movement that would have been the envy of any astronaut.

He carefully extended his arms and legs until he was spread-eagled. After angling the pincers into the seabed and locking the joints, he wedged his elbows against the upper carapace with his hands splayed below. Everything now depended on his ability to rip the battery pod from the vice of rock that was holding it.

With every fibre in his being Jack heaved upwards. As he arched back into the harness he was convulsed by pain from his gunshot wound. He knew it was now or never, that his body had been pushed to the limit and would soon lose the strength to do his bidding.

He was about to collapse in exhaustion when there was a grinding sound and a barely perceptible upward movement. He threw in all his reserves and strained one last time.

Suddenly the ADSA broke free and sprang up on its feet, the jolt throwing him against the console.

He was free.

After flooding the buoyancy reservoir to prevent the ADSA from rocketing upwards, he looked around him. Ahead were undulations where slow-flowing rivers of lava had solidified into bulbous pillows of rock. To his right was a huge lava pillar, a hollow cast five metres high where quick-flowing lava had trapped water which had then boiled and pushed the cooling rock upwards. Next to it was another eruption of igneous rock, this one more like a miniature volcano that showed up yellow and red-brown in the floodlight. Jack guessed that the scorching blast of heat that had jolted him had come from a hydrothermal vent, an open pore in the seabed where superheated water belched up from the magma lake below the rift. As he looked at the miniature volcano, the cone ejected a jet-black plume like a factory chimney. It was what geologists called a black smoker, a cloud laden with minerals that precipitated to blanket the surrounding sea floor. He thought back to the extraordinary entrance chamber to Atlantis, its walls shimmering with minerals which could well have originated in a deep-sea vent thrust upwards as the volcano formed.

Hydrothermal vents should be teeming with life, Jack thought uneasily, each one a miniature oasis that attracted larval organisms drifting down from far above. They were unique ecosystems based on chemicals rather than photosynthesis, on the ability of microbes to metabolize the hydrogen sulphide from the vents and provide the first links in a food chain utterly divorced from the life-giving properties of the sun. But instead of armies of blood-red worms and carpets of organisms, there was nothing; the lava chimneys loomed around him like the blackened stumps of trees after a forest fire. In the poisonous depths of the Black Sea not even the simplest bacteria could survive. It was a wasteland where the wonder of creation seemed to have been eclipsed by the powers of darkness. Jack suddenly wanted to be away from this place that was so utterly devoid of life, that seemed to repudiate all the forces that had brought him into existence.

He tore his gaze away from the bleak scene outside and scanned the instrument display. The sonar showed he was 30 metres from the western face of the chasm and 150 metres shallower than the wreck of *Seaquest*, his absolute depth now reading just over 300 metres. He was a third of the way to the island, which now lay just over two kilometres due south.

He looked ahead and saw a milky haze like a towering sand dune. It was the leading edge of a drift of unstable sediment, an indication that the area of substrate exposed by the avalanche was coming to an end. All round him were scour marks caused by previous slides. He needed to be above the zone of turbulence in case his motion triggered another avalanche. He closed his left hand round the buoyancy control and his right hand on the thruster stick, at the same time leaning forward for a final look outside.

What he saw was a terrifying apparition. The wall of silt was slowly, remorselessly swirling towards him like some vast tsunami, all the more horrifying because there was no noise. He barely had time to press the buoyancy trigger before he was engulfed in a whirling storm of darkness.

27

Costas blinked furiously as the scalding water dripped off his face. He had been sent sprawing on the rock floor after being thrust for an appalling moment into the vapour column, the vast pillar of white that rose in front of him to the oculus far above.

He was back in the audience chamber, back where he had last seen Jack. He had passed out so many times over the last few hours that he had lost all measure of time, but he guessed that a night had gone and it was now a full day since they had stumbled out of the labyrinth into the glare of Aslan's searchlight.

He steeled his mind for what would come next. *How did you get from the submarine?* Over and over again, so often his body had become a continuous mass of welts and bruises. Yet Costas was a born optimist, and each time Aslan's thugs beat him he felt a sliver of hope, a hint that Ben and Andy had stayed the course and were still holding out against the intruders.

With his face pressed against the floor he could just make out a veiled and blindfolded figure seated on the throne a few metres from him. As it came into focus the blindfold was ripped off and he realized it was Katya. She looked at him without recognition, and then her eyes widened in horror at his appearance. He gave her his best effort at a smile.

What happened next sent a chill of helplessness through him. A short, stocky figure came into view, wearing the standard black overall but clearly identifiable as a woman. She held a vicious curved knife of Arab design against Katya's throat, then slowly trailed it towards her midriff. Katya shut her eyes but the whites of her knuckles showed where her hands gripped the throne.

'If I had my way we would end this now.' Costas could just make out the Russian words spat into Katya's face. 'And I will have my way. That veil will be your shroud.'

With a sickening jolt Costas realized it was Olga. The drab, yet handsome woman he had seen on the helipad at Alexandria, whose voice he had heard so many times over the last hellish hours. She must be a monster. As Olga continued to taunt Katya, Costas struggled to raise himself but was brought down by a paralysing blow to the back.

There was a commotion at the edge of the chamber where sunlight streamed through the entranceway. With his one good eye Costas saw Aslan heaving into view, supported on either side by a black-clad figure. He shuffled down the steps until he stood panting and wheezing in front of Olga, waving away his two helpers impatiently.

For a second Costas caught Aslan's eyes darting to and fro between the two women, a hint of doubt in his expression before he settled on Olga. At that moment Costas realized she was no mere minion, that she held more sway than Aslan could ever have acknowledged. Katya's expression showed that she too knew the truth, that his megalomania had been stoked by another evil force that had twisted the last vestiges of fatherhood from him.

'You will leave now.' Aslan spoke in Russian to Olga. 'Fly *Vultura*'s helicopter back to Abkhazia and contact our customer. I believe our merchandise will be ready for transport shortly.'

Olga casually swept the knife past Katya's face as she turned and mounted the steps with the two men. She was shaking slightly, her lips trembling with the sick excitement of what she had nearly done. Costas stared in horror, marvelling at the malevolence that emanated from her.

After they had gone Aslan laboriously bent towards Costas, his face now a terrifying image of rage. He yanked Costas' head up and held a pistol under his chin. Costas could smell his breath, like stale meat. His eyes were bloodshot and puffy, his skin oily and deadened. Costas recoiled, but returned Aslan's gaze.

'Before you emerged yesterday I sent three of my men down the same tunnel,' Aslan hissed. 'They have not returned. Where are they?'

Costas suddenly remembered the bubbles coming up from the volcanic vent in the final stretch of underwater passageway.

'Took a wrong turning, I guess.'

Aslan whipped the pistol across his face and Costas jerked back in agony, blood spattering over the throne.

'Then you will lead us the right way.' He waved the gun

over the diving equipment now arrayed on the floor, then gestured towards the adjacent throne where Katya was struggling against two of his thugs. 'Or my daughter will be initiated into the rites of *sharia* rather earlier than she might have expected.'

As Jack rocketed up through the silt he focused all his attention on the navigation system. The radar terrain-mapper showed he was ascending perilously close to the eastern wall of the canyon; its rim was now less than fifty metres above. The depth read-out was rising at more than two metres per second, a rate that would increase dramatically as the external pressure reduced but which Jack could ill afford to slow until he was clear of the rift.

Suddenly a red light flashed as the radar sweep alerted him to a hazard overhead. In the split second that he saw the lip of the canyon he spun east and gunned the stern thrusters. He braced himself for an impact that miraculously never came, the ADSA just missing the overhang which would have eviscerated the propulsion and buoyancy pack and sent him plummeting to his death.

As soon as he had cleared the canyon, he bled the reservoir until he was neutrally buoyant, and then tilted forward using the vectored thrusters. He seemed to be flying above a giant slow-moving storm, a surging mass that lapped the rim of the canyon and obscured the yawning crevasse below. Jack had colleagues who would itch to return to this place, using sub-bottom probes to rediscover the hydrothermal vents, but he sincerely hoped he had made his only foray into a wasteland that seemed to encapsulate all the worst nightmares about the ocean abyss.

And now in the gloom ahead was the discovery that had brought them here, a prospect that made Jack's heart race as he gunned the submersible towards the co-ordinates of the island. The depth gauge read 148 metres, almost the level of the submerged ancient shoreline. He was still in the reducing environment below the oxycline and the blue-grey mud was devoid of visible life. After several minutes he began to make out a ridge, a continuous low berm which he realized must be the ancient beach escarpment.

He would be entering the lost city over its eastern quarter, at the opposite end from the sector he and Costas had explored in the Aquapods two days previously. The first sight of silt-clad structures brought back the intense thrill he had felt then, the wonder of their discovery suddenly eclipsing the trials of the past twenty-four hours. With mounting excitement he rose over the berm and surveyed the scene in front of him.

His mind turned immediately to his friends. By now *Sea Venture* would have heard nothing from her sister ship for hours and would have alerted the Turkish and Georgian authorities. But they had agreed to inform the Russians of the submarine discovery first and a concerted response might take days.

Help could still come too late.

He prayed that Ben and Andy still held fast. Aslan's men would try to make their way through the labyrinth, to take them by surprise. The only way they could do that would be to have Costas or Katya as a guide, to force them to tap the code on the submarine's casing that would make the crewmen open the hatch. Jack knew they would have little chance of survival after that. He must do all he could to contact Ben and Andy, then somehow make his way back to the audience chamber and defend the passageway as best he could.

The battery was running dangerously low and he knew he must conserve it for the final effort. He dropped to the seabed and began to walk the ADSA along a wide roadway, each step detonating a small cloud of silt. To the right was a line of curiously familiar shapes blanketed in sediment. Jack realized with astonishment that he was looking at the world's first carts, more than 2000 years older than the first wheeled transport recorded in Mesopotamia.

To his left was a deep gully, once an inlet from the sea, which widened into a rectilinear basin about thirty metres across. He passed neatly stacked piles of logs, probably fir, aspen and juniper ancestral to the forests that still shrouded north-eastern Turkey, all perfectly preserved in the anoxic environment. The view beyond surpassed his wildest expectations. On the foreshore were two semi-complete hulls, each about twenty metres long and raised up on wooden formers. It could have been an image from any modern boatyard on the Black Sea. The vessels were open-hulled and narrow-beamed, designed to be paddled rather than rowed, but otherwise as sleek and refined as Viking longships. As he approached the first hull a gentle tap with the manipulator arm to dislodge the silt revealed sewn-plank joinery, precisely the technique he and Mustafa had guessed for the Neolithic mariners.

Further on the foreshore was littered with stacks of adzed planks and coils of thick cordage. In between lay five sets of formers aligned side-by-side towards the basin, each large enough for a hull forty metres in length. The supports were empty and the shipwrights long gone, but for a few desperate weeks in the middle of the sixth millennium BC they must have been a hive of construction activity unmatched until the Egyptian age of the pyramid builders. As the waters drowned the lower reaches of the city the people must have moved their tools and timber up the slopes, unable to comprehend that their home would soon be lost forever. Jack had found one of the key staging posts of history, the place where all the energy and wisdom of Atlantis had been poised to ignite civilization from western Europe to the Indus Valley.

The terrain-mapper began to reveal the contours of the slope ahead. He switched to submersible mode and jetted beyond the ancient coastal plain over a plateau the size of a racetrack, a wide opening in its centre. He remembered the water conduit in the volcano and guessed this was the second stage in the system, a huge rock-cut reservoir that served as a dispersal point for aqueducts fanning down into the industrial and domestic quarters of the city.

He continued in a southerly direction up the slope. According to the sketch map he had fed into the computer he should now be approaching the upper reaches of the processional way. Seconds later the terrain-mapper provided vindication, the 3-D display showing the stepped face of the eastern pyramid. Just beyond it the irregular outline of the volcano was beginning to materialize, and in between was a telltale cylindrical shape that blocked the gap between the pyramid and the jagged rock face.

Out of the eerie gloom a mass of twisted metal came into view. The ADSA seemed insignificant beside the submarine's immense bulk; the hull casing towered higher than a four-storey building and extended the length of a football pitch. Cautiously he made his way over the sheared-off propeller, thankful that the electric motor in the ADSA was barely audible and the water jets produced minimal turbulence. He deactivated the floodlights and dimmed the LCD displays.

As he passed over the rear escape hatch behind the reactor chamber, he thought briefly of Captain Antonov and his crew, their irradiated corpses another addition to the harvest of death reaped by this grim sea. He tried to dispel the gruesome image as he approached the soaring form of the conning tower. In the gloom beyond he could just make out the halo from a searchlight array above the starboard foredeck. The lights were mounted on a submersible that had settled like a predatory insect on the DSRV where it was docked to the submarine's forward escape hatch. Aslan's men had gained access to the *Kazbek* by docking to the DSRV's rear hatch, using a single-lock mating ring.

Jack set the ADSA down gingerly on the anechoic coating of the submarine. He pushed his hands into the manipulator arms and extended them outwards until he could see the joints at the elbows and wrists. The metal was yellow and pitted from the hydrogen sulphide but the sealings had held. He flexed both arms inwards until they touched the outer of the two metal boxes he had strapped to the front of the suit above the battery pack. He used the three metal digits at the end of each arm to prise open the box and extract the contents. He then cut the binding with the pincer and unravelled a mesh of ping-pong sized balls, all joined together by a web of fine filaments.

Normally the mines were divided into strands and deployed as a floating umbrella over an archaeological site. Each of the two hundred charges was primed to explode on contact and was potentially lethal to a diver. Kept together they formed a single high-explosive charge, enough to put a submersible out of action permanently.

After activating the detonator he withdrew his hands and grasped the control stick, using the buoyancy trigger to rise cautiously off the submarine. Although he was beyond the main arc of illumination, he was wary of being spotted and flew in a wide sweep off the port side of *Kazbek* and back again dead astern of the enemy submersible. He closed in behind the metre-wide drum that protected the submersible's propeller, putting the buoyancy system on automatic to ensure he would remain neutral while his hands were off the controls. He feathered the stern thruster until he was as far forward as he could go and then quickly reinserted his hands in the manipulator arms.

Just as he was about to secure the mines under the shaft with a carabiner, he was thrown back from the propeller housing. He began to spiral like an astronaut out of control, the orb of light from the submersible receding alarmingly as he struggled to right himself using the lateral thrusters. After finally coming to a halt he looked back and saw the turbulence coming from the propeller shaft. He had already felt uneasy that the submersible's floodlights were on, an unnecessary drain of battery reserves, and now he saw a radio buoy being winched inside.

He gunned the stern thrusters and jetted back towards *Kazbek*'s conning tower. The bubble mines were precariously balanced where he had left them on the submersible's propeller housing. If they slipped off, his enterprise was doomed. He would need to blow the charge as soon as he was behind *Kazbek*'s fin and out of range of the explosive shock wave.

He reached into his chest pocket to ready the remote detonator, a small unit almost identical in appearance to a hand-held radio. He had preset the downlink to channel 8.

Jack allowed himself a quick glance to starboard as he approached *Kazbek*'s upper casing. To his dismay the submersible had decoupled and was now less than ten metres away, its cylindrical form rising towards him like a predatory shark. Through the viewport a face stared directly at him, its expression showing shocked surprise and fury.

Jack had to think fast. He could never hope to outrun the submersible. He was closely familiar with the type, a derivative of the British LR5 rescue sub with hydraulic thrusters tiltable through 180 degrees that gave it the agility of a helicopter. It was too close to risk detonating the charges, not only because of the danger to himself but also because the shock wave might damage *Kazbek*'s emergency life support system and destabilize the warheads. His only chance was to stand and fight, to lure the submersible into a duel that would seem suicidally one-sided. His gamble rested on the dead weight of the submersible. With a full passenger complement it would be sluggish, and each lunge would require a wide turning circle which might take it beyond the danger zone.

Like some space-age matador, Jack landed upright on the casing of *Kazbek* and turned to face his assailant. He barely had time to flex his legs before the submersible was on him, its pontoons missing him by a hair's breadth as it sped over the hull. He prepared for another onslaught with his arms outstretched, a toreador taunting a bull. He saw the submersible vent its ballast tanks and slow down as it climbed the cliff face and pivoted round for another dive. It swooped down with terrifying velocity, the floodlights blinding him as he fell face down on the casing. As it rocketed overhead, the ferment rolled him onto his back and the dangling end of the bubble mines swept perilously close. There was no way the mesh could survive another roller-coaster ride without slipping off or becoming entangled in the propeller, a potentially deadly outcome if it triggered an explosion too close to the submarine.

Jack watched as the submersible hurtled off to a new starting point, its diminishing form framed against the vast southern face of the pyramid. This time Jack remained prostrate on the casing as he estimated the distance. Twenty metres. Twenty-five metres. Thirty metres. It was now or never. Just as the submersible began to turn he pressed channel 8.

There was a searing flash followed by a succession of jolts that pummelled his body like sonic booms. The explosion had torn off the submersible's rudders and left the wreckage spiralling crazily towards the seabed. The shock wave would have killed the occupants instantly.

28

'Life support systems functional? Over.'

Jack was using the manipulator arm to tap his question through the submarine's casing at the point where the rock-cut stairway disappeared under it. Despite the dampening effects of the anechoic coating, his first taps had provoked an immediate and gratifying response. In a few sentences of Morse code he learned from Andy and Ben that Katya's threat to destroy the submarine had held their assailants at bay. They had backed off in an uneasy truce while the two IMU men stood their ground in alternate watches at the top of the weapons loading chute.

'We could use a brew. Over.'

Jack hammered out his final sequence.

'Full English breakfast on its way. Await return. Out.'

Twenty minutes later the ADSA had rounded the eastern promontory of the island and risen to thirty metres below sea level. Jack knew he had to find a route over the volcano to the audience chamber, but first he had a visit to pay. In Aslan's headquarters Jack had memorized the GPS co-ordinates from the SATSURV image of *Vultura*, and he had programmed them into the ADSA's navigation tracking system. The radar terrain-mapper had amply proved its worth, the 3-D virtual-reality display providing detailed bathymetry for hundreds of metres on either side as well as surface contacts which were impossible to see in the Stygian gloom.

The unmistakable image of a large surface vessel appeared bang on target two hundred metres ahead. Jack felt like the driver of a midget submarine infiltrating an enemy harbour, one whose occupants had no reason to suspect an intrusion. As far as they were concerned, he was long gone, a nuisance disposed of for ever when the ravaged hulk of *Seaquest* entombed him in the abyss.

The terrain-mapper showed he was approaching the stern of the vessel, the twin screws and rudder assembly clearly visible on the screen. Twenty metres below, Jack began his final ascent, slowly injecting air into the buoyancy chamber and corkscrewing upwards using the lateral thrusters. At fifteen metres the dark outline of the hull became visible to the naked eye and he could see the sun shining off the waves on either side. As he came closer he could make out scars where the valiant efforts of York and Howe had left their mark, and he could hear the muffled clanging of repair work on the turbojet tubes directly above.

He nestled the ADSA against the rudder assembly and repeated the procedure he had carried out on the submersible less than an hour before. He extracted the second bubble-mine mesh and wrapped it round the rudder pintle, this time securing the ends with an additional strand beneath the screw. As he clicked on the detonator he glanced up and saw the wavering forms of two figures leaning against the starboard gunwale. Fortunately the oxygen rebreather produced none of the telltale exhaust of scuba gear, and he would not be seen against the inky depths.

He knew there was a chance that Katya and Costas were in the vessel above him. The explosive would cause massive damage to the screw and rudder but should be deflected by the armour plating of the hull. It was a risk he had to take. Yet again he mouthed a silent prayer.

He had gambled that the crew would be preoccupied with topside damage from the gun battle the day before and would already have carried out an inspection below the waterline. To minimize the risk of detection he opted to descend using the lateral thrusters rather than the buoyancy chamber, even though it meant draining the battery reserve.

A mere ten minutes after first sighting the hull, the ADSA disappeared as silently as it had come, dropping into the murky depths and stealing off without being seen or heard by any of the crew on *Vultura*.

Using the terrain-mapper to navigate, Jack jetted half a kilometre towards the western shore of the island and found a cove out of sight of *Vultura*. As the rocky seabed rose up to meet him, all power suddenly ceased. The battery was dead. He reduced his buoyancy and dropped down to complete the final leg on foot, striding upwards over the billowing folds of lava towards the surf line.

He found a flat rock in two metres of water and cautiously broke surface. He locked the limbs of the ADSA and decoupled the neck ring. As he pushed open the helmet, he blinked furiously in the sunlight and gasped repeatedly, his lungs filling with fresh air for the first time since he had tumbled into the command module on *Seaquest* more than three hours previously.

He hauled himself out and squatted on the rocky ledge. It was a brilliant summer afternoon, the sun glinting off the waves that lapped at his feet. Over the barren shore the precipitous slopes of the island rose ahead of him. Above the uppermost ridge he could see a plume of white framed against the sky.

He had no time to savour the relief of survival. The pain from his wound was searing his side and he knew he had no time to lose.

After quickly looking around to make sure he was alone, he removed the items he had brought from the weapons locker. He was still wearing the helicopter flight suit and shoved the detonator transceiver into one thigh pocket and the two Semtex charges into the other. He took out the Beretta, pushed the slide forward to cock it and replaced it in his chest holster. He then extracted the SA80 and the three magazines, pushing one in place and sliding the other two into his waist pockets. After checking the sound suppressor, he pulled the bolt and slung it over his back.

He closed the helmet and gently toppled the ADSA back beneath the waves. It had been his lifesaver, his reminder that Costas had been with him in spirit. But now no amount of technology would guarantee his safe passage. It was up to him alone, to his physical stamina and strength of will.

He swivelled round to contemplate the rocky slope ahead.

'Payback time,' he muttered under his breath.

The jagged wall of rock loomed above Jack as he made his way inland. Between him and a plateau some eighty metres above were three terraces, each culminating in a razor-edged row of pinnacles and punctuated by fracture lines and gullies. The basalt was hard and coarse and gave an excellent grip. He had no alternative but to climb it.

He slung the SA80 more tightly and began to ascend a vertical chimney that rose the entire height of the first pitch. About halfway up, it narrowed and he inched higher with his legs braced on either side, eventually heaving himself onto a narrow platform some thirty metres above his start point. The second pitch was precipitous but straightforward, Jack's ample reach proving advantageous as he worked his way up a series of finger-holds and ledges. He continued past the second row of pinnacles onto the third pitch until he reached a point just below the summit where an overhang jutted out almost a metre along the entire length of the cliff.

As he balanced spread-eagled against the rock face, he knew that any hesitation would only weaken his resolve. With his mind blank to the consequences of failure, he threw his right arm outwards and curled his fingers round the edge. Once he was certain of his hold he released his other hand and snapped it beside the first. He was hanging over eighty metres of vertiginous rock that would tear him to shreds if he fell. He began to swing his legs, slowly at first and then with increased momentum. On the second attempt he hooked his right leg over the top and scrambled to safety.

The scene that confronted him was breathtaking. He crouched down to recover his strength and looked out over a wilderness of solidified lava. Some two hundred metres to his right lay the cone of the volcano, its chimney spewing out a voluminous cloud of vapour that rose in a swirling column high into the sky. Partway down the cone he could see an unassuming low entrance above a rock-cut stairway that meandered down the saddle towards him and disappeared out of sight to the left. It was evidently an ancient route up the volcano on the outside, the one taken by Aslan and his men when they first reached the island.

The lesser peak some thirty metres ahead was a massive upwelling of jet-black lava. The top was level like a landing pad, an impression reinforced by the Kamov Ka-28 Helix parked in the middle. Round the perimeter Jack counted four black-clad figures, all armed with AK or Heckler & Koch submachine guns.

The most astonishing sight was the structure surrounding the helicopter. Encircling the platform was a ring of giant megaliths, upright stones at least three times the height of a man and two metres in girth. The stones were weathered from millennia of exposure but had once been finely finished. They were capped by massive flat slabs that formed a continuous circular lintel. Inside were five free-standing trilithons, each pair of stones with its lintel arranged in a horseshoe pattern that opened west towards the volcanic cone.

Jack realized with awe that he was looking at the precursor of Stonehenge. It was where the Atlanteans had observed the difference between the solar and lunar year they had seen tabulated in the passageway far below. The cone of the volcano was a sighting device, the position of the sun on either side indicating the season of the year. At the vernal and autumnal equinoxes the sun would appear to sink into the volcano, an event which would have affirmed the life-protecting powers of Atlantis.

Jack concentrated on using the stones to his tactical advantage. After flipping off the safety on the SA80 he slipped into a fissure that ran like a trench towards the platform. By sprinting in short bursts he quickly reached the nearest megalith and flattened against it. He cautiously peered round and saw the helicopter was unoccupied with no guard in sight. After pulling out the Semtex he darted forward through the inner horseshoe and placed one block in the exhaust and the other under the cockpit, clicking on the detonators as he did so.

He turned to leave and was suddenly face to face with a black-clad figure emerging from behind one of the trilithons. For a split second both men were immobilized by surprise. Jack was the first to react. Two thuds from the SA80 and the man dropped like a stone, killed instantly by the high-velocity 5.56 millimetre slugs that tore through his neck.

The clatter of the man's weapon alerted the other men. Jack ran directly into their path as they converged on the helicopter. Before any of them could raise their weapons he emptied his entire remaining magazine in a tight arc from the hip. The bullets spattered and ricocheted off the rock and all three men fell sprawled over the ground.

He slammed in another magazine and plunged headlong down the ramp towards the stairway. He had gambled that the rest of Aslan's men were either on *Vultura* or in the volcano.

He reached the entrance at the top of the steps without any indication that he had been detected. The portal was more imposing close up, the opening wide enough for the processions that must have passed between the stone circle and the audience chamber. He could see the passageway veering off to the left in a dog-leg towards a distant source of light. After catching his breath, he levelled his weapon and cautiously advanced over the worn steps into the gloom beyond.

Ten metres on he rounded the corner and saw a hazy rectangle of light. Then the column of vapour came into view and he realized he was approaching the same raised platform they had stood on the day before, only from a different doorway. He concealed himself in the shadows and sidled up for a look inside.

Far above he could see the skylight in the dome. In front of him the ramp led directly down and he had an unimpeded view of the central space. On the central dais were five figures, two of them black-clad guards flanking a woman on the throne. Her head was covered by a veil but her face was visible.

It was Katya. She looked dishevelled and exhausted but mercifully free from injury. Jack closed his eyes for an instant, his relief overwhelming.

To her right was a man facing away towards the vent. With his flowing red robe and the nimbus formed by the vapour behind his head he seemed a grotesque parody of the priests of old, some denizen of Hades sent to perform a macabre ritual and taint the sanctity of Atlantis forever.

Aslan shifted slightly and Jack caught sight of another figure, a familiar form kneeling in the gap between the thrones with his head bowed dangerously close to the vapour chimney. He was bound hand and foot and was wearing the tattered remnants of an IMU E-suit. To his horror Jack saw that Aslan was levelling a pistol at the back of Costas' head in classic executioner's pose.

Instinct took over and Jack sprang onto the ramp brandishing his weapon. Even as he ran he knew he had no chance. There was a vicious blow to his lower back and the SA80 was snatched from his hands.

'Dr Howard. What a pleasant surprise. I had not imagined we would be rid of you so easily.'

Jack was pushed roughly down the stairs by the guard who had been lurking beside the entrance. His Beretta was removed from his flight suit and passed to Aslan, who began idly flicking rounds from the magazine. Katya was staring at Jack as if he was a ghost.

'They told us you were dead,' she said hoarsely. 'That explosion, the helicopter . . .' She looked dazed and bewildered. Her eyes were red-rimmed and had dark rings under them.

Jack flashed her a reassuring smile.

Aslan waved the gun dismissively and turned back towards the figure crouched between the thrones.

'Your friend did not have a comfortable night. If my daughter had told us what she knew, things might have been easier for him.'

Costas turned his head and managed a crooked smile before one of the guards slapped him back into place. Jack was shocked at his appearance. His E-suit was a mess and his face was covered in welts and bruises, and was flushed red where he had been scalded by the vapour chimney. One eye was closed and swollen and Jack guessed his head was not the only place he had been beaten.

'Your friend had just agreed to guide my men through the tunnels to the submarine.' Aslan gestured at three sets of mixed-gas equipment laid out beside the ramp and then back at the ravaged figure in front of him. 'As you can see it took some persuading. But now you are here he is expendable. You have destroyed three of my helicopters and there is a price to pay.'

Aslan levelled the Beretta at Costas' head and pulled back the hammer.

'No!' Jack cried. 'He is the only one who knows the route back. His job was to memorize waymarkers while Katya and I studied the archaeology.'

Aslan smiled slyly and eased forward the hammer. 'I do not

believe you. But I am willing to spare your Greek friend for the time being if you agree to my demands.'

Jack said nothing but stared at Aslan impassively. His training had taught him always to let the hostage-taker feel they had the upper hand, that they were in total control. If Aslan had known that half his men were dead and that his favourite piece of hardware was about to blow, he would probably have exploded in blind fury.

'First, this.' Aslan produced the copy of the gold disc from his tunic. 'I took the liberty of relieving you of this when you were my guest. A small return for my hospitality. I assume it is some form of key, perhaps to a secret vault.' Aslan swept his arms expansively round the doors that lined the chamber. 'I wish to own all the treasures of this place.'

He placed the disc on the throne beside Katya and stepped onto the circular platform. The vapour was abating and they could see down the cleft a few metres from Aslan's feet. It was like a suppurating wound, a yawning gash that exposed the awesome tumult beneath the surface of the volcano. Far below them a surge of magma welled up, its lurid tendrils erupting like a solar flare over the river of lava that had borne it. In the distance they could hear bangs and crashes where pockets of gas were breaking through with explosive force.

Aslan turned back from the spectacle, the heat giving his swollen features a demonic glow.

'And my second demand,' he continued. 'I assume your other vessel, *Sea Venture,* is on its way. You will call them off and tell them *Seaquest* is safe and sound. I assume you have an understanding with the Turkish and Georgian governments. You will tell your captain to relay the information that you have found nothing and are leaving the island. You have a dedicated radio transmitter? Search him.'

The guard quickly found the detonator transceiver in Jack's left pocket and held it up for Aslan to see.

'Give it to me. What is the channel?'

Jack caught Costas' eye and nodded almost imperceptibly. He watched Aslan's fat fingers curl round the receiver before replying with quiet assurance.

'Channel 8.'

The instant Aslan punched in the number there were two explosions outside, followed seconds later by a deeper boom that rolled up from the sea. The split second of paralysis was all that was needed for Aslan's men to lose the advantage. Costas rolled on his side and kicked his guard's legs from under him, and Jack took out his captor with a ferocious punch to the neck. Katya immediately saw what was happening and kicked out with lightning speed at the third man, hitting him hard in the solar plexus and leaving him retching on the floor.

Aslan bellowed hideously when he heard the explosions, his face contorted with rage. He hurled the detonator into the chasm and tottered precariously on the edge, his arms flailing wildly as he struggled to remain upright and away from the searing blast of the vent.

Katya screamed as she saw what was happening. Jack reached up to hold her back but it was already too late. The ground was shaken by a series of violent tremors, the explosions having set off a seismic disturbance. Aslan was sucked in by the centrifugal force of the chimney, his expression fleetingly showing the heightened awareness of a person facing death, at once aghast and strangely accepting, before his body burst into flame like a self-immolating idol. The scalding heat of the vapour consumed his robe and melted his skin until all they could see were the bones of his hands and the white of his skull. With a piercing shriek he toppled over and plummeted into the chasm, a living ball of fire swallowed forever into the inferno of the volcano.

The river of death had claimed its last victim.

29

'Jack Howard. This is *Sea Venture*. Do you read me? Over.'
Costas passed the portable VHF receiver they had taken
from *Vultura* a short time before and Jack pressed the recall
button.

'I read you loud and clear. What's your status? Over.'

Jack was thrilled to hear Tom York's confident tones again.
He had expected the worst, that York could never have
survived the onslaught that wreaked such devastation on
Seaquest's foredeck.

'We're hove to three nautical miles north-west of the island.
A flight of four Seahawks with Turkish marines and Georgian
anti-terrorist commandos is heading your way. They should
be in sight about now.'

Jack had already heard the distant clatter and guessed their identity.

'How did you make it off *Seaquest*?' he asked.

'I was blown clear when *Vultura* attacked. Luckily the crewman in charge of the escape sub recognized the vibrations from the gun battle and came back to investigate. I have a nasty gash on my leg but am OK.'

'And Peter?'

York's voice when it came back was taut with emotion. 'We're still searching. I have to be straight with you, Jack. It doesn't look good.'

'I know. You've done your best.'

Though Jack was overjoyed that York had made it, Peter Howe had been a boyhood friend. It was like losing a brother, and the cost suddenly seemed far too high. Jack closed his eyes.

York put the receiver on hold and returned a few moments later.

'We've just had a message from Ben and Andy in the *Kazbek*. They've managed to float a radio buoy. They're standing by.'

The roar of the approaching helicopters began to drown out the conversation.

'We're going to have to terminate while the cavalry arrive,' Jack shouted. 'Tell the captain to sail to the following co-ordinates and maintain position until further notice.' Jack read out a map reference corresponding to a point one kilometre north of the submerged pyramids. 'I have some unfinished business to attend to. You'll be hearing from us. Out.'

Jack was in an emotional turmoil, anguished at the fate of Howe yet elated that the others had survived their ordeal. He looked at Costas' battered face and was amazed at his friend's unruffled demeanour.

They were squatting on the steps outside the rock-cut doorway. They had left Katya seated just inside the audience chamber, a Heckler & Koch MP5 resting on her legs. Jack had tried to comfort her after the death of her father but she had been unable to talk about it or even make eye contact. He knew there was nothing he could do until the initial shock had worn off.

In addition to the three bodyguards lashed together on the central dais, there were twenty men from *Vultura*. The crew had surrendered after Jack and Costas boarded the disabled vessel and informed them of their leader's demise. Despite his injuries Costas had insisted on coming along, claiming that he was in no worse condition than Jack had been on their journey through the volcano. Katya had asked to be allowed to guard the prisoners, a way of being alone with her thoughts.

'The good guys are finally winning,' Costas said.

'It's not over yet.'

Costas followed Jack's gaze beyond the island where *Sea Venture*'s Lynx was carrying out a grid search over the site of York and Howe's stand. Four Zodiacs were combing the waves beneath.

The first of the Sikorsky S-70A Seahawks thundered overhead, the downdraught a refreshing blast of cool air. Above the stone circle beside the other peak the doors sprang open and disgorged heavily armed men who rappelled past the smoking wreckage of the Ka-28 Helix. As they made their way up the steps towards them, Jack and Costas looked at each other and mouthed their age-old refrain.

'Time to kit up.'

Just over an hour later the two men stood dripping inside the torpedo room of the submarine. Using fresh equipment airlifted from *Sea Venture* they had made their way back through the labyrinth, following the tapes that Costas had paid out on the way up. In the membrane chamber they had heaved shut the gold-plated doors and tapped a signal on *Kazbek*'s casing. Moments later the pump emptied the chamber and the hatch swung open to reveal the gaunt faces of Ben and Andy.

'We haven't got long,' Ben warned. 'The hydrogen peroxide CO_2 scrubbers are saturated and the reserve air tanks on the DSRV are nearly empty.'

They quickly doffed their equipment and followed the crewmen round the edge of the torpedo room and up the weapons loading chute. The door to the sonar room with its macabre sentinel was closed and they could hear a muffled banging inside.

'Two of Aslan's men,' Andy remarked. 'Left behind as guards after the rest fled in the submersible. They surrendered almost immediately. We thought they'd like to keep our KGB friend company.'

'The others weren't so lucky,' Jack said grimly.

Ben and Andy's haggard appearance matched their own, but Jack still marvelled at their stamina after so many hours holed up in the submarine.

Moments later they were inside the control room. Jack stood at the spot where he had taken the bullet that so nearly cost him his life. In the corner a blanket covered the body of the dead Kazakh gunman. The evidence of their firefight had become part of the scenery, another layer to the devastation caused years earlier during the crew's desperate last stand.

'Where's the ballast control?' said Jack.

'Over here,' Andy replied. 'It's pretty smashed up, but luckily we don't have to do anything sophisticated. We think there's enough pressure left in the air banks to carry out an emergency blow. All you have to do is yank these handles and the valves open manually.' He pointed at two mushroom-shaped protrusions on top of the panel, both designed to be pulled down by an operator standing in front of the console.

'Right,' Costas said. 'Time to saddle up. You guys deserve some R & R.'

While he and the two crewmen went aft to disengage the DSRV, Jack went over the next stage in his plan, the final act that would extinguish Aslan's evil empire once and for all.

When Costas returned from the escape trunk, Jack was seated behind the weapons panel in the fire control alley. It was one of the few areas to have escaped damage.

'What are you doing?' Costas enquired.

'I have a score to settle.' Jack glanced at him with cold eyes. 'Call it loss adjustment.'

Costas looked intrigued if a little dumbfounded. 'You're the boss.'

'Leaving Aslan's headquarters intact is asking for trouble. There'll be plenty of good intentions but neither the Georgians nor the Turks will touch it for fear of escalating the civil war and provoking the Russians. And we're not talking about just another warlord. The place is a tailor-made terrorist centre, a dream for the al Qaeda operatives who must already have had Aslan's number and been waiting for just this kind of opportunity.' Jack paused, thinking of Peter Howe. 'And this is personal. I owe it to an old friend.'

Jack activated the two LCD screens in front of him and ran a series of operational checks.

'Katya gave me a briefing before we left. Apparently even junior intelligence officers of her grade were trained to shoot these weapons. In a nuclear holocaust they might be the last survivor in a submarine or bunker. All systems were self-contained and designed to be operable in extreme conditions. Katya reckoned the back-up computer would still be functional even after all this time.'

'You're not going to fire a cruise missile,' Costas breathed.

'Damn right I am.'

'What about the works of art?'

'Mostly in the domestic complex. It's a risk I have to take.' Jack quickly surveyed the monitors. 'I checked after we defused those warheads. Number four tube is occupied by a complete all-up Kh-55 Granat ready to fire. The canister is still sealed by the membrane pressure cap. Eight metres long, three thousand kilometre range, mach point seven zero cruising speed, one thousand kilogramme direct-impact fused HE charge. Basically a Soviet version of the Tomahawk land-attack missile.'

'Guidance system?'

'Similar terrain-contour-matching software and GPS to the Tomahawk. Fortunately the course is a direct over-sea route so no need to program in evasive tactics. I have the exact target co-ordinates so we won't need the seeker head and search pattern system. I'll be able to bypass most of the complex programming procedures.'

'But we're too deep for a launch,' Costas protested.

'That's where you come in. I want you to operate the emergency blow valves. As soon as we reach twenty metres you give the order to fire.'

Costas slowly shook his head, a crooked smile creasing his ravaged features. Without a word he took up position in front of the ballast control panel. Jack remained hunched over the console for a few moments and then looked up with grim determination.

'Developing fire-control solution now.'

Their movements gave no hint of the momentous force

they were about to unleash. Jack was fully focused on the monitor in front of him, his fingers tapping a sequence of commands with brief pauses while he awaited each response. After inputting the necessary presets, a pattern of lines and dots appeared on the screen. In a typical operational scenario the solution would represent a best-fit search area, but with the destination co-ordinates known, the screen simply showed a linear projection of range and course with the target pinpointed.

'I've loaded a mission profile into the TERCOM computer and am warming up the missile,' Jack announced. 'Initiating firing sequence now.'

He swivelled his chair to the fire control console, sweeping the crust of precipitate from the launch control panel to reveal the red firing button. He checked that the electronics were active and looked across at Costas behind the buoyancy control station. Jack needed no affirmation that he was doing the right thing, but the sight of his friend's bludgeoned face hardened his resolve even further. The two men nodded silently at each other before Jack turned back towards the screen.

'Engage!'

Costas reached up and pulled the two levers down with a resounding clank. At first nothing happened, but then a deafening hiss of high-pressure gas seemed to fill every pipe above them. Moments later it was joined by a rumbling like far-off thunder as the rush of compressed air purged the ballast tanks between the two layers of hull casing.

Slowly, almost imperceptibly, there was movement, a creaking and groaning that rose in a shrieking crescendo and seemed to whip from one end of the boat to the other. It was as if some long-dormant creature were stirring awake, a sleeping giant grudgingly roused after an eternity of undisturbed slumber.

Suddenly the bow tilted upwards at an alarming angle, throwing the two men sideways. There was an ear-splitting wrenching sound as the remains of the propeller and rudder assembly sheared away.

'Hold on!' Costas shouted. 'She's about to go!'

With a final screech the stem lurched upwards and nine thousand tons of submarine was free. The depth gauge in front of Costas began to cycle through with alarming rapidity.

'On my mark!' he yelled. 'Eighty metres . . . sixty metres . . . forty . . . thirty . . . shoot!'

Jack punched the red button and there was a sound like a vacuum extractor from the front of the submarine. The launch system automatically opened the hydraulic door of the tube and set off an explosive charge that blew the missile into the water. Just metres in front of the hull the booster rocket thrust the missile with colossal force towards the surface, its course now set for a deadly rendezvous away to the north-east.

On the bridge of *Sea Venture* Tom York stood in crutches beside the captain and the helmsman. They had been watching the last of the Seahawks as they lifted off from the island on their way to a maximum security compound for terrorist prisoners in Georgia. Now their attention was focused on *Vultura*, its hull low in the water where Jack's explosives had mangled the stern. They had just despatched three Zodiacs with twin 90 hp outboards to tow the hulk further offshore above the deep-sea canyon.

As York glanced back at the island, his eye was suddenly caught by a disturbance on the sea about a kilometre away. For a moment it looked like the shock waves from an underwater explosion. Before he had time to alert the others a spear of steel burst through the waves, its exhaust kicking up a vast orb of spray like the plume from a rocket launch. Thirty metres up it tilted lazily and hung motionless for a second while the burnt-out booster ejected and the wings folded out. Then the turbofan ignited with a thunderous roar and the missile streaked off on a level trajectory towards the east, soon reaching high subsonic as it skimmed the waves like a fast-receding fireball.

Seconds later a vast eruption turned all eyes on *Sea Venture* back to the sea. *Kazbek* broke surface like a mighty whale, its bow rising clean out of the water and then flopping down with an immense crash. As the huge black shape settled into the waves, the only evidence of its prolonged immersion was a faint yellowing on some parts of the casing and the damage to the stern quarter. For a brief moment until it settled underwater they had seen the circular hole where the EH-4 membrane had ripped off, the torpedo room now flooded but sealed off behind a bulkhead by Costas. The sheer size of the submarine was overwhelming, an awesome image of one of the most lethal war machines ever devised.

To many former servicemen on *Sea Venture* it was a sight that would once have provoked apprehension and fear, an image as potent as the U-boat to a previous generation. But now it was met by a ragged chorus of cheers, its appearance one less chance that weapons of mass destruction would fall into the hands of terrorists and rogue states that were now the common enemy of all the world's navies.

'*Sea Venture*, this is *Kazbek*. Do you read me? Over.'

The crackling voice came through on the bridge radio and York picked up the receiver.

'*Kazbek*, we read you loud and clear. Thanks for the fireworks. Over.'

'Here are some co-ordinates.' Jack read out a twelve-digit

number and repeated it. 'You might want to set up a SATSURV link with Mannheim. The satellite should be overhead now. In case any of the crew are wondering, these are the guys who took out *Seaquest*.'

A few minutes later everyone had crowded into *Sea Venture*'s communications room, priority of place being given to the crew from *Seaquest* who had been picked up by the rescue sub. They were joined by Ben and Andy, who had just finished docking the DSRV. Everyone braced themselves against the final waves of disturbance from the surfacing submarine and stared intently at the screen as the image came on line.

In hazy grey it showed a group of buildings ranged like the spokes of a wheel round a central hub. To the right the infrared sensor picked up the heat signatures of a dozen or so people bustling around two huge double-rotored helicopters, transport machines which had arrived after Jack's escape. Along with a second group visible on the seafront, they seemed to be in great haste. They were ferrying objects that looked suspiciously like paintings and statues.

Suddenly there was a blinding flash and a concentric ripple of colour pulsed out at lightning speed from the centre of the screen. When it cleared the scene was one of utter devastation. The central hub had been atomized, its dome pulverized into a million fragments. The thermal imagery showed where the blast had seared down the passageways leading from the hub. The shock wave had gone further, toppling the helicopters and all the people who had been visible, their lifeless bodies in disarray among the packages they had been carrying. They could not have known what hit them.

There was muted applause from the crew. They knew this was no mere act of retribution, that the stakes were much higher.

30

'We were grieved to hear about Peter Howe.'

Maurice Hiebermeyer had clambered out of the helicopter and walked straight past the stone circle to put his hand on Jack's shoulder. It was a moving gesture, evidence of a friendship that went beyond shared professional passion.

'We haven't given up hope yet.'

Jack stood with Katya and Costas at the bottom of the steps that led up to the entrance into the volcano. They had spent a well-earned night on board *Sea Venture* and were now basking in the morning sun as it rose in the east behind the stone circle. The blue IMU overall concealed Jack's freshly bandaged chest, but Costas' face was a very visible reminder of what he had been through. Katya was still subdued and withdrawn.

'Warmest congratulations on your discovery. And on overcoming a few obstacles along the way.' James Dillen spoke as he shook hands with Jack. His gaze took in Katya and Costas.

Dillen was followed from the helicopter by Aysha Farouk, Hiebermeyer's assistant who had first revealed the Atlantis papyrus in the desert and had now been invited to join them. Standing to one side was the genial figure of Efram Jacobovich, the billionaire software tycoon who had provided the endowment that made all their research possible.

To Jack the conference in the castle at Alexandria seemed a lifetime ago. Yet it had only been four days. And they were still one step away from their goal, from the fount of all that had driven the priests to preserve and covet their secret over so many generations.

Just as they were about to file up the rock-cut stairs, Mustafa Alközen came bounding over the platform carrying two diver's flashlights.

'My apologies for being late,' he said breathlessly. 'We have had a busy night. Yesterday evening a Turkish Air Force Boeing 737 early warning aircraft detected an explosive shock wave on the coast of Abkhazia near the Georgian border.' He winked at Jack. 'We decided it was a threat to national security and sent a Special Forces rapid reaction team to investigate.'

'The works of art?' Jack asked.

'Most were still inside Aslan's domestic quarters, and most of those being removed were outside the main blast area. As we speak they are being transferred by Navy Seahawks to Istanbul's Archaeological Museum for identification and conservation and then will be returned to their rightful owners.'

'A pity,' Costas interjected. 'They'd make a unique travelling exhibit. Examples of the finest art from all periods and cultures, never before seen together. It would be an astounding show.'

'A few anxious curators might want to see their property first,' Jack said.

'But an excellent idea.' Efram Jacobovich pitched in with quiet enthusiasm. 'It would be an appropriate use for the funds confiscated from Aslan's accounts. Meanwhile I can think of one private benefactor who might provide the seed money.'

Jack smiled appreciatively and turned back to Mustafa. 'And the security situation?'

'We have been seeking an excuse to go into Abkhazia for some time,' Mustafa replied. 'It has become the main transit point for drugs from central Asia. With the terrorist link now firmly established we have been assured of full co-operation from the Georgian and Russian governments.'

Jack tried hard to conceal his scepticism. He knew Mustafa was obliged to toe the official line even though he was well aware that the chances of concerted action beyond the present situation were minimal.

They looked towards the low shape of *Kazbek* and the flotilla of Turkish and Russian FAC craft which had arrived overnight, evidence of the process already underway to ensure the nuclear warheads were removed and the submarine returned to its home port for decommissioning. Following disposal of the reactor core, the bodies of Captain Antonov and his crew would be left on board and the submarine sunk as a military grave, a final monument to the human cost of the Cold War.

'What about the hardware?' Jack asked.

'Anything reusable will go to the Georgians. They need it

most. We had hoped to offer them *Vultura*, but I now see that will no longer be possible.' He grinned at Jack. 'So they get a brand-new Russian Project 1154 *Neustrashimy*-class frigate instead.'

'What will happen to *Vultura*?' Katya asked quietly.

They all looked out at the distant hulk which had been towed into position above the underwater canyon. It was a pitiful sight, a smouldering pyre that was the last testimony to the avarice and hubris of one man.

Mustafa checked his watch. 'I believe you will have the answer about now.'

Exactly on cue the air was rent by the high-pitched screech of jet aircraft. Seconds later two Turkish Air Force F-15E Strike Eagles thundered overhead, their twin afterburners flaring red as they flew in close formation towards their objective. About two kilometres beyond the island a canister dropped from the left-hand jet and skipped over the sea like a dambuster bomb. As the two aircraft tore away to the south, the sea erupted in a wall of flame that engulfed the wreck in an awesome display of pyrotechnics.

'A thermobaric bomb,' Mustafa said simply. 'The tunnel-buster first used by the Americans in Afghanistan. We needed a live-fire target to test the delivery system on our new Strike Eagles.' He turned as the noise rumbled past them and gestured towards the door. 'Come. Let us go in now.'

The cool air of the passageway provided a welcome respite from the sun which had begun to beat down uncomfortably on the rock outside. For those who had not yet seen it, their first view of the audience chamber with its vast domed ceiling far exceeded anything they had imagined. With all evidence of Aslan gone, the chamber was pristine, the thrones standing empty as if awaiting the return of the high priests who had vacated them more than seven thousand years earlier.

The chimney was now dormant, the last of the rainwater having dissipated overnight, and instead of a vapour plume a brilliant shaft of sunlight illuminated the dais like a theatrical spotlight.

For a few moments there was silence. Even Hiebermeyer, not usually at a loss for words and accustomed to the splendours of ancient Egypt, took off his misted-up glasses and stood speechless.

Dillen turned to face them.

'Ladies and gentlemen,' he said, 'we can now take up where the text left off. I believe we are one step from the supreme revelation.'

Jack never ceased to be amazed by his mentor's ability to switch off from the excitement of discovery. Wearing an immaculate white suit and bow tie, he seemed a throwback to another age, to a time when effortless elegance was as much a part of the scholar's tools of trade as the sophisticated gadgetry of his students' generation.

'We have precious little to go on,' Dillen cautioned. 'The papyrus is a tattered shred and the Phaistos disc is equally elusive. We can infer from the entranceway inscription that "Atlantis" refers to this citadel, this monastery. To outsiders it probably meant the city as well, but for the inhabitants it may have specifically denoted their most sacred place, the rocky slopes and caves where the settlement began.'

'Like the Acropolis in Athens,' Costas ventured.

'Precisely. The disc implies that within Atlantis is a place I translate as "place of the gods", Katya as "holy of holies". It also mentions a mother goddess. As far as I can tell none of your discoveries fits this bill.'

'The nearest would be the hall of the ancestors, the name

we gave to the cave painting gallery,' Jack said. 'But that's Palaeolithic and contains no representations of humans. In a Neolithic sanctuary I'd expect to see anthropomorphic deities, a grander version of the household shrine we saw in the submerged village at Trabzon.'

'What about this room, the audience chamber?' Efram Jacobovich asked.

Jack shook his head. 'It's too large. This space is inclusive, designed for congregational gatherings like a church. What we're looking for is something exclusive, hidden away. The holier the place, the more restricted the access to it. Only priests would be allowed entry, as befitted their status as intermediaries with the gods.'

'A tabernacle,' Efram suggested.

Katya and Aysha appeared on the ledge beside the ramp. While the others had been talking they had carried out a quick reconnaissance of the doorways surrounding the chamber.

'We think we've found it,' Katya said, the excitement of once again exploring and discovering the secrets of Atlantis pushing aside the nightmare of the last few days. 'Altogether there are twelve entrances. Two we can discount because they're the passageways we know about, one from outside and the other coming up from below. Of the remainder, nine are either blanks, false doorways leading nowhere, or passageways leading down. I assume we're going up.'

'If this is truly the mother of all peak sanctuaries,' Jack replied, 'then the higher the better.'

Katya pointed towards the door at the western extremity of the chamber, directly opposite the entrance passageway. 'That's the one. It also happens to be capped by the sign of the outstretched eagle god.'

Jack smiled broadly at Katya, glad to see her beginning to recover from her ordeal, and turned to Dillen.

'Professor, perhaps you would lead us in.'

Dillen nodded courteously and walked beside Jack towards the west door, his dapper form a striking contrast to his former student's weather-beaten appearance. They were followed by Katya and Costas and then by the other four, with Efram Jacobovich unobtrusively bringing up the rear. As they neared the entrance Jack glanced back at Costas.

'This is it then. A gin and tonic by the pool awaits.'

Costas cast his friend a crooked smile. 'That's what you say every time.'

Dillen paused to inspect the carving on the lintel; it was an immaculate miniature of the spread-winged eagle god the others had seen in the hall of the ancestors. Jack and Costas switched on their flashlights and shone them into the darkness ahead. Like the walls of the submerged passages, the basalt had been polished to a lustrous hue, its mottled surface sparkling with mineral inclusions which had welled up from the earth's mantle as the volcano formed.

Jack stepped aside to let Dillen take the lead. About ten metres in he suddenly halted.

'We have a problem.'

Jack came alongside and saw that a massive stone portal blocked the passageway. It melded almost seamlessly with the walls but close up they could see it divided into two equal halves. Jack aimed his beam at the centre and saw the telltale feature.

'I believe I have the key,' he said confidently.

He reached into his IMU overalls and extracted the copy of the golden disc which he had rescued from the dais after Aslan's abrupt departure. As the others watched, he slotted it into the saucer-shaped depression. The instant he withdrew his hand the disc began whirling clockwise. Seconds later the doors sprang open in their direction, the accumulated patina providing little resistance to the weight of the slabs as they pivoted on each side of the passageway.

'Magic.' Costas shook his head in amazement. 'Exactly the same mechanism as the door on the cliff face and still functioning after seven and a half thousand years. These people would have invented the computer chip by the Bronze Age.'

'Then I'd be out of a job,' Efram chuckled from the back.

The odour that greeted them was like the musty exhalation of a burial vault, as if a draught of stale air had wafted through a crypt and brought with it the very essence of the dead, the last residue of the tallow and incense which had burned as the priests made their final ablutions before they sealed their hallowed shrine for ever. The effect was almost hallucinogenic, and they could sense the fear and urgency of those last acts. It was as if two hundred generations of history had been swept away and they were joining the custodians of Atlantis in their final desperate flight.

'Now I know how Carter and Carnarvon felt when they opened the tomb of Tutankhamun,' Hiebermeyer said.

Katya shuddered in the chill air. Like the tombs of the pharaohs in the Valley of the Kings, the passage beyond the doorway was unadorned, giving no hint of what lay beyond.

'It can't be far now,' Costas said. 'According to my altimeter we're less than thirty metres below the summit.'

Dillen suddenly stopped and Jack stumbled into him, his beam flailing wildly as he righted himself. What seemed another doorway was in fact a ninety-degree turn to the left. The passageway angled upwards in a series of shallow steps.

Dillen moved forward and stopped again. 'I can see something ahead. Shine your beams to left and right.' His voice was uncharacteristically edged with excitement.

Jack and Costas obliged and revealed a fantastic scene. On either side were the front quarters of two enormous bulls, their truncated forms cut in bas-relief and facing up the stairway. With their elongated necks and horns arched high overhead, they were less composed than the beasts in the underwater passageways, as if they were straining to break free and leap into the darkness above.

As they mounted the stairs, they began to make out a succession of figures in front of the bulls in lower relief, their details exactingly rendered in the fine-grained basalt.

'They're human.' Dillen spoke with hushed awe, his usual reserve forgotten. 'Ladies and gentlemen, behold the people of Atlantis.'

The figures exuded a bold confidence appropriate to the guardians of the citadel. The carvings on either wall were identical in mirror image. They were life-sized, tall figures, marching ramrod straight in single file. Each figure had one arm extended, with the hand clasped round a hole which had once held a burning torch of tallow. They had the hieratic, two-dimensional stance of the relief carvings of the ancient Near East and Egypt, but instead of the stiffness normally associated with the profile view, they exhibited a suppleness and grace which seemed a direct legacy from the naturalistic animal paintings of the Ice Age.

As the beams highlighted each figure in turn, it became clear that they alternated between the sexes. The women were bare-breasted, their close-fitting gowns revealing curvaceous but well-honed figures. Like the men they had large, almond-shaped eyes and wore their hair down their backs in braided tresses. The men had long beards and wore flowing robes. Their physiognomy was familiar yet unidentifiable, as if the individual features were recognizable but the whole was unique and impossible to place.

'The women look very athletic,' Aysha remarked. 'Maybe they were the bullfighters, not the men.'

'They remind me of the Varangians,' Katya said. 'The Byzantine name for the Vikings who came down the Dnieper to the Black Sea. In the cathedral of Santa Sofia in Kiev there are wall paintings that show tall men just like this, except with hooked noses and blond hair.'

'To me they're like the second millennium BC Hittites of Anatolia,' Mustafa interjected. 'Or the Sumerians and Assyrians of Mesopotamia.'

'Or the Bronze Age peoples of Greece and Crete,' Jack murmured. 'The women could be the bare-breasted ladies from the frescoes at Knossos. The men could have walked straight off those beaten gold warrior vases found in the royal grave circle at Mycenae last year.'

'They are Everywoman and Everyman,' Dillen asserted quietly. 'The original Indo-Europeans, the first Caucasians. From them are descended almost all the peoples of Europe and Asia. The Egyptians, the Semites, the Greeks, the megalith builders of western Europe, the first rulers of Mohenjo-Daro in the Indus Valley. Sometimes they replaced original populations entirely, other times they interbred. In all these peoples we see some trace of their forebears, the founders of civilization.'

They gazed with renewed awe at the images as Dillen led them up the steps. The figures embodied strength and determination, as if they were marching inexorably towards their place in history.

After about ten metres, the alternating men and women gave way to three figures on either side, apparently leading the procession. They carried elaborate staves and wore strange conical hats that reached all the way to the ceiling.

'The high priests,' Jack said simply.

'They look like wizards,' Costas said. 'Like druids.'

'That may not be so far-fetched,' Katya replied. 'The word

druid derives from the Indo-European *wid*, "to know". These were clearly the holders of knowledge in Neolithic Atlantis, the equivalent of the priestly class in Celtic Europe five thousand years later.'

'Fascinating.' Hiebermeyer was pushing his way up through the group. 'The hats are remarkably similar to the beaten gold caps found in votive deposits of the Bronze Age. We discovered one in Egypt last year when the secret treasury in the Khefru pyramid was opened.'

He reached the first of the figures on the left-hand wall, a woman, and took off his glasses for a closer look.

'Just as I thought,' he exclaimed. 'It's covered with tiny circular and lunate symbols exactly like the Bronze Age hats.' He wiped his glasses and gave a dramatic flourish. 'I'm certain it's a logarithmic representation of the Metonic cycle.'

While the others crowded round to examine the carving, Jack caught Costas' puzzled glance.

'Meton was an Athenian astrologer,' he explained. 'A contemporary of Socrates, Plato's mentor. He was the first Greek to establish the difference between the solar and the lunar months, the synodic cycle.' He nodded towards the carvings. 'These were the guys who devised the calendrical record of sacrifices with the leap months we saw carved in that passageway.'

Dillen had detached himself from the group and was standing in front of a portal at the top of the steps in line with the leading priests.

'They were lords of time,' he announced. 'With their stone circle they could chart the movements of the sun in relation to the moon and the constellations. This knowledge empowered them as oracles, with access to divine wisdom that allowed them to see into the future. They could predict the time of sowing and the annual harvest. They had mastery over heaven and earth.'

He gestured grandly towards the low entrance behind him. 'And now they are leading us towards their inner sanctum, their holy of holies.'

31

The group stood clustered round the portal and peered into the dark passage beyond. Again they felt the brush of ancient vapour, a musty waft that seemed to carry with it the distilled wisdom of the ages. Out of nowhere Jack conjured up an image of Solon the Lawmaker and the shadowy priest in the temple sanctuary at Saïs. In a moment the phantasm was gone, but he was left convinced they were about to delve the inner secrets of a people who had passed out of history thousands of years before.

After a few metres they reached the end of the passageway and Jack panned his light forward. Beside him Dillen blinked as his eyes adjusted to the unaccustomed brilliance of the scene ahead.

'What is it?' Hiebermeyer could not contain his excitement. 'What can you see?'

'It's a single chamber, approximately ten metres long by six metres wide,' Jack replied in the measured tones of a professional archaeologist. 'There's a rock table in the middle and a dividing screen towards the rear. Oh, and there's gold. Thick gold panels on the walls.'

He and Dillen stooped through the entrance and the others followed cautiously behind. Once they were all inside, Jack and Costas adjusted their flashlights to wide beam and shone them down the length of the chamber.

Jack's laconic description scarcely did it justice. On either side the walls were embellished with massive slabs of polished gold, each two metres high and a metre across. They shone with dazzling splendour, their surfaces pristine and mirror-like in the protective atmosphere. There were ten panels altogether, five on either side of the walls, evenly spaced with a gap of half a metre between each. They were covered with markings instantly recognizable as the Atlantis symbols.

'Take a look at her,' Costas whispered.

His beam had caught a gargantuan shape towards the rear of the chamber. It was barely recognizable as human, a grotesque parody of the female form with pendulous breasts, protuberant buttocks and a bloated belly that gave the torso a nearly spherical appearance. She was flanked by life-sized bulls that faced up towards her. The tableau was like a triptych or heraldic group that screened off the rear of the chamber.

Jack stared at the colossus and then glanced at Costas. 'She's what prehistorians flatteringly call a Venus figure,' he explained with a grin. 'About eighty have been found in Europe and Russia, mostly small statuettes in ivory or stone. This one's phenomenal, the only one I know of bigger than life-size.'

'She's a little different from the comely maidens in the passageway,' Costas observed ruefully.

'She's not meant to be a pin-up.' Katya's tone was gently admonishing. 'Look how they haven't even bothered to finish the feet or the arms, and the head's just a blank. Everything's deliberately exaggerated to emphasize fecundity and good health. She may not conform to the modern western ideal of beauty, but for people living with the constant fear of starvation, an obese woman symbolized prosperity and survival.'

'Point taken.' Costas smiled. 'How old is the lady?'

'Upper Palaeolithic,' Jack replied immediately. 'All the Venus figurines fall between 40,000 and 10,000 BC, the same range as the paintings in the hall of the ancestors.'

'They used to be thought of as mother goddesses,' Hiebermeyer added pensively. 'But there's no certainty Stone Age European societies were matriarchal. They're probably best seen as fertility idols, worshipped alongside male deities as well as animal spirits and inanimate forces.'

There was a brief silence, which Jack broke. 'For hundreds of thousands of years hominids lived an unchanged existence during the Old Stone Age, right up to the Neolithic revolution. It's no surprise the Atlanteans so soon after still revered the time-honoured gods of their ancestors, the hunter-gatherers who first painted wild beasts in the hall of the ancestors during the Ice Age.'

'The ancient Israelites of the Old Testament still worshipped a fertility god,' Efram Jacobovich interjected quietly. 'Even the early Christians of the Mediterranean incorporated pagan fertility deities into their rituals, sometimes in the guise of saints or the Virgin Mary. The Venus of Atlantis might not be as far from our own beliefs as we might imagine.'

The stone table in front of the statue was massive. It extended almost to the entrance, terminating just in front of them in a raised ledge capped by an irregular globular shape about a metre across. In the light reflected off the gold it seemed preternaturally white, as if it had been burnished by the countless supplicants who had come to pray before the great goddess.

'It looks like a sacred stone,' Jack speculated. 'What the ancient Greeks called a *baetyl*, a rock of meteoric origin, or an *omphalos*, a centre or navel. In Bronze Age Crete there were baetyls at the entrance to holy caves. In classical Greece the most famous omphalos was in front of the chasm where the oracle sat at Delphi.'

'Marking the threshold into the House of the Divine, like the bowl of holy water at the entrance to a Catholic church,' Efram suggested.

'Something like that,' Jack agreed.

'It's definitely meteoric.' Costas was examining the bulbous form more closely. 'But it's curious, almost like a warped sheet of metal rather than a solid nodule.'

'The kind of thing Stone Age hunters might have picked up on the ice cap,' Jack mused. 'Most fresh meteor fragments are found on ice because they're easy to spot. This could be a sacred object passed down from their ancestors, another link to earliest prehistory.'

Aysha had edged her way along the far side of the table and stopped before reaching the goddess. 'Come and look at this,' she exclaimed.

The two beams swept forward along the surface of the table. It was littered with slats of wood, some joined at right angles like the corners of boxes. They could make out a jumble of carpenter's tools, familiar forms including chisels and files, awls and mallets. It looked like the paraphernalia of a cabinet-maker's workshop, all hastily abandoned but immaculately preserved in the dust-free environment.

'This is more than it seems.' Dillen bent over beside Aysha and carefully swept the wood shavings from a raised surface facing him. It was a wooden frame like a portable lectern. As he straightened up they caught a glimpse of gold.

'It's a copyist's table,' he announced triumphantly. 'And there's a gold sheet on top.'

As they crowded round, they could see the upper third of the sheet was densely covered with Atlantean symbols, some aligned erratically as if done in a hurry but all separated into phrases like the Phaistos disc. From a small box at the side, Dillen held up three cigar-sized stone punches, each terminating in an obverse instantly recognizable as the Mohican head, the sheaf of corn and the canoe paddle. Another one lying on the table terminated in the Atlantis symbol.

'It is identical to the inscription on the wall opposite,' Katya said. 'The copyist was replicating the symbols on the second panel from the left.'

They looked where she indicated and could just make out the individual symbols, a sequence faithfully transcribed up to the twelfth line where it had been abruptly abandoned.

Efram Jacobovich remained at the head of the table. He was staring intensely at the clutter of wooden slats, clearly lost in thought. Without looking up he cleared his throat and began to recite.

'And it came to pass on the third day of the morning, that there were thunders and lightnings, and a thick cloud upon the mount, and the voice of the trumpet exceeding loud; so that all the people that was in the camp trembled. And Moses brought forth the people out of the camp to meet with God; and they stood at the nether part of the mount. And mount Sinai was altogether on a smoke because the Lord descended upon it in fire; and the smoke thereof ascended as the smoke of a furnace, and the whole mount quaked greatly.'

He closed his eyes and continued.

'And Bezaleel made the ark of shittim wood; two cubits and a half was the length of it, and a cubit and a half the breadth of it, and a cubit and a half the height of it; and he overlaid it with pure gold within and without, and made a crown of gold to it round about. And he cast for it four rings of gold, to be set by the four corners of it; even two rings upon the one side of it, and two rings upon the other side of it. And he made staves of shittim wood, and overlaid them with gold. And he put the staves into the rings by the sides of the ark, to bear the ark.'

There was a stunned silence. He looked up. 'The Book of Exodus,' he explained. 'Those of my faith believe God gave Moses the Covenant, the Ten Commandments, and inscribed them on tablets which were borne by the people of Israel in the Ark. Biblical references to the pharaohs put the event in the second half of the second millennium BC. But now I wonder whether the story contains the kernel of a much older account, of a people thousands of years earlier who were forced to flee their homeland, a people who took with them copies of their ten sacred texts from their holy sanctuary near the summit of a volcano.'

Jack looked up from where he had been examining a stack of blank gold sheets. 'Of course,' he exclaimed. 'Each of the migrating groups was to have a copy. Clay tablets would have been too fragile, stone inscriptions would have taken too long and copper would have corroded. Gold was in good supply from the Caucasus and was durable and soft enough for rapid inscription with punches. Each set of ten tablets was encased in a wooden crate just like the Ark of the Covenant. The priests worked right up to the last minute and abandoned the final copy only as the city was overwhelmed by the floodwaters.'

'These may be sacred texts but they are definitely not the Ten Commandments.' Katya had extracted her palm computer and was scrolling through the concordance of the Atlantis symbols with Minoan Linear A. 'It'll take time to translate them completely, but already I have a general sense of the meaning. The first tablet to the left refers to grains, legumes, even vines, and to seasons of the year. The second, the one our scribe was copying, refers to animal husbandry. The third is about copper and gold metallurgy and the fourth about architecture, the use of building stone.' She paused and looked up. 'Unless I'm mistaken these tablets are a kind of encyclopedia, a blueprint for life in Neolithic Atlantis.'

Jack shook his head in wonder. 'Aslan would have been disappointed. No royal cache, no fortune in works of art. Only the greatest treasure of them all, priceless beyond measure. The keys to civilization itself.'

While Katya and Dillen busied themselves translating in Jack's torchlight, Costas made his way beyond Aysha to the goddess and the bulls. The gap between the front legs of the right-hand bull and the voluminous thigh of the goddess formed a low entryway worn smooth by generations of use. Costas crouched down and disappeared from sight, his presence only revealed by the beam of light that silhouetted the bulls where they reared up towards the head of the goddess.

'Follow me.' His voice was muffled but distinct. 'There's more.'

They all scrambled through and stood with their backs against the far side of the statues. They were inside a narrow annexe in front of an irregular rocky face.

'This must be the holy of holies.' Dillen's eyes darted around as he spoke. 'Like the cella in a Greek temple or the sanctuary in a Christian church. But it's surprisingly bare.'

'Except for that.' Costas trained his beam on the rock face.

It was adorned with three painted figures, the central one almost as large as the mother goddess and the other two slightly smaller. They seemed to mimic the arrangement of the goddess and the bulls. They were dull red, identical to the pigment used in the hall of the ancestors, except here the colour had faded. Stylistically they were also reminiscent of Ice Age art, with broad, impressionistic strokes that gave a strong sense of animation yet were essentially outline representations. But in their form the figures were like nothing else they had seen in Atlantis.

Instead of powerful animals or statuesque priests they were scarcely recognizable as earthly beings, abstract renditions that barely captured the essence of the corporeal. Each had a bulbous, pear-shaped body with limbs jutting awkwardly sideways, the hands and feet terminating in ten or twelve digits that splayed out. The heads seemed grossly out of proportion to the bodies. The eyes were outsized lentoids edged in black, reminiscent of the *kohl* marks of ancient Egyptian portraits. They were like a child's attempt at the human form, yet with something oddly deliberate about the shared characteristics of all three.

'These are old, very old,' Jack murmured. 'Late Ice Age, maybe five thousand years before the flood. They're executed on the living rock, just like the animals in the hall of the ancestors. There are plenty of minimalist depictions of the human form in rock art around the world, in the petroglyphs of Africa and Australia and the south-western United States. But I've never seen prehistoric figures like this.'

'These cannot be serious attempts at the human form.' Costas was shaking his head in disbelief. 'There's no way Ice Age art was this primitive. Those animals in the hall of the ancestors are amazingly naturalistic.'

'They're probably humanoid rather than anthropomorphic,' Jack countered. 'Remember these are thousands of years older than the Atlanteans carved in the passageway, really more like shamans or spirits, or gods who had no defined physical form. In some societies the human form was sacrosanct and portraiture never attempted. The Iron Age artists of Celtic Europe were wonderfully accomplished, but if you saw the representations of humans they began producing under the Romans you'd think they were primitive in the extreme.'

Jack's beam rose to a small carved device atop the central figure. It was a single cartouche half a metre long and contained two of the Atlantean symbols, the perched eagle and the vertical paddle.

'That's more recent than the paintings,' Jack commented. 'The surface is cleaner and the carving would have required metal tools. Any idea of the translation?'

Katya knew most of the syllabary and did not bother to consult her computer. 'It's not in the concordance,' she asserted confidently. 'It could be a verb or noun we haven't encountered. But in the context I'd say it's most likely a proper name.'

'How is it pronounced?' Efram spoke from the far corner of the room.

'Each of the Atlantean symbols represents a syllable, a consonant preceded or followed by a vowel,' Katya replied. 'The perched eagle is always *Y* and the vertical paddle *W.* I'd suggest one word reading *ye-we* or *ya-wa*, the vowel sounds short rather than long.'

'The Tetragrammaton!' Efram sounded incredulous. 'The name that shall not be spoken. The First Cause of all things, the Ruler of Heaven and Earth.' As if by instinct he shied away from the images on the wall, his eyes averted and his head bowed reverentially.

'Yahweh.' Dillen sounded scarcely less astonished. 'The principle name of God in the Hebrew Old Testament, the divine name only to be uttered by the high priest in the Tabernacle, in the holy of holies, on the Day of Atonement. In Greek it was "The Four-Lettered Word", the Tetragrammaton. The early Christians translated it as Jehovah.'

'The God of Moses and Abraham.' Efram slowly recovered his composure as he spoke. 'A tribal god of the Sinai at the time of the Israelite exodus from Egypt, but he may have revealed himself much earlier. Unlike the other gods who tempted the Israelites, he was highly interventionist, uniquely effective on behalf of his worshippers and able to alter current events in their favour. He led them in battle and exile and gave them the Ten Commandments.'

'And saved them from the flood.'

The words came from Costas, who unexpectedly began to recite from the Book of Genesis.

'And God said unto Noah, This is the token of the covenant, which I have established between me and all flesh that is upon the earth. And the sons of Noah that went forth of the ark, were Shem, and Ham, and Japeth; and Ham is the father of Canaan. These are the three sons of Noah; and of them was the whole earth overspread.'

Jack was aware of his friend's Greek Orthodox upbringing

and nodded slowly, the gleam of revelation in his eyes as he spoke.

'Of course. The Jewish God caused the land to be inundated and then signalled his pact with the chosen by revealing the rainbow. It's just as we thought. The building of the ark, the selection of breeding pairs of animals, the diaspora of Noah's descendants around the world. The ancient flood myths not only tell us about river inundations and the great melt at the end of the Ice Age. They also tell of another cataclysm, of a flood in the sixth millennium BC that consumed the world's first city, extinguishing a precocious civilization unequalled for thousands of years to come. Plato is not the only source of the Atlantis story after all. It's been staring at us all along, encoded in the greatest work of literature ever written.'

32

After carefully examining the rest of the inner sanctum, they filed back into the main chamber. They assembled at the far end around the mysterious metallic orb. Dillen emerged last and picked up a chisel from the debris on the table.

'This is bronze,' he said. 'An alloy of copper and tin, smelted some time prior to the abandonment of this room in the middle of the sixth millennium BC. An extraordinary discovery. Before today, archaeologists would have said bronze was first made around 3500 BC, possibly in Anatolia, and only became widespread during the following millennium.'

Dillen replaced the chisel and put his hands on the table.

'The question is, why did it take so long for bronze to reappear after the Black Sea flood?'

'Presumably the civilization of Atlantis developed in isolation,' Costas said, 'and much faster than anywhere else.'

Jack nodded, and started pacing up and down. 'At the right time, in the right circumstances, progress can be phenomenal. When the Ice Age ended ten thousand years ago, the southern Black Sea region was already rich in flora and fauna. Because the Bosporus was blocked, the great melt had only a limited effect. The soil around the volcano was highly fertile, the sea teemed with fish and the land with aurochs, deer and boar. Add to this the other natural resources we know about: timber from the mountain forests; salt from the coastal evaporation pans; stone from the volcano; gold, copper and, perhaps most significant of all, tin. It was a cornucopia, a Garden of Eden, as if some power had concentrated all the ingredients for the good life in one place.'

Costas was staring pensively at the corpulent figure of the mother goddess. 'So,' he said, 'a particularly dynamic band of hunter-gatherers move into this area about forty thousand years ago. They discover the labyrinth inside the volcano. The animal paintings in the hall of the ancestors are theirs, and this chamber is their holy shrine. At the end of the Ice Age they invent agriculture.'

'Good so far,' Jack said. 'Only agriculture probably emerged about the same time across the entire Near East, an idea that cropped up more or less simultaneously and spread rapidly. Sophisticated Neolithic settlements existed elsewhere as early as the tenth millennium BC, most famously at Jericho in Palestine and Çatal Hüyük in southern Anatolia, the two sites that most closely parallel our Neolithic village off Trabzon.'

'OK,' Costas went on. 'Like the people at the Anatolian site, the Atlanteans hammer copper but they take a giant leap forward and learn how to smelt and alloy the metal. Like the people of Jericho they create monumental architecture, but instead of walls and towers they build arenas, processional ways and pyramids. From about 8000 BC something incredible happens. A farming and fishing community transforms into a metropolis of fifty, maybe one hundred thousand people. They have their own script, a religious headquarters the equal of any medieval monastery, public arenas that would have impressed the Romans, a complex water supply system – it's unbelievable.'

'And none of this happened anywhere else,' Jack said. He stopped pacing. 'Çatal Hüyük was abandoned at the end of the sixth millennium BC and never reoccupied, possibly a result of warfare. Jericho survived but the fabled walls of Biblical times were a pale shadow of their Neolithic precursors. While the Atlanteans were building pyramids, most of the Near East was just beginning to grapple with pottery.'

'And bronze, above all, must have facilitated such a prodigious development.' Mustafa leaned forward over the table as he spoke, his bearded face caught in the torchlight. 'Think of all the uses for hard, sharp-edged tools that could be made into virtually any shape and then recycled. Without adzes and chisels no ark would ever have made it off the drawing board. Bronze tools were crucial for quarrying and stone-working and agriculture. Ploughshares, picks and forks, hoes and shovels, sickles and scythes. Bronze truly spurred a second agricultural revolution.'

'In Mesopotamia, modern Iraq, it also spearheaded the world's first arms race,' Hiebermeyer remarked, wiping his glasses as he spoke.

'An important point,' Dillen said. 'Warfare was endemic in the early states of Mesopotamia and the Levant, often as a result of the avarice of the elite rather than any real competition for resources. It's a dangerous modern fallacy that warfare accelerates technological progress. The benefits of advances in engineering and science are far outweighed by the exhaustion of human ingenuity in devising methods of destruction. Perhaps by exercising total control over the production and use of bronze, the priests of Atlantis could prevent it being used for weapons.'

'Imagine a society with no warfare yet abundant access to bronze so soon after the Ice Age,' Hiebermeyer said. 'It would have accelerated the development of civilization like nothing else.'

'So if the Atlanteans were alone in discovering how to produce bronze, was the knowledge somehow lost when Atlantis flooded?' Costas asked.

'Not lost, but kept secret,' said Dillen. 'We need to return to Amenhotep, the Egyptian high priest in the temple scriptorium at Saïs. I believe he was a caretaker of knowledge, one in an unbroken succession stretching back five thousand years to the time of Atlantis. The first priests of Saïs were the last priests of Atlantis, descendants of the women and men who fled this very chamber and embarked on a perilous journey west to the Bosporus. Their role was to to regulate human behaviour according to their interpretation of divine will. This they achieved not only by enforcing a moral code but also as guardians of knowledge, including knowledge they knew could be destructive. After Atlantis disappeared, my guess is they kept the secret of bronze for generation after generation, master to novice, teacher to pupil.' Dillen gestured towards the shimmering plaques on the walls.

'Here we have the entire corpus of knowledge of the priesthood of Atlantis, codified as a sacred text. Some knowledge was open to all, like the rudiments of agriculture.

Some was the preserve of the priests, perhaps including medicinal lore.' He swept his arm towards the untranslated plaques to his left. 'The rest we can still only guess at. There may be ancient wisdom in these writings the high priests kept exclusively to themselves, to be revealed only at a time appointed by the gods.'

'But surely the rudiments of bronze technology would have been common knowledge, available to all,' Costas insisted.

'Not necessarily.' Jack was pacing behind the orb. 'When I flew the ADSA over the eastern quarter of the city I noticed something strange. I saw woodworking areas, stonemasons' yards, pottery manufactories, kilns for drying corn and baking bread. But no forges or metalsmiths' workshops.' He looked questioningly at Mustafa, whose doctoral thesis on early metallurgy in Asia Minor was the benchmark for the subject.

'For a long time we thought the tin used in the Bronze Age all came from central Asia,' Mustafa said. 'But trace-element analysis of tools has pointed to mines in south-eastern Anatolia as well. And now I believe we are looking at another source, one that could never have been guessed at before this discovery.'

Jack nodded enthusiastically while Mustafa continued.

'Smelting and forging are not household activities. Jack is right that a community of this size would have required a substantial metal-working facility well away from the residential districts. A place where intense heat could be harnessed, heat conceivably from a natural source.'

'Of course!' Costas cried. 'The volcano! The minerals brought up in the eruption must have included cassiterite, tin ore. It was a mine, a honeycomb of galleries that followed veins of ore deep into the bowels of the mountain.'

'And since the mountain was already hallowed ground,' Dillen added, 'the priests could control access not only to the means of producing bronze but to an essential ingredient of it as well. They could erect a further barrier, too, a wall of piety. A priesthood exists because it professes an understanding of truths beyond the grasp of lay people. By consecrating bronze they could elevate metallurgy to a rarefied art.'

Jack stared intently at the table in front of him. 'We're standing on a catacomb of ancient technology, a protean forge worthy of the fire god Hephaistos himself.'

'So what actually happened at the time of the Black Sea exodus?' Costas asked.

'Now we come to the nub of the matter,' Dillen answered. 'When the Bosporus was breached and the floodwaters rose, the people must have assumed the worst, that the end was nigh. Even the priests could not have come up with a rational explanation for the relentless approach of the sea, a phenomenon as supernatural as the rumblings of the volcano itself.'

He began to pace, his gesticulations throwing strange shadows onto the walls.

'To appease the gods they fell back on propitiatory sacrifice. Perhaps they dragged a giant bull up the processional way and cut its throat on the altar. When that failed they may have turned in desperation to the ultimate offering, to human sacrifice. They slew their victims on the preparation slab in the mortuary chamber and flung their bodies from the funerary ledge into the heart of the volcano.'

He paused and looked up.

'And then it happened. Perhaps a magma surge, maybe accompanied by a violent rainstorm, a combination that would have produced that remarkable vapour column and then a glorious rainbow. It was the long-awaited sign. A final mark was hastily scratched into the wall. Yahweh had not abandoned them after all. There was still hope. It convinced them to leave rather than await their doom.'

'And then they set off in their boats,' Costas said.

'Some took the shortest route to high land, east towards the Caucasus and south across the floodplain past Mount Ararat towards Mesopotamia and the Indus Valley. Others paddled west to the mouth of the Danube, some of their number eventually reaching the Atlantic coast. But I believe the largest group portaged round the Bosporus to the Mediterranean. They settled in Greece and Egypt and the Levant, some even as far west as Italy and Spain.'

'What did they take with them?' Efram asked.

'Think of Noah's Ark,' Dillen responded. 'Breeding pairs of domestic animals. Cattle, pigs, deer, sheep, goats. And bushels of seeds. Wheat, barley, beans, even olive trees and grape vines. But there was one item of immense significance they left behind.'

Costas looked at him. 'Bronze?'

Dillen nodded gravely. 'It's the only possible explanation for the complete absence of bronze in the archaeological record for the next two thousand years. There would have been space in their boats to take their tools and implements but I believe the priests ordered them not to. Perhaps it was a final act of appeasement, an offering that would safeguard their passage into the unknown. They may even have thrown the tools into the sea itself, an offering to the force that had doomed their city.'

'But the priests took their knowledge of metallurgy,' Costas said.

'Indeed. I believe the high priests made a pact with their gods, a covenant if you like. After the omen gave them hope of escape they set to work with the greatest urgency copying out the words of their sacred text, transcribing the ten tablets onto sheets of beaten gold. We know their wisdom included the rudiments of agriculture and animal husbandry and stonemasonry, along with much else which will only be revealed when the translation is complete.' He glanced at Katya. 'Each set of tablets was encased in a wooden coffer and entrusted to a high priest who accompanied each of the departing flotillas.'

'One group had an incomplete set,' Jack interjected. 'The unfinished gold sheet in front of us, abandoned partway through copying the fourth tablet.'

Dillen nodded. 'And I believe one group was larger than the others, including most of the high priests and their retinue. By despatching a copy of their sacred text with each group, the priests ensured their legacy would endure whatever befell the main flotilla. But their intention was to find a new holy mountain, a new Atlantis.'

'And you're saying their descendants just sat on their knowledge for two thousand years,' Costas said incredulously.

'Think of the priests at Saïs,' Dillen replied. 'For generation after generation they concealed the story of Atlantis, a civilization that perished eons before the first pharaohs came to power. As far as we know Solon was the first outsider made privy to their secrets.'

'And the priests had plenty to offer besides the mysteries of metallurgy,' Jack said. 'They could still use their astronomical knowledge to forecast the seasons and prescribe the most propitious dates for sowing and harvesting. In Egypt they may have transposed their authority to the annual flooding of the Nile, a miracle that required divine intervention. The same was true in the other cradles of civilization where rivers inundated the land, the Tigris-Euphrates in Mesopotamia and the Indus Valley in Pakistan.'

'And we should not overlook what could well be a more direct legacy of bronze,' Mustafa added. 'During the sixth and fifth millennia BC, workers in chipped flint and polished stone reached their pinnacle, producing exquisite knives and sickles. Some are so similar to metal forms they could have been made with the memory of bronze tools. At Varna on the coast of Bulgaria a cemetery has produced a dazzling array of ornaments in gold and copper. The site dates to before 4500 BC, so the first settlers could have been Atlanteans.'

'Nor should we forget language,' Katya said. 'Their greatest gift may have been the Indo-European inscribed on those tablets. Theirs was the true mother tongue, the basis of the first written languages in the Old World. Greek. Latin. Slavonic. Iranian. Sanskrit. Germanic, with its descendant Old English. Their extensive vocabulary and advanced syntax boosted the spread of ideas, not only abstract notions of religion and astronomy but also more mundane matters. The clearest common denominator among Indo-European languages is vocabulary for working the land and animal husbandry.'

'Those abstract ideas included monotheism, the worship of one god.' Efram Jacobovich seemed in the throes of another revelation as he spoke, his voice tremulous with emotion. 'In Jewish tradition we are taught that the Old Testament stories derive mainly from events of the late Bronze and early Iron Age, from the second and early first millennium BC. Now it seems they must incorporate a memory almost inconceivably older. The Black Sea flood and Noah. The golden tablets and the Ark of the Covenant. Even the evidence for sacrifice, possibly human sacrifice, as the ultimate test of fealty to God, evoking the story of Abraham and his son Isaac on Mount Moria. It's all too much for coincidence.'

'Much that was once held true will need to be revised, much rewritten,' Dillen said solemnly. 'A series of remarkable chances led to this discovery. The uncovering of the papyrus in the desert. The excavation of the Minoan shipwreck and the discovery of the golden disc, with its precious concordance of symbols. The translation of the clay disc from Phaistos.' He looked at Aysha and Hiebermeyer, Costas and Jack and Katya in turn, acknowledging the contribution of each. 'A common thread runs through all of these finds, something which at first I dismissed as mere coincidence.'

'Minoan Crete,' Jack responded immediately.

Dillen nodded. 'The garbled version of the Atlantis story from Plato seemed to refer to the Bronze Age Minoans, to their disappearance after the eruption of Thera. But by great good fortune the surviving fragment of papyrus showed Solon had recorded two separate accounts, one that did indeed refer to the cataclysm in the Aegean in the mid-second millennium BC but the other describing the disappearance of Atlantis in the Black Sea four thousand years earlier.'

'Events that were completely unconnected,' Costas interjected.

Dillen nodded. 'I had assumed Amenhotep was giving Solon an anecdotal account of great natural catastrophes in the past, a list of civilizations lost to floods and earthquakes, something that pandered to the Greek taste for the dramatic. A century later the Egyptian priests fed Herodotus all manner of stories about bizarre goings-on in far-off places, some of them clearly spurious. But now I think differently. I have come to believe Amenhotep had a higher purpose.'

Costas looked perplexed. 'I thought the only reason the priests were interested in Solon was his gold,' he said. 'They would never have divulged their secrets otherwise, especially to a foreigner.'

'I now believe that was only part of the story. Amenhotep may have sensed the days of pharaonic Egypt were numbered, that the security which had allowed his forebears to carry their secrets for so many generations could no longer be counted on. Already the Greeks were establishing trading posts in the Delta, and only two centuries later Alexander the Great would storm through the land and sweep away the old order for ever. Yet Amenhotep may also have looked hopefully at the Greeks. Theirs was a society on the cusp of democracy, one of enlightenment and curiosity, a place where the philosopher might truly be king. In the Greek world people might once again discover Utopia.'

'And the sight of the supplicant scholar may have rekindled memories of a fabled land over the northern horizon, an island civilization shrouded in legend that once held the greatest hope of resurrection for the priesthood.' Jack's face lit up with excitement. 'I too believe Amenhotep was a latter-day priest of Atlantis, a direct descendant of the holy men who guided a group of refugees five thousand years earlier to the shores of Egypt and shaped the destiny of that land. High priests, patriarchs, prophets, call them what you will. Other groups landed in the Levant, in western Italy where they were the forebears of the Etruscans and Romans, in southern Spain where the Tartessians were to flourish. But I believe the largest flotilla sailed no further than the Aegean.'

'The island of Thera,' Costas exclaimed.

'Before the eruption, Thera would have been the most imposing volcano in the Aegean, a vast cone dominating the archipelago,' Jack replied. 'To the refugees the distant profile would have been startlingly reminiscent of their lost homeland. The latest reconstructions show the Thera volcano with twin peaks, remarkably similar to the view we first had of this island from *Seaquest*.'

'That monastery revealed in the cliffs of Thera after the earthquake last year,' Costas said. 'Are you saying it was built by the Atlanteans?'

'Ever since the discovery of prehistoric Akrotiri in 1967 archaeologists have puzzled over why such a prosperous settlement had no palace,' Jack said. 'Last year's revelation proves what some of us thought all along, that the main focus on the island was a religious precinct that must have included a magnificent peak sanctuary. Our shipwreck clinches the matter. Its cargo of ceremonial accoutrements and sacred artefacts shows the priests possessed the wealth of kings.'

'But surely the wreck is Bronze Age, thousands of years later than the Black Sea exodus,' Costas protested.

'Yes, Akrotiri was a Bronze Age foundation, a trading emporium by the sea, but Neolithic pottery and stone tools have been found all over the island. The earliest settlement probably lay inland and upslope, a better location at a time when sea-raiding was rife.'

'What was the date of the monastery?' Costas asked.

'It's astonishingly old, fifth to sixth millennium BC. You see how everything falls into place. As for the shipwreck, probably not just the gold disc but many other sacred artefacts on board will prove to have been much older, venerated heirlooms dating back thousands of years before the Bronze Age.'

'So how does Minoan Crete fit in?'

Jack gripped the edge of the table, his euphoria palpable.

'When people think of the ancient world before the Greeks and Romans, it tends to be the Egyptians, or the Assyrians and other Near Eastern peoples mentioned in the Bible. But in many ways the most extraordinary civilization was the one that developed on the island of Crete. They may not have built pyramids or ziggurats but everything points to a uniquely rich culture, wonderfully creative and perfectly attuned to the bounty of their land.' Jack could sense the mounting excitement in the others as they began to make sense of everything they had juggled in their minds since the conference in Alexandria.

'It's difficult to visualize today, but from where we are now the Atlanteans controlled a vast plain that extended from the ancient shoreline to the foothills of Anatolia. The island of Thera is also highly fertile but too small to have sustained a population anything like this size. Instead the priests looked south, to the first landfall two days' sail from Akrotiri, an immense stretch of mountain-backed coast that must have seemed like a new continent.'

'Crete was first occupied in the Neolithic,' Hiebermeyer commented. 'As I recall, the oldest artefacts from under the palace at Knossos are dated by radiocarbon to the seventh millennium BC.'

'A thousand years before the end of Atlantis, part of the great wave of island settlement after the Ice Age,' Jack agreed. 'But we already suspected another wave arrived in the sixth millennium BC, bringing pottery and new ideas about architecture and religion.'

He paused to marshal his thoughts.

'I now believe they were Atlanteans, colonists who paddled on from Thera. They terraced the valleys along the north coast of Crete, establishing vineyards and olive orchards and raising sheep and cattle from the stock they brought with them. They used obsidian which they found on the island of Melos and came to control as an export industry, just as the priests of Atlantis had controlled bronze. Obsidian came to be used in ceremonial gift exchanges that helped to establish peaceful relations all over the Aegean. For more than two thousand years the priests presided over the development of the island, exercising benign guidance from a network of peak sanctuaries as the population gradually coalesced into villages and towns and grew wealthy from agricultural surplus.'

'How do you explain the appearance of bronze more or less simultaneously across the entire Near East in the third millennium BC?' Costas asked.

Mustafa answered. 'Tin was beginning to trickle into the Mediterranean from the east. It would have led to experimental alloying by coppersmiths all over the region.'

'And I believe the priests bowed to the inevitable and decided to reveal their greatest secret,' Jack added. 'Like medieval monks or Celtic druids I think they were international arbiters of culture and justice, emissaries and intermediaries who linked together the developing nation states of the Bronze Age and maintained peace where they could. They saw to it that the legacy of Atlantis was a common currency in the culture of the region, with shared features as grandiose as the courtyard palaces of Crete and the Near East.'

'We know they were involved in trade from the shipwreck evidence,' Mustafa said.

'Before our wreck there had been three excavations of Bronze Age ships in the east Mediterranean, none Minoan and all of later date,' Jack went on. 'The finds suggest it was the priests who controlled the lucrative metal trade, men and women who accompanied the cargoes on long-haul voyages to and from the Aegean. I believe that same priesthood first unveiled the wonders of bronze technology, a revelation orchestrated over the whole area but conducted in greatest earnest on the island of Crete, a place where careful nurture during the Neolithic had ensured conditions were right for a repetition of their grand experiment.'

'And then the multiplier effect.' Katya's face seemed flushed in the torchlight as she spoke. 'Bronze tools foster a second agricultural revolution. Villages become towns, towns beget palaces. The priests introduce Linear A writing to facilitate record-keeping and administration. Soon Minoan Crete is the greatest civilization the Mediterranean had ever seen, one whose power lay not in military might but in the success of its economy and the strength of its culture.' She looked across at Jack and nodded slowly. 'You were right after all. Crete was Plato's Atlantis. Only it was a new Atlantis, a utopia refounded, a second grand design that continued the age-old dream of paradise on earth.'

'By the middle of the second millennium BC, Minoan Crete was at its height,' Dillen said. 'It was just as described in the first part of Solon's papyrus, a land of magnificent palaces and exuberant culture, of bull-leaping and artistic splendour. The eruption of Thera shook that world to its foundations.'

'Bigger than Vesuvius and Mount Saint Helens combined,' Costas said. 'Forty cubic kilometres of fallout and a tidal wave high enough to sink Manhattan.'

'It was a cataclysm that reached far beyond the Minoans. With the priesthood all but extinguished, the entire edifice of the Bronze Age began to crumble. A world that had been prosperous and secure slid into anarchy and chaos, torn apart by internal conflict and unable to resist the invaders who swept down from the north.'

'But some of the priests escaped,' Costas interjected. 'The passengers in our shipwreck perished but others made it, those who left earlier.'

'Indeed,' Dillen said. 'Like the inhabitants of Akrotiri, the priests in the monastery took heed of some forewarning, probably violent tremors which seismologists think shook the island a few weeks before the cataclysm. I believe most of the priesthood perished in your ship. But others reached safe haven in their seminary at Phaistos on the south coast of Crete, and a few fled further to join their brethren in Egypt and the Levant.'

'Yet there was to be no new attempt to revive Atlantis, no further experiment with utopia,' Costas ventured.

'Already dark shadows were falling over the Bronze Age world,' Dillon said grimly. 'To the north-east the Hittites were marshalling in their Anatolian stronghold of Boghazköy, a gathering storm that was to scythe its way to the very gates of Egypt. In Crete the surviving Minoans were powerless to resist the Mycenaean warriors who sallied forth from the Greek mainland, the forebears of Agamemnon and Menelaus whose titanic struggle with the east was to be immortalized by Homer in the siege of Troy.'

Dillen paused and eyed the group.

'The priests knew they no longer had the power to shape the destiny of their world. By their ambition they had rekindled the wrath of the gods, provoking once again the heavenly retribution that had obliterated their first homeland. The eruption of Thera must have seemed apocalyptic, a portent of Armageddon itself. From now on the priesthood would no longer take an active role in the affairs of men, but would closet itself in the inner recesses of sanctuary and shroud its lore in mystery. Soon Minoan Crete like Atlantis before it would be no more than a dimly remembered paradise, a morality tale of man's hubris before the gods, a story that passed into the realm of myth and legend to be locked for ever in the mantras of the last remaining priests.'

'In the temple sanctum at Saïs,' Costas ventured.

Dillen nodded. 'Egypt was the only civilization bordering the Mediterranean to weather the devastation at the end of the Bronze Age, the only place where the priesthood could claim unbroken continuity back thousands of years to Atlantis. I believe Amenhotep's was the last surviving line, the only one still extant at the dawn of the classical era. And that too was doomed to extinction two centuries later with the arrival of Alexander the Great.'

'And yet the legacy endures,' Jack pointed out. 'Amenhotep passed on the torch to Solon, a man whose culture held promise that the ideals of the founders could one day be resurrected.' He paused and then continued quietly, with barely suppressed emotion. 'And now that sacred duty has fallen to us. For the first time since antiquity the legacy of Atlantis has been laid before mankind, not only what we have seen but untold wisdom not even Amenhotep could have divulged.'

They left the chamber and made their way slowly down the stairway towards the well of light at the bottom. On either side the carved figures of the priests and priestesses seemed to ascend past them, a solemn procession forever striving for the holy of holies.

33

There was a commotion at the end of the passageway and Ben came hurrying towards them along with two of *Sea Venture*'s crewmen.

'You should get out at once. We have a possible intruder.'

Jack shot Costas a glance and the two of them immediately strode ahead with the crewmen.

'What's the situation?'

'Unidentified aircraft flying in low directly at us. The radar picked it up five minutes ago. It doesn't answer any call signs. And it's fast. High subsonic.'

'Bearing?'

'Trajectory 140 degrees. South-south-west.'

They reached the audience chamber and strode together

round the platform to the exit on the opposite side. Even skirting close to the edge they could feel the scalding heat coming from the central chimney, a sudden upsurge of volcanic activity while they had been inside the passageway.

'It looks like we're in for an event.'

'In more ways than one.'

Jack gestured for the others to hurry and waited while Hiebermeyer and Dillen caught up, taking up the rear as they stumbled through the exit tunnel. A wave of scorching gas blew past them as they huddled to one side in the brilliant sunlight outside the entrance.

'It's an upwelling in the core.' Costas raised his voice against the increasing roar from the chamber they had just left. 'One of those events the Atlanteans recorded in their calendar. There might be some lava.'

'Tom York has already ordered a complete evacuation because of the intruder,' Ben shouted. 'It's for your own safety.'

'We're with you.'

They quickly followed Ben down the steps towards the makeshift helipad, blinking furiously in the glare of daylight. The last of the Seahawks had just taken up position offshore and the only remaining aircraft was *Sea Venture*'s Lynx, the rotors powered up and two crewmen hanging out of the side door ready to help them in.

'It's a military jet.' Ben was pressing in his earphone against the cacophony as he ran. 'They've never seen one like it here before. The Russian FAC captain thinks it's a Harrier.'

Jack suddenly felt a sickening wave of certainty as he helped Dillen towards the helicopter.

Aslan's blast-proof hangars. Olga Ivanovna Bortsev.

'They think it's heading for the submarine. They've got a missile lock. They're not taking any chances. They've fired.'

As he leapt into the helicopter Jack saw the streak of two missiles from the FAC craft nearest *Kazbek*. As they sought their target, a black dot appeared over the waves on the horizon to the east.

She's not coming for the submarine. She's come to join her lover in hell.

'Go!' Jack yelled. 'It's coming for us!'

As the pilot wrenched the helicopter off the ground they saw the aircraft hurtle over the submarine, followed by the contrails of the two missiles. Jack spun back towards the open doorway just in time to see the missiles impact and blow off the Harrier's tail. The Lynx rose with dizzying speed as the wreckage hurtled beneath them, the helmeted figure in the cockpit visible for an instant as the explosion engulfed the forward part of the fuselage. Before they could register what had happened, an immense shock wave threw the helicopter upwards, nearly bouncing Jack and the doorman out of the aircraft as the others held on to anything they could.

The burning Harrier hit the cliff face with the impact of a comet. The aircraft had been aimed directly at the volcano entrance and its remains continued on into the audience chamber, vanishing as if they had been sucked into the maw of the volcano. For an extraordinary moment the fire and noise disappeared completely.

'She's going to blow!' Costas yelled.

As the helicopter rose above a thousand feet and veered to seaward they stared aghast at the scene beneath them. Seconds after the concussion there was a mighty roar and a jet of flame burst out of the entrance like an afterburner. The Harrier's impact had compressed and ignited the volatile gases which had collected inside the audience chamber. The cone of the volcano seemed to blur as the colossal rumbling of the detonation reached them. A geyser of fire shot up hundreds of metres where the vapour chimney had once been.

From the edge of the billowing cloud of dust that obscured the cone as it collapsed they saw a rim of fire, tongues of molten magma that began to roll inexorably down the slopes towards the sea.

Atlantis had revealed its secrets for the last time.

Epilogue

The last rays of the setting sun cast a warm glow over the waves that lapped at the stern of *Sea Venture*. Away to the east the sea merged with the sky in a lurid haze, and to the west the sinking orb drew in the remaining light in vast converging trackways across the sky. In the aftermath of the eruption everything was suffused with pastel colours, the shrouded site of the volcano a vortex of dust and vapour surrounded by a halo of pink and orange.

Jack and the others were sitting on the upper deck above the bridge, the entire panorama of the last few days visible before them. After the extraordinary discoveries of the morning and their narrow escape they felt drained but exuberant, and now were quietly basking in the warmth at the end of the day.

'I wonder what your old Greek would have made of all this.' Costas was leaning back on one arm, his battered face turned towards Jack.

'He probably would have scratched his head for a moment, gone "ah" and then taken out his scroll and begun recording it. He was that kind of guy.'

'Typical archaeologist,' Costas sighed. 'Complete failure to get excited about anything.'

The site of the island was still concealed by clouds of steam where the lava had entered the sea but they knew nothing now remained above water. The underground labyrinth had progressively collapsed after the audience chamber imploded with the weight of the magma welling up above. For several alarming hours that afternoon they had experienced a version of the Thera aftershock as the larger chambers caved in, the sea sucking in and rebounding in minor tsunamis that challenged even *Sea Venture*'s stabilizer system. Even now they knew the eruption was continuing deep underwater, disgorging rivers of lava that were flowing down the ancient roadways and taking the outer reaches of the city in their embrace.

'Excavation might still be possible,' Costas said. 'Look at Pompeii and Herculaneum, even Akrotiri on Thera.'

'Pompeii's taken two hundred and fifty years and they're only halfway there,' Jack replied. 'And it's under ash and fallout, not lava. And it's not underwater.'

They consoled themselves that other marvels remained to be discovered along the ancient shoreline, perfectly preserved sites like the village off Trabzon that would answer many of their questions about how the people of this extraordinary culture flourished more than seven thousands years ago.

For Jack there was nothing more important than the revelation about Atlantis and its remarkable place in history. If they had known they were on borrowed time they might never have entered the volcano at all; their dive through the labyrinth and the discovery of the sanctuary now seemed hallowed experiences, never to be repeated.

He was certain that safeguarding the submarine and destroying Aslan may have prevented nuclear holocaust. Their achievement was a ray of hope, a small sign that people still had the ability to shape their own destiny. For the sake of those priestly visionaries at the dawn of civilization they must ensure their discovery was remembered not just as a revelation of past glory but also as a promise for the future. That was the true legacy of Atlantis.

The dying ripples of wind ruffled the sea in sheets of mottled orange, each gust sweeping off towards the west. To the north they could just make out the oily smudge that was all that remained of *Vultura*; her burnt-out shell had slipped almost unnoticed beneath the waves an hour before. Close inshore the scene was dominated by the huge bulk of *Kazbek*. Its escort had opened up to allow a Russian salvage vessel to manoeuvre into position. Further out lay another cordon of warships whose number had increased steadily through the day. They were taking no chances, the events of the past few days showing that rogue elements had the ruthlessness and daring to take on the most potent international forces.

Efram Jacobovich was talking quietly into a cellphone with his back to the group. Using the negotiating skills that helped make him one of the world's richest men, he had already brokered a deal which would see Aslan's wealth split between the three main parties. The Turks would get a much-needed reserve for earthquake relief and the Georgians the means to raise a powerful security force. IMU would be able to build *Seaquest II*, with more than enough left over to finance a programme of research along the entire Black Sea shore.

Jack looked at Costas.

'Thanks for the ADSA, by the way. If you hadn't insisted on installing it in the command module I'd be a permanent fixture on the seabed by now.'

Costas raised the large gin and tonic which had thoughtfully been provided for him. 'And thanks for showing up in the nick of time,' he replied. 'Where I was, things were getting distinctly hot.'

'I have one question,' Jack said. 'What would you have done if I hadn't arrived?'

'I'd just agreed to lead Aslan's men back down through the volcano to the submarine. Remember the final section of underwater tunnel, the lava extrusion just before we broke surface? I would have taken them down the left-hand passageway.'

'Directly into the magma chamber.'

'I was going there one way or another,' Costas said ruefully. 'That way I'd at least have taken a couple of Aslan's men with me and given Katya a chance. For the greater good, as you would say.'

Jack looked across at the pensive form of Katya, her face gilded by the sun as she leaned on the rail with her eyes fixed on the sea. They had discovered such incredible things over the past few days, yet she had been through a searing experience Jack could never have predicted when they first met in Alexandria a few short days ago.

He looked back at the battered features of his friend.

'For the greater good,' he repeated quietly.

Dillen was sitting quietly to one side, staring at the horizon, his face a picture of studious contemplation as he sucked on his antique clay pipe. After they had finished speaking, he turned and looked quizzically at Jack.

'And I have one question for you,' he said. 'That incomplete set of plaques. Which group do you think had them?'

Jack thought for a moment. 'They had everything up to the fourth tablet, the rudiments of agriculture and animal husbandry and stonemasonry. They could have gone to western Europe, where the Bronze Age began later than in the Near East, to Spain or western France or Britain.'

'Or further afield,' Dillen prompted.

'Some of the artefacts from early prehistory found in Mesoamerica and China have never been properly explained,' Jack said. 'When urbanism developed in the Americas it produced architecture incredibly similar to Old World forms, pyramids and courtyards and processional ways. It could be that the legacy of Atlantis was a truly global phenomenon, that the world was knit together then as never before or since.'

The landing lights on the stern helipad came on and Jack turned to watch. The helipad had been a hive of activity all day. Earlier that afternoon *Sea Venture*'s Lynx had arrived with a UN nuclear weapons inspection team for transfer to *Kazbek*, and now it had returned on a refuelling stop from Abkhazia with a precious cargo of works of art from Aslan's shattered headquarters. As it lifted off on its way to Istanbul, they could hear the deeper drumming of two Westland transport helicopters which had taken holding positions and were awaiting their turn to land.

Despite their fatigue, Jack knew he had been right to call a press conference immediately. In little more than an hour the reporters would all be back at the IMU staging headquarters at Trabzon and news of the discovery would be flashed around the world in time to fill the next morning's headlines.

As the first helicopter settled on the helipad and began to disgorge scurrying teams of cameramen, Jack stood up, his rugged features framed against the dying light of the day. Just before walking down the steps to face the limelight he turned to the others.

'I'm here with *Sea Venture* until the search is called off,' he said. 'Peter wouldn't have wanted it but I owe it to him. I brought him here and he was my friend.'

'He was a hero,' Katya said softly. 'The world is a better place than it was five days ago.'

They looked over to where she still leaned on the rail, staring to the east. She turned to him and held his gaze. The emotions of the last few days were etched on her face, but the soft copper hues of the evening light seemed to wipe away her cares and radiate the warmth of a brighter future. She got up, and, smiling tiredly, came over and stood beside him.

Jack took a deep breath and then looked back at the others.

'Oh, and any of you are welcome to take some R & R at my expense.'

'Sorry, old boy.' Dillen smiled warmly at Jack, his pipe clenched firmly between his teeth. 'I have a conference on palaeolinguistics to chair and this little diversion has disrupted my preparations completely. I'm afraid I have to get back to Cambridge tomorrow.'

'And I have Noah's Ark to find,' Mustafa said nonchalantly. 'Not on Mount Ararat but on the shoreline where the southern group beached their vessels before going overland. I need to organise an IMU survey team.'

Jack turned to Hiebermeyer and Aysha. 'And I suppose you have some boring old mummies to excavate.'

Hiebermeyer allowed himself a rare smile. 'As a matter of fact, yes.'

'Just don't find any more treasure maps.'

'Now you mention it, we've just had an intriguing report of a discovery in the Hellenistic quarter of the necropolis. Something to do with Alexander the Great, a secret shipment across the Indian Ocean to a far-off mountain kingdom.'

They could see Jack's interest was immediately excited, his mind already racing over the possibilities.

'And in case you'd forgotten, we still have a Minoan shipwreck to excavate.' Costas had put aside his drink and was surveying the latest reports on his palm computer. 'They've just brought up some amazing artefacts, golden sheets covered with strangely familiar symbols.' He grinned and looked up at his friend. 'So where's our next project?'

'That's another story.'

Author's Note

The discovery that underpins this story is fictional. However, the archaeological backdrop is as plausible as the story allows, taking account of the current state of knowledge and debate. The purpose of this note is to clarify the facts.

The Black Sea Flood. The Messinian salinity crisis is an established event, a result of tectonic and glacio-eustatic processes which cut off the Mediterranean from the Atlantic; the crisis has been dated to 5.96 to 5.33 million years BP (Before Present), with inundation over the Gibraltar land bridge occurring rapidly at the end. The level of the Mediterranean rose about 130 metres further during the 'great melt' at the end of the Ice Age some twelve to ten thousand years ago.

Recently evidence has been marshalled to suggest that the Black Sea was cut off from the Mediterranean for several thousand years more, and did not rise to the same level until a natural dam across the Bosporus was overwhelmed in the sixth millennium BC. Core samples from below the floor of the Black Sea suggest a change from freshwater to seawater sediments about 7,500 years ago, a date pinpointed by radiocarbon analysis of mollusc shells from either side of the horizon. The West Antarctic Ice Sheet may have experienced a rapid retreat phase about this time, and it could be that such an event, combined with tectonic activity, pushed the sea over the Bosporus.

In 1999 researchers using sonar and a dredge found a probable berm from an ancient shoreline 150 metres below sea level off northern Turkey near Sinope. Although there is much debate about the date, rapidity and volume of the Black Sea flood, its existence is widely accepted.

The Neolithic Exodus. Many experts believe that Indo-European language originated in the Black Sea region some time between the seventh and fifth millennia BC. Well before the Black Sea flood hypothesis, leading archaeologists argued that Indo-European language evolved among the first farmers of Anatolia about 7000 BC, that it reached Europe about 6000 BC and that its spread went hand in hand with the introduction of large-scale agriculture and animal husbandry. This model has provoked much controversy, not least over whether diffusion primarily involved the spread of people or ideas, but it remains central to any debate over the origins of civilization.

★

Atlantis. The only source for the Atlantis story is the dialogues *Timaeus* and *Critias* written by the Greek philosopher Plato in the first half of the fourth century BC. The credibility of the story rests on two leaps of faith: first, that Plato was not simply making it up; second, that his avowed source, the Athenian scholar Solon several generations earlier, had not himself been spun a tale by the priests at Saïs in Egypt who were his supposed informants some time in the early sixth century BC.

It seems likely that Egyptian priests did indeed have records stretching back thousands of years. The Greek historian Herodotus, who gathered reams of information from the priests when he visited in the mid-fifth century BC, much of it verifiable, was shown a papyrus with the succession list of 'three hundred and thirty' Egyptian monarchs (Herodotus, *Histories* ii, 100). He sounds a note of caution: 'Such as think the tales told by the Egyptians credible are free to accept them for history' (ii, 122).

By the time of Solon, Mediterranean seafarers knew of distant shores beyond the Red Sea to the east and the Pillars of Hercules to the west. Yet there is no need to look so far afield for Atlantis. To the Egyptians in the sixth century BC, isolated for centuries following the collapse of the Bronze Age world, the island of Crete was a mysterious land beyond the horizon which had once housed a brilliant civilization. All contact had been lost following a cataclysm which they may have experienced in the pall of darkness and plague of locusts recorded in the Old Testament (*Exodus,* 10).

Today, many who accept the veracity of Plato's story see Atlantis in the civilization of Minoan Crete and its disappearance in the eruption of Thera in the middle of the second millennium BC.

★

A Minoan shipwreck has yet to be excavated. However, several wrecks of later Bronze Age date have been found, including one in 1982 off south-west Turkey hailed as the greatest discovery in archaeology since the tomb of Tutankhamun. The finds include ten tonnes of oxhide-shaped copper and tin ingots; a cache of cobalt-blue glass ingots; logs of ebony, and ivory tusk; beautiful bronze swords; Near Eastern merchant's seals; gold jewellery and a magnificent gold chalice; and an exquisite gold scarab of Nefertiti that pins the wreck to the late fourteenth century BC. The metal was enough to equip an entire army and may have been royal tribute. The finds even include items of religious significance interpreted as the accoutrements of priests. These treasures are now magnificently displayed in the Museum of Underwater Archaeology at Bodrum.

★

In 2001 a hominid skull discovered at Dmanisi, in the Republic of Georgia, was dated to an astonishing 1.8 million years BP, almost a million years before the earliest hominid fossils from Europe. A much later migration from Africa brought *Homo sapiens sapiens*, who began painting exquisitely lifelike animals on the walls of caves around 35,000 years ago.

The 'hall of the ancestors' is based not only on the famous cave paintings at Lascaux in France and Altamira in Spain, dated respectively to 20,000 BP and 17,000 BP, but also on two more recent finds. In 1994 at Chauvet in south France cavers discovered a complex which had been blocked off by a rock fall in prehistory. The paintings have been dated to 35,000 BP, making them among the oldest ever found; they show that Stone Age artists reached the pinnacle of their skill only a few thousand years after anatomically modern humans arrived in the region. The depictions include giant woolly mammoths and other Ice Age megafauna. Another cave reported in 1991 near Marseilles contained more than 140 paintings and engravings, a particularly remarkable discovery because the entrance lies 37 metres below sea level. The Cosquer Cave shows that other treasures may remain undiscovered in caves submerged at the end of the Ice Age.

It was to be many thousands of years before language was represented by a script, the earliest known being the cuneiform of Mesopotamia and the hieroglyphs of Egypt around 3200 BC. Yet finds from the Upper Palaeolithic (35,000–11,000 BP), contemporary with the cave art, include bones incised with lines and dots that may represent numerical sequences, possibly the passing of the days or the lunar calendar. The idea of writing may thus have been established well before the first need for extensive record-keeping in the early Bronze Age.

★

The fictional priests of Atlantis are an amalgam of the shamans and medicine men of hunter-gatherer societies with the priest kings of the early city states. They are also distant precursors of the druids, the elusive priests known largely from Caesar's *Gallic Wars*. The druids may have been powerful mediators who bound together the disparate tribes of Celtic Europe. Their forebears may have worn the conical golden 'wizard's caps', intricately embellished with astrological symbols, which have recently been identified among Bronze Age finds; the symbols suggest an ability to chart and predict the movement of the heavens, including the lunar cycle, a knowledge also revealed in the megalithic observatories such as Stonehenge. The earliest cap dates from about 1200 BC and so far none have been reported outside western Europe.

★

The first farmers on the Mediterranean islands had breeding

pairs of domestic animals, including deer, sheep, goats, pigs and cattle, that were not indigenous and must have been brought from the mainland in paddled longboats. Excavations on Cyprus suggest these migrations began as early as the ninth millennium BC, very soon after the inception of agriculture in the 'Fertile Crescent' of Anatolia and the Near East.

The earliest dated wooden boats are dugout fragments from Denmark of the fifth to fourth millennium BC. Whereas the first Egyptian and Near Eastern boats may have been bundles of reeds, recalled in the 'papyriform' shape of later funerary vessels, the abundance of timber along the southern Black Sea shore suggests that vessels built there may have been wooden even before metal tools became available.

A model for Noah's Ark is the 'Dover Boat', a remarkably well-preserved hull found in the English port of that name in 1992. Though it dates from the Bronze Age, it is a generic shape that may have been typical of the earliest seagoing vessels. It was about fifteen metres long and constructed of planks sewn together with yew withies which could be disassembled for repair and overland transport. With eighteen or twenty paddlers it could have transported passengers, livestock and other cargo across the English Channel. A fleet of such vessels is more likely for a Neolithic exodus than a single vessel the size of the Old Testament ark, especially if metal carpentry tools were absent and effective sailing rigs had yet to be developed.

*

The most important early Neolithic sites so far discovered are Jericho and Çatal Hüyük (also Çatalhöyük). Jericho, the Biblical city identified as Tell es-Sultan in the Jordan Valley of Israel, was surrounded by a massive stone wall built about 8000 BC during the pre-pottery Neolithic. Elsewhere there is little direct evidence for warfare before the sixth millennium BC, in the form of fortifications, burned settlements or massacre sites, and a recent reappraisal argues that the Jericho 'defences' were in fact protection against floods.

Çatal Hüyük in south-central Turkey flourished from the late seventh to the mid-sixth millennium BC, when it was abandoned. The image of its pueblo-like buildings, their cult rooms furnished with bull's horn symbols and decorated with exuberant wall paintings, provides an authentic blueprint for structures imagined beneath the Black Sea. The finds include clay and stone figurines of a grotesquely corpulent mother goddess, reminiscent of a stylized female image in clay recently found on the Black Sea coast of Turkey at Ikiztepe.

One of many extraordinary images from Çatal Hüyük is a fresco found in a cult room dated to about 6200 BC showing a volcano venting a great plume of ash. With its twin cones and intervening saddle the volcano looks remarkably like the bull's horn images from the shrines. Beneath it lies a town, extending outwards as if along a seashore, the buildings reminiscent of Çatal Hüyük but separated into tightly packed rectilinear blocks. The volcano may represent a cinder cone in the Karapinar volcanic field, some fifty kilometres to the east, and the town may be Çatal Hüyük itself; or it may instead be a distant scene where a seaside town really did nestle beneath the twin peaks of a volcano. The painting is the oldest known image of an active volcano and of a planned town.

Around the Black Sea the clearest evidence for precocious development comes from Varna in Bulgaria where a cemetery has produced an enormous cache of gold and copper artefacts alongside objects made from flint and bone. The finds reveal not only the extraordinary achievements of early metallurgists but also a society with stratification reflected in material wealth. The cemetery dates from the late

Neolithic, a period also referred to as the 'Chalcolithic' or Copper Age, and was in use by the middle of the fifth millennium BC.

★

Eighty kilometres north of Crete lies the volcanic island of Thera. Only part of the prehistoric town of Akrotiri has been uncovered, but as it emerges from its tomb of ash and pumice it looks like a Bronze Age Pompeii. The inhabitants had some forewarning of the eruption, probably a series of violent earthquakes. As yet no 'monastery' has been unearthed, but the splendid marine fresco from Akrotiri, showing a procession of ships and a palatial seaside structure, suggests that religious observance and ceremony played a major part in island life.

Many archaeologists have placed the eruption around 1500 BC, based on evidence for the destruction of the palaces on Crete and the arrival of the Mycenaeans. However, scientists have recently suggested a 'best fit' of 1628 BC in the acidity layers of Greenland ice, radiocarbon determinations and dendrochronological analysis of Irish oak and California bristlecone pine. Whatever the precise date, there can be no doubt of the colossal scale of the eruption that obliterated the settlement on Thera, smothered a huge swath of the east Mediterranean and caused tsunamis which pummelled the north coast of Crete and would have overwhelmed ships for miles around.

★

Alexandria, the great port founded by Alexander the Great in 331 BC on Egypt's Mediterranean coast, is the setting for the conference early in this book. It takes place in the Qaitbay Fortress, the fifteenth-century AD castle built on the foundations of the ancient lighthouse at the entrance to the harbour. Many fragments of masonry and sculpture have been charted on the seabed where the lighthouse collapsed in the fourteenth century.

More than two thousand kilometres to the west lies Carthage, location of the fictional Maritime Museum. Since 1972 the UNESCO 'Save Carthage' programme has ensured that the city is among the most studied from antiquity, despite having been razed by the Romans in 146 BC and again by the Arabs almost nine hundred years later. Today an outstanding feature is the landlocked circular harbour where excavations have revealed slipways that once housed a fleet of war galleys.

★

Solon is a genuine historical character who lived from about 640 to 560 BC. He was chief archon of Athens in 594 BC and famous as a statesman whose reforms paved the way towards the democratic city state of the Golden Age. Afterwards he travelled extensively in Egypt and Asia Minor and was revered as one of the 'seven wise men' of Greece. His only writings to survive are a few fragments of poetry, but there can be no doubt that like Herodotus a century later he would have taken extensive notes from the priests and other informants he met on his travels.

The 'Atlantis Papyrus' is fictional, though the circumstances of its discovery are inspired by a remarkable series of finds in western Egypt. In 1996 at the oasis of Bahariya a donkey broke through the sand into a rock-cut necropolis that had lain undisturbed for fifteen centuries. Since then more than two hundred mummies have been uncovered, many gilded and painted with portrait faces and religious scenes. They are from the Graeco-Roman period, dating after Alexander's conquest in 332 BC, but in 1999 archaeologists digging beneath the oasis town of El Bawiti discovered the tomb of a governor of Bahariya during the Twenty-sixth Dynasty (664–525 BC), the period of Solon's travels.

The ruins of Saïs lie under the modern village of Sa el-Hagar in the western Delta near the Rosetta branch of the Nile, less than thirty kilometres from the Mediterranean. Like Carthage and Alexandria, little remains of the riverside metropolis, its masonry plundered and its foundations lying beneath metres of silt. Nevertheless, Saïs was probably an important cult centre at the dawn of Egyptian history, even before the Early Dynastic Period (*circa* 3100 BC). By the time of Solon's visit it was the Royal Capital of the Twenty-sixth Dynasty, a place the Greeks would have known well from their nearby emporium of Naucratis.

Pilgrims came from far and wide to pay their respects at the temple of the goddess Neith, a vast complex described by Herodotus when he visited the following century. He met with the 'scribe', his term for the high priest, who 'kept the register of the sacred treasures of Athene (Neith) in the city of Saïs', a man who regrettably 'did not seem to me to be in earnest' (*Histories* ii, 28). The temple had towering obelisks, colossal statues and human-headed sphinxes (ii, 169–171, 175). Today it requires a leap of the imagination to envisage anything like this at the site, but a low limestone wall suggests a precinct as large as the famous complex at Karnak in Upper Egypt.

The excavations which produced the early heiroglyphs and the priest list are fictional. However, by extraordinary chance the name of the man who may have been the very priest met by Solon is known: Amenhotep, whose impressive statue, in greywacke sandstone, probably from Saïs, probably dedicated in the temple and of the Twenty-sixth Dynasty, is in the British Museum (no. EA41517). He holds a *naos*, a shrine containing a cult image of the goddess Neith.

★

Bronze Age sailors intent on reaching the Nile from Crete may have departed from the recently excavated port of

Kommos, on the south coast within sight of the palace of Phaistos. From its magnificent position the palace dominates the Mesara plain and abuts Mount Ida with its sacred caves and peak sanctuaries. Three kilometres away lies the complex known as Hagia Triadha, traditionally interpreted as a royal villa but perhaps some form of seminary for the Minoan priesthood. It was here in 1908 that the famous Phaistos disc was discovered. The 241 symbols and 61 'words' have so far defied translation but may relate to an early language spoken in western Anatolia, and thus to the Indo-European spoken in the early Neolithic. The shape of marking termed here the 'Atlantis symbol' actually exists, uniquely on this disc: several of them from one die are clearly visible, one close to the centre on one side.

No second disc has been discovered. However, visitors can ponder the existing disc close up in the Archaeological Museum at Heraklion, where it is displayed alongside other treasures of the Minoan world.

*

Hagia Triadha in Crete also produced a painted sarcophagus depicting a bull trussed on an altar, its neck bleeding into a libation vessel. Some fifty kilometres north at Arkhanes archaeologists found evidence for a different kind of offering: a youth bound on a low platform inside a hilltop temple, his skeleton propping up a bronze knife incised with a mysterious boar-like beast. Moments after his death the temple collapsed in an earthquake and preserved the only evidence yet found for human sacrifice in the Bronze Age Aegean.

Arkhanes lies under Mount Juktas, the sacred peak overlooking the valley leading to Knossos. Among the many extraordinary finds at Knossos were several thousand baked clay tablets, the majority impressed with symbols christened Linear B but several hundred with Linear A. Linear B was brilliantly deciphered as an early form of Greek, the language spoken by the Mycenaeans who arrived in Crete in the fifteenth century BC. They adopted the script but rejected the language; Linear A is similar, also being syllabic with a number of shared symbols, but dates from before the Mycenaean arrival and remains substantially untranslated.

Two other Bronze Age sites mentioned are Athens and Troy. On the Acropolis one of few survivals from prehistory is a rock-cut tunnel leading to a subterranean spring; it was this that inspired the idea that there may yet be hidden chambers from the classical period. At Troy, palaeogeographical research has pinpointed the line of the ancient beaches and may one day reveal evidence of a Bronze Age siege.

★

The Black Sea is indeed dead below about 200 metres, a result of huge accumulations of hydrogen sulphide caused by the biochemical process described in this book. In its deep recesses are deposits of brine which formed when the sea was cut off from the Mediterranean and began to evaporate, causing the salt to precipitate.

To the south the sea lies astride one of the world's most active geological boundaries, one which came to world attention in 1999 when a magnitude 7.4 earthquake devastated north-west Turkey. The North Anatolian Fault between the African and the Eurasian plates runs as far east as Mount Ararat, itself an extinct twin-peaked volcano, and could be associated with imaginary features in this book including the volcanic island, the tectonic rift and the hydrothermal vents.

Several wrecks of ancient merchantmen have been found in the coastal waters of the Black Sea, including one located by a submersible off Bulgaria in 2002. In 2000 the team that pinpointed the ancient shoreline near Sinope found a shipwreck from late antiquity in 320 metres of water, its wonderfully preserved hull an indication of the archaeological marvels that may lie elsewhere in the anoxic depths of the sea.

★

With the exception of the fictional EH-4 'magic sludge', and some aspects of laser application, most of the technology presented in this book is grounded in current developments, including matters relating to diving and archaeology. *Kazbek* is a fictional variant of the *Akula*-1 class Soviet SSN attack submarine, and thus an imaginary addition to the six boats of this class known to have been commissioned between 1985 and 1990.

★

The quotes from Plato in Chapter 3 are from *The Dialogues of Plato* translated by Benjamin Jowett (1817–93). The Bible quotes in Chapter 3 are from *Exodus* 10: 21 and in Chapter 31 from *Exodus* 20: 16–18, *Exodus* 37: 1–5 and *Genesis* 9: 17–19, King James Version.

Now you can buy any of these other bestselling
books from your bookshop or
direct from the publisher.

FREE P&P AND UK DELIVERY
(Overseas and Ireland £3.50 per book)

The Last Gospel	David Gibbins	£6.99
Crusader Gold	David Gibbins	£6.99
Wicked	Gregory Maguire	£7.99
Out of my Depth	Emily Barr	£6.99
Run The Risk	Scott Frost	£6.99
Pretty Dead Things	Barbara Nadel	£7.99
Flint's Code	Paul Eddy	£6.99
Power Play	Joseph Finder	£6.99
Lean Mean Thirteen	Janet Evanovich	£7.99
The Roaring of the Labyrinth	Clio Gray	£7.99

TO ORDER SIMPLY CALL THIS NUMBER

01235 400 414

or visit our website: www.headline.co.uk

Prices and availability subject to change without notice.

Crusader Gold

David Gibbins

THE HOLIEST OF TREASURES

The gold menorah, symbol of the Jewish faith, stolen by Romans who sacked Jerusalem's Holy Temple.

A HISTORICAL SYMBOL

Carried in triumph through Rome, it came to represent the Empire's ruthless conquests. When the Romans moved to Constantinople, the menorah went with them . . .

THE FINAL CRUSADE

. . . But it had vanished by the time bloodthirsty Crusaders pillaged the city in 1204.

AND TO THIS DAY NO ONE KNOWS WHERE IT IS.

Turkey, present day. In Istanbul's harbour, on a dive for lost Crusade treasure, archaeologist Jack Howard discovers something wholly unexpected. Meanwhile, in an English cathedral library, a long-forgotten medieval map is unearthed. Together they could alter history. Suddenly the clock is ticking for Jack – and the stakes are already too high . . .

What unfolds is a thrilling but lethal quest, stretching from Harald Hardrada, greatest of the Viking conquerors, to the fall of the Nazis and the darkest secrets of the modern Vatican.

An exhilarating blend of history, fact and fiction, CRUSADER GOLD is another unputdownable read from the author of the worldwide bestseller *Atlantis*

'What do you get if you cross Indiana Jones with Dan Brown? Answer: David Gibbins' *Mirror*

978 0 7553 2424 8

headline

The Last Gospel

David Gibbins

JACK HOWARD IS ABOUT TO DISCOVER A SECRET. PERHAPS THE GREATEST SECRET EVER KEPT . . .

WHAT IF
– one of the Ancient World's greatest libraries was buried in volcanic ash and then rediscovered two thousand years later?

WHAT IF
– what was found there was a document that could shatter the very foundations of the western world?

WHAT IF
– you were the one who discovered this secret? And were then forced to confront terrifying enemies determined to destroy you to ensure it goes no further?

David Gibbins' electrifying new novel is the story of one last Gospel, left behind in the age of the New Testament, and of its extraordinary secret, one that has lain concealed for years. Follow Jack Howard, man of action and the greatest archaeologist of his day, as he unearths the mystery – and must prevent others from doing the same . . .

You won't be able to put THE LAST GOSPEL down. You won't be able to forget it.

Praise for David Gibbins, international bestselling author of ATLANTIS:

'What do you get if you cross Indiana Jones with Dan Brown? Answer: David Gibbins' *Mirror*

'Every ounce of energy is spent propelling the plot . . . I couldn't put this one down' *Sydney Morning Herald*

978 0 7553 3516 9

headline